MW01463117

Little Crow

A Novel

Albert Sandberg

Copyright © 2023 Albert Sandberg
All rights reserved.

Little Crow is a work of fiction. All characters, with the exception of historic figures, are products of the author's imagination. Any similarity or resemblance to any real people, real situations or actual events is purely coincidental and not intended to portray any person, or people, in a false, disparaging, or negative light. Where historic characters appear, the situations and dialogues are fictional and are not intended to depict actual events.

The scanning, uploading and distribution of this book via the Internet or via any other means without the permission of the publisher is illegal and punishable by law. Please purchase only authorized electronic editions, and do not participate in or encourage electronic piracy of copyrighted materials. Your support of the author's rights is appreciated.

ISBN: 9798387709586

Imprint: Independently published

"When I fought to protect my land and my home, I was called a savage. When I neither understood nor welcomed his way of life, I was called lazy. When I tried to rule my people, I was stripped of my authority."

Chief Dan George, July 1, 1967

Arapaho Encampment
Sand Creek, Colorado
1864

Faint tremors pulsed from the ground below the sleeping boy. The tremors grew into a steady trembling, waking him. The boy sat up and looked to where his parents slept. His father, Tall Pony, was also sitting up, his brow furrowed as he turned his head to a sound from outside the tipi. Then, he turned and looked into the boy's eyes. "Stay here," he said and then ducked through the tipi's door.

The boy crawled on his hands and knees and lifted a corner of the flap to peer outside. He shivered when he felt the cold, crisp air drift in. The vibrations were stronger now, and the boy could hear the drum of hundreds of horse hooves rolling into one sound, like distant thunder. Then, in the light of dawn's early glow, he saw his father and Chief Black Kettle raising a pole that held the American flag at the top and a white flag lower down.

Why were they doing that?

"Little Crow, get away from there," said the boy's mother, Morning Star.

"But I want to see the horses!"

Morning Star knelt beside her son and looked outside. Now, the thunder of hooves became a rolling roar, and then they appeared. Hundreds of mounted blue-coated soldiers charged across Sand Creek and into the camp, yelling and firing their rifles. Soon, the screams of Arapaho and Cheyenne women and children added to the din. The boy saw his father running toward their tipi, waving his arms and shouting unintelligibly until a bullet struck him and he fell to his knees. Then a soldier rode by and slashed down with his saber, cutting into Tall Pony's head. Tall Pony remained on his haunches, staring directly into the boy's eyes, and then another bullet struck his back and drove him forward. Little Crow gasped and tried to run to his father, but his mother held him back. Then she quickly dressed herself and her son.

Morning Star knelt in front of her son, grasped his frail shoulders, and said, "Little Crow, we need to hide by the creek. If anything happens to me, do not look back. Just keep running and find a place to hide."

Little Crow stood trembling, tears running down his face.

"Listen to me. We have to run to the creek, now!"

Morning Star shook his shoulders firmly, and when he finally nodded, she grabbed his hand and dragged him out the tipi's door. Little Crow cried out from the pain of her grip, but still she hung on as they wove through tipis and charging cavalry. Suddenly, Morning Star stopped short, jerking Little Crow backward. He turned and saw his mother had fallen to her knees and a small red spot had blossomed between her breasts. She pulled Little Crow to her, her grip on his hand weakening. He stood before his dying mother as she struggled to speak. She looked into his eyes and said "run." She gasped, blood erupting from her mouth, and then she fell to the ground.

A soldier charged toward them with a raised saber, snapping Little Crow out of his stupor. He dodged the soldier's slash and then ran through the melee, bouncing off one horse's flank and avoiding another saber slash before he made it to the creek. From his time playing at the creek with his friends, Little Crow knew a good hiding place, and he stumbled along the bank toward the spot. It was an old muskrat run burrowed into the bank. Unfortunately, several people already occupy it, so he ran farther and dropped down behind a clump of bush. A girl he knew was crouched nearby, staring at him with frightened eyes. Like himself, she was in her fifth year, and they had often played together. Now, he waves her to him, and then they huddle together and watch the attack.

Through the clouds of acrid gun smoke, he saw White Antelope walking toward a group of soldiers, waving his hands in the air, begging them to stop the killing. Bullets struck his chest and he fell. To Little Crow's horror, a soldier dismounted and straddled White Antelope. Little Crow covered the girl's eyes. She struggled, but he held firm, intent on hiding the brutality from her. Then, a gurgle escaped Little Crow as he watched the soldier triumphantly raise something in the air.

"Waynoka! There you are; come with me."

A woman grabbed the girl and dragged her away, leaving Little Crow by himself.

"Where's my mom?" the girl cried.

"She's gone."

"Can we take him with us?" She pointed at Little Crow.

"No."

Little Crow watched as Waynoka looked back at him with tear-filled eyes while she was being dragged away. When she tripped and fell, the woman cuffed her head and continued to drag her along.

Now alone, Little Crow sat behind that clump of bush for two hours, unmoving and staring at the distant mound that was his mother. His terror turned to rage when he watched a soldier walking through the village, driving his sword into wounded men, women, and children that lay in his path. A groan escaped Little Crow when the soldier drove his blade into his mother's body and then moved on as if she were nothing. Little Crow stood and began to run toward the soldier, but a woman with blood-encrusted hair reached out, grabbed his wrist, and pulled him along behind her. When he struggled to get away, she tightened her grip and dragged him onto the trail the others had taken. They joined other survivors, and eventually Little Crow ceased his struggles, but he did not stop looking back toward the village until it was out of sight.

So, they walked for several days, Little Crow silent in his deep grief as he stumbled along. Finally, they reached Dakota territory where the rest of the tribe had stopped. Unfortunately, the woman accompanying Little Crow died shortly after their arrival, leaving him alone once again. He never spoke during the trek; in fact, it would be another five years before Little Crow would utter another word.

During those five years, he stumbled around the camp in a daze and survived on scraps others tossed to him. Perhaps he was afraid to care for and lose another person, or perhaps there may have been some other reason, but Little Crow resisted the attempts of families to adopt him. He never stayed with a family longer than a few nights. In the winter months, he would sleep inside a family's tipi near the door, but in the morning, he would always be gone. Most nights, he curled up out of the wind under a ratty old buffalo hide, usually with a few of the camp dogs wedged up against him.

Then, when he was ten, Rabbit Tooth, a boy near Little Crow's age, had fallen through the river's ice and drowned. Rabbit Tooth's parents had not survived the Sand Creek Massacre, and his grandmother had been raising him. The old lady wailed for days and would wander around camp calling her grandson's name. Then one day she saw Little Crow sucking the marrow from a discarded bone. Two emaciated dogs stood in front of him, growling and ready to attack, when the old lady screamed, picked up a branch, and stumbled toward Little Crow. The dogs turned on the old lady, but she was saved when a man came to investigate the screaming. He chased the two dogs away and then turned to see the old lady hugging Little Crow.

"Rabbit Tooth, I knew I would find you!" she cried as she rocked the boy.

The man stood, uncertain what to do, so he went to consult the chief. The chief saw no harm in letting the old lady care for the boy who wouldn't speak, so Little Crow stayed with the old lady. But his diet didn't improve much—he still relied on handouts and scraps—only now, he shared the leftovers with the old lady. But at least he had a tipi to sleep in. So finally, after a month of being called Rabbit Tooth, he mumbled, "My name is Little Crow; I am the son of Tall Pony and Morning Star"

1

Saskatoon, 1910

Edward Humphries, a slight bespectacled man and unemployed newspaper writer, nearly jumped out of his skin at the sudden pounding on his door. That would be Doyle, the son of the boarding house's owner, Siobhan Donnelly. Doyle was a simple-minded brute who worked as a bouncer in one of the roughest saloons in Saskatoon. Edward did have the amount he owed Mrs. Donnelly, but paying her his rent would leave him penniless. So, Edward had a decision to make: pay for his room and stay in Saskatoon with no prospects of gainful employment, or skip out on the Donnellys and purchase a train ticket out of the city. The relentless pounding on the door, and the thought of facing Doyle, made up Edward's mind. The fact that he hadn't sold a story in weeks also factored into his decision. It was time for a change of scenery.

"Open up, you little shite!" Doyle Donnelly yelled through the door.

Edward stood on shaky legs and stared wide-eyed at the door. He grabbed his crotch and squeezed when he felt his bladder begin to loosen. Then the sound of a key turning in the lock broke him out of his paralysis and he ran to jam a wooden chair under the knob. He then turned and raced across the room and almost wept when the room's only window wouldn't budge. He could hear the doorknob jiggling, and then a loud bang shook the room. Doyle, the big ape, was throwing his shoulder against the door, and to Edward's horror, the chair's top rail cracked loudly. He looked around frantically for something that could break the window panes and spied the chamber pot under the bed. He grabbed the pot and hurled it at the window. The half-full pot shattered one pane before bouncing back into the room. Edward jumped back, narrowly avoiding a splash of urine.

"What are you doing in there?" Doyle yelled from the hall. "You are going to pay for damages, one way or another!" He followed his threat with another slam into the door, further cracking the chair's oak frame. It would not survive another blow. Edward grabbed his worn old carpetbag and was about to break the rest of the window panes with it when he noticed the window lock was engaged. Chocking back tears of relief, Edward turned the clasp and the window smoothly slid up. Then, careful to avoid the urine on the window sill, he slipped through the opening onto the boarding house's rear lean-to roof.

Edward gingerly walked to the edge of the roof and peered over; it was a seven-foot drop to the dirt yard below. Then, hearing another bang and the sound of the chair breaking into kindling, Edward dropped his valise over the edge and watched it land with a thud. He then turned, lay on his stomach, and pushed his feet and legs over the roof's eave. Edward dangled there for a second, then dropped three feet to the ground, landed softly, and leaned against a row of firewood stacked against the house's back wall. Relieved that he had survived the drop unscathed, Edward picked up his bag just as the back door flew open, and a red-faced Siobhan charged out. At the same time, he heard loud cursing from above. Siobhan stopped, and they both looked up when Doyle yelled, "he pissed all over the window!"

"Why you filthy, little shite!" roared Siobhan.

"Eep," Edward croaked, and then he picked up a piece of firewood from the woodpile and hurled it toward Siobhan. Without looking back, Edward broke into an ungainly lope down the back alley. He saw neither the piece of firewood connect squarely with Siobhan's forehead nor her drop to the ground. But Doyle saw it, and he leaped off the roof and ran to his mother's aid.

"Mam?" Doyle cried, rocking his body while cradling his mother's head in his lap as he sat on the ground beside her, "Mam?"

"Mmph."

"Mam!"

"Did you get him?" she slurred when her eyes opened.

"No, I came to check on you first."

"Well, for fek's sake, idjit!" Siobhan cried, then winced. "Go get him before he gets away!"

"Okay, Mam!" Doyle leaped up, dropping his mother's head, and ran toward the alley.

"Idjit!" Siobhan cursed when her head bounced off the ground. Then she turned and vomited in the dirt.

Edward ran like he had from bullies that tormented him in his youth, cutting through yards, weaving around clothes and sheets hanging on lines, and leaping over picket fences. Finally, he made it to the Grand Trunk Pacific Railway train station. Bent over, gasping for breath, and massaging a hitch in his side, Edward looked behind him. No sign of Doyle, but that did not mean the brute had given up. He walked onto the platform, entered the station, and studied the schedule board. He saw an eastbound train was scheduled to leave in a few minutes. Looking out the bank of windows, Edward could see people boarding. He hurried to the ticket agent's cage and asked how much a ticket to Winnipeg cost, the next large city east of Saskatoon. The amount was more than Edward had thought it would be, and it left him with just a few dollars to spare. He got his ticket and was about to rush out onto the boarding platform when he saw Doyle rounding the corner of the station and stepping onto the boardwalk. Edward ducked back inside the station and knelt below the glass insert of the door. He rose and peered out at Doyle, who was walking along the train, looking in its windows, and studying each passenger's face as he strode by.

Edward waited until Doyle walked by his spot and then crept quickly to the train and climbed the steps. He stood at the back of the railcar and watched Doyle through the windows, ducking back when his pursuer stopped, turned around, and retraced his steps, still looking up at the train's windows. Edward held his breath when Doyle walked past his hiding spot near the train's steps and then exhaled with relief when the train jerked and began to slowly move forward. Edward walked down the aisle and searched for an empty seat. There were none, so he walked through to the next car as the train began to pick up speed. This car appeared full, too, except for the very back where a stern-looking Indian man sat beside a smiling round-faced woman, also Indian, in a booth by themselves.

The Indian man scrutinizing Edward as he approached was dressed in jeans with the cuffs rolled up, square-toed cowboy boots, and a faded denim shirt. A round black felt hat with two feathers in the hatband sat on the overhead luggage rack beside what looked like a trapper's packsack. It was quite a contrast to Edward's patent leather lace-up shoes, brown pinstriped suit, and carpetbag with its floral design. Somewhere along his escape route, he had lost his bowler hat. The woman, short and stocky with a very dark complexion, wore a floral dress and, despite the warmth in the train car, had a shawl draped around her shoulders. Her hair was in two braids secured on the ends with strips of deerskin.

Edward slowly sat in the lone empty seat across from the couple. For the first several minutes, Edward put his cheek to the window, trying to look as far back as possible, hoping to see Doyle standing on the train station platform. Still, he couldn't see that far, at least not until the train turned slightly, and then there he was, standing on the platform with his hands on his hips, staring after the train. Finally, Edward turned in his seat and smiled. The couple smiled back.

"You are being chased," the man said. It was a statement and not a question.

Edward shook his head and then looked out the window. He watched as the city gave way to open prairie. When he looked back, the Indian's man's eyes were closed, and the woman, sitting next to the window, was watching the scenery go by. The conductor began making his way through the car, taking tickets, punching a hole, and passing them back. When he got to their booth, the Indian opened his eyes and handed their tickets over.

So, he hadn't been asleep after all.

"My name is Edward Humphries," he said after the conductor left, extending his right hand.

"Little Crow," the man said, shaking Edward's hand. "This is my wife, White Dove."

Edward shook her hand as well and then asked Little Crow, "So, where are you two going?"

"New York City."

"New York! Why are you going there?"

"A trip with friends. We are meeting them in Winnipeg."

"A holiday, then."

"Little Crow doesn't like the word holiday," White Dove said before lowering her voice to a whisper. "He thinks holidays are for lazy people."

"It's just a trip somewhere new to spend time with friends; I only see them once a year," Little Crow clarified. "This year, it's New York."

That sure sounded like a holiday.

"You go somewhere new each year?" he asked.

"Yes."

"Are your friends, uh, are they like you?" Edward asked, trying not to insult them.

"Yes, two of them are men, and the other two are women," Little Crow said.

"No, I mean, uh . . ."

"He knows what you mean!" White Dove said. "And no, our friends, Jacque and Genevieve Daoust, are Métis, and Tom Flynn, he's a policeman. He's white, but his wife, Annie, is Cree. I am Sioux, and Little Crow is Arapaho."

"Wow, that is quite a mix. How did you all meet?"

"That is a long story, Edward." Little Crow said.

"Well, we have lots of time."

"Be careful what you ask for, Edward; Little Crow likes nothing better than telling stories of his brave deeds." White Dove said and laughed heartily.

"Please, I would like to hear your story."

"Okay," Little Crow said with a sigh, and then he began to tell a story that was so fascinating, Edward had to stop him while he searched for pen and paper.

"Okay, I'm ready," Edward said after digging in his bag and producing a journal and pencil.

"You are writing this down?"

"Yes, is that okay?"

"I guess, but what I'm about to tell you is not just my story. It is White Dove's, Jacque and Genevieve's, and Tom and Annie's stories too."

"Your friends, the ones you are going to meet?

"Yes. Our lives have crossed many times over the years, and now we are family."

"I don't understand," Edward said.

"You will, Edward, once you hear my story."

* * *

Where do I start? I think I will begin my story when I was seventeen, in what is now called Montana, in June of 1876. My name is Little Crow; I am the son of Tall Pony and Morning Star. My parents were killed at the Sand Creek Massacre in 1864 when I had only seen five snows.

I was a warrior; I had a war pony. One morning, I followed Yellow Eagle and four others when they rode out of our camp near Fort Robinson, Nebraska. You see, Edward, our chief had signed a treaty with the whites, and we Arapaho were reduced to drawing rations from the fort. But the young men of our tribe were growing restless, and these five decided they were going up into Montana territory to look for Shoshones and to pick a fight with them. The Shoshone, Crow, Pawnee, and Utes were all enemies of the Arapaho, Cheyenne, and Sioux brothers. Why, you ask? I don't know, nor do I know how long we had been enemies. We just were.

"Go home, Little Crow," Left Hand yelled when he saw me following them. "You are too young to ride with warriors."

"I am a warrior!" I cried.

Left Hand had always treated me badly. It was my fault though; a few years earlier, I had joined in with a group of young boys who were taunting the heavy-set man. You see, even though Left Hand lived among the Arapaho, he was actually half Blackfoot and half Cheyenne, and that is why we were teasing him. He never forgot that day, and he would hit my shins with his stick every chance he could whenever there was a game of stickball. Everyone saw it, but no one ever did anything since Left Hand was a warrior and I was only an orphan. But he was also a big man; maybe that is why no one helped me. Who knows?

So, Sage said, "It is good that he is with us; how else will he become a warrior?"

"Bah! Stay out of my way, Little Crow." Left Hand warned me.

They had all turned on their ponies and were looking back at me, Sage, Left Hand, Yellow Eagle, Yellow Fly, and Waterman, our leader. I pointed beyond them and said, "Lakota."

There was a small party of Lakota Sioux about a half-mile away, sitting on their ponies and looking our way. Waterman turned and saw them.

"How can you tell they are Lakota, Little Crow?" He asked.

It was hot and hazy, as most June days are on the prairie, but yet I could see them.

"By their headdresses."

"You can see their headdresses?"

"Yes," I said, "they are Lakota."

"Come ride up here beside me," Waterman said.

Left Hand scowled at me as I trotted my pony past him. We rode to meet the Lakota, who sat and waited for us. They were twelve in number, a fierce looking lot who all bore scars of past battles.

"You let a child lead you?" one of the Lakota said when we approached them, and they all laughed.

"He sees the world through the eyes of an eagle," Yellow Fly said, pointing two fingers to his eyes and then to the sky.

I did not like the way these warriors were looking at us. I saw two of them with their hands on their tomahawks, knuckles white and bodies tense. There was malevolence in their eyes.

The Lakota leader nodded and said, "We are going to the sun dance; you should come with us."

"We are scouting for Shoshone," Waterman said. He cast an annoyed glance at Yellow Fly. Waterman was the leader of our scouting party and should have been the one to have spoken first.

"There are no Shoshone within two days ride of here. So, you will come with us to our sun dance."

The Lakota leader turned and rode off, followed by his party. One of his warriors galloped ahead of the rest and was soon out of sight. As it would have been considered an insult to refuse such an invitation, we agreed to join their sun dance. They led us toward a large encampment at a place called Greasy Grass near the Little Bighorn River, and several more warriors rode out to meet us. They formed a circle around us, and three warriors slid off their ponies and demanded our weapons. We told them we were their brothers, but they would not listen.

Waterman nodded to us and handed over his tomahawk and gun. I did not have a rifle, so I slipped off my buckskin quiver and handed it over with the bow Spotted Tail had given me several months before. He had taken them from a Crow warrior he had killed in battle. Spotted Tail was a great Cheyenne warrior who sometimes taught me in the ways of hunting and war.

When we arrived at their camp, I was amazed to see hundreds of tipis stretching for as far as I could see. There must have been thousands of people here. Warriors dragged us off our ponies and herded us into a tight circle. Dozens of Lakota warriors surrounded us, many had cocked their rifles, and war cries erupted. Some women called for our deaths in retaliation for their husbands' deaths. They thought we were scouts for the white soldiers.

I was terrified, I will admit that. I would accept my death, but only in battle, so I went into my fighting stance. For some reason, this amused some of our captors. Waterman clamped a hand on my shoulder, and I relaxed my stance. I looked across this vast camp and saw many Sioux and Cheyenne but no Arapaho.

We were encircled by a group of angry Lakota warriors who pushed hard at us with their rifles, crowding us into a tight circle that kept getting tighter. From all around us, there were shouts of "Kill them!" Many of them had lost family members when white soldiers had attacked their camps. These soldiers were led to the camps by Indian scouts from other tribes, and they must have thought we were some of those scouts.

Suddenly, we heard shouting from the rear. Two Cheyenne warriors had pushed through the crowd, and one said loudly, "Wait, we are standing in front of Two Moon's lodge; it is for him to decide the fate of these men!" A murmur spread through the crowd, and then one of the Lakota stepped toward the tipi and called for Two Moon to come out, but he was not inside. Then a boy was sent to find the Cheyenne war chief.

We were pushed down to the ground, and we sat in a circle, back-to-back, as Lakota warriors kept their cocked rifles pointed at us. It was uncomfortable knowing that any of those guns in the anxious men's hands could go off at any moment. Then Waterman began to sing his death song. The others soon joined in with their own death songs. I am ashamed to say that I did not have a death song, so I copied Yellow Fly's; I liked his song, and he smiled when I sang it. The Lakota respected the ritual and did not interrupt us.

Sometime later—and I don't know how long—Two Moon and five other Cheyenne chiefs arrived. We stopped singing, and they looked at us with stony faces as they walked by and entered Two Moon's lodge. We remained silent, along with the Lakota, as we waited. I looked up and saw a warrior staring at me with a malicious grin; he swung his rifle toward me, and I watched his finger on the trigger. I braced for impact when I saw his finger twitching. He pulled the trigger and I heard a click and I jerked forward. His rifle was not loaded, and those around him laughed before an older warrior angrily shoved him away. I tried to hide the shaking that racked my body by drawing my knees up and hugging them tight to my chest as I pressed my forehead to my knees.

The shakes subsided, and Waterman helped me up when we were called into Two Moon's lodge. We were seated across from six war chiefs who stared stony-faced at us. Gray pipe smoke hung in the gloomy air, and I had to stifle a cough. It was quiet for some time as they studied us.

"What are you called?" Two Moon asked.

Waterman began, and I was the last to say my name. I was embarrassed when it came out in a croak, and I had to clear my voice before repeating my name.

"You are Little Crow, the orphan?" Two Moons asked.

"Yes." I stammered.

Act like a warrior, I told myself.

"Spotted Tail speaks highly of you."

My companions, confused, turned and looked at me.

2

You see, Edward, I had first met Spotted Tail while hunting deer the previous fall. I carried a sapling that I had carved smooth and burned a point in one end to use as my hunting spear. Unfortunately, it would not fly true, so I was forced to sneak up close to my prey. After an hour of slowly crawling toward a grazing buck, I felt I was close enough, so I rose up and drew my spear back when an arrow whizzed by my ear and struck the deer in its ribs. The animal leaped up and ran several yards before falling on its side. I turned and held my spear at the ready, not knowing if it was a friend or foe behind me. The Cheyenne war chief, Spotted Tail, and several other warriors sat on ponies fifty yards away. He said something to his warriors, and then he trotted up to me and sat staring at me while the others quickly gutted and loaded the deer onto one of their ponies. Finally, one of them walked over to us and handed Spotted Tail a piece of liver. Spotted Tail tore a chunk off with his teeth and then passed the rest to me. I ate it in one bite, not having eaten anything in two days.

"Who are you?" he asked me.

"I am Little Crow, son of Tall Pony, the great Arapaho warrior!" I declared with a strong voice and pounded my narrow chest with a fist.

Spotted Tail suppressed a grin and nodded.

"The son of Tall Pony should carry a strong bow!"

His companions murmured agreement, and Spotted Tail handed me his bow. I hesitated, but he lifted it slightly, and I took it from him. Then, he unslung his quiver full of arrows and gave it to me. I was speechless as I stared in awe at the beadwork on the quiver. When I looked up, I was relieved that they had turned and trotted away, for there were tears in my eyes. The following winter, I had been summoned to Spotted Tail's lodge a few times, and he would tell me stories and teach me how to shoot the bow and arrow. I cherished those visits and had been waiting several months to be summoned once again, but no summons had come since the spring.

Now, where was I? Oh, yeah, inside Chief Two Moon's tipi.

"You are here to fight the soldiers with us?" Two Moons asked us.

"Yes, they are our enemies too," Waterman said.

Two Moon nodded and indicated to us that we were to leave his tipi. The chiefs followed us out, and then Two Moon declared to the crowd that we were their friends and were there to help fight the white soldiers. So, we were released and given our weapons back. Unfortunately, my bow was broken when it was handed back to me; I feared I had dishonored Spotted Tail. Seeing my anguish, Waterman put a hand on my shoulder, but it was little comfort.

You see, Spotted Tail was my mentor. He was the one who had taught me how not to hate the whites. I found that hard to do, but he had explained that they were scared of us and that shamed them. I still did not understand and told him so.

He said, "When someone is scared of you, they are capable of doing bad things when they gain the upper hand. It is not their fault."

"Do you hate the whites?" I asked Spotted Tail.

"No," he said. I waited for more but he never spoke about it again. I thought about his words for many months until I realized I no longer held a hatred for those soldiers. At first, it felt like it was a betrayal to my parents, but I think they would be proud of me. Anyway, back to my story.

A Lakota warrior called Two Elk, the one who had dry fired at me, walked up to us and said, "Come with me."

My companions and I looked at each other. Then Waterman shrugged, and we followed the young man. We came to a tipi, and he indicated for us to wait outside. Two Elk poked his head into the tipi and said something to the occupant. Then Two Elk withdrew his head and walked by us and yelled "Bang!" when he was abreast of me. I hated that I jumped noticeably, so I started after the laughing warrior, but Sage grabbed my arm and shook his head.

We were surprised when the Lakota war chief, American Horse, came out of the tipi.

"Come eat with me," he said and went back inside.

After recovering from the shock of meeting the great war chief, we followed him into his lodge.

"This is my wife, Walks With." American Horse smiled at his wife when he said this.

I waited for him to finish her name, but that's all it was, just Walks With. Hiding behind her was a young girl about my age. She gradually came out from behind Walks With and sat beside her, head lowered shyly. But when she looked up, I was struck by her beauty. I could not take my eyes off the girl. She saw me looking and quickly looked down. A memory suddenly flashed in my mind. A scared little girl, her tear-streaked face flickering in the light of burning tipis and the air filled with the sounds of screaming, shooting, and pounding horse hooves. Could it actually be her?

* * *

Edward looked up from his writing and glanced at White Dove. Was she that girl? Her face was turned, looking out the train's window so he could not see her reaction to her husband's mention of the girl in American Horse's tipi. Edward looked around him, sensing they weren't alone, and was surprised to see several men and women standing near their booth, listening to the story. Edward looked down at his journal and resumed his frantic writing as Little Crow continued talking.

* * *

Our backsides had barely touched the ground before American Horse began to regale us with exploits from his youth. I listened raptly with the others to how he and several companions had been about to attack a party of Shoshone who had encroached on Cheyenne territory when American Horse spotted a deer. Being hungry, he shot the deer with his bow and arrow, and his companions joined him as he gutted the deer. He cut the liver out of the still quivering animal, sprinkled it with bile from the gall bladder for taste, and passed it around to be eaten raw. With renewed energy from the deer's gift, he and his companions then attacked the Shoshone and drove them away. While we dutifully oohed and aahed, I looked at the girl, and we locked eyes. I felt a strange flush in my chest that ran down to my groin; it was not an unpleasant feeling. Our host saw me looking, and he turned to see the girl smiling. Her smile was partially hidden behind long raven-black hair.

"This is Waynoka, a Cheyenne girl." Then American Horse looked directly at me and asked, "What do you have to offer her?"

I choked on my food, and my friends laughed at me; Yellow Eagle slapped me on the back.

"I, uh . . ."

Could she be the same Waynoka from Sand Creek? There were Cheyenne camped with the Arapaho when the soldiers attacked, so it was possible.

American Horse laughed as Waynoka cried out and ran from the tipi.

"She is too young for marriage, Little Crow, as are you."

"I am a warrior!" I said. "Wait, how do you know my name?"

"Spotted Tail has spoken of you."

"You know Spotted Tail? Is he here?"

"Of course I know Spotted Tail; he is a great warrior, but no, he is not here."

"Where are Waynoka's father and mother?" I asked, breaking a brief silence that had settled over us.

"Waynoka was found hiding in some sagebrush near Sand Creek. Her parents were killed by the soldiers. Now, she helps my wife," American Horse said.

So, it was her!

"My parents were also killed there."

We went quiet and lowered our heads. Those twelve snows before, the white soldiers had attacked our sleeping village of Cheyenne and Arapaho. The soldiers had slaughtered and mutilated almost everyone in the encampment, including women and children. Those who had escaped the massacre had fled north to the Black Hills of Dakota.

"Thank you for the food; it was an honor to sit with a great warrior!" Waterman said as he rose.

"We will meet again." American Horse was looking at me when he said this.

I turned to look back as we walked away, and I saw a slim shape in the shadows beside the tipi.

Our scouting party stayed in the camp for several days, taking part in the sun dance and sleeping near our ponies at night. In the afternoons, I played stickball with boys my age, and some older men participated. I received many sticks to the shins from Two Elk. He would go out of his way to torment me, but I was used to that. Finally, after one severe blow to my shin from Two Elk's stick, I had had enough. I dropped my stick, charged at him with a yell, and tackled him around the waist. We went down to the ground and rolled in the dirt as the rest of the players formed a circle and cheered us on. I heard more cheers for Two Elk than for me, but a few were calling my name.

Two Elk quickly rolled on top of me and pushed his forearm onto my neck. I panicked when I couldn't breathe, and I grabbed at his arm, but he rose and pushed his weight onto my throat. I frantically kicked at him, and my knee accidentally connected with his testicles, hard. Finally, the pressure on my neck eased, and I managed to roll him over. He was clutching his groin as I grabbed his head in both hands and pushed one side of his face into the dirt. The crowd stood around us in shocked silence, and then two older Cheyenne boys, Limber Bones and Closed Hand, lifted me off Two Elk. I was still in fighting mode and threw a kick toward Two Elk, but Limber Bones jerked me back, and my foot narrowly missed Two Elk's head. He lay on his side, and his eyes bored into mine as the two Cheyenne pulled me back. Several of his friends tried to help him up, but he roughly pushed their hands away.

After my pulse had returned to normal, I walked back to American Horse's lodge and saw Left Hand and Sage sitting outside. Sage gave me an appraising look as I approached. Was it a look of respect? I like to think so. Sage was a quiet man, thoughtful and well respected among the Cheyenne. When he looked at me, I always felt as though he could see into my mind. It was unnerving, but whenever I needed counsel, it was Sage who I would seek for guidance.

Anyway, American Horse let it be known that we were welcome to share evening meals with his family during our stay, and we did not refuse his hospitality. Unfortunately, with such a large encampment, food was scarce, so Waterman sent out our best hunters, Yellow Eagle and Yellow Fly while he, Left Hand, and Sage would try to catch trout in the river. I asked Waterman what I was supposed to do.

"American Horse wants you to go with Waynoka for her protection while she gathers prairie turnips," Waterman said.

I tried to hide my joy at this news, but from the smirks on Left Hand and Sage's faces, I did not do a good job of it.

* * *

Little Crow stopped his narrative, leaned over to White Dove, and whispered, "Is it okay if I tell this part of the story?"

She nodded but did not smile.

"Are you sure?"

"Yes, it is not my favorite part to hear, but I know she was an important part of your life's journey. There's no need to leave her out on my account," she said with a small smile as she patted his hand.

Across the booth, Edward had heard the whispered conversation and had seen Little Crow's chest swell as he looked at his wife. Then he turned and continued his story.

* * *

Early the next morning, Waynoka and I had taken the ponies to the river. We waded in and threw water onto the ponies. Waynoka playfully splashed me, and I scooped up water and threw it at her. She screamed, and when I chased her, she turned and threw water in my face. We were laughing and splashing each other when we heard the first gunshots. We stopped and looked toward the camp and saw warriors running about, catching ponies, and riding toward the sound. I led the ponies out of the water and leaped onto mine. I yelled for Waynoka to go home. Then I saw my friends, so I rode to them, handed them their pony's ropes, and we raced with other warriors toward a large cloud of dust. I had no weapon, but I was too excited to think about that.

* * *

Little Crow again stopped his story, this time when the car door opened and the conductor loudly announced sandwiches and drinks for sale. He pushed a cart down the aisle and the people standing near our booth returned to their seats for their lunch.

"Mr. Little Crow," said a woman who had stopped by their booth before returning to her seat, "please wait until I return before continuing your story."

Little Crow smiled and nodded. Edward took out his pocket watch and checked the time. It was just after twelve. His stomach rumbled at the thought of food, but could he afford it?

"Just water," Edward said when the cart stopped at their booth.

"Us too," Little Crow said.

"There are cups and a water dispenser at the other end of the car," the conductor gruffly told them and then moved to the next booth.

After the conductor and his food cart left the car, Little Crow and Edward went to get paper cones of water. When they returned, White Dove dug into one of her bags and produced two sandwiches, handing one to Little Crow and unwrapping the other one for herself. When Edward's stomach rumbled loudly, she glanced at her husband, who nodded. Then she removed another sandwich from her bag and handed it to Edward. He made a show of refusing, but his eyes belied the gesture, and White Dove lifted the sandwich up and down in front of him with a smile until he took it.

"Thank you."

Edward lifted one piece of the thick homemade buttered bread and saw roast beef covered with onions. He took a bite and moaned with pleasure. White Dove's face lit up, and Little Crow said, "Our tribe raises our own cattle."

"It may well be the best sandwich I have ever eaten!" Edward gushed between bites. He finished eating quickly and now waited patiently as Little Crow and White Dove leisurely ate their lunch.

3

Finally, after the lady who had spoken to him earlier and the rest of his audience had assembled once again, Little Crow resumed his story. Edward noted that the crowd had grown since the last time he had checked.

**

I heard many guns firing in rapid succession and war cries of the Lakota and Cheyenne, and my excitement built.

"Go hide with the children, Little Crow!" Two Elk yelled over his shoulder at me. "You do not even have a gun."

"I do not need a gun!" I yelled with all the false bravado that came with surging adrenaline as I raced past him. My pony looked plain, but it was fast. I heard Two Elk whoop behind me as he tried to catch up. I crossed the river with a group of Lakota and Cheyenne, and I could see a group of white soldiers surrounded on a ridge. I raced forward, heart-pounding, heedless of the shooting around me, when a soldier swung his carbine at my pony like a club. I was thrown over my pony's head as it skidded to a stop. I rolled when I hit the ground and jumped to my feet to meet the enemy in a crouch.

The soldier raised his carbine and aimed it at me, but a horse slammed into him before he could shoot, knocking him down. Two Elk jumped off his horse and drove his tomahawk into the man's head.

"Take his gun!" he called as he leaped back on his horse and galloped away.

I shook my head and looked around for my pony, but he was nowhere in sight, so I ran forward on foot, empty-handed. I would not kill anyone. Instead, I will count coup and show my bravery by touching the enemy with a stick and letting him live. Then I saw Left Hand ride toward an Indian on foot and drive his lance into him. I ran past the dead man and saw that he was a Lakota warrior. Why did Left Hand kill him? The broken end of Left Hand's lance lay several feet past the dead warrior, so I picked it up as I ran forward.

I ran past white soldiers, tapped them on the head or shoulder with the lance, and yelled my war cry. They turned toward me. Some screamed and cowered, others aimed their guns and shot, but no bullets found me. Then, through the clouds of dust and gun smoke, I saw Crazy Horse looking at me; he yelled his war cry and shook his Winchester in the air before disappearing in the dust.

Suddenly, shots erupted from the other end of the encampment, and many warriors turned and raced that way. I saw the white soldiers running away from this ridge, so I turned and followed the others toward the new threat. It sounded like a fierce battle. Then I saw my pony, but he was limping, so I caught a white soldier's riderless horse and leaped on him. He bucked and tried to throw me off, but I held on tight and dug my heels into his ribs until he obeyed my commands.

When I arrived at the fighting, I continued to use the broken lance as my coupstick. The gunfire here was so intense—the staccato sounds of pop-pop-pop so furious—it seemed to meld into one continuous sound. I choked on the clouds of gun smoke that burned my eyes, yet I still counted coup and the soldiers still shot at me. I saw their leader, Long Hair, on his horse, yelling orders to his men, when a woman warrior holding a club charged toward him. I thought that was the end of her because Long Hair swung his saber at her, but she ducked and struck Long Hair with her club, knocking him off his horse.

*   *   *

"Wait, there was a woman fighting?" a large man asked.

"Yes, that was Buffalo Calf Road Woman, and Pretty Nose was also there," Little Crow said.

"And you're saying this Buffalo Calf woman knocked General Custer off his horse?"

"Buffalo Calf Road Woman. Yes, she did, but he wasn't a general."

"What?" the man asked loudly.

"He was a Lieutenant-Colonel."

"I don't think so."

"Jake!" A lady tugged at his arm. "Let the man tell his story."

"No, I will not stand here and listen to this bullcrap any longer!" Jake said, then added, "Well, are you coming?"

The woman smiled apologetically to Little Crow and all the others in the audience as she followed her husband through the car door.

"Who were these women?" Astrid asked Little Crow after Jake and his wife exited the car.

"She was a Cheyenne woman. A lot of women fought in the battles, not just Cheyenne but Arapaho and Sioux women also."

"But who was Buffalo Calf Road Woman?"

"Well, even before Greasy Grass, she was famous for saving her bother, Chief Comes in Sight, at the Battle of the Rosebud. Comes in Sight had been wounded, knocked off his horse, and surrounded by soldiers during the battle, and when Buffalo Calf Road Woman saw him, she charged through the soldiers, grabbed her brother, and swung him onto her horse, carrying him to safety. So, from then on, the Cheyenne have called the Battle of the Rosebud, the Fight Where the Girl Saved Her Brother."

"That's amazing!" Astrid said.

"Yes, and at Greasy Grass, she knocked Long Hair from his saddle and then claimed his saber after the battle. She would wear the saber into a few more battles, but then everything must come to an end. Still, the Cheyenne have protected her identity to this day."

"Why?"

"For fear of retribution against her."

"I see, and who was the other woman?"

"Pretty Nose?"

"Yes."

"I saw her once, in the fight at Greasy Grass, but I don't know what happened to her afterward."

"And the person you call Long Hair is Gener…, Lieutenant-Colonel Custer?"

"Yes. Three years before the Little Bighorn fight, Sitting Bull and Crazy Horse fought against Custer in Montana, along the Tongue River. Tales of the encounter with the long-haired white soldier had been retold many times before we knew the man's real name."

"I see."

"Shall I continue?"

"Yes, please."

* * *

So, the white soldiers formed a ring around their leader, and then I saw Crazy Horse charge through their center, but none of the soldiers' bullets struck him. Instead, his and Buffalo Calf Road Woman's bravery rallied the Lakota and the Cheyenne warriors, and they soon overwhelmed the soldiers.

I counted many more coups throughout the furious fighting before a bullet found me and I fell off the soldier's horse. I came to a little while later. The shooting had stopped. I sat up slowly, and through a blue haze of gun smoke, I saw warriors stripping the dead soldiers. My head spun, and suddenly I was back at Sand Creek, and I could hear the screams of women and children as the white soldiers cut them down. I began to shake so hard I thought it would never stop. But it did, and the screams faded, and I was back on a hill at Greasy Grass. Tears blurred my vision, and I smelled the iron of blood. I wiped my eyes and felt dried blood on the side of my face. I got to my feet and had to fight a wave of dizziness and nausea. When my head cleared, I stumbled through the carnage in a daze. Eventually, I stopped near a Lakota warrior and asked him why he had cut off a dead soldier's arms. My words sounded like they came from far away.

"So he cannot fight me in the next life," he said with a wild look on his blood-smeared face.

I did not understand this, so I kept wandering through the battlefield.

"How many coups have you counted this day, Little Crow?" someone called.

I turned and saw Crazy Horse looking down at me from his war pony.

"I don't know," I said, unsure of how I was supposed to address this great warrior.

"I saw many, twenty at least!" he shouted, which caused a lot of whooping from nearby warriors. Crazy Horse exaggerated; of course, I do not think it was twenty. When he trotted his horse away, several Lakota slapped me on the back or clutched my shoulder. I saw American Horse a hundred yards away among a group of Cheyenne warriors. He grinned and held his rifle high, and then his warriors followed suit.

What I saw that day I will never forget, and I will not try to explain it. I stood swaying as I scanned the battlefield, and everything was moving funny, like my eyes were not working properly, and it scared me.

"Little Crow!" I heard but did not see my tormentor, Two Elk, yell.

Then the world spun, and I fell.

Sometime later—they told me it was a whole day—I woke thirstier than I could ever remember being. My tongue felt like a stick in my mouth, and I tried to swallow, but it made my throat hurt. Then I heard someone cry, "He's awake: Little Crow's awake!"

It was Waynoka. She rushed to me, and I made a drinking gesture with one hand. Lifting my head caused blinding pain, and I winced and laid my head back down. I felt the brim of a cup and drops of water on my lips. I licked my lips, and more water dripped into my mouth. I tried to take the cup and drink it down, but Waynoka pulled it away.

"Go slow," she said. "American Horse told me you need to drink only a little."

I did not understand this. Why would American Horse say that? There was plenty of water in the river. I drifted off again.

"Little Crow!"

I felt water drip in my mouth. I licked my lips and opened my eyes and saw American Horse's grinning face inches above me.

"We must go."

"Go where?" My words came out in a croak, and he handed me a cup of water.

"Drink slow. Sitting Bull wants us to leave this place. All the tribes are going in different directions. We will go to the Dakotas. The white soldiers are angry; they are coming to avenge the death of Long Hair. More soldiers than we have ever seen."

"Why did they attack us, American Horse?"

"They say we broke a treaty, but Sitting Bull did not sign any treaty."

"I don't understand. What is this treaty?"

"Some Lakota have signed a treaty saying that they would stay on a reservation. Sitting Bull did not sign any treaty with the whites, and they used that as an excuse to attack our camps."

I still did not understand, but my head hurt, so I did not ask any more questions. American Horse helped me up, and I swayed until the dizziness passed. He helped me walk outside the tipi, and I shut my eyes against the blazing sun. Most of the tipis in the encampment were gone; others were being taken down. There was a sense of urgency bordering on panic among the remaining Indians. Walks With and Waynoka were wrapping furs onto a travois tied to American Horse's only pony. My pony walked over and nudged me, his limp miraculously healed. American Horse told me he needed my pony to pull his tipi. Despite everything that had happened, and the fact that we were fleeing, I felt joy that day. I was part of their family now. No words were said; it was just so.

"Where are my friends?" I asked.

"They left," American Horse said. "They feared for their families' safety."

I understood that. I had no family back at the Arapaho camp, but I understood.

"There are some who say an Arapaho killed a Lakota warrior during the fight." He looked at me with a raised eyebrow.

"I saw that. The Lakota could have been mistaken for a soldier's scout. It was hard to see clearly in all the smoke and dust."

"Ah." He nodded.

I drank more water as I waited for them to finish packing. My head ached, and there was a bandage wound around my forehead.

"What happened to my head?"

"A bullet bounced off your skull. Good thing your head is made of stone!" He laughed, and I saw Waynoka grinning.

I saw a new bow and a headband with an eagle feather on their travois and assumed it belonged to American Horse. It didn't.

"Two Elk brought these from Crazy Horse," American Horse said.

"Two Elk?"

"Yes, he came here twice to check on you. He told me to tell you that he is sorry for treating you badly. He said you are a brave warrior and he would be proud to call you a friend."

I had not expected that from my tormentor. Maybe he wasn't so bad after all.

* * *

Little Crow stopped his recitation there, saying he had need of the washroom. Edward noticed that everyone in the car had been listening to the story.

"It does not bother you when Little Crow speaks of Waynoka?" Edward asked White Dove after Little Crow left.

"It did, years ago, but not anymore," she said. "They were never married."

"But it must still bother you to hear him talk about how much he had cared for her?"

"Yes, in the past, we had argued about speaking her name, but then I realized that she is the reason he appreciates me so much."

"I don't get it."

"He has lost one love in his life; he doesn't want to lose another."

"Ah, I think I get it now."

Little Crow returned and took a drink of water. A woman holding a little girl's hand asked, "Excuse me, Mr. Little Crow, would you mind waiting until we get back before resuming your story?"

The little girl stood staring at Little Crow, eyes wide and sucking her thumb.

"Yes, of course, but hurry back because I am going to tell what really happened at Slim Buttes."

"Slim Buttes?" the lady, Astrid, asked.

"Yes, the stories you may have read or heard about Slim Buttes are not entirely true. I will tell you the true story."

"Come, Greta," Astrid said and then hurried toward the lavatory.

When they returned, she flashed a smile and said, "Thank you. Can I ask you a question, Mr. Little Crow?"

"Of course."

"Who was Long Hair?"

"His full name was George Armstrong Custer." Little Crow glanced at Edward who nodded.

"Oh, and he is famous?"

"Yes, from the Little Bighorn Battle."

"But you call it something else?"

"Yes, we call it the Battle at Greasy Grass."

"Thank you, Mr. Little Crow."

4

In September of the same year, we were camped near Slim Buttes, in Dakota territory, and I was sitting with Two Elk in front of his lodge. When I had first arrived there with American Horse and his family, Two Elk had approached me and apologized for treating me so roughly at Greasy Grass. Since then, a close friendship had slowly developed between us. Now, we would often sit together without talking, both of us comfortable in each other's presence. And we were doing just that one day when a face poked out from his tipi and beckoned to Two Elk. It was his wife, Laughing Woman. She had always been a puzzlement to me. She was short and rotund, and I often wondered what a tall strong warrior like Two Elk saw in her. And I suspected Laughing Woman had wanted to laugh with me too from the way I would catch her looking at me when she thought her husband was not watching. Two Elk nodded to her and then said to me, "Come, Little Crow. My wife has something for you."

I bent and followed my friend into his tipi and let my eyes adjust to the gloom. Laughing Woman was standing with a wide grin on her face and holding a large blanket of many colors. It was beautiful. I looked at Laughing Woman, and she smiled proudly. I did not understand.

"It's a courting blanket; my wife has made it for you," Two Elk announced proudly.

"But she is already married to you!" I said, shocked.

Two Elk and Laughing Woman looked at each other in confusion and then burst out laughing. Now, Laughing Woman's laugh was something to behold! It began with a whoop, was followed by braying as she bent over and slapped her knee, and ended with an intake of breath. It was an infectious laugh.

* * *

Little Crow then stood and imitated Laughing Woman's laugh, including the whoop and braying, which caused Greta to laugh gleefully and clap her hands.

* * *

"It's for you to court Waynoka!" Two Elk cried, still chuckling and shaking his head at the thought of me courting Laughing Woman.

"Waynoka!" I said. "But she is too young."

"She is seventeen, same as you, and there are others who look at her. If you don't take her for your wife, someone else will," Laughing Woman said.

"But I have nothing to offer American Horse."

"After you court her, we will go steal some Crow ponies and present them to American Horse," Two Elk declared.

* * *

"Now, I see some shocked faces, and I presume it is because of Two Elk's suggestion that we steal horses from another tribe," Little Crow said to his audience. "So, let me try to explain the customs of the time. You see, wealth was measured by how many ponies a family owned, and an Indian, both men and women, earned status among their tribe by 'borrowing' prized ponies from another tribe, so much so that they would paint their brave deed on their tipi. I say 'borrowing' instead of 'stealing' because people from our tribe would borrow ponies from another tribe, and a few months later, they would come in the dark of night and borrow our ponies. It was all a game to prove how brave we were. But, in this instance, it was customary to present the bride's father with ponies when asking for her hand. And since I didn't have any ponies, it was a time to borrow some ponies from another tribe. I hope that explains our customs and you see that Indians are not thieves. On the contrary, we are raised to be honorable men and women. We did not break any of the treaties we signed."

"Yes, that is most helpful, Mr. Little Crow," Astrid said.

"I'm glad. Now, I will continue my story."

* * *

"We are going to take ponies from the Crow?" I asked.

Now the Crow, they are a formidable people, strong and fearless, so the thought of entering their camp and taking their ponies from under their noses caused my body to tingle with both fear and anticipation.

"Yes, there is an encampment three days' ride from here."

"How do you know this?"

"Cut Nose told me."

I stood, looked at Two Elk and Laughing Woman's grinning faces, and came to a decision.

"Okay."

Laughing Woman shrieked, and I worried what others may think was going on in here. The next few minutes were a flurry of directions from both Two Elk and his wife. Laughing Woman quickly shot down Two Elk's advice.

"I tried not to laugh when you spoke those words to me, bah!"

Two Elk gaped at her, and then the argument started. I picked up the blanket and snuck out of the tipi.

I folded the blanket so it wouldn't drag on the ground and carried it on one arm. The air buzzed as I made my way through the tipis toward American Horse's lodge. People, primarily women and young girls, pointed, whispered, and giggled as I passed. Then I glimpsed Red Dog, an ugly and cruel man, glaring at me. I suspected he was one of the warriors who Laughing Woman had noticed was interested in Waynoka. I smiled and waved at him as I passed. His hand dropped to his tomahawk, but his father was standing beside him and stayed his hand. I would do well to watch Red Dog.

I considered turning around and running during my walk. Yet I kept going as my entire body flushed with both fear and anticipation, even more than it had at the thought of borrowing Crow ponies. Waynoka must have been watching me approach, for when I neared American Horse's tipi, she stepped out and stood, waiting for me with her hands behind her back and her head lowered. I could see a couple round faces through a gap in the door flap.

I stopped in front of Waynoka, unfurled the blanket, flipped it over my shoulders, and held out a flap for her. I held my breath when she made no move toward me. Had I misread her feelings? But then she tilted her head up, smiled, and stepped forward, tucking herself under my arm. Then I lifted the blanket over our heads.

Now, I cannot repeat what was said under that blanket because my head was in a whirl the entire time. But I know I promised her the earth and everything on it until she reached up and placed a finger on my lips. Then she replaced her finger with her lips, and I almost passed out. How long we stayed under that blanket, I do not know. All I know is that I wished it would last forever.

* * *

Edward glanced at White Dove when she grunted. At the beginning of this session, she had been sewing glass beads onto a patch of smoked moosehide. The geometric beadwork resembled a series of little colorful tipis; it was beautiful work. Edward had watched in fascination at how effortlessly she threaded the needle through the tough hide, securing the beads. But now her face was grim, and she was aggressively jabbing the needle through the leather. Edward glanced at Little Crow as he stopped his narrative and leaned over to whisper in White Dove's ear for several seconds. Her face slowly lost its scowl and then brightened considerably. She turned and smiled at her husband and nodded. Little Crow smiled back at her and then turned to face the crowd who had leaned in as if to eavesdrop on their private conversation. He smiled and apologized for the interruption.

* * *

When I lifted the blanket, I was surprised to see how many people were standing around us. Of course, most were smiling, but I did see a few scowling warriors, Red Dog among them.

"I will be back in seven days," I told her, "With many ponies to offer American Horse."

"I will wait for you, Little Crow."

I walked through a gauntlet of men who grinned and slapped me on the back or shoulder as the women rushed toward Waynoka and surrounded her, all chattering excitedly.

Two Elk was waiting for me with our ponies. He smiled and said, "Let's go make American Horse a rich man!"

Three days later, we approached the Crow camp on foot, having tied our ponies a mile away. We knew their ponies would greet ours with a whinny if we brought them closer. Their camp was on the valley floor, beside a small stream. Ponderosa pines and sagebrush dotted the low valley walls.

It was several hours before dawn, but the moon shone intermittently as it traveled between clouds. A rattlesnake warned us that we were getting too close, and then we saw a figure, sitting against a tree several yards away, lift his head. It was a Crow sentry who had turned to look toward the sound of the rattle. I was too close to the snake to make any sudden movements, so it was up to Two Elk to take care of the sentry. I was still watching the snake in front of me when I heard a bonk and, out of the corner of my eye, saw the sentry fall quietly to the ground. I carefully backed away from the snake and then crawled toward the ponies. Two Elk had taken the unconscious sentry's headband to mask some of his scent from the ponies.

There should have been another guard, so we lay in wait until the moon peeked through the clouds, and then I spotted him. Like the first sentry, he was sitting against a tree when he yawned mightily. Two Elk handed me the knotty branch he had used to knock out the other sentry, and I crept stealthily toward the man. As it turned out, the sentry was just a boy, and he had fallen asleep by the time I got to him. So, I carefully eased his head band off, and all he did was reposition himself and continue sleeping. He looked so young and peaceful sleeping there that I felt sympathy for him, for the berating he would get in the morning when the tribe discovered the missing horses. But I knew that I would face ridicule of my own if I backed down now, so I continued on.

A string of twenty ponies sensed our nearness, but they were not alarmed once they caught the Crow sentries' scents on us. We went to either ends of the line, untied the rope, and slowly walked the ponies away from the camp. I kept a close eye on the sleeping boy, but he did not move. We led the animals to our own ponies, and not surprisingly, they greeted each other as if they were old friends. I had seen that before, when visitors from another tribe had come into our camp and our ponies seemed to have known some of their ponies. I guess, with all the "borrowing" going on over the years, they may well have known each other at one time or another.

We rode fast the first day; we did not take all the Crow's ponies, so we knew they would be riding hard after us. On the second day, in the evening, we stopped on a hilltop overlooking a coulee and saw a dust cloud several miles behind us. We knew it was a Crow war party raising that dust, and we knew they would have seen us silhouetted against the sky on the ridge, and we knew they would not stop until they had caught up to us. The prospect of being captured by a large group of angry warriors was not something we cared to contemplate, so we rode through the night.

We crested a hill the next morning and saw a large hunting party sitting their horses a hundred yards away. We instinctively grabbed our rifles, ready to fight against impossible odds, when we realized they were Oglala and at the head of the group was Crazy Horse himself. After we rode to them and explained the situation, Crazy Horse shook his head and said with a grin, "Did you tap the Crow on their heads when you took their ponies?"

"Well, Two Elk did, but I just sung a lullaby and put the other guard to sleep."

"Hah, you are either crazy or very brave!" Crazy Horse said. "Come, Little Crow, let's go see how badly these Crow want their ponies back."

We turned our ponies toward the Crow, and Crazy Horse yelled, "Put your war feather on, Little Crow. Let them know they are dealing with the famous Arapaho coup counter!"

We charged toward the Crow, who quickly scattered and ran when they saw Crazy Horse in the lead. We stopped, and Crazy Horse looked at the twenty ponies behind us.

Without hesitation, I said, "I would be honored, Crazy Horse, if you'd accept my gift to you of ten ponies."

"It is I who should be honored, Little Crow."

It was later that evening and raining steadily when Two Elk and I drove the remaining ten ponies into American Horse's camp.

"Do you think ten ponies will be enough?" I asked.

"It will have to be, Little Crow. I do not want to go back for more," Two Elk replied wearily.

We were exhausted and looking forward to a good night's sleep but, unfortunately, all hell would break loose before the night was over.

* * *

By now, several passengers from other cars had heard about the Indian man telling a story, and they now stood in the aisle listening. Edward could see that Little Crow was enjoying himself and that his voice had gotten louder as his audience had grown. Edward had been writing furiously, trying to get every word down. Still, there were some blank sections where he had fallen behind and had to skip ahead to keep up. He would have to fill those in from memory.

5

It was well after dark and raining heavily by the time I lay down to sleep. Before the rain had started, Two Elk and I had staked the ponies on the grass behind the encampment after watering them at a creek. After six days of hard riding to the Crow camp and back, I looked forward to a good night's sleep without having to take turns on sentry duty. That night, I slept in Two Elk's tipi.

It was still dark when gunshots entered the fog of my dreams. I was dreaming of the Battle at Greasy Grass and that I was in hand-to-hand combat with Long Hair while bullets whizzed by my head. I heard the soldiers' shouts and our women's screams, and then realized I was not dreaming. The camp was under attack! The door flap was tied shut to keep the rain out, and Two Elk had cut through the hide at the back of the tipi.

I grabbed the rifle and cartridge belts that Two Elk had found on the battlefield at Greasy Grass and slipped out of the tipi behind him. I had left my bow in American Horse's lodge.

"Run to the hills, Little Crow!" Two Elk yelled at me, and then he realized Laughing Woman hadn't come out of the tipi. I hesitated for a few seconds after he went back through the slit. The gunfire from the soldiers was intense. They shot blindly into tipis and at anything that moved.

I ran toward American Horse's lodge to get Waynoka. I was halfway there when I met American Horse and his family.

"Where is Waynoka?" I asked.

"She is safe," American Horse said. "Red Dog came and took her to the hills."

"Red Dog!" I cursed.

"Come with us, Little Crow!" American Horse pushed me in front of him, making it clear he would not tolerate dissent. There were three warriors and about twenty-five women and children with him. The warriors and I provided covering fire for American Horse's family until we reached a dry gully almost twenty feet deep and hidden behind trees and brush. It wove a couple hundred yards into the hills behind the encampment. The warriors and I backed toward the gully, still shooting at the whites, and then we descended the slope and ran to catch up with the others. It was then that I felt the fear and the shaking started. I tried to hide it from the others, but then I noticed one of the warriors was also shaking. You know, when I had been worried about Waynoka, and then later when I had been protecting American Horse's family during our flight, I had felt no fear. It wasn't until we were relatively safe in the gully that the fear came.

Then soldiers began chasing us along the bank and firing blindly into the gully. Fortunately, they underestimated the depth of the wash, and the bullets flew harmlessly over our heads. Nevertheless, we knew the soldiers would eventually find an opening, and then we would be sitting ducks. And wouldn't you know it? When we were in danger again, the fear left me!

I could hear continuous gunfire coming from the camp, but my duty was to protect my chief. I was also confident Red Dog had taken Waynoka to safety; I suspected he would prefer to run than fight. Anyway, we came to a large cave that the camp's children had dug into the side of the gully's bank to play in. Once inside, I noticed a damp earthy smell, and I looked up at the ceiling of the cave. Exposed tree roots poked through the soil, and I wondered how safe it was in there. But what choice did we have? American Horse led us further inside and directed the women and children to the back. At the same time, we scooped dirt up into breastworks near the cave's mouth to defend our position.

One of American Horse's warriors, an old man called Bald Bull, spotted a soldier riding by on the bank across from our cave. He fired two shots and knocked the soldier from his horse with the second shot. Several more soldiers appeared in front of the cave, and we opened fire on them. We were well entrenched and had plenty of ammunition.

"Come on out!" a voice called in Lakota. We assumed it was one of their scouts, and we trained our guns toward the cave opening, hoping to get a clear shot at the speaker. "You are surrounded and don't have a chance!"

"Go home, traitor, while you still can." American Horse yelled the insult. "Crazy Horse's camp is not far from here, and we have sent runners to summon him."

We caught movement to the side of the opening and fired a sustained volley at the spot. We could hear curses once the ringing in our ears stopped. There were a few anxious seconds until the gun smoke cleared away and children could be heard coughing behind us. We cheered when shots and war cries came from the other side of camp. Our warriors were fighting back! But the shooting died down, and then a period of quiet settled over the encampment.

Either the stinging gun smoke that hung in the air or my lack of sleep made my eyes feel itchy, so I laid my head down on my arms and rested my eyes, just for a minute. Then the sound of horse hooves striking earth and the clang of jostling canteens and swords woke me from my slumber as thousands of soldiers marched toward us. I was surprised that I had drifted off, considering the danger I was in.

It wasn't long before we saw soldiers on the other bank of the gully, but none presented a good target to shoot at. Then, suddenly, a barrage of gunfire erupted from the opposite bank into our cave, and all we could do was crouch down behind our earthen breastworks and wait it out. But once it stopped, we poured fire back at the attackers and were pleased to see them scramble back from the bank.

We assessed the damage and found two women dead and several more wounded. As the women and children wailed in their grief, American Horse ordered the two bodies be moved to the back of the cave. Because the bodies would be exposed to gunfire, I disagreed with his command and stayed where I was while other warriors moved to carry out the unpleasant task. I saw American Horse scrutinizing me out of the corner of my eye, so I continued staring straight ahead, watching the cave opening. I saw a few dozen soldiers sneaking toward the mouth of our cave with torches, and I alerted the others. We poured a deadly barrage of gunfire at them, and they quickly retreated.

After a lull in the siege, American Horse sent Scared of Dogs forward to see what was happening outside the cave. Scared of Dogs' name does not give a true measure of the man; he was a brave warrior, and he did not hesitate as he crawled toward the right side of the opening and peered out. He must not have seen anyone, for he continued to crawl until he was behind a stunted cedar tree. He looked up and aimed at something above the cave. Scared of Dogs shot, and a long-haired scout fell and landed a few feet in front of the cave opening. We could see Scared of Dogs reaching toward the dead man's pistol when another scout dropped from above onto Scared of Dogs, and they rolled away from the opening. The other warrior in our group, Running Bull, jumped up to help his friend, but American Horse raised a hand, stopping him.

Scared of Dogs did not come back. Instead, we heard cheers from the soldiers. Running Bull's shouted curses at the soldiers were soon drowned out by a thundering barrage of bullets that didn't end for many seconds. We fired back when their fusillade subsided somewhat, but it must have sounded pitiful compared to their firepower.

The women behind us began singing their death songs while children screamed and cried. Several had been wounded, and some were killed. The bodies that had been placed in rear of the cave had been struck many times during the fusillade.

Suddenly, we heard shouted orders, and eventually the soldiers stopped firing. The only sounds then were the death songs of the women and the whimpering of the children. Then, finally, a scout approached the cave from the side and yelled to us.

"General Crook offers safety for the women and children."

American Horse considered and yelled back, "They will not be harmed in any way once they leave here?"

"You have the general's word."

"His word is shit!" Bald Bull muttered.

"Okay, hold your fire; they are coming out!" American Horse yelled.

We shepherded the women and the children, most of whom were in cradle boards, toward the mouth of the cave, and they reluctantly stepped outside. They were led away by the soldiers, and all we could do was hope the general kept his word. Three women—wives of American Horse and his warriors, one with an infant–refused to leave.

We could see more soldiers forming lines across the gully, and then for the next two hours, a rain of bullets poured onto our position. Our breastworks were reduced to a low berm. We could only muster a few shots between lulls in the relentless barrage. Yet even above the onslaught of shooting, we could still hear women and children wailing from the camp, along with numerous dogs barking.

Finally, the firing stopped, and we heard a scout offer us safe quarter if we surrendered.

"What is this quarter they want to give us?" Bald Bull asked.

"It means they will not harm us if we surrender," American Horse explained.

"Well," Running Bull sighed, "I don't think they harmed the women, and we are almost out of bullets."

American Horse nodded grimly, and then I noticed he was holding his midsection. He saw me looking and said matter-of-factly, "I have to hold my guts in. Come, Little Crow, it is time for us to go."

We stood and reluctantly followed our leader. I will never forget how I felt at that moment: fear of my unknown fate, self-disgust for surrendering, and sorrow for the dead friends I was leaving behind. But I was not ashamed of my tears. And yet we walked proudly behind American Horse, who, despite his injury, walked with a straight back and raised head to the general and handed him his rifle. The general accepted the gun, noticed American Horse's wound, and quickly called for his white medicine men. Many soldiers were angrily yelling "No quarter!" but the general promptly silenced them.

As we were led away, we saw one of their medicine men move American Horse's hand away from his stomach, and his entrails spilled out. We yelled our objections but were pushed roughly away. I knew American Horse would soon be dead when I heard him begin singing his death song. We cheered and yelled our support for our chief and were rewarded with rifle butts slamming into our kidneys.

* * *

"Is there tea?" Little Crow hoarsely asked the crowd. We all saw the tears glistening in his eyes, and Astrid said she would bring him some tea. Edward noticed most of the other women were dabbing their eyes. Greta pulled her hand out her mother's and went to stand beside Little Crow, leaning her head against his arm.

Little Crow smiled and said, "I will continue the story after my tea."

Edward's excitable mind was elsewhere. This could be a magazine series or even a book!

"Don't start again until I come back," he said to Little Crow, and after Little Crow nodded, Edward joined the queue that had formed in front of the lavatory.

6

Edward watched Little Crow drain his cup, smack his lips, and sigh. Greta had crawled up onto Little Crow's lap and curled into the crook of his arm. Little Crow passed the cup back to the woman and thanked her again.

"Come, Greta, don't bother the nice man," Astrid said.

"She is no bother," Little Crow said. "Now, is everyone ready to hear more of my story?"

He grinned broadly when everyone cheered, and then he resumed talking.

* * *

Running Bull, Bald Bull, and I were placed in front of American Horse's lodge with several women while a white man set up a box on long sticks. This box, I later learned, was a camera for taking photographs. We were lined up, and a couple of soldiers stood on either side of us. They were grinning, proud of their massacre; it was a humiliating experience.

Then, our spirits rose when we saw Crazy Horse arrive with what looked like a thousand warriors. Our joy turned to horror when we saw the soldiers were setting a trap for Crazy Horse. Most of the two thousand soldiers hid while a few hundred others milled about, presenting a tempting target. Noticing the trap too late, Crazy Horse led the charge and was met by overwhelming firepower when the bulk of the white army rose up and opened fire. Lakota and Cheyenne warriors parted and rode along the perimeter of the soldier's positions in both directions, firing bravely and dying just as bravely.

The soldiers maintained a continuous hail of bullets, and the warriors scattered in all directions. It was a sight I thought I would never see. Crazy Horse did not return, and we were left in the hands of the soldiers—soldiers who had attacked our camp at Slim Buttes in retaliation for the deaths of Custer and his men two and a half months earlier.

We spent the night shivering in the cold rain while the soldiers slept under our buffalo robes. In the morning, the soldiers packed what they wanted from our camp: buffalo hides, meat, berries, weapons, and the war prizes we had taken from the Battle at Greasy Grass. I saw one soldier carrying my beaded quiver away, and another had my courting blanket rolled up behind his saddle. They took all our ponies, including the ten that Two Elk and I had borrowed from the Crow.

They laid waste to everything else. We were told we could go. Go where? We were homeless now that they had destroyed or stolen everything we had owned. But most of the survivors wandered away in the direction of Crazy Horse's camp. Running Bull and several women, tired of war and now destitute, decided to go with the whites, who said they would take them to a Cheyenne reservation.

"Come with us, Little Crow," Running Bull said.

"No, I have to find Waynoka."

"I need your help; I cannot make this trip alone, not with all these women and their babies to look after. When we get to the reserve, then you can go seek your woman."

It was a plea for help from a respected warrior, one I could not refuse.

"Okay, Running Bull, I will help you."

It was a cold four-day march through rain and mud to the camp they called Deadwood. I was not pleased with Running Bull; he spent a lot of time talking with or following General Crook and leaving me to help and watch over the women and children. No wonder he had wanted me to come with him.

We were paraded through Deadwood. There were first cheers for the soldiers, then shouted curses for us. Mud and stones followed, and I tried to protect the children, but some were hit and bleeding. I was proud of them for not crying out, even though blood flowed into their eyes. I picked up a girl of about three years who had been knocked unconscious by a large rock. My head was exposed and covered in mud, which cushioned some of the blows from the stones. The soldiers did not help, and I saw Running Bull walking between the general and another soldier's horse where he was protected from the onslaught. I raised my head to yell at him when a rock hit the side of my head. I saw bright lights and heard a ringing in my ears as I fell. Even though I was losing consciousness, I protected the girl on the way to the ground. I covered her against the stones before blacking out.

Later, I opened my eyes and wondered where I was. When my vision cleared, I saw a wooden roof above me. Exploring my surroundings, I saw two walls made of stone and hard mud and two walls of steel bars. I had heard about these places—jails with cells and cots—from Cut Nose, who had spent some time in one after being caught pilfering food. As I lay on that hard cot with the smelly blanket covering me, I understood I was a prisoner of the white men. I saw another cot in the cell beside mine where someone was snoring loudly under a blanket with a tuft of red hair poking out. He passed gas, and I gagged at the smell.

I took stock of my injuries, and I was not surprised to feel a bandage wrapped around my head. How many times could I be hit on the head before I became witkó—one who behaves erratically? My left eye had swollen shut, and I had bruises on my shoulders and arms. I moved each limb to see if anything was broken, but the blows had not been thrown with enough force to break bones.

Where was everyone?

My throat was dry, so I sat up to search for water, and the room spun, and I vomited on the floor. The noise woke the man, and he peeked out from under his blanket. He yelled and I heard metal clinking. Then another man, a guard, came through a heavy wooden door.

The guard and the other prisoner yelled at each other, the prisoner waving a hand toward me, and even though I couldn't understand his words, I could tell he was not happy about me being there.

Years later, when I understood the language and remembered one of his words, it struck me as ironic. That dirty, smelly man had called me a savage when he was more of a savage than me.

Anyway, the guard chuckled and then pantomimed holding a rope up above his head while tilting his head at an angle and sticking his tongue out the side of his mouth. That really set off my cellmate, for he began spewing what I could only guess were swears. But that only made the guard laugh harder, until he saw the vomit on the floor of my cell. Then he too began cursing.

I raised my palm up in a drinking gesture to let him know I wanted water. He turned and walked out of the room but soon returned with a bucket, sloshing water over its rim as he walked. Relief flooded through me, but it was short-lived. He threw the water over my vomit, followed by a filthy rag. Then he gestured at me, swirling his right hand around before turning and leaving the cells. He obviously wanted me to clean up my mess.

My cellmate said something to me and then reached under his cot. He raised a metal cup, drank, sighed contentedly, and sneered at me before laying back down.

"What happened to the little girl?" I asked, but of course, he could not understand me.

I lay down and closed my eyes.

A while later, I heard bars rattling, and then two men fell upon me and dragged me off my bunk. I landed in my waterlogged vomit, and the cloth was shoved in my face. The guards grabbed me by my hair and shoved my face into the vomit. The pain was excruciating, but I remained silent. I heard laughter from the guards and my cellmate. Another filthy rag and a bucket of water were set on the floor beside me. I lifted the bucket, tilted it up, and drank deeply from the brackish, soapy water before it was knocked out of my hands. More laughter followed, and I was kicked in the ribs. The guard pointed to the vomit, so I wiped it up as best I could while the men laughed and made comments I did not understand. Finally, they picked up the bucket and left. I crawled back onto my cot, humiliated but grateful that at least I had drunk some water.

I woke up, and the angle of light coming through the window told me that I had slept for several hours. Outside, I heard banging and men laughing and hollering at each other. I saw the man in the next cell standing on his cot and looking out a small barred window. I had a window too, so I slowly stood and looked outside. My ribs were sore where I had been kicked, but nothing felt broken. It was late afternoon, and I saw men building a platform. This seemed to upset the man in the next cell.

My cellmate cursed and then saw me looking at him. He pointed at me and then pointed to the structure outside and copied the guard's earlier pantomime, which I now understood was meant to mimic a person hanging from a rope. I pointed a finger back at him, which seemed to upset him more. Then he erupted into a litany of curses, grabbed the bars between us, and tried to shake them loose. His face was the darkest red I had ever seen on a man. I lay back down and closed my eyes.

Sometime later, I don't know how much later, I woke and heard someone crying. When I looked to my right, I saw the man in the next cell sitting on his cot with his head in his hands, sobbing quietly. I sat up and looked at him; I had never seen a grown man cry before.

He noticed me and quickly wiped his eyes with a corner of his blanket. He cursed at me and I didn't understand a word of it, so I pointed to my chest and said, "Little Crow."

He grunted and stared at the floor. Then, after a while, he jabbed a thumb to his chest and muttered, "Zeke."

I nodded. I had slept too long and I was restless, so I began to pace around my cell. Zeke soon joined me, and we passed near each other now and then. He would say something to me each time we passed near each other. His words seemed pleasant enough, so I would nod and smile as I passed him. After a while, my ribs started to ache, so I lay back down.

It was dark when next I woke. Zeke was quietly calling my name. I looked at him and saw that he was beckoning for me to come closer to him in the gloom. I did not trust this man, so I sat up and stared at him. He continued to beckon me over. He looked friendly enough, so I stood and took a few steps toward him. He continued to beckon toward me, so I carefully stepped nearer. He whispered something quietly, and I bent to hear him. I don't know why I did that; I couldn't understand his words. Then he reached through the bars swiftly, grabbed me by my shirt, pulled me against the bars, and began yelling loudly. I struggled, but the man had a death grip on me, and I couldn't get leverage against the bars.

I heard the door open, and the guard stepped into the room carrying a lantern and began yelling at us. Then he set the lantern down and fumbled with his keys in the lock of my cell door. He took out his pistol, entered, and yelled at me. Zeke wouldn't let go, so the guard came toward us, yelling threateningly as he came. I felt one of Zeke's hands release my shirt, and I looked down and saw that his hand held a spoon that had been sharpened into a makeshift knife. I pushed on the bars and tore my shirt in my panic to get away from the blade. The guard pointed his gun at me, and I feared he was going to kill me; then Zeke reached through the bars, grabbed the guard by his shirt, pulled him against the bars, and stabbed him in the throat. The guard gurgled and slid down the bars. He had a shocked look on his face, which may have matched the shock on my own face. I had not expected that. Then the guard slowly died. Zeke reached through the bars and took the pistol and keys from the guard.

I sat down on my cot and watched Zeke unlock his door. He stepped out, picked up the lantern, walked toward the door, stopped, and waved for me to follow. I understood his meaning, and it seemed better to leave than stay there until the other white men came and found the guard dead. My cell door was still open, so I stood and followed Zeke into the outer room, which was dimly lit. Zeke set the lantern on a table before going to a wall where several rifles hung. He selected one and loaded it. He looked back at me, chose another rifle, and handed it to me. From my experience in the cave, I knew the value of abundant ammunition, so I picked up an empty sack and filled it with every box of bullets I could find.

Zeke shook his head and said something, but I didn't understand him, so he just shrugged. He walked to a window, parted the curtains, and peaked outside. Nodding, Zeke beckoned for me to follow him and then opened the door slowly. We stepped out into the darkness of the boardwalk, walked to the corner of the building, and then trotted down an alley. We got to a wood structure with horses inside, and Zeke motioned for me to stay outside. He went inside and came out a little later leading two horses, one saddled and one not.

Zeke handed me the reins to the bareback horse. It was much larger than the ponies I was used to, and I must say, I was a little intimidated by the animal's size. Zeke mounted, and I leaped onto the horse. It tried to shy away from me, but I hung on, and Zeke grabbed the horse's bit and quieted him. Then he said something to me, followed by "Little Crow." I think he may have said, "Let's go," but I'm not sure.

Anyway, we walked the horses out of the camp they called Deadwood and then kicked them into a gallop when we were well out of earshot. I took the lead and headed in the direction of Slim Buttes. I heard Zeke yelling in protest, but he followed just the same.

7

"We are going to Deadwood!" a middle-aged lady cried, her husband shushing her.

"Yeah?" Little Crow said. "I suppose it is different now."

"My husband wants to go see Wild Bill's grave."

"Wild Bill?" Little Crow asked.

"Yeah, Wild Bill Hickok, the famous gunfighter." She gushed.

"Never heard of him."

"Really? He is quite famous."

"Okay," Little Crow said, clearing not interested in discussing Wild Bill any further. "Now, where was I?"

"You had just escaped from the jail in Deadwood," someone said.

"Oh, yeah."

* * *

So, we rode fast for several hours, and then my head began to ache, and I fought to stay on my horse as wave after wave of dizziness washed over me. The sun was up by then, and it penetrated my skull like a constant flash of lightning. I had to find Waynoka! The horizon turned on its side and then I saw the sky and hit the ground hard. I turned and vomited water, as that was the only thing left in my stomach. The world spun, and blackness crept into my vision and slowly blocked my sight. Then, nothing.

I wondered how long I had slept when I awoke hanging upside down on a horse's back. Seeing long shadows under the horse's belly, I figured it was dusk. I tried to lift myself up, but I was tied down. My first attempt at speaking came out in a croak. Then I began to dry heave. Finally, the horse stopped, and I heard the creak of leather and then the crunching of boots on the ground as someone walked toward me.

Zeke bent low and looked up at my face and said something. I remember the word "rabbit." I felt ropes loosen from my hands and feet, and he began to slide me gently off the horse. The horse shied away, and I was dumped onto the ground. The blood rushed from my head, and the dizziness returned. Zeke was talking, but I was focused on the canteen he was tilting to my lips. Lukewarm water had never tasted so good, and with great willpower, I pushed the canteen away. I recalled Waynoka's advice to go slow with the water the last time I had woken from a head injury.

I looked around and asked instinctively in Arapaho, "Where are we?"

He just grunted, and I closed my eyes against another wave of nausea. I was determined to keep the water down. We were on the bank of a river, so I pointed at the ground and held my palm up in a questioning manner. Zeke seemed to understand my meaning. He pointed at the lazily flowing water and spoke. The only words I remember are "Missouri River," but at the time they meant nothing to me, so I reached for his canteen and drank some more water.

Zeke lit a fire, skinned a jackrabbit, and hung it over the fire with a stick. I did not see a bullet hole in the rabbit's hide, and I wondered how he had come to catch this rabbit. To this day, his method remains a mystery to me. Anyway, he walked over and moved behind me, and I heard him snapping branches, all the while mumbling to himself. What a strange man, I thought. It hurt to move my head, so I ignored what he was doing and breathed in and out to ward off nausea. The smell of the roasting rabbit flipped my stomach.

He said something and then grabbed me under my arms and dragged me backward. I made a feeble attempt to struggle against his grip but soon gave up and let him pull me. He had made a bed of spruce boughs at the base of a tree and covered them with a blanket. He dragged me onto the bed and propped me up against the tree, and I nodded my gratitude to him.

Sometime later, Zeke shook my shoulder, and I came awake. He was holding a rabbit leg out to me. My nausea was gone, my stomach rumbled, and I took the offering. I greedily stripped all the meat from the bone, and then broke the bone and sucked the marrow out. Zeke sat on his haunches, watching me; was it with revulsion or curiosity? I will never know. Anyway, he handed me a canteen, and I drank greedily until he pulled it away from me. Water spilled down my neck as I leaned back with a sigh and closed my eyes.

My eyes flew open when a hand covered my mouth and my shoulder was being shaken. The sun was low in the sky, and I was about to struggle when I saw it was Zeke above me. He put a finger to his lips, and I nodded. Then he removed his hand from my mouth and pointed downriver, where seven Crow warriors were riding their ponies and heading in our direction. They hadn't seen us yet, but it wouldn't be long before they stumbled into our camp. Were we in their territory? It was possible, but it did not matter. I was an Arapaho warrior, an enemy of their people, and they would not hesitate to kill me. Zeke handed me my rifle and crab-walked behind the remnants of an old fallen tree. I crawled behind the tree at the head of my bed and set my bag of ammunition nearby. My senses were on high alert, and although I was still a little tired, I felt the exhilaration of a coming fight.

The Crow warrior in the lead was studying the ground when suddenly he stopped and looked in our direction. I heard a loud bang and saw him flip over the back of his pony. I opened fire with the lever-action rifle but failed to hit any targets as they scattered low on their ponies. The Crow melted into the surroundings. They were skilled warriors; I'll give them that. Of course, the Crow were always worthy adversaries.

I moved backward and crawled toward the river. I knew they would be spreading out and hunting us. A short time later, I heard Zeke's first scream. Where were they? I realized my only route of escape was the river. The cold took my breath away when I slid over the bank and into the water. I was careful to hold the rifle and canvas sack of ammunition above the surface. I peeked over the bank and saw several warriors grouped around Zeke. They had stripped him naked. Was that all of them? I suspected not. I couldn't stay where I was, so I waded upstream as quietly as I could. Finally, I rounded a bend, but a downed tree blocked my progress. I was about to climb the bank when I thought, why not float with the log down the river and use it for cover?

I worked the log loose from the bank; it was quite a large log, almost a fully intact spruce tree. I wedged the ammunition between some branches, laid my rifle on top, and pushed the tree out to the middle of the river. The current pulled it downstream, and I dove underneath and came up on the other side. I was hidden from the Crow, or so I thought. I heard a yell and then shots. Bullets hit the tree, and I worried that they might hit legs when I saw water splash in front of me, but none did. It occurred to me that I should be firing back at them as they were running along the bank and shooting at me. So, I lifted my rifle, rested my elbows on the tree, and took aim. There were still seven of them, so Zeke must have missed the lead warrior.

The first Crow I shot at stumbled and fell, and I levered another round and hit one more. I shot the third before the rest scattered and took cover. That was one fine rifle, let me tell you. Anyway, off to my right, I heard a splash and saw Zeke in the water. Three of the remaining warriors ran to the river bank and started shooting at him, but he dove underneath, so I turned back to the one Crow that remained focused on me. He was trotting from tree to tree as he followed my progress down the river. I took aim and timed his next run perfectly and hit him mid-stride.

Deciding I had better see if I could help Zeke, I placed the rifle on top of the log and dove under to the other side. I pushed the tree to the shore opposite of the Crow, took the gun and ammunition, and climbed the bank. Working my way back across from the warriors, I found a good spot behind a deadfall tree and reloaded my rifle. The first box of cartridges I opened didn't fit, but luckily, the next box did. I hadn't realized until then that bullets came in different sizes. The three warriors had retrieved their ponies and were entering the water. I saw no sign of Zeke. I waited until the Crows were mid-river and shot the last one in line, hitting him in the head. I quickly turned my aim to the middle warrior, and the bullet found his throat. The leading warrior dropped into the water and swam behind his pony, but the current was pulling them toward me. I waited until he was across from me, and even though I hated to do it, I shot the pony. Then the animal slowly dropped below the surface, leaving the Crow in the open. He dove under the water, and I fired several shots where I thought he should be and then waited. Several minutes later, he emerged on the opposite bank and ran for cover before I could react. I heard the pounding of hooves and knew he had caught a pony and was going for help.

Where was Zeke? Was he even still alive? I walked along the bank until I found a shallow area of the river and waded across. Though it was shallow, I still felt panic when the water came up to my chin in the center of the river. I held my rifle and ammunition above my head and struggled to keep my balance in the current. Finally, after sliding one foot in front of the other, the water began to drop below my chin. I climbed the bank, walked toward our camp, and saw one of the Crow's ponies standing near our horses. Movement near the bank drew my attention, and I raised my rifle. It was Zeke! He was crawling on his hands and knees. I walked over to him and let him know it was me.

He turned to look at me with wild eyes, waved his hands around, and pleaded with me. He seemed to have lost something and was searching franticly. I came close to him and saw his wound. The top part of his scalp had been removed, and I could see the white of his skull through streaks of dried blood. He still had hair around the bottom half of his head, below the tops of his ears, but none would ever grow above that again. He looked at me, waved his hands in a circle, and cried out. I understood then what he was looking for, and I scanned the ground, but I was sure his scalp was tied to one of the dead warriors' waistbands, floating down the river.

After a while, I left him to his search, found some dried buffalo meat in a sack tied onto the Crow pony, and hungrily devoured several chunks. Then, finally, I felt my strength begin to return, and I headed to the river, brushed aside floating reeds and cattail fluff, and scooped water to drink.

Zeke was sitting on the ground with legs extended, hunching forward, and mumbling quietly. I gathered his clothes, walked over to him, and placed a hand on his shoulder. He yelped and jumped away, scooting backward on his arse, whimpering. He didn't seem to recognize me, so I set his clothes and boots down, sat across from him, and spoke to him. He couldn't understand Arapaho, but I kept my voice low and steady to reassure him. Zeke sat and stared at me with large eyes, still mumbling incoherently. I had seen this before, in children taken from other tribes after battles. It would eventually pass. I set some dried buffalo before him and then took the horses and the Crow pony to the river. After they had their fill of water, I staked them out on the grass near my bed and lay down. They would warn me if anyone approached, including Zeke. I watched him search for his topknot until the sun went down, and then I closed my eyes.

8

"Does anyone need a break?" Little Crow asked.

"No!" everyone said almost in unison.

"Please continue," Astrid said.

Little Crow had noticed she had covered the little girl's ears when he had talked about the killings and the scalping of Zeke, and he was pleased that she had. As gruesome as it had been, it was an integral part of his story.

* * *

I woke to find a knife at my throat. Zeke's face was inches from mine as he stared into my eyes. He looked confused, so after my heart slowed, I whispered, "Zeke." A light seemed to come on in his eyes, and I felt the knife move away from my skin. Finally, he stood to his full height and tossed his head in a "let's go" gesture. I was glad to see he was fully clothed.

He saddled his horse, and I walked over to the Crow pony and the other Deadwood horse and led them to the river. Zeke followed me and let his horse drink. His eyes were constantly moving, searching for more Crow, no doubt. I supposed we should put as many miles as we could between them and us. After the horses had their fill, I mounted the Crow pony and turned north. I looked over my shoulder when I didn't hear the other horses following me. Zeke was riding south, leading the other horse behind him.

"Hey!" I yelled in Arapaho. "You are going the wrong way!"

He didn't slow or give any other indication that he heard me.

"Hey!"

I watched as Zeke kicked his horse into a trot. I was in a quandary; should I follow Zeke or head north to find Waynoka? Zeke had looked after me when I had been too sick to ride, but I had also saved him from those Crow warriors, so I figured we were even. And Waynoka meant more to me than Zeke did, so with my mind made up, I continued north. It dawned on me that Zeke had led me south the entire time I had been sick. How far had we gone? I was also acutely aware that I was going in the same direction that the Crow had come from. Had we traveled through their territory? If so, I would have to cross it again to get back to Cheyenne and Sioux territories. The difference this time was the Crow were aware of my presence.

Damn that man for leading me south!

Travel was slow as I followed the river, made detours to higher ground, and carefully approached blind corners. I was only about ten miles from our last camp by dusk. My nerves were frazzled from being constantly on high alert. I had eaten the last of the dried buffalo meat at noon, and I had no prospects for supper. If I shot at food, I would alert the Crow. I longed for my bow and arrows. I found an embankment with an overhang that provided cover from three sides and some shelter from above. I laid my rifle beside me with ammunition at the ready and tied my pony's rope to my left wrist. I watched his ears in the twilight, as they would be my first warning of an enemy presence.

My eyes flew open at the first tug on my wrist. If I had slept, it was a near-conscious sleep at the very edge of wakefulness. I knew my pony's ears may have been twitching long before it had tugged the rope, so the Crow could be nearby. I slid my hand to my rifle and eased the hammer back. It was predawn, that time of morning when shapes are visible but not clearly defined. I carefully slipped the rope from my left wrist, and my pony didn't notice. That was good.

Apart from my scent and the pony's, I detected the sweet smells of pine and juniper, the sharp aroma of cedars, and something else, something faint.

Smoked buffalo hide.

They were near.

I squinted at the surrounding terrain, trying to spot them.

Was that a man?

No, just a stunted cedar.

Suddenly, a pony charged, running perpendicular to my recess. Its rider was hanging on the opposite side of the pony, using its body for cover, and he fired under the pony's neck as he passed. He was gone before I could react, and then another went by and shot. My pony broke away and followed their ponies.

So much for a fast getaway.

I did not doubt the skill and bravery of the Crow, so I accepted that I would die there. But I would not go down without a fight. I suspected that the only reason they hadn't poured fire into the embankment was because they had revenge on their minds. The revenge for killing six of their warriors would be prolonged and extremely painful. I decided to deny them the satisfaction of inflicting pain on me, and I rose to a crouch. Then, before I could reconsider, I charged from my lair and swung my head both ways, looking for targets.

I had barely cleared the embankment when a warrior landed on my back from above. The wind was knocked out of me as he crushed me to the ground, and my rifle discharged harmlessly as more warriors descended upon me. I struggled under their weight to draw air into my lungs, and it occurred to me that suffocating may be my best option. The alternative was to endure the tortures they would impose on me, so I stopped struggling. Turns out that was a mistake. They rose off me, no longer having to restrain me, and I involuntarily gulped air.

The four of them stripped me bare and tied my hands and feet. They cut six saplings and tied four of them into a large rectangle. They used the final two to prop up the rectangular frame at an angle, like an artist's easel, and I knew what that meant. First, they lifted me by the arms and dragged me to the pole frame. Then they hoisted me up, untied my wrists, and retied them to the top corners. My feet dangled, and they repeated the process with my ankles so that I was suspended and tied spreadeagle to the four corners. The mid-September sun had now risen above the trees with the promise of a warm day. But there was a dampness in the cool air that coated my naked body with oily moisture. I was pleased that my death would come on a pleasant crisp morning and smiled while I listened to birds singing and water bubbling over rocks in the river.

My captors left me hanging while they built a fire and prepared their breakfast. They were in good humor as they cooked fish. When had they caught those fish? The smell made my stomach rumble. After many years of taking prisoners from each other—some for adoption, others as slaves—many Crow and Cheyenne were fluent in the other's language, but not usually in Arapaho. One Crow asked me in Cheyenne if my stomach was empty. I nodded, and he said, "We will soon find out!" He waggled his knife and laughter erupted. I suspected that most of them understood Cheyenne. I cursed them in Arapaho to see if they understood; they didn't.

"I do not fear you; I am seven warriors!" I spontaneously shouted in Cheyenne.

They stared at me and glanced nervously around.

"What do you mean, camp dog?"

"I am Little Crow. I have taken the strength of the six Crow that I killed, and I have taken their souls into my body! When you kill me, you are killing those warriors too."

I had to suppress my smile as I watched them look at one another and whisper frantically among themselves. Then, having come to a consensus, the warriors stood and placed arrow points in the fire. My ruse appeared to have failed, so I tried another ploy.

"My spirit will follow you into battle and foul your weapons! I will give your presence away when you are stealing ponies!"

"Shut up, dog," said the one who appeared to be their leader.

Out of the corner of my eye, I saw movement.

Was there someone hiding behind those juniper bushes?

The warriors were moving; one took an arrow out of the fire and inspected the glowing point. Then, finally, he nodded, and they converged on me.

"Now, mongrel, where is your friend, the white man?"

"Are you scared of him, 'He Who's Breath Smells Like Dog Shit'?" I asked with a sneer.

His companions laughed heartily, and his face clouded over. He slapped the arrowhead against my chest and held it there as my flesh burned. It was all I could do not to scream at the searing pain or gag at the smell of burning flesh. My flesh. He grinned as he pulled the arrowhead from my charred skin. I saw movement to my right. It wasn't windy, so I knew someone or something was behind that bush.

"Where is your friend?"

"He is coming for you, 'He Who Lies with Dogs'!" I spat.

"Get me another arrow!" he ordered angrily, and one of the warriors ran to the fire.

When another arrow was handed to him, he held the glowing point near my cheek and sneered at me. I opened my mouth, and he slapped the brand against my face. I hissed, but that was all. The pain was excruciating.

* * *

"This is the mark he left on me," Little Crow said. He touched a finger to the rough scar on his cheek and everyone in the car strained to get a look. Edward noticed that Astrid and Greta were still in their seats, away from the description of torture that had entered the story.

* * *

After he removed the arrowhead from my cheek, he said, "The next one will be against your sack."

The others laughed, and I chanced a glance toward the juniper bush. I was relieved to see Zeke's face. Why was he just crouching there? The pain from the burns on my chest and cheek were constant now. I watched my tormentor walk to the fire and select another arrow. He came back, grinned, and held the glowing arrow point in front me.

"I will give you one chance, 'He Who's Breath Smells Like a Fart,' to surrender and untie me," I said to him.

That struck my captives as hilarious.

"You are funny, 'Little Sack'!" he said. "And if we don't let you go?"

"I will summon the Awwakkulé."

The mention of the mythical ferocious little people momentarily shocked them. I had learned of the stories the Crow used to frighten children from Spotted Tail, during one of my visits. These Crow recovered and laughed, but their laughter seemed forced, and I saw two of them glance behind them. The leader moved the arrowhead toward my genitals.

"You have been warned," I said to him and then yelled loudly, "Now, Zeke!"

Nothing happened, and they laughed once again. As the arrowhead touched my flesh, I gritted my teeth and silently cursed Zeke. Then, all of a sudden, I heard a scream, and looked toward the sound. Zeke, wild-eyed and covered in dried mud, was running toward us. The arrow was mercifully dropped as the Crow warriors yelled and ran to their weapons. Zeke levered and fired his rifle as fast he could, fatally hitting two of my captors, and when his gun was empty, he tossed it aside and pulled a tomahawk from his belt. Zeke hadn't stopped screaming as the two remaining warriors, wild-eyed and hands trembling, fumbled with their guns. Zeke threw his tomahawk, which bounced harmlessly off the leader before Zeke tackled him around the waist. The other warrior ran to their ponies, mounted one, and galloped away. Zeke and the Crow leader rolled on the ground, each trying to gain the upper hand.

Zeke wound up on the bottom, and I feared for him. I moved my midsection back as far as I could and then thrust my body forward, feeling the rear poles leave the ground before settling back down. My position now seemed more vertical, and I suspected the support poles had moved forward. I looked toward the two fighters and saw them holding each other's throats. I repeated the thrusting motion, and this time the rack tilted straight up, hung there for a second, and then fell forward. I turned my face to protect my burned cheek, hit the ground, and my burned chest slammed into the grass. After the initial pain of impact, the dewy grass helped ease the pain of my burned flesh.

I couldn't see the fight anymore; I was turned away from them and couldn't raise my head. I listened to the grunting and scuffling until it went quiet. I heard some movement but couldn't discern what it meant. And then I heard the unmistakable thwack of a scalp being removed.

Zeke had lost.

Wait, Zeke had already lost his scalp!

It was quiet again, and then I heard footfalls coming toward me. Then they stopped. I couldn't see who it was until Zeke's face appeared inches from mine.

"Little Crow!" he cried, all smiles.

His eyes looked wild, but he seemed to have snapped out of his trance. He cut my ties with a knife, probably once owned by the Crow's leader, and then helped me up.

"Why did you wait until after they started burning me to help?" I demanded in Arapaho as I rubbed my wrists.

He waved his hand in a dismissing gesture, as if I had thanked him. I didn't bother saying anything else to him since we didn't understand a word the other was saying. It was then that I noticed the new hair on his head. I shuddered at the sight. He grinned back, his eyes wild, and I shuddered again.

After I recovered and put my clothes back on, I went to secure the Crow's ponies and found three of them staked in the trees; the one I had rode here was standing untethered beside them. Zeke wandered away and came back a little later, leading the two horses we had taken from Deadwood. We were definitely in Crow territory, and I had no doubt that the one who got away would return with more warriors.

I gingerly mounted my pony and led the others to the northwest, and then I heard Zeke holler at me. He had turned his horse to the south. We looked at each other, and I waved and kicked my pony forward. I did not look back, but I heard him curse, and from the sound of his horse's footfalls, I knew he had turned and was following me. That pleased me.

9

The conductor pushed his dinner cart through the door at the other end of the car.

"What is going on in here?" he said. "Everyone, please return to your seats."

White Dove lifted her bag onto her lap, took out a sandwich, and was handing it to Little Crow when an older gentleman said, "Please, allow me to treat you to supper."

"Oh, you don't have to do that, sir." Little Crow said.

"It would be my pleasure."

"Well, okay."

"Would you like to join us?" White Dove asked the man.

"Yes, I would like that!" He looked down at Edward until Edward sighed and slid over to the window.

"I am Bertram Carmichael," he said. "I know your names, but not this gentleman's."

"I'm Edward Humphries."

"Pleased to meet you, Edward. I saw you were chronicling Little Crow's adventures."

"Yes, I write for various magazines."

"Really, like Harper's Magazine?"

"Uh, yeah. Sometimes."

"Will Little Crow's stories appear in Harper's Magazine?"

"If Little Crow is okay with that?" Edward looked at Little Crow, who shrugged indifferently.

"Well, it seems you would get paid quite handsomely by Harper's, or any other magazine, for Little Crow's story," he said, "but shouldn't Little Crow get some of that money?"

"Uh, . . ."

Who the hell was this man?

"Little Crow, allow me to present my card," Bertram said, handing a business card to Little Crow, who accepted it and then looked at it briefly before handing it back.

"You can keep it."

White Dove leaned toward Bertram and whispered, "He can't read."

"Oh, my apologies," Bertram said. "Perhaps you could take it?"

White Dove blushed and looked down, and then Bertram realized his mistake. Neither of them could read.

"The card just says that I am a lawyer. I would suggest you enter into a contract with Mr. Humphries here before agreeing to allow your story to be published, in any form."

"Why would I do that?" Little Crow asked.

Edward silently cursed the lawyer.

"So, you will be compensated fairly for your life's story!" Bertram said. "Will you be stopping in Winnipeg for long?"

"Yes, it's a two-day stopover."

"Where are you staying?"

"At our friend Jacque's son's home."

"Well, if you give me the address, I can draw up the contract and bring it to you." He turned to look at Edward. "I assume you will also be available?"

"Uh, yeah," Edward said, "but tell me, Mr. Carmichael, what's in it for you?"

"Well, of course, there will be a small fee for my services."

"And who pays this fee?" Edward persisted.

"Well, that would be Mr. Little Crow, but let's not dwell on that right now," Bertram said. Then, as the food cart arrived, he said, "Select anything you want, Little Crow and White Dove."

It was not lost on Edward that his name was not included in Bertram's offer, and he wondered what he could afford from the notoriously overpriced train food. But White Dove saved him by discreetly handing him the beef sandwich she had taken out earlier. He smiled his gratitude.

Little Crow and White Dove were not shy when it came to selecting food from the cart. They chose several sandwiches, pies, and cakes as well as tea and milk.

"Pass me a long berry, Little Crow," White Dove said.

Edward, curious to see what a long berry was, grinned when Little Crow picked a banana from the cart and handed it to her. After supper, passengers began filtering back to hear more of Little Crow's story. Little Crow, of course, was only too happy to oblige. When he had his full audience, he picked up where he had left off.

* * *

The pain from my burns was constant, and it wasn't until midafternoon that I finally found a chokecherry bush. Aside from being mindful of the danger we were in; I had been scanning the terrain for these bushes. I dismounted and took a knife to cut some of the branches. These I would pulverize between two stones and then chew to a pulp before applying it as a poultice to my burns. I had no way to secure the plasters, so I decided to make camp there. Zeke had stayed behind me up to this point and seemed to have accepted the role of follower.

He disappeared as I prepared and applied the poultice. I was laying in the shade of a spruce tree, basking in the relief the plasters provided, when a rabbit was tossed beside me. I turned to look, but no one was there. I caught a wisp of fragrance in the air and realized it was the hair Zeke wore. I knew I was going to have to do something about it soon. The rabbit's neck was broken. No other wounds, just the broken neck. I cleaned the animal, careful not to dislodge my poultices, and left it lying under its hide until Zeke returned.

The scent of a broiling rabbit woke me. It was dusk, and I must have dozed off, not the best thing to do while deep in enemy territory. Zeke had his back to me near the fire. I removed and set aside the poultices before walking over to him.

"Little Crow!" he said. I once again heard the word "rabbit."

I looked at him, puzzled at the swings in his demeanor. At times he seemed terrified with a haunted look in his eyes, and at other times, he was the same Zeke I had met in the Deadwood jail cells. I decided it was time to learn his language. He caught on to my intent after I held up different items, and he would tell me the English words for them. I could only do this when he was in his right mind. The other times, I pretended to ignore him yet kept a watchful eye on him, as he was unpredictable when in a crazed state.

The next day, when the sun was at its highest, we saw the Crow. They were in a line along a ridge, twelve in total. Zeke, as it happened, was in one of his crazed moments, and when he saw those warriors, he let out a bloodcurdling scream and leaped off his horse. He ran back and forth, doing some type of dance that looked like a frog running on water while shouting obscenities at them. In another time and place, it would have been funny. I was sure he had gone barking mad. The Crow stared at him; they were too far away for me to read their facial expressions, but I suspected they were puzzled by this man. Finally, after a few tense moments, the Crow leader, judging by the number of feathers in his headband, pointed a lance toward the string of ponies behind me.

I understood his meaning; he wanted the ponies back. I dismounted, staked those ponies to the ground, and then remounted my pony. I looked at the warrior, and he pointed his lance in my direction. No, he was not pointing at me; it was my pony that he wanted.

I dismounted and tied the pony with the rest. When I walked over to the unsaddled horse tied to Zeke's mount, he shied away from me, but I leaped on him and called to Zeke. He stopped his crazy dance and looked at me. He looked at the horse I was on and then seemed to snap out of his crazed state. He remounted his horse without once looking at the warriors, and we rode away at a trot. After several moments, I looked back and saw a warrior leading the ponies away.

The rest of the trip back to Slim Buttes was uneventful, other than Zeke's odd behavior. It would be quiet, and then all of a sudden, he would scream, and not just an ordinary scream. This was a primal scream that never failed to make me jump. When we arrived, the camp no longer existed. I saw burn marks where tipis once stood, but nothing else.

What had I expected?

Of course, why would anyone come back to this place after what had happened here?

Crazy Horse and his Oglalas had camped not far from here. I doubted that were still there but decided I would check. But before leaving, I knelt on my haunches and surveyed the campsite. Then Zeke walked over and knelt beside me. He clapped a hand on my shoulder and looked at the bare land in front of us. He didn't say anything. I nodded my head and knew that he understood my sorrow. I stood and held out my hand to help him up, and then we went to our horses. I considered looking in the cave but decided there was nothing I wanted to see or remember in that place.

As expected, Crazy Horse's camp was abandoned. There were many tracks from shod and unshod horses, drag marks from travois, and wagon wheel ruts. There had been no battle here, but the army had been on Crazy Horse's trail. Tomorrow, we would follow their tracks, but that night, there would be more English lessons. That was, of course, if Zeke was not off on one of his spells. Some nights, he would be sitting quietly, and then a scream would signal another spell. He would then run into the darkness and reappear in the morning, red-eyed and acting as if nothing had happened. Those mornings, I tended to stay close to him in case he dozed off and fell asleep on his horse.

Fortunately, Zeke had a good night, and I learned more English. We were getting to the point where we could have brief conversations with each other. He had no interest in learning Arapaho, Cheyenne, or Sioux, so that made it easy.

"Where to?" he said with a wave of his hand at the grassy expanse before us.

"Yellowstone," I told him.

He nodded and followed me. We met a Brule Sioux hunting party made up of eight warriors near midday, and I recognized Grey Hawk from the days before the Battle at Greasy Grass. I could tell Zeke was nervous, and I worried about how he was going to react. I placed a hand on his shoulder, pointed to the warriors, and said, "Friend." He had taught me that word, hugging me and shaking my hand while he repeated it one night. He seemed to understand and relaxed a little. We rode our horses to where they were waiting for us. The Brule warriors appeared nervous, too. I could tell they didn't know what to make of this wild-eyed white man beside me.

"Grey Hawk, it is good to see you again," I called in greeting.

"Little Crow," he smiled broadly, "you are alive! I had heard you were killed in the white settlement."

"They tried, but my friend here helped me escape," I said, placing a hand on Zeke's shoulder. "This is Zeke, he who survived being scalped and sought a scalp in revenge!"

The Brule warriors studied Zeke and then shook their guns in the air and yelled their war cries in approval. I squeezed Zeke's shoulder to try and calm him, but I could see he was getting agitated.

"Is he witkó?"

I thought about that; did Zeke have spells of erratic behavior? Unfortunately, he did.

"Yes, he is."

They nodded their heads and mumbled words of understanding. I was their brother, and they would accept a friend of mine into their company.

"Have you seen any buffalo?" Grey Hawk asked.

"No, we haven't seen any game for a few days now."

He nodded to a warrior who dismounted and dug inside a buffalo-hide bag. He produced portions of dried meat and walked over to us, handing one piece to me and one to Zeke. Zeke hesitated, but I nodded, and he took the offering.

"I am looking for Sitting Bull's camp," I said before taking a bite of the meat.

"I heard he is camped somewhere along the Yellowstone."

"And the Oglala?"

"The last I heard they were constantly on the move," he said. "The army is chasing them."

"The army should be careful," I said, "in case they catch up and have to deal with Crazy Horse!"

I regretted saying that when they repeated the war cries and rifle shaking. I looked at Zeke and saw his eyes roll up, and then he fell over the side of his horse. I quickly dismounted and went to him, joined by the warrior who had handed us the meat. Zeke appeared to be uninjured but remained unconscious. I staked the horses and built a shade structure for Zeke. The Brule warriors decided to stay and visit, and two of them went in search of wood and another for water.

"He is haunted from battle?" Grey Hawk asked.

"Yes; we have fought our enemies together."

That seemed to satisfy him.

"You are safe here, Little Crow, both of you. Many of our enemies have moved to reservations, and the army is several suns away."

"What are reservations?"

"A place where tribes are put. They cannot leave and there is nothing to hunt, but the army feeds them," Grey Hawk said.

"Sounds like the prison I was in."

"Prison?"

"A small room that I was locked inside. It had stone walls and steel bars. The guard fed me dog food and insulted me."

He looked at me, the question on his face unspoken.

"My honor is safe, Grey Hawk. I drew the guard into my cell, and Zeke killed him."

He looked down at Zeke with newfound respect.

"He is a warrior?"

I told the gathered men the story of our battles with the Crow. They sat rapt as I told them how I was tortured and how Zeke saved me. They wanted to see my burns, and when I showed them, they oohed and aahed at the scarred flesh. When Zeke stirred, he was momentarily confused but then saw friendly faces and relaxed. The Brule smiled and patted him on his shoulder. Zeke looked at me and asked, "Friends?" I nodded and he smiled back. One of the warriors walked to his pony and returned with a tanned scalp. He sat down and pointed to Zeke's head and held up the tanned scalp.

"Trade," I said in English, hoping it was the right word.

Zeke looked from me to the warrior and back. I nodded, and when he hesitated, I nudged him. And then, to my relief, Zeke made the trade. Zeke put the new hair on his head, adjusted it, and then looked at me. I nodded and smiled, and then the warriors cheered and smiled at Zeke. He visibly relaxed and smiled back. His stomach rumbled, and the warriors quickly prepared a meal of dried buffalo and berries. I noticed the warrior walk off into the bushes with the putrid scalp, and when he returned, his hands were empty.

It was a sad moment when they mounted and rode away. I was tempted to join my new friends, but the call to find Waynoka was stronger. If she thought I was dead, as Grey Hawk had, she may allow someone else to court her. The thought made me anxious to get moving.

We arrived at the Yellowstone River three days later. The banks here were steep and densely covered in willow, so we followed it to the west until we came to a bend in the river where the bank sloped gently down to the water. A portion of the shore was covered in sand with scattered clumps of willow and grass, and the area was surrounded by stands of willow trees. We set up camp in one of the stands so that we were partially hidden from view. I cut a willow stalk and sharpened the points where two branches began, making a two-pronged fishing spear. Zeke watched me and then looked for a similar willow. I tried not to snicker at his attempt at a fishing pole. We stood in shallow water waiting for fish to pass. Not for the first time, I wondered if Zeke's time would be better spent hunting rabbits when he slowly raised his spear and then swiftly plunged it into the water. I was shocked to see a wriggling trout on the end of his spear. He began to hoot and dance in the water until the fish fell off his spear. Zeke cried out and dove after the fish, and all I saw was water roiling around his thrashing body. I feared he was drowning, so I waded toward him, but then he emerged triumphant, holding the trout by the gills. He carried it to shore and struck its head with a rock and then, with a huge grin, held it up for me to see.

I saw that his hair had fallen off during the scuffle with the fish, so I pointed at the top of my head and then at him. He touched his bare head, let out an anguished howl, threw the fish onto the bank, and ran into the water, frantically looking for his hair. I scanned the water's surface and saw it floating with the current. I ran along the bank until I was a little ahead of the hair and then swam out to retrieve it. I held it high and yelled to Zeke. He stopped his frantic splashing, looked toward me, and saw it in my hand. His face lit up and he splashed toward me, the smile never wavering. He took it from my hand and put it back on his head. Then he surprised me by giving me a bear hug, lifting me off my feet. He dropped me and then walked back to look for his fishing spear.

"One more fish for you," he said with a grin when he found it.

I laughed and watched him stand still in the water, pole raised and ready to strike. I walked to the trout he had caught and started to clean it when I heard a splash. He had caught another trout. He dropped the fish at my feet and then said he would build a fire. To this day, whenever I smell fish cooking over an open fire, I think of that time with my friend.

"There is a skill to catching fish, Little Crow," Zeke said between bites. "I will teach you how if you want."

I glared at him, and he burst out laughing; flakes of fish flew out of his mouth. I was about to join in his laughter when he started coughing. I watched with concern as he went to his hands and knees and began hacking and spitting. His scalp fell to the ground. It did not stick to his head like the greasy one he had traded away.

"A bone," he gasped, pointing to his neck.

"There is a skill to eating fish, Zeke. I will teach you how if you want," I said with a grin.

"Fek you!"

I didn't understand the words at the time, but I suspected they were not said in appreciation of my humor.

"Let me help."

He reluctantly turned and sat, and I knelt before him. I opened my mouth wide, indicating that was what I wanted him to do. He did, and I leaned in for a look. It was hard to see, so I turned his face to the sun, grasped his chin and nose, and looked inside. There it was, far in the back of his mouth, near that floppy thing that hangs down. I let go of his chin and reached in with my fingers, but my hand was too big and he gagged, so I looked around and found two sticks. I removed the bark so they were smooth and showed him that I would pinch the bone between the twigs and pull it out. He nodded and opened his mouth. I held a stick in each hand and carefully moved them toward the bone. One twig came in contact with the floppy thing, and he gagged once more. On my second attempt, I managed to pinch the bone and pull it out. Zeke saw the bone and grinned broadly.

Then, when he looked over my shoulder, his eyes widened and his grin disappeared.

10

I turned and saw three Cheyenne warriors sitting on ponies high up on the riverbank, watching us. They turned and disappeared over the bank. I looked back at Zeke, who was still quite close to me, and then it dawned on me and I chuckled. They must have thought we were two-spirit. There is no shame in that among our tribes, but I thought it best not to explain it to Zeke, not knowing what his views were.

I wanted to ask them if they knew where Sitting Bull's camp was, so I ran up the bank, yelling for them to come back, but they were nowhere in sight.

Where did they go?

I saw their tracks, and it looked like they were going east along the river.

Should I follow them or continue west?

I decided there was nothing to be gained other than explaining to them what we had been doing, so I went back to our fire and finished my meal. Zeke was carefully picking at his fish, eating a little more slowly now. After we were finished, we sat by the river with Zeke in front of me as I braided the old and new hairs together on his head.

That should keep it in place.

When I finished, Zeke gave a few gentle tugs on his hair and grinned in approval. Then, as the sun dropped below the horizon, I heard coyotes howling. The first howls came from across the river and then were answered by calls from our side. Coyotes could be unpredictable when in packs, so we took turns sleeping and standing watch, just in case.

* * *

Little Crow yawned and said, "It's late, time for sleep."

Everyone voiced their disappointment, and many began to plead with him to continue for at least a bit longer.

"Did the coyotes attack you?" a teenage boy from another car asked.

Once again, passengers from other cars had come to hear Little Crow's stories.

"The answer, I'm afraid, will have to wait for another day."

His audience responded with groans and scattered applause.

The next morning, shortly after breakfast, the people began crowding around Little Crow's booth, jostling for positions near the storyteller.

"Easy, my friends," Little Crow said. "I will speak loud enough for everyone to hear."

Edward studied Little Crow's expression. The man sure was enjoying all the attention.

"Now, is everyone here?" Little Crow said loudly, "Good. Then I'll begin. Be sure to call out if you can't hear me."

* * *

It was October of 1876 when we found Sitting Bull's camp on the banks of the Yellowstone River, near the Missouri River. We had wasted several weeks by going west instead of east, and avoiding the soldiers and white buffalo hunters also slowed us down. They had been everywhere.

The camp had been warned that an Indian and a white man were coming, so we were met by a large group of heavily armed warriors.

"Little Crow!" I recognized the yell that came from behind the forward group. "I heard you were dead!"

"Two Elk!" I cried and slid off my horse. Some of the Lakota recognized me now, but they were still wary of Zeke. Two Elk dismounted and ran through the ponies to meet me. Our joy was infectious, and the warriors around us grinned as they watched us clasp each other's shoulders and dance in a circle. It was good to see my friend! Zeke dismounted and was smiling, which put most of the warriors at ease. They crowded around him and stared at his hair. His natural red locks at the hairline were still braided with the black hair on top.

"This is Zeke, a friend," I said to everyone. "He saved my life. Twice."

"I have heard of a two-spirit Arapaho traveling with a white man," Cut Nose said, one brow arched.

"I have also heard that," I said, "but we did not meet them."

"Ah," Cut Nose said, clearly unconvinced.

"Is Waynoka here?" I turned and asked Two Elk.

He lowered his head and shifted uncomfortably. "She has gone with Red Dog to Fort Robinson."

"He surrendered and took my betrothed with him?"

"They were married after news of your death reached us."

I collapsed onto the ground; my legs unable to hold my weight any longer. First, Zeke came and sat down beside me, and then Two Elk sat on my other side. The remaining warriors raced toward camp, each wanting to be the first to tell the news of my arrival with the strange white man.

After I had recovered from the shock of hearing Waynoka had married, we wandered into the camp. It didn't take long to see that there was little food here. I had noticed that most of the warriors who had met us were lean, but the exposed ribs of the children told a far more worrisome story. I asked Two Elk about this as we walked through the camp.

"Hundreds of white men have come to this land and are killing the buffalo for their hides." He glanced at Zeke as he said this. "They leave the meat to rot in the sun. Pretty soon, there will be no more buffalo."

"We cannot stop them?"

"There are too many, and they are protected by the soldiers."

"Two Elk!" A boy ran up to him. "Tatanka Iyotake wants him to come to his lodge." He used his lips to point at me.

"Go," Two Elk told me. "I'll see to your horses. They'll be behind my lodge."

"Where will I find your lodge?"

"In front of your horses." He looked at me with puzzlement and then led our horses away. I watched him for a while to get the general direction of his tipi.

"Come on!" The boy bolted away, bony elbows and knees flying in all directions.

"Come, Zeke," I said. "Let's go meet Tatanka Iyotake."

He stared at me with a confused look, so I said, "Sitting Bull."

Of course, he knew that name. As we walked, I saw him brushing off his clothes and spitting in the palm of his hand to slick down his hair, both the new hair and his own.

"Little Crow!" Sitting Bull said when we entered. "Tell me about this man you are with, and then tell me of your adventures after Greasy Grass."

"Sitting Bull, it is an honor to sit with you in your lodge. This my friend, Zeke. He saved my life, more than once."

I told him everything that had befallen me, starting with the fight at Slim Buttes. The stories ended as Seen by Her Nation, Sitting Bull's wife, brought us food. I stood when she entered the tipi, for I have great respect for Seen by Her Nation, and most Indian women, for that matter.

* * *

"Why?" Edward asked, earning scowls from the women in Little Crow's audience.

"Why, you ask?" Little Crow said. "Well, everyone in an Indian village has a role to play. The men would hunt, fish, and protect the village from enemies, and the women would raise the children, who were loved and cared for not only by their own mothers but by all the women in the tribe. If a child's parents died, another family would step forward to rear the orphan within their lodge. The women also made clothing, blankets, and shelter from the buffalo hides they tanned. So, you see Edward, women held as much respect in the tribe as a man."

Edward nodded and saw White Dove lay a hand on Little Crow's sleeve and smile when he looked at her.

"Excuse me, Mr. Little Crow?" Astrid said. "You say the women would look after orphans?"

"Yes?"

"Then how come no one looked after you when you were orphaned?"

Little Crow looked down, and after several minutes, the people standing in the aisle began to shift their feet restlessly. The silence was becoming uncomfortable, and some were about to leave when Little Crow raised his head and spoke.

"I was not truthful when I told that part of the story. I am ashamed of that, as I am ashamed of my behavior during that time."

Little Crow inhaled deeply and expelled a long breath, seeming to come to a decision.

"I did not make it easy for the women of the tribe to look after me. I would obey neither them nor the men. At night, I would dream of Sand Creek and wake up screaming. If anyone touched me, to try to comfort me after a nightmare, it would only make me scream louder. Finally, Rabbit Tooth's grandmother took me in, and that was good. The nightmares stopped and I began my recovery."

"What happened to her?"

"Grandmother? She died in her sleep when I was fourteen. I mourned her death for several months."

"Thank you for telling us, Mr. Little Crow," Astrid said.

"Just call me Little Crow, Mrs. . . ."

"Astrid Jonsdotter."

Little Crow smiled. "Now, where was I?"

"Seen by Her Nation, is that right? She brought you food."

"Yes, that's right."

* * *

"I am ashamed that I cannot offer you more, Little Crow, and you also, Zeke," Sitting Bull said to us. "But food is scarce in these times."

"I understand; the whites are destroying the buffalo."

"Maybe your friend can spear some fish for the camp?" Sitting Bull said with a smile. He had enjoyed that part of the story. "How many snows have you seen, Little Crow?"

"Seventeen . . . I think."

He looked at me for a long time and then nodded. He looked tired, so I rose and left his tipi with Zeke following close behind.

We did not catch any fish before the camp was moved. It moved a lot over the next month and into the winter. We were pushed by the white soldiers' relentless pursuit and by our need to find game. In that winter with Sitting Bull's Hunkpapa, I was the hungriest I had ever been. Many of the people had left the camp and surrendered to the whites. No one could blame them for leaving. They had children to feed, and they would be provided for on the reservations. But the rest of us were not ready or willing to give up our way of life, and we would continue the fight to protect it.

We received word that Crazy Horse's band was in the Black Hills harassing the white prospectors there. Two Elk, who had not remarried since Laughing Woman's death at Slim Buttes, told me he was going to the Black Hills. I was tempted to join him, but I felt a strong sense of loyalty to Sitting Bull.

My heart was healing; thoughts of Waynoka no longer caused me sadness. There were plenty of available women, mostly older than me, who had lost their men in battle, but I had no interest in them. Cut Nose had been pushing me to take his eldest daughter for a wife, but I told him I was still grieving the loss of

Waynoka. Zeke, on the other hand, had married Walking Woman, a Hunkpapa widow whose husband had died at Greasy Grass.

It didn't take long for Zeke to be accepted into the tribe. At first, the children would run up and count coup on him, striking the back of his legs with a stick. Then Zeke would turn and growl like a grizzly bear and chase the screaming children. This alarmed their parents at first, but they soon realized it was all in fun. It was not uncommon to see Zeke wandering through the camp followed by dozens of children. His spells of erratic behavior had stopped completely, and he had become quite a colorful character. He had grown a white beard, his own hair remained red, and the hair on top, black.

Zeke had also become one of the camp's best food providers, often going out on his own and returning days later, pulling a laden travois. Sometimes his travois would be carrying deer and other times it would be fish, beaver, or muskrats. Regardless of what he provided, the people were grateful for his contribution. It pleased me that he had made a home among the Hunkpapa people. It was midwinter when Walking Woman's belly began to grow. There was much speculation, and many wagers, on what color the child's hair would be.

I found myself alone much of the time, so I joined hunting and scouting parties and spent more time away from camp than in it. It was spring when everything changed.

* * *

"Winnipeg!" called the conductor. "Everyone, please return to your seats. We will be arriving in Winnipeg in fifteen minutes."

Edward checked his pocket watch and was surprised to see it was noon. Where had the time gone? He looked at his journal and realized he was almost out of pages to write on.

"But we won't hear the rest of your story!" one man lamented.

"I will chronicle the rest, with Little Crow's consent, and publish the story," Edward said.

He looked at Little Crow for concurrence and was pleased to get a slight nod. The lawyer Bertram harrumphed, but Edward ignored him.

"Keep an eye on magazines and newspapers for my name, Edward Humphries!"

"But how did things change in the spring?" Astrid asked. "Was it for the better or for the worse?"

"Well, that depends on how you look at it," Little Crow said, tousling Greta's hair and earning a grin.

Astrid, on the other hand, only frowned at Little Crow's response.

11

The train chugged into the Winnipeg station, came to a stop, and blasted steam across the platform. Edward waited while Little Crow and White Dove gathered their things. He wanted to follow them out so he could see who was there to meet them.

"Well, I will see you in two days then?" Edward asked.

"Yes, so long, Edward," Little Crow said as he and his wife moved to the aisle. He held his hand out, as did White Dove, and Edward shook them both.

"Here, Edward, you may as well take these; we won't need them anymore."

She held out a small sack that held two wrapped sandwiches and two oranges.

"Thank you."

At least tonight he would have something to eat.

While the line slowly moved through the car, Edward glanced out a window and scanned the people on the platform. Two tough-looking men caught his eye.

Why did they look familiar?

He watched them watching the people getting off the train.

Who were they?

Then it came to him: they looked like Doyle Donnelly. Both of them. Were they Doyle's relatives? Had the Donnellys wired ahead and asked their relatives to watch for him and then waylay him? Edward turned and walked against the flow of passengers to the rear of the car. He went through the rear door and stepped onto an open steel deck with steps leading down on either side. Edward stepped down the stairs on the opposite side of the station, and then ran on gravel alongside the train cars until he came to the last car. He peeked around the corner of the caboose toward the platform. He saw the two men walking up and down the platform, looking up at the train's windows. When several people walked between Edward and the two men, he bolted out into the open and ran across the tracks, hoping to circumvent the station and sneak onto the city streets. He almost made it to the corner of the station undetected.

"There he is!"

The shout sent shivers of fear through Edward as he ran alongside the station and out into traffic. Stumbling off the curb, Edward dodged a horse and wagon, saw a streetcar approaching, and leaped onto the steps. Holding the handrail, he watched as the two men emerged from the station, looking up and down Main Street. One of them spotted Edward, pointed at him, and shouted to his partner.

They're catching up! Edward thought with alarm as he watched the men chase the trolley. Edward jumped off the streetcar, stumbled into a wobbling run, and then fell flat on his face. He lay there and succumbed to the realization that the men chasing him were going to catch him and do him harm.

"Edward?"

Edward rolled onto his back and looked up at White Dove as she leaned over the side of a wagon.

"What are you doing down there?" Little Crow asked.

"Little Crow, the man needs help," White Dove said.

Two sets of hands grabbed Edward under his arms and lifted him up. Edward looked side to side and saw Little Crow on one side and a stranger on the other. They lifted him onto the back of the wagon, and Edward saw the two Donnellys standing a hundred yards away, glaring at him. Edward smiled and made an obscene gesture toward them. One of them stepped forward but the other held him back.

"Do you know those men, Edward?" White Dove asked; she was also in the rear of the wagon.

"They were trying to rob me."

"They're following us. Gabriel, could you go a little faster?" Little Crow said to the man driving the wagon.

"You bet!" He snapped the reins, and Edward had to quickly grab the wagon bed's rails to avoid rolling off the back. He watched with satisfaction as his pursuers were left behind and soon out of sight.

"I can get off here. Gabriel, is it?"

"Yes," Gabriel replied. "Are you sure? You're welcome to come to our house and get cleaned up. That's a nasty scrape on your chin."

"Thank you, but I need to find a telegraph office."

"Alright, there's one a few blocks ahead; I will let you off there."

"Gabriel is my friend Jacque's son," Little Crow said by way of introduction. "Edward is the man who is going to write my stories."

"Really? In a book?"

"Magazine, or maybe newspapers," Edward corrected.

"Ah, you should hear some of my dad's stories," Gabriel said.

"Yeah?"

"Yes, especially when he went voyageuring in Egypt for the British army."

"What's that?"

"My father and several hundred other voyageurs paddled supplies and soldiers up the Nile River to a place called Khartoum, to aid in the battle against the Africans. Quite the story, that one."

"But how does it fit in with Little Crow's story?"

"Our paths crossed several times over the years, including the fight at Batoche," Little Crow said.

"Batoche?"

"During the North-West Resistance."

"Is your father home now?" Edward asked Gabriel, his interest suddenly piqued. "I would like to meet him."

"Not until tomorrow," Gabriel said. "I'll give you my address, and you can drop by tomorrow evening if you like."

"Yes, I would like that."

They stopped beside a telegraph office, and Edward alit from the wagon.

"Are you sure you're going to be okay, sir?" Gabriel asked. "We can wait for you."

"No, I've put you out enough already. Thank you for the ride and for rescuing me."

"You're welcome; see you tomorrow."

What began as an introductory telegram to the offices of Harper's Magazine in New York City turned into numerous back-and-forth wires that significantly depleted Edward's meager funds. Edward had pitched the idea of a true story of one Indian's participation in the Custer massacre and his flight from American retribution. The magazine sent a telegram informing Edward that he would receive a telephone call in the lobby of the Royal Alexandra Hotel from the magazine's editor in chief at noon the following day to discuss particulars.

Happy with the prospect of having one of his works appear in the famous magazine, Edward stepped out of the telegraph office and looked up and down the street. There was no sign of the two men who had chased him. He counted the remainder of his money and was dismayed to see he would be lucky to have enough for another journal to write in. But he needed one, and probably two, if he were to keep taking notes on Little Crow's stories and possibly his friend's stories as well. He also required loose paper to begin drafting Little Crow's adventures.

Spotting a sign across the street that read "Bookseller and Stationer," Edward waited for a break in the traffic and trotted across. Entering the shop, Edward looked around and immediately relaxed. This was his domain; the aromas of ink, paper, musty books, coffee grounds, and sweet pipe tobacco hung in the air.

"Can I help you, sir?" The question came from a small bespectacled man who bore a striking resemblance to Edward.

"Yes, I need writing journals. Unfortunately, I am a little strapped for cash at the moment, so I can't afford my usual quality."

"You have bought here before?"

"Oh, no, I meant purchases in other cities."

"Ah, I see. Well, let me show you what we have. Follow me, sir."

Edward looked through the array of journals and writing pads, flipping them over and checking prices before replacing them on the shelf. When he put back the last option and sighed, the owner asked, "Perhaps you could tell me your budget, and I will see what we have in the back."

"Uh," Edward mumbled. He knew precisely what he had, fingering the fifty-cent piece in his pocket, but he was ashamed to admit it. Still, seeing no other option, he let out a breath and said, "Fifty cents."

"Fifty—uh, hmm, I'll be right back."

Edward browsed the bookcases while he waited. One day he would own a bookstore like this and have all the classics on the shelves.

"You're in luck, sir." The man said, coming out the back. "I found a couple discontinued journals that I can let you have for fifty cents."

"Oh, thank you, sir!" Edward paid the man and put the journals in his carpetbag.

"Edward," the store owner said.

"How did you know my name?"

"Huh?"

"My name, Edward."

"That is my name too!"

They grinned like fools and then shook hands.

"Pleased to meet you, Edward!"

"Likewise, Edward!" the store owner said. "But call me Eddie."

The most distinguishing feature between the two men was their age; Eddie's receding hairline marked him as a bit older than the thirty-five-year-old Edward. But aside from their slight age difference, the two men could have been twins. Edward caught movement in the front window and looked that way. He was shocked to see one of his pursuers' menacing face peering in.

"Is there a back door, Eddie?"

"Yes, is there a problem?"

"That man is after me. I do not know why, but he means me harm."

"Oh dear, yes, of course, straight through that door. Keep going straight and unbolt the rear door; it leads out to the alley."

"Thank you, sir." Edward shook Eddie's hand and then ran through the door and into the back room, seeing the rear exit straight ahead. He twisted the knob, panicked when the door wouldn't open, and then remembered to slide the bolt open. Edward stumbled through the door, stepped into air, and crashed to the dirt alley a foot below the door's threshold. He got to his feet, looked around for his bag, and saw the other pursuer running toward him. The man was closing in on him, so Edward abandoned his bag and ran down the alley. As he neared the building's corner, the man who had peered into the front window stepped in front of Edward and drove a beefy fist into his face.

A half hour later, a Winnipeg police constable knelt over Edward when he opened one eye. The other eye had swelled shut.

"Are you okay, sir?" the policeman asked.

"Uh, I think so." The punch to his eye seemed to be the only injury Edward had sustained.

"I'm Constable Jackson, James Jackson. Here, let me help you up." The constable lifted Edward by the armpits and braced him until he seemed able to stand without swaying. "Can you tell me what happened, sir?"

"Two men have been chasing me since I got off the train," Edward said. "I don't know why."

"Well, robbery seems to be the motive; your pockets arn turned inside out. How much money did you have on your person?"

"On me?" Edward was reluctant to tell this policeman that he was penniless lest he be arrested for vagrancy. "Not a lot, certainly not enough to justify robbery."

"Well, that's a good thing, I suppose. Let's go inside."

"Hang on, I need to find my glasses."

"Uh, I already found them. They appear to have been crushed under a heel," Jackson said, handing the fragments out to Edward.

He looked at the fragments in the constable's hand and sighed. Both lenses were missing, and the wire frame was bent beyond repair. Edward was nearsighted; anything farther than thirty feet appeared blurred. As they approached the rear door of the bookstore, Edward saw his carpetbag lying among waste bags on the ground near the door.

"There's my bag!" Edward said, and then picked up his bag and looked inside. He exhaled with relief when he discovered nothing was missing. The constable looked at the bag's condition and then seemed to scrutinize Edward's worn and soiled clothing for the first time.

When they entered the bookstore, Edward was shocked to see it had been thoroughly ransacked, but what was more alarming was the sight of Eddie being wheeled out the front door on a gurney by two men dressed in white. Edward followed the men out to the ambulance and called Eddie's name as they were lifting him into the back.

"He can't hear you," one of the men said.

"Your brother was beaten pretty bad, but nothing life-threatening that I can see," the other ambulance attendant said.

"He's not my brother; I just met him," Edward said. "Where are you taking him?"

"Winnipeg General."

"Could we have a word, sir?" Constable Jackson said to Edward. "This is Constable Liam O'Reilly."

Constable O'Reilly was a solid-looking fireplug of a man with red hair and muttonchops that were running to gray.

"Yeah, okay."

Constable Jackson asked the questions, and Constable O'Reilly wrote down Edward's responses. They seemed to have an established procedure and appeared to be long-time partners. Edward answered the questions as best he could, but other than knowing the store owner's first name, he had little to offer regarding what was missing. As for the suspects, Edward told Jackson that they resembled the Saskatoon Donnellys. Edward admitted to a dispute with the Donnellys over unpaid room and board. Fortunately, the constables weren't concerned about Edward's issues in Saskatoon and didn't dwell on it.

"Do you think they are cousins?" Jackson asked. "Possibly with the same surname?"

"I wouldn't be surprised."

"Alright, you're free to go."

"Thank you, sirs. Uh, where is the hospital?" Edward said, moving toward the door.

"It's on McDermot Avenue. Go to Main Street, turn left until you get to McDermot, turn left again, and it will be on the right. You can't miss it."

"Okay, thanks."

"Wait!"

Shit!

"Could you take these with you?" Constable Jackson held out a pair of spectacles that looked similar to Edward's ruined glasses and nodded toward the departing ambulance. "They belong to him."

"Sure." Edward said with relief. He hadn't been sure if he would go to the hospital, but now he felt obligated to. So, taking the glasses, he left the store and began walking toward Main Street. At least Edward didn't have to worry about his pursuers anymore. If the Donnellys had sent them, then they had completed their task. Edward lifted Eddie's glasses to his good eye and was surprised to see they were a similar strength to his own. In fact, if Edward had picked them up by mistake, he would not have known they weren't his.

After a long walk, Edward arrived at the hospital to some curious stares at his battered face and rumpled clothing. Not concerned stares, just curious ones. He had rehearsed what he would say, but as he neared the front desk, he realized how suspicious it might seem for him to only know the man's first name.

"Hi, I'm here to see Eddie, Edward," he said. "He was just brought in by ambulance."

To his relief, the woman behind the desk asked, "Edward Shuttleworth?"

"Yes."

"He is still in the operating room, sir." She looked up at Edward and asked, "Is he your brother?"

"Yes," Edward lied.

"I see. Do you want a doctor to have a look at that eye?"

"No, it's just swelled."

"Well, you're welcome to have a seat in the waiting room. I'll let you know when you can see Eddie, but it may be a while."

"Thank you."

Edward used the time to continue drafting Little Crow's story. He was even given a cup of coffee by a friendly orderly. However, it was late in the day before a nurse came to tell him he could see Eddie.

"He's still pretty groggy, but he is awake."

"How is he?"

"Fractured cheekbone, orbital bone, and several broken ribs; they really worked him over. So, they got to you too?" she asked, nodding at his swelled eye.

"Yeah."

"Well, you were luckier than your brother."

"He's—" Edward caught himself and then let the comment pass. It may not hurt to let the staff here think he was related to Eddie. He took off Eddie's glasses and put them inside his pocket as he followed the nurse down a hallway. He may as well hang on to them since Eddie wouldn't be needing them for a while.

"Here we are. Don't tax him; he needs rest to recover."

"I won't. Thank you."

Edward was shocked to see the condition of Eddie's face. One side was completely covered in bandages. On the other side, his eye was a closed purple lump and his cheek had swelled, the skin stretched so tight it was almost translucent.

"Eddie?"

"Hmph?" Eddie grunted.

"It's me, Edward."

"Edward! What a relief; I didn't know if you were dead or alive."

Edward had to lean in close and concentrate to understand Eddie's muffled and slurred speech.

"I'm sorry, Eddie; this was all my fault."

"Yes, it was."

"How can I make it up to you?" Edward figured it was a safe offer, considering Eddie knew he was penniless.

"Could you look after my store until I'm up and around?"

Edward had not been expecting that.

"I'm sorry, Eddie, they did a lot of damage to your store. Books are torn apart, knickknacks and all your pipes are broken, glass display cases are shattered, and the front windows and door are broken. They will have to be boarded up. But, more importantly, I have to go with my friends to New York in two days."

"Well, then, could you see about boarding the place up and securing the doors, maybe clean it up a little?"

"Sure, I can do that. Uh, I will need some money for the boards," Edward said, embarrassed.

"Oh," Eddie said, and then was quiet for so long, Edward turned to leave.

"Look under the counter; there's a small safe there," Eddie said, startling Edward. "There's money inside, but only take what's needed to secure the store and leave the rest. I will give you the combination."

"Okay."

Edward stayed long enough for Eddie to fall asleep and to finish the supper the nurse was kind enough to give him. She whispered, even though no one else could hear her, for him to keep it their little secret. She followed that up with a wink.

Well, that hadn't happened since, well, ever.

But Edward couldn't dwell on that. He had work to do. Assuming the lumber yards would be closed at that hour, he decided to go straight to the bookstore and attempt to clean up the mess. He had a spike of panic walking down the last block before the bookstore. Two men were outside the store, but relief flooded through him when he saw they were hammering nails into boards.

"Excuse me?" he asked, not knowing what else to say.

"Eddie?" one of the men asked and then did a double take when he realized Edward wasn't the store's owner. "Who are you?"

"My name is also Edward. I'm Eddie's friend. He asked me to clean up the mess inside."

"Ah, looks like you were also attacked?"

"Yes, I just left the hospital. Eddie got the worst of it."

"How is he?"

"Pretty beat up, but he's resting now."

"That's good. I mean, we didn't know if he was going to make it or not."

"Where'd you get the boards?" Edward asked.

"Lumberyard."

Of course, it would have still been open when these men had picked them up. They were almost finished boarding up both windows and the door.

"What's your name?" Edward asked them. "I'm sure Eddie would want to know about your generosity."

"I'm Frank and this is Gerald; we are the Johanssons," Frank said, pointing across the street at a store with a sign that read, "Johansson's Funeral Home." "And the lumber yard donated the boards when they heard about the robbery."

"That was good of them; I will let Eddie know."

"Okay, so long, Edward. We'd stay and help you clean up, but we have a few clients to prepare."

Edward suppressed a shudder and tried not to cringe when he shook their moist hands. Inside, he went straight to the safe behind the counter, which appeared to be bolted to the floor, and spun the dial to the numbers Eddie had given him. It took a few tries, but it eventually clicked open. Edward's good eye bulged when he saw the stack of banknotes among the papers inside. Picking up the cash, he counted and then recounted. Four hundred and twenty-five dollars! He shut the safe and spun the dial. Edward didn't know why he did that. He should put the money back, shouldn't he? He would have to think about it. But for now, it felt good to carry it around, occasionally fanning the bills under his nose and breathing deeply the distinct aroma of paper money. He found some rubber bands, so he rolled up the cash and secured it with a thick band.

He wandered through the store lit by the fanlight windows that were nestled above the picture windows and had escaped damage. They let in enough light to see by, as long as the sun was still up. He saw a stack of loose writing paper and shoved a thick ream into his bag.

He was in the significantly darker back room when he heard the rear door rattle. His heart leaped into his throat, and he looked around frantically for a place to hide. There was nothing except a door in the corner that he hadn't noticed before. He tried the knob, and the door opened onto stairs leading down into the cellar. Edward did not like cellars, but the creaking and cracking of the back door being forced open left him no choice, so he shut the door behind him and descended the stairs into the dank earthen-floored space. Rough wood planks covered the walls, and the floor joists above were exposed and covered in cobwebs.

Edward found and hid behind a steamer trunk and dragged an old linen dustcover over himself. The floor above creaked under the weight of at least two people. Edward peaked out from under the dustcover and tracked their progress to the front of the store and then to the space behind the counter. He looked up and saw the nuts on the bolts that secured the safe to the floor. The bolts suddenly started to move, and dust filtered down. The boards began to creak and bow upward. They were trying to steal the safe by using a lever bar! With a loud cracking that made Edward jump, the boards broke. Edward quickly re-covered himself with the dustcover in case they looked through the hole they had made in the floor and caught sight of him. He could hear their grunting and boots shuffling across the floor as they dragged the safe toward the back room.

Edward waited for twenty minutes after it went quiet upstairs before leaving the cellar. While hiding, he had heard rustling in the corners and had to suppress the urge to run up the stairs sooner. The store was empty. He peeked through the gap in the rear exit door. The lock had been forced and would not latch shut anymore. The alley was deserted, as far as he could tell in the gathering gloom of early evening. What to do now? Edward could not stay there, and what should he do with the money? Should he take it to the hospital and give it to Eddie? Wait, as far as anyone would know, the safe and all its contents had been stolen. This money could fund Edward's trip to New York, and the police and Eddie would blame the Donnellys for the theft of the cash.

Edward felt a pang of guilt, which he suppressed just as quickly. Finally, his mind made up, Edward decided to go in search of a hotel. Not a dive, of course, now that he had money, but a grand hotel. He smiled as he slipped out the back door and crept along the building to the corner. Something rustled behind him and the hairs on the back of his neck stood on end as he bolted out of the alleyway.

12

Edward woke in a strange room, momentarily confused as to where he was. He had slept deeply in the luxurious bed. The room was fashionably furnished, large, and high ceilinged. Then the events of the previous day came rushing back: first, being chased and beaten by relatives of the Donnellys; then finding a large amount of money in Eddie's safe; flying through dark alleys where shadows hid miscreants and evildoers, if only in his imagination; and finally finding the large stone-and-brick hotel with all the main-floor windows brightly lit. The clerk had been about to call the security guard to remove him from the premises when Edward had peeled off a ten-dollar note from the wad of bills and slapped it on the counter. After that, he had been treated like royalty. Now, he sat up, stood, walked to the window, and looked outside. The street below was busy, and it took Edward a minute or so to understand its significance. He found his vest and took his pocket watch out.

Ten to twelve.

His phone call!

Edward quickly dressed, ran down the lobby to the elevator door, and pushed the call button. He watched the iron dial above the doors slowly move from one to two and then three; what floor was he on? The wood doors slid open when the dial reached four, and an attendant pushed the inner cage doors open for him.

"To the lobby, sir?"

"Yes."

When they reached the ground floor, he brushed by the attendant's outstretched hand and walked quickly to the guard standing by the front door.

"Excuse me, how do I get to the Royal Alexandra Hotel?"

The guard looked at him incredulously and said, "This is the Royal Alexandra."

Relief flushed through Edward, and then he turned and walked to the front desk. He shuffled from foot to foot as a lady in front of him with a yappy little dog argued with the clerk. Checking his watch, he saw he had one minute left before the appointed time of his telephone call.

"Excuse me, I am expecting a call from New York at noon," Edward announced, interrupting the woman, who glared at him as if he were something nasty she had found on the bottom of her shoe.

"Mr. Humphries?"

Edward nodded.

"It's coming through now." He pointed to a phone booth set against the wall.

Edward walked quickly to the phone inside the booth and picked up the receiver.

"Hello?"

"Mr. Humphries?"

"Yes."

"Please hold for Mr. Ogden."

As Edward waited, he realized he didn't have to beg for an advance on his story now; he could concentrate solely on pitching Little Crow's story. And that he did. Mr. Ogden wasn't overly excited about another story involving Custer's Last Stand. Still, his interest piqued when Edward told him about Little Crow's friend, the voyageur. He was especially interested in the voyageur's adventures at Khartoum. When Edward added that the two had later met during a North-West Resistance battle, Ogden was sold. The amount to be paid to Edward for the story would be negotiated after Ogden reviewed the final draft. Edward was assured that Harper's pays the highest prices among their competitors. Flush with money, Edward was more than happy just to be published in Harper's, but he kept that to himself.

After breakfast, Edward went shopping. He purchased two off-the-rack suits, a new pair of shoes, a hat, and a leather traveler's bag. This time, when Edward walked into the Royal Alexandra, the front-desk clerk did not turn his nose up at him.

"Another night, my good man," Edward said in his haughtiest voice.

"Yes, sir!"

He could get used to this. It was time for lunch and then a nap. In the evening, he would go to Gabriel's home to meet the voyageur, Jacque Daoust.

What if Jacque refused to relate his story? The thought had never occurred to him until that moment, and it caused the acid to rise in his stomach. But no, from what White Dove had told him, Little Crow and Jacque liked nothing better than to tell their stories. So, he pushed his anxiety down and went to the dining room for lunch. If that snooty woman with the yappy dog was there, and if she was single, perhaps he could charm his way into a free lunch? But, alas, she was not in the room.

Later that evening, Edward came to a stop in front of a modest, clapboard home near the river. A hansom cab had dropped him off a block away, and he had walked the rest of the way. He did not want to appear as a man of means and, to that end, had changed back into his old clothes, but even freshly laundered, they somehow now felt dirty on him.

"Edward, come on in!" Gabriel said. "My father is anxious to meet you."

Edward followed Gabriel into the living room, where he was glad to see Little Crow and White Dove sitting on a couch with a woman their age. And, in an armchair, sat a stocky man with a ruddy face half covered behind a full beard. He stood when Edward entered the room.

"Father, this is Edward, the writer we told you about," Gabriel said to the man. Then turning to Edward, he said, "This is my father, Jacque Daoust."

They shook hands, and then Gabriel said, "And this is my mother, Genevieve." Edward bent over and shook her hand. Genevieve did not stand and seemed cold toward him.

"I hear you want to write my life story?" Jacque said in his heavy French accent after Edward sat on a wooden kitchen chair that Gabriel had carried in from the kitchen.

"No, sir, just the interesting parts," Edward said.

Jacque looked at Edward for a few seconds and then laughed heartily.

"Sorry, Little Crow, I'm going to have to leave you out of my story; he only wants the interesting parts!"

"Ah, hie!" Little Crow grumbled, but he was grinning when he said it.

Edward watched the two men and could see the bond they shared.

"Shall I begin?" Jacque asked. He was obviously eager to tell his story to someone new.

Edward had hoped to arrive in time for supper, but it looked like they were early diners.

"Yes, of course." Edward had carried a journal with him for this purpose and now opened it on his lap. With a pencil poised, he nodded to Jacque.

* * *

I will begin my tale in Fort Chipewyan in the year 1877. I am, of course, Métis, and I was beginning my career as a voyageur for the Hudson's Bay Company. My father, Francois Daoust, and my mother, Antoinette, were both Métis. They are gone now. I had signed a three-year agreement with the company and received one-third of my first season's pay, of which I gave most to my mother. Besides the pay, I also got clothing, a blanket, and several pounds of tobacco. As I didn't smoke back then, I gave the tobacco to my father, and he handed me back a few twists "for trading," he said.

My father had also been a voyageur, as had his father before him. My grandfather had come to the Red River region of Manitoba from Quebec to work for the company. That is where he had met my grandmother Eliza, a Cree woman. My grandfather was a devout man, so he took her by canoe to Trois-Rivières, Quebec, to be married in a church by a catholic priest. My grandmother told me the stories of that trip, how she and five other native women had traveled by canoe with six Frenchmen all the way to Quebec.

One of the hardships they faced on that journey was that none of the women spoke French, and the Frenchmen spoke only broken Cree, Ojibwe, or Sioux. Yes, besides three Cree, there were two Ojibwe women and one Sioux. Back then, the Sioux and Ojibwe considered themselves enemies, and one morning, my grandmother woke to find the Sioux woman gone. A heated argument ensued between the Sioux woman's fiancé, Emile, and the other men. Emile blamed the other Ojibwe for her disappearance, even going so far as accusing them of killing her. A fight then ensued between Emile and the men protecting the honor of their Ojibwe brides-to-be. As a result, the bloodied Emile left the camp searching for his Sioux bride-to-be. Neither were ever heard from again.

My grandmother would sit with the other women in the evenings and talk about the Frenchmen. Meanwhile, the Frenchmen would sit together, tell stories, and smoke their pipes. When they arrived in Trois-Rivières, the priest refused to marry them, pointing out that Indians were not Catholics. So, the Frenchmen went from church to church in Quebec until they found an agreeable priest to perform the ceremonies.

That was a long time ago. Me, I was born at Fort Chipewyan on the shores of Lake Athabasca in 1861. And, at sixteen years of age, I was about to embark on my first canoe run to the settlement at Grand Rapids on the north end of Lake Winnipeg. A part of me wished I was traveling with my father and another part was glad I wasn't. I wanted to prove I could be a voyageur without his help.

My father had suffered a hernia the previous season. He had slipped on rocks while portaging. He told me he would have been fine had he just dumped his packs instead of trying to recover his balance. My father shown me the hernia. It looked like an egg under his skin. I vowed that I would dump my packs if I slipped on rocks.

My father told me what I must do as a middleman, as that would be my job. Middlemen sit between the bowsman and the steersman and do all the paddling. The bowsman stands in the front and guides the canoe through rapids and past logs while the steersman steers the canoe. Both of them use long poles.

We began our journey at three in the morning. There were eight of us in the canoe I was assigned to, with six middlemen between the bowsman and steersman. We were part of a brigade of eight canoes. We loaded our twenty-five-foot birchbark canoe with bales of furs, beaver pelts for the most part. This canoe was called a "canot du nord" by some and a "north canoe" by others. I was unsure when it was my turn to climb in, but Étienne, another middleman, directed me. We pushed off from shore and began our journey paddling down the Athabasca River. I looked back and saw my mother and father waving and shouting, "Farewell!" They were the only ones seeing us off, and I was deeply embarrassed.

"Ah, isn't that sweet? Brings a tear to my eye, it does!" Rene, the middleman in front of me, crooned loudly. Everyone in our boat, and several voyageurs in nearby canoes, laughed.

We stopped every so often for "pipes." And for that, I was grateful, not because of the smoking but because it allowed my muscles to rest. I could feel the aches across my chest, shoulders, and arms. But the worst pain was in my legs. I was not used to kneeling in one position for long periods, and even at pipes, I couldn't stretch my legs. Étienne admonished me the first time I tried moving around.

"Stop what you are doing, Jacque!" he cried. "You will crack the seams in the bark!"

Since then, I sat as still as they did while trying to flex as much as possible, but it did little to ease the pain. Then, after another stop for pipes, we resumed our journey and heard rushing water as we rounded a bend in the river.

"There are rapids ahead, Jacque. We will need to portage."

We steered toward the shore to a well-used landing area.

"We must jump out of the canoe at the same time, Jacque, so we don't tip over."

"Jump?"

"Yes, we must guide the canoe in. Do exactly as I do."

I watched and mimicked his movements, grasping the gunwale beside me with one hand and the thwart in front of me with the other, and leaned forward.

"Use your arms to lift yourself out of the canoe. Only use light pressure with your feet." Étienne told me, and then he lifted himself out of the canoe. I panicked when my feet wouldn't move, and the man behind me grabbed me under my arms and heaved me overboard. The canoe rocked violently, and I lost my grip on the gunwale. My legs had locked up, and I began to sink. I took a deep breath before going under and then thrashed my arms in panic. My heart was pounding, and my lungs began to ache. I was drowning!

Just before I lost all hope and was about to let the ice-cold water rush into my lungs, two hands grabbed my shirt and roughly dragged me to the surface and onto the beach. I lay gasping as seven faces looked down on me. They were angry faces. I coughed and sucked air into my lungs.

"Get up, Jacque," Étienne said quietly. "We have to portage."

"I can't straighten my legs," I gasped. "It feels like there are balls stuck behind my knees."

"I have seen this before," Pierre, a middleman, said. "Lay on your stomach."

I was rolled over before I could attempt to do it on my own.

"Here, bite on this." Pierre handed me a stick.

"Hold him down," he said to the other men.

I felt hands on my shoulders and back, and then Pierre grabbed hold of one ankle and began rocking my lower leg back and forth. A muffled scream escaped around the stick as the pain he was inflicting on me was beyond anything I had ever felt. Then Pierre yanked my ankle down, and my knee popped. I gasped, but the pain gradually subsided.

"Now, the other one."

Oh, God, not again!

Pierre repeated the process, and the pain was no less excruciating the second time around. I lay whimpering, and Pierre looked down at me.

"Get up, ya lazy arse, we have work to do!" Jean, the steersman, cried.

I started to get up, but Pierre put a hand on one shoulder.

"Do not bend your legs right away, or they will cramp again."

He and Étienne grasped a hand each and pulled me straight up. I walked in circles stiff-legged until I felt my knees were back to normal. It was futile trying to wave away the clouds of mosquitoes that enveloped my head. I spit as several enter my mouth.

"Do not spit out the mosquitoes, Jacque; they are good for the protein," Pierre said.

I didn't know what he meant by protein, but from then on, I swallowed every mosquito that entered my mouth.

"Will they will bite my innards?"

They found this funny, and yet no one answered me. I looked up and saw the other canoe crews had passed us by, and we were now in the rear. I stood in front of Étienne so he could load the first bale onto my back. Each pack weighed approximately ninety pounds. Étienne pulled the tumpline over my forehead, and then added another pack on top of the first. I now had one hundred and eighty pounds on my back. We climbed the embankment and carried the furs around the rapids. It took several trips, and then we moved the canoe. It was then time for breakfast. We'd eat before reloading the canoe and continuing down the river.

Breakfast turned out to be a potage of peas, pork, and biscuits boiled in water until it formed into a mush. I had never eaten a meal that tasted so good. I was beginning to doze when Jean yelled for us to load the canoe. It was not without great effort that I rose from the ground. Had I known what was to come, I may well have not gotten up at all.

* * *

"What do you say we go sit on the porch while there's still light?" Jacque asked.

"I would like to keep going, sir," Edward said.

"We will, but first I want to go outside for pipes."

"Pipes?"

"Yes, to smoke our pipes."

"I don't smoke," Edward said.

"Well, that's unfortunate. You don't know what your missing; good for the digestion."

"Would you men care for some tea?" Therese, Gabriel's wife, asked.

"Yes, that would hit the spot!" Jacque declared.

Had they never heard of coffee? Edward managed to keep his comments to himself.

13

After tea was served, the cream and sugar mixed in, and cookies selected, Jacque continued his story.

* * *

Fifteen hours! That was how long we paddled that day. My knees didn't lock up again, and we had two more portages before stopping for the day. We unloaded the canoe while Anton, the brigade's cook, went about making our dinner. We turned our canoe over on the high ground and propped one side up. It would serve to cover our heads for the night, and in case of rain, we attached canvas tarps to the canoe and made a canopy for us to sleep under.

Because the mosquitoes attacked us in relentless droves whenever we were still, we would sit downwind of the cooking fire so the smoke would keep some of the ravenous bloodsuckers at bay.

"Do you have a woman, Jacque?" Étienne asked me after we had settled down to wait for our supper.

"No."

"Well then, we will have to find you one when we get to Grand Rapids!" he said and winked at other voyageurs who were sitting nearby.

"Have you been with a woman yet, Jacque?" Jean asked.

"What do you mean?"

"Have you bedded a woman?"

"Uh—"

"Just as I thought!" Jean cried gleefully. "Voyageurs, we must see to the boy's education!"

Murmurs of assent all around.

"Uh—"

"Okay, Jacque, the best advice I can give you is to learn from the best."

"And, I suppose that is you, Jean?"

"Hah," Gabriel, another middleman, laughed. "He would like to think so, but no, it is not Jean who you want to speak to."

"Then who?"

"Well, that would be Anton."

"Anton?" Now I knew they were joking. Anton, as good a cook as he was, was also the smelliest man I had ever come across. He reeked so high of body odor that it would make a skunk gag.

"Oui, Jacque," Jean said. "Don't let his appearance fool you. Once he gets cleaned up, why, there's not a woman who could resist him."

I was still not convinced, but I decided that if I wanted this crew to accept me, I should play along.

"So, what you need to do is get on Anton's good side, compliment him on how handsome he is, and then you can ask him to teach you in the ways of love," Jean said. "You will be forever grateful, mon ami."

"Ah, alright." It couldn't hurt, I supposed, aside from everyone getting a good laugh at my expense. So, I got up and approached the cook.

"It's not ready yet," Anton said gruffly.

"No, that's not why I'm here."

"Well, what the hell do you want?"

"I just wanted to say, Anton, how handsome you are, and if you would be so kind as to teach me above love?"

Now, thinking back, I suppose I could have worded that a little better because, when he looked at me, his eyes bulged out, and his face slowly turned a deep red, redder than I had seen on any other person. He then reached for his meat cleaver and started toward me.

"You little fek!" he bellowed and came at me, cleaver raised high. I bolted, and I was thankful my knees felt strong, although the sight of that man coming at me made them shake a little. The others were rolling on the ground laughing as I ran by.

Later, when it was time to eat, everything seemed to have settled down, so I approached the cook slowly, and he smiled and said all was forgiven.

"Jacque, the boys told me what they did." Anton chuckled. "Here, I made this special for you. No hard feelings?"

I accepted the bowl of food he handed me and asked what it was.

"You don't know rubbaboo?" Anton asked with an amazed look on his face.

"No, what is rubbaboo?"

"Why, it is pemmican boiled in water with flour."

"Okay, but what is special about mine?"

He leaned toward me and whispered, "Saskatoon berries," winking one eye. I forced myself not to recoil from the man's sour breath.

I sat with the others and spooned the food in.

"Is it supposed to taste bitter?" I asked when I saw the others shoveling their rubbaboo into their mouths with great zeal.

"No, why? Does yours taste bitter?" Étienne mumbled through a half-filled mouth.

"A little, maybe it's the saskatoons."

"What saskatoons?"

"The cook said he added some to mine."

"Let me see." Étienne took my bowl. He poked at some of the berries floating in the potage and said, "These aren't saskatoons."

"What's wrong, Jacque?" Jean asked with some alarm.

I had bent over as a severe cramp gripped my stomach, and then I ran hunched to the bushes when I felt my bowels loosening. I caught sight of a grinning Anton through the bushes as I relieved myself.

The bastard!

I was not the strongest paddler the next day. I woke up shivering and weak. I drank some water and turned down breakfast when we made the stop. At midafternoon, we were paddling toward shore for another portage when our canoe capsized. It could have been my fault, but who knows? We shall not speak about that. Anyway, all our cargo got soaked through, so we had to spend the rest of the day opening bundles and laying the contents out to dry. Jean, mercifully, told me to go lay down somewhere until I got my strength back. I think he just wanted me out of their way, which was fine by me.

On day three, I felt like my old self again. The other canoes in our brigade were far ahead of us; we would have to paddle hard to catch up to them. By the time we had repacked everything and finished the portage, it was time for breakfast.

The crew were in good spirits. They always were, for that matter. They sang their songs boisterously all day, never seeming to tire. I don't know how they did it. Maybe I would be the same after a season or two. Étienne asked me if I planned to be a voyageur for life, and I told him yes.

"That may not be too long; look at your father," he said. "Early forties, and he may never paddle another company canoe."

"But that was an accident," I said. "I will not suffer the same fate."

"The life of a voyageur is a dangerous one, Jacque. There are many ways to injure yourself, or even die, out here."

"Why are you telling me this, Étienne? I know it is dangerous."

"You need to think about what you will do afterward when it is too hard to keep up with younger paddlers."

"What about you?" I asked.

"I will be a buffalo hunter."

"But I heard the buffalo herds are dwindling."

"And that's why I will make lots of money!" Étienne exclaimed. "The demand will be high, and I will make a lot of money for every buffalo I shoot."

I looked at him and wondered if he was making a joke, but he looked off in the distance with a contented smile. Although, it did make me think.

What would I do after voyageuring?

We encountered a cow moose and her calves that evening. Pierre spotted them swimming across the river a few hundred yards ahead of us. He wanted to take one of the calves for the cooking pot and called for a gun, but Jean refused. He said the calves would grow and feed more bellies, and we didn't have time to waste after losing most of yesterday drying out our cargo. Pierre grumbled and glared at me. Was everything my fault? I spent the rest of the day dreaming up different ways to get even with the cook for giving me the runs. I was glad he traveled in one of the other canoes.

Our canoe slowed when the other middlemen lifted their oars where the banks began to narrow. Everyone removed their hats, so I followed suit, and then Jean started a prayer. I wondered what was happening, and then I saw them: dozens of crosses on the banks of the river and, beyond them, rapids. I assumed we would turn toward shore for another portage, but we continued toward the roiling water.

"Why are we not going to shore?" I asked.

"Because of the fractured cliffs, portaging here is more dangerous than shooting the rapids," Étienne said. "But remember, Jacque, you must paddle hard when we enter them."

"Shouldn't we try to go slower?"

"That is what the men those crosses honor may have thought. But no, we will go fast and trust our steersman and bowsman to guide us safely through."

I felt the first mist of water spray my face as I matched the others' paddling. I watched Peter, the bowsman, skillfully steer through the rocks with his long pole as everyone sang loudly. Then our canoe picked up speed, and it was difficult to paddle as my oar seemed to be swept back with each dip into the water through no effort on my part. Water soaked me whenever we crashed through a crest, and I kept one eye on the level of water in our canoe. Had that water splashed in, or was it seeping in through cracks in the birchbark?

I looked up just as Peter's pole got stuck between two boulders. He refused to give up his grip on his pole and was pulled overboard. I saw his bulging eyes as he flew past. Our canoe then hit a large rock and capsized. The ice-cold water shocked me, and then my back slammed into a boulder. It knocked the breath out of me, but I gasped and drew in gulps of air and swallowed some water as I was carried down the rapids. I bounced off a few more boulders and wondered if other voyageurs would remove their hats and say a prayer when they saw my cross. But then I found myself in calmer waters. I looked around and saw bales floating by me, so I grabbed one and kicked my feet toward shore.

I watched, prayed, and waited for the others, occasionally wading out to snag another bale floating close to shore. Finally, with great relief, I saw a voyageur hanging onto a bale. He entered an eddy and began turning in a circle. I hollered to him, but he didn't respond. It was peaceful here with the roar of the rapids behind us, and yet he couldn't hear me. I saw his head slide down toward the water and knew I had to do something. The cold water took my breath away as I dove in, but I grew accustomed to it after a few strokes. Would I be able to break out of the eddy once I reached the man? The vortex didn't look very strong, but that could be deceiving.

Without another thought, I swam into the eddy, and the swirling water immediately swept me into its vortex. Yet I stroked hard and reached the man; it was Étienne. He was unconscious with both hands jammed into the bale's strapping. I tried to escape the eddy with Étienne and the bale, but it seemed futile. I silently willed Étienne to wake up so he could help me, but he remained unconscious. I stopped my efforts and rested my body for another push when something bounced off me. It was Jean, and Pierre was there too. They each grabbed the bale and the three of us kicked our legs hard and we finally managed to break free of the eddy. No one spoke until we reached the shore. Jean and Pierre freed Étienne's hands from the bale and dragged him up the bank. I pulled the bale onto dry land and walked over to them.

"He is alive!" Jean declared. "Tear off your sleeve, Jacque."

"Why mine?" I said and then instantly regretted it.

I tore off my left sleeve and handed it to Jean, who used it to bandage a cut on Étienne's head.

"Hey!" Pierre yelled. "There's Gabriel!"

And there he was, floating by on his back. He heard Pierre, rolled over, and swam to shore. Then Jean, Pierre, Gabriel, and I waited at the river, but no others passed by. We lowered our heads and said a silent prayer for our friends.

"The canoe!" Gabriel shouted, then ran into the water, grabbed the canoe by its bow, and swam with it back to shore. There were two large holes in the birch skin and several broken cedar ribs.

Jean looked it over and said, "Well, boys, it looks like we got some mending to do, so let's get to it. Gabriel, you and Jacque find some birch trees and cut some bark. Pierre, you go cut some spruce roots, and I'll see if I can find some cedar trees for the ribs and oars."

Étienne regained consciousness and, other than a painful headache, had suffered no other injury. We patched the canoe and saved eight bundles of fur, but we had no food. Andre and Rene's bodies floated by, and we recovered and buried them near our campsite. As long as voyageurs navigated this river, they would remove their caps and say a prayer as they passed their crosses. Of Peter, we found no sign, but we placed a cross for him too.

* * *

Jacque stopped talking and wiped his eyes. Seeing this, Genevieve moved closer and wrapped an arm around his shoulder.

14

"Shall we take a break?" Edward asked.

"No, I can continue," Jacque said hoarsely and then wiped his eyes with the backs of his forefingers.

* * *

Four weeks later, we could see Grand Rapids ahead. We turned toward shore, and I asked Étienne what we were doing.

"We cannot enter the settlement looking like this!" Étienne said, waving his arm at the others.

"Hey, what about you, mon ami?" Pierre cried.

They were all in good humor, and that surprised me.

"How can everyone be happy when we are arriving less three men?" I asked.

"Jacque, we all signed on as voyageurs knowing the dangers we'd face," Gabriel said, "and we all accepted those dangers. Andre, Peter, and Rene all died courageously, and we will honor them every time we pass those rapids."

I lowered my head, ashamed for calling them out for being happy. Étienne walked over and placed a hand on my shoulder.

"We are brothers, us voyageurs; never forget that," he said. "Now, build us a fire, little brother, so I can have a shave!"

I nodded and looked around. The others had stripped and were bathing at the river bank. Unfortunately, all our spare clothes were lost in the rapids, so we had to wash what we wore.

We were in damp clothes, but we sang and paddled with great gusto as we approached the landing. Our bellies were empty and we were exhausted, but we were determined to arrive looking as fresh as when we had left Fort Chipewyan.

Each of us reported to the company commander and told our story. Then we were relieved of duty until he determined whether our stories agreed and if the loss of cargo was accidental or was in any way our fault. My friends decided to do a little drinking, and since I was too young to have developed a taste for alcohol, I went in search of a good meal.

The smell of boiling sturgeon drew me to an older native woman sitting on a tree stump in front of a fire. Behind her stood a small log cabin. She was stirring a large iron pot, and I stood inhaling the wonderful aroma.

"Would you like some fish?" she asked in Cree.

"Yes, I can pay."

"Next time. For now, just tell me a story." She lifted out a sturgeon steak, placed it on a metal plate, reached beside her, broke off a chunk of bannock from a slab, and handed me the plate. "Here's some lard for the bannock," she said as she set a small tin cup in front of me. "Sorry, I have no salt."

I tasted the fish and moaned my pleasure, which made her laugh.

"I'll make some tea, and you can tell me your story."

"Mmph," was all I could manage as I stuffed my mouth with the glorious food. Then, over tea and more bannock and lard, I told her about the trip from Fort Chipewyan. She nodded and smiled in all the right spots, but I suspect the stories were not as interesting as I had thought, or maybe they were commonplace among the voyageurs that passed through here.

"Thank you for the good food and the company, . . . ?"

"Maggie."

"Maggie, I am Jacque."

"Come back anytime, Jacque, and bring some more stories with you."

I was halfway back to our canoe when I realized I was famished.

How could that be?

I had just enjoyed a good and plentiful meal.

I asked a man where I could get something to eat, and he directed me toward a small log cabin. As I walked through the open doorway, my senses were assaulted by grease, fried meat, fish, and body odor. A long table ran lengthwise with benches on either side, and at one end of the table was the kitchen. The seats were half-full, so I sat near some friendly-looking men. Fishermen, I learned. A Métis server stopped in front of me and asked, "What happened to your sleeve?"

"I tore it off to use as a bandage."

She looked me over, then said, "For what?"

"My friend's head."

"Ah, what can I get you?"

"Sturgeon."

"Sturgeon?" she asked with a confused look on her face. "What is this sturgeon you speak of? Is it some kind of animal?"

"No, no, it is a large fish," I said and spread my arms wide. "They have whiskers."

"Whiskers!" she cried. "Even the lady sturgeon?"

"Well, I suppose . . ."

At this point, the diners could not contain their humor any longer and let loose with gales of laughter. The serving girl grinned from ear to ear, basking in the glory of being the jokester. She eventually turned and gave my order to the cook, an older man, also Métis.

The man next to me, still chuckling, slapped me on the shoulder and said, "Welcome, friend. I am Gaston."

"Jacque."

"You are a voyageur?"

"Yes, are you?"

"I was."

I waited for him to continue, but no further explanation seemed to be forthcoming.

"It's funny, I just had a large meal of sturgeon and bannock, yet I am still hungry."

"Is that a fact?" Gaston asked. "And where did you have that?"

"A nice woman offered me a meal if I told her a story."

Once full of boisterous conversations and eruptions of laughter, the room suddenly went quiet. I looked around to see every set of eyes upon me, including those of the cook and server.

"What was this woman's name?" Gaston asked.

"Maggie."

"Ah. After we eat, you will show me this woman."

"She's not in any trouble, is she?"

"No, no."

The serving girl set my plate in front of me, the humor now gone from her face.

"Hey, where are the whiskers?" I demanded.

"What?" She gave me a look as if I had insulted her.

"The whiskers, they are the best part!"

"Uh . . ."

I slid the plate toward her. "Take this away and bring it back with the whiskers!"

She instinctively reached for the plate, but I grabbed it and slid it back to me while grinning at her. Again, the room erupted in renewed laughter, this time at her expense. Then, she huffed and spun on her heel and stomped away.

"Oh, Jacque, you will pay for that," Gaston said. "Genevieve is not one to trifle with."

I finished the meal, and Genevieve took my plate.

"How much do I owe you?"

"More than you can ever pay, but the meal is on me since you didn't get your whiskers."

Everyone either whistled or hooted at the exchange, and Genevieve sashayed back to the kitchen.

Gaston stared at me and said, "Well, that hasn't happened before."

I shrugged, and he and a few others followed me out of the cabin.

Oh, yeah, they wanted to meet Maggie.

"Um, maybe she won't be happy if I show up with a bunch of men," I said, second-guessing the idea of bringing these men to her. They were a rough-looking lot, and it had crossed my mind that they may be planning to rob me.

"Oh, no, Maggie enjoys visitors."

"Well, if you have already met her, why am I showing her to you?"

"I want to be sure we are talking about the same woman."

"Why?"

"You will see."

I could see no way out of this, so I took them to Maggie, but I took a roundabout route to ensure we'd always be within sight of others in the village. I stopped short when I neared Maggie's camp. The cabin was no longer there. What was left were a few rotten logs and the remnants of a caved-in roof. The clearing where I had sat with Maggie an hour earlier was now filled with thick weeds, and the circle of stones marking the firepit that had warmed us now held nothing but growing green grass and wild sage.

"What the . . ."

"It has been a while since Maggie showed herself to anyone."

"What is this?" I asked.

"Maggie was the wife of a voyageur. He drowned many years ago, shooting rapids. When Maggie was told, she refused to believe it. She would cook lunch every day for her husband, but of course, he never showed up. And then, one day, she was gone."

I stood transfixed, and when he didn't say any more, I asked, "Where did she go?"

"Her clothes were found on the riverbank, neatly folded."

The men stood quietly. Some looked around, obviously spooked. Goosebumps rose on my arms, and my hair stood on end. We walked back, Gaston leading the way.

"Don't worry, Jacque, we will not harm you."

I felt shame, not for thinking that but for them knowing that I had suspected them. I decided to change the subject.

"How come you stopped paddling?"

"There's no more work for everyone. You were lucky to get a contract."

"How come there's no more work?"

"Steamships, York boats, and rail lines. There is less and less need for hauling furs by canoe." Gaston sighed. He stopped and faced me. "Take my advice, Jacque; save all the money you can because you will not get another contract after this one."

"Buy some land or go fishing," one of the others put in.

I nodded and continued walking, head down, deep in thought.

"Good luck in your travels, Jacque!" Gaston said as they peeled off in another direction.

"So long, friends!"

It was dusk when I returned to our canoe. The others were still out drinking somewhere. I thought I had better get some sleep while I could because I suspected they would be loud when they returned. Little did I know that no one would return to rouse me from the ghost that would haunt me that night.

* * *

"It is getting dark; perhaps we can continue inside?" Edward said, looking around at the growing shadows in Gabriel's yard.

"Yes, of course," Jacque agreed.

15

Jacque and Edward sat on the couch in the living room, but Gabriel, Little Crow, White Dove, and Genevieve moved to the kitchen to play cards.

"I've heard the story many times, Edward," Little Crow said before leaving the room, "and it gets longer and more heroic with each telling."

Jacque laughed good-naturedly and then said to Edward, "He's just jealous that my stories are more interesting than his."

"Ah, hie," Little Crow said and walked out of the room, grinning all the way.

* * *

I had a nightmare that night. A noise from the river woke me, and when I sat up, Maggie rose out of the water and waded toward me. When I was a boy, I had witnessed the recovering of a drowning victim, an older boy, who had been in the water for several days. Maggie's face had that same look. It was one of those dreams where I knew I was dreaming, but my limbs refused to move. When she came near me, she croaked, "Would you like breakfast?" Her breath made me gag, and then a worm crawled out of her mouth. I broke free of the dream and woke with a pounding heart.

It was dawn, and there was no sign of my friends. They couldn't still be out drinking! Or maybe they could; they didn't seem to do anything half-heartedly. I stretched and yawned mightily. I would go look for them later, but for now, breakfast. With some trepidation, I approached the river to scoop some wash water into a bucket. I watched the surface, half expecting the dead woman to appear, but the river remained calm. After walking back to the canoe, and with more than a few glances over my shoulder, I washed my face. I thought of seeing Genevieve again, and the anticipation sent a tingling throughout my body.

Entering the cabin, I was disappointed to see a young boy, maybe twelve years old, serving the diners. I didn't see Gaston or his friends, so I sat near some men who didn't appear to be hungover or drunk. Some further down the table had that look. Three men seemed half asleep at one end of the bench. One sported a black eye, and another had a fat lip. There was a gap between them and the next diners, and I caught a faint whiff of their body odor. It was that sickly metallic smell of processed alcohol seeping out of skin pores.

"Where's Genevieve?" I asked when the boy came to take my order.

He shrugged and mumbled, "What do you want?"

I glanced around and saw everyone had a bowl in front of them.

"What they are having."

The boy left, and the man next to me said, "I don't know why he asks; they only have porridge."

I nodded, pointed my chin toward the hungover men, and asked, "What happened to them?"

"Several men were drinking behind the bootlegger's shack, and a fight broke out. Looks like they got the worst of it."

"Huh," I grunted and wondered if my friends had been there. I was finishing my meal when a Mountie entered, and the boy handed him a large pail of porridge.

"Hang on, there," one of the hungover men hollered. "Let me spit in that first!"

A smattering of forced laughs ensued, but I doubt anyone other than the other hungover men found the comment humorous. The Mountie, who didn't look much older than me, smiled tolerantly at the men and then walked out the door.

"Sore losers," my neighbor whispered out the side of his mouth.

"What's going on; why would they want to spit on good porridge?" I asked.

"It's for the men that beat them up; they are locked up in the dead house."

"The dead house?"

"Yeah, it's behind the church."

"Why is it called the dead house?" I asked, suspecting the men locked up were my partners.

"The church stores dead bodies in the building during the winter months, until the ground is thawed enough for burial. In the summer, the Mounties use it as a jail."

I jumped up, paid for my breakfast, and chased after the Mountie.

"Hey!" I called to him, and he turned warily toward me. He moved the pail to his left hand and placed his right hand on his holster. "I think you have my friends in your jail."

"Yeah?"

"Yeah, voyageurs, four of them."

"Well, they did say they were voyageurs. Kept me up half the night signing French songs. But there's five of them, not four."

"Huh, when are they being released?"

"After I wake them up and feed them, they can pay their fines and leave."

"Can I come along to see if they are my friends?"

"Sure." He shrugged and visibly relaxed.

"How come the three men in the cookhouse weren't arrested?"

"I have only one jail, and I can't put two fighting groups together. Besides, I know those three men. They're basically harmless," the policeman said. "Now, the ones in jail, I don't know them from Adam."

"Makes sense, I guess," I said. "I'm Jacque Daoust."

"Constable Tom Flynn," he said, extending his right hand. "You came in yesterday?"

"Yeah, we lost three men on the trip when our canoe capsized in rapids," I said, shaking his hand.

"Sorry to hear that. Did they get a proper burial?"

"Two did. We couldn't find the other."

"Ah, that's too bad."

We walked the rest of the way in silence.

"Wait here," he told me when he unlocked the heavy door on the small log building and went inside. I heard him hollering, and then he came back outside.

"After they eat, you can go inside and see if they're your friends," he said and then sat down on the steps. He took out a pipe and packed some tobacco in it from his pouch. When he lit it, I was taken by the aroma.

"That smells good, better than what my friends smoke."

"It is expensive, but it's my one indulgence," he said, offering me his pouch.

I shook my head and said, "I don't smoke."

He shrugged and put the pouch away.

"My friends' tobacco smells like they're burning rotten socks."

He laughed and said, "How did you get mixed up with that bunch?"

"They're good men; they just can't hold their liquor, I suppose. And I don't get to choose who's in the canoe I'm assigned."

He nodded and then tapped his pipe out in a tin can beside the steps. After scraping the bowl, he heaved himself up and said, "Let's go see if these men have the money to pay their fines."

I followed him inside, and I was not surprised to see my friends sitting on the floor. If I thought the men in the eatery were hungover and beaten, they had nothing on these men. The stink and heat in the room were oppressive. It smelled of body odor, liquor, vomit, urine, and an underlying scent that reminded me of the room back home where we hung wild meat. What caused that smell is something I try not to think about.

"Jacque!" Étienne cried. "I told you he would come."

The others looked at me bleary-eyed and gave me a half-hearted grin. Anton, the brigade cook, was the fifth man; they all had various cuts, bruises, and swellings.

"You're free to go once you pay your fines," Tom informed them.

"How much is the fine?" Étienne asked, and they all began checking their pockets.

"A dollar each."

"Tabernac, someone took all my money!" Gabriel cried.

One by one, they all said, "Mine too."

"Those bastards robbed us!"

"Are you sure you didn't spend all of it on liquor?" Tom asked.

They looked at each other, and then Étienne shrugged and mumbled, "Maybe."

"Do you have money, Jacque?" Pierre asked. "We will pay you back."

"Yeah, but I only have four dollars and fifty cents," I said. "Sorry, Anton, I have to look after my crewmates first."

"Putain!" Anton threw the insult at me and then asked Tom, "What happens if I can't pay my fine?"

"Five days in the dead house."

"The dead house?" Anton looked slowly around the room.

Tom waved around the room and said, "This is the church's dead house, where they store bodies for burial."

"Merde!" he whispered, wide-eyed.

I handed Tom the four dollars and said I would wait outside. The smell was overpowering in the unventilated building.

I waited outside and grinned when my four friends walked out, and I heard Anton's colorful curses that continued until we were out of earshot.

"That place smelled something fierce!" Jean mumbled.

"I don't know why you're complaining," I said. "Other than the dead-body smell, it was all you guys."

"Hey!" they yelled and chased me, but they didn't stand a chance of catching me in their condition, and they quickly gave up the chase. They spent most of the day alternating between sleeping under the canoe and lying in the river. No one offered to pay me back once we got back to our little camp, so I suspected they had squandered all their pay.

Suppertime. My fifty cents would buy me two more meals, so I would have to find some work until we were outfitted for the return trip to Fort Chipewyan. I had been waiting patiently for a chance to see Genevieve again. And, this time, when I walked through the door, she was there, serving the customers. She returned my smile as I walked in, and it made my stomach flutter. I looked over at the man nearest me as I sat down and caught the aroma of his meal.

"What's that?" I asked him in a friendly way.

"Pork," he mumbled over a full mouth. His beard glistened with grease in the candlelight when he turned my way.

I watched Genevieve approach, and I wiped my sweaty palms on my thighs.

"I'll have the pork."

She made a face and said, "Well, hello to you too!" She spun and sauntered away. Dammit! I hadn't even said hello to her, just made an order.

"Hello, Jacque."

I turned and saw Constable Flynn enter. He rounded the table and sat opposite me.

"Hello."

"Where are your friends tonight? Not drinking again, are they?"

"No, they have no money, and they aren't in any condition to do much at the moment anyway."

Genevieve appeared and set my plate in front of me.

"Hey, this isn't pork!"

"No, it's not," she said and turned to Tom. "You need food for prisoners tonight?"

"No, the jail's empty, for now. I'll have what my friend here is having."

"Good choice, Tom," she said and placed a hand on his shoulder.

Jealousy burned inside me when I saw that, but I tried to hide my emotions.

"You and Genevieve are friendly?"

"I suppose you could say that," Tom said.

"I ordered pork, and she gave me beef; why would she do that?"

"She must like you."

"Is the pork bad then?" I asked in a whisper and glanced at the man nearest me.

"I'm sure it's fine," Tom said.

Then it hit me. "You released Anton?"

"Yeah, a voyageur came and paid his fine." Tom hesitated, then said, "Anton was plenty sore at you, Jacque."

"At me? Why?"

"He thinks you had enough money to pay his fine."

"That's ridiculous."

"He won't bother you."

"How you can be so sure?"

"He doesn't want to spend another night in the jail, that's for sure, and I assured him you didn't have enough for his fine."

"But he was still mad?"

"Yeah, he said he was the brigade's cook and outranked the others," Tom said, "and that you were paying him back for the berries, whatever that means."

"He slipped some poison berries in my rubbaboo," I said a little too loud. "Gave me diarrhea!"

Genevieve made a face as she set Tom's plate down in front of him. I hadn't even seen her coming. Once again, she placed a hand on his shoulder and said, "Enjoy your meal, Tom." I noticed a quick flick of her eyes toward me before she turned and left.

"I'm glad my wife's not here," Tom said. "She would not put up with that."

Relief flooded through me, and I grinned like an idiot. It would be many years before I found out that Tom had not been married when he had made his comment; he told me that he saw the way Genevieve and I looked at each other and did not want to be caught in the middle.

I caught Genevieve looking sidelong at me with a frown on her face. She quickly turned her head when she saw me looking back at her. I lingered over coffee with Tom and was just about to leave when Genevieve came to us and asked Tom if he would like anything else.

"Thank you, but I am fine," he replied.

I stood and reached into my pocket for money.

"Put your money away, Jacque," Tom said. "I'm buying tonight."

"Why, thank you, Tom!"

"No problem."

"Have a good night," I said. "You too, ma'am."

Her face darkened, and I turned to leave. I opened the door and was grinning like a fool when a meaty fist drove into my face. The force of the punch propelled me backward; my ears rang and I saw stars. I rolled to one side and rose up on one knee and shook the cobwebs from my brain. Anton was bearing down on me, so I charged down low and heard him grunt when I hit his stomach with my shoulder. I kept propelling my feet forward as we went through the door and fell off the front steps. We rolled on the ground and punched at each other. Anton was large and strong, but he was suffering from a hangover. Yet even in his state, he still wound up on top. He squeezed my throat with his left hand and reached for a rock with his right. I was pounding at his left arm with both fists as panic set in when I realized I couldn't breathe. He raised the stone and was about to bring it down on my head when a pistol pressed against his temple and its hammer clicked. Anton froze as Tom said, "Drop the rock and let him go, Anton."

Anton gave one final squeeze and then let go of my neck. I gulped air. It felt like I had swallowed a dozen knives.

"Get up," Tom told him.

Anton placed one hand on my chest and drove his weight into me as he pushed himself off. Once free, I rolled onto my hands and knees and alternated between coughing and gasping for air. Then I felt an arm placed across my shoulders, and it took me a moment to realize that Genevieve was talking to me.

"Are you okay, Jacque?"

I nodded and continued coughing and gasping. Tears had filled my eyes, and when I looked to my left, I saw the blurred shapes of Tom walking behind Anton toward the jail. Then I realized I couldn't breathe through my nose and saw strings of blood hanging from both nostrils. My nose felt heavy. Finally, I got my breath back, and I sat on my rear on the ground, legs splayed in front of me. As gently as I could, I brushed the tears from my eyes, but it still sent waves of pain through my nose.

"Come inside, Jacque," Genevieve said. "I'll clean you up."

I nodded, and two men lifted me by my armpits and walked me into the cabin.

"That nose is broken, my friend," one of them said. After they sat me down on the bench, he bent in front of me and inspected my nose. Genevieve had gone into the kitchen for water and a cloth.

"Yup, it's broken. Grab hold of him, Jim," he said to his partner. Then, before I realized what was happening, Jim grabbed my arms from behind, and the man placed his thumbs on my nose and pushed down hard. I heard a crunch and saw stars.

"What the hell are you doing, Jake!" Genevieve yelled at the man.

"I fixed his nose."

"Get away from him; you're no doctor!"

Jake grumbled as he backed away. I heard the word "ungrateful," but that was about it.

"Tilt your head back, Jacque," she said and then started washing the blood away.

If it hadn't hurt so bad, I would have enjoyed her nearness, soft touch, and attention. Well, maybe I did enjoy it a little, but it was still painful.

"You'll sleep on the floor in here tonight," the cook said, "or the mosquitoes will feast on you outside."

I asked how he knew I slept outside, but it came out in a slur. Jim, who may have been the only person in the room who understood my words, said to me, "Everyone knows everything about everyone else in this town, my friend." I found out later he sold liquor illegally out of his cabin and was used to listening to slurring drunks, which was what I must have sounded like. Everything after that was a blur. I remember being helped onto a makeshift bed on the floor and promptly falling asleep.

16

It hurt to swallow the next morning, and my nose was plugged. I opened my eyes and was startled to see a face mere inches from mine. It was the morning serving boy.

"What happened to you?" he asked.

"Told the cook his food tasted bad."

"Yeah?" he said with large eyes. "You are a brave man."

"No, I was lying. It was a drunken man who attacked me."

"Oh," he physically relaxed and then pointed at my nose. "Does that hurt?"

"It hurt worse when Jake fixed it."

"Jake?" he asked, shocked. "The bootlegger?"

"I guess."

"Have you checked your pockets?"

I reached into my pants pockets and was relieved to find my fifty cents still there.

"Why did you ask that?"

"Jake and his partner, Jim, the like to steal money from passed-out drunks."

"I wasn't drunk."

"But were you awake when they were near you?"

"Mostly, but there were a lot of people around."

"Well, then you're lucky."

"Who are you?"

"Norbert. Genevieve is my sister. She likes you."

"Really? My name is Jacque," I said, suddenly feeling a whole lot better.

"I know."

Jim's comment about everyone knowing everything about everyone in this village came back to me. Had Jake and Jim stolen my friends' money? I couldn't see how my friends could have spent all their money in one night, right down to the last halfpenny. I would have to discuss this with Tom.

"Help me up, Norbert," I said, holding a hand out to him.

He effortlessly pulled me up. The boy had strength.

"You going to eat?" he asked.

"Yeah, can I get a basin of water so I can wash up?"

"There's one on the back porch and a rain barrel too. Make sure you rinse and put fresh water in the basin when you're done."

"Thanks, Norbert."

Theophile, the cook, who I later found out was also the owner, didn't even glance my way when I walked through the cabin and out the screen door. It squeaked on rusty springs and then slapped closed with a bang.

I stood on the covered porch and leaned over the edge. I blew my nose and had to grab the corner post for support when a wave of pain and dizziness staggered me. When my vision returned, I noticed drops of blood in the washbasin. I swirled the pink water after washing my bruised face and flung it off the porch.

"You look like you've been dragged through a knothole, Jacque."

"Hi, Maggie." I was not startled when I saw her standing in the willows. "I know who you are."

"Of course, you do; we met the other day."

"No, I mean . . . ah, never mind."

As she stood there watching me, I looked into her eyes, and it felt like they were fake eyes with no depth. I shivered and said, "I saw you the other night."

"Yeah?" Maggie said.

"In the river."

Suddenly, she screamed and flew toward me. Just before she reached me, she veered off and disappeared like wisps of smoke in the wind. I felt my skin pimple, and a flush of fear coursed through my body. Later, I found Constable Flynn and related my suspicions that my friends had been robbed by Jake and Jim.

"That would not surprise me; I've had complaints about them before but could never prove anything."

"I just don't see how they could have spent all their pay in one night."

"How much are we talking?"

"I don't know. A lot."

"Well, let's go see them and ask."

As we walked toward our camp by the river, I said, "I saw a ghost."

"Maggie?"

"Yeah, have you met her?"

"No, but I have heard the stories about her."

"Do you believe them?"

"You mean, do I believe in ghosts?"

"Yeah."

He was quiet for a while, and then he said, "Well, a lot of people claim to have seen her, and some, like you, claim to have talked to her . . ."

"Doesn't really answer my question, Tom."

"No, I suppose it doesn't."

It was obvious to me that he didn't believe in ghosts and that he was too kind to admit it because, if he had said so, he would have effectively been calling me a liar.

But was there such a thing as ghosts? Could my conversations with Maggie have all been a figment of my imagination, like the dream I had of her emerging from the river?

"What happened to you, Jacque?" Étienne cried when Tom and I reached the camp. "You look like a raccoon!"

"Anton attacked me after he was released from jail."

"What, that dirty—"

This was followed by a chorus of curses from the others. Although Anton was the brigade's cook and they had known him far longer than me, I was their crewmate.

"He's back in jail," I said with a hand held up to quell their outrage.

"Jacque tells me you carried a lot of money with you when you went to Jake's place," Tom said to the group.

He was answered with a chorus of grumpy affirmatives.

"Can you tell me how much each of you had on you?" Tom took a notebook and pencil from one of his pockets.

As one, they looked to the sky and moved their lips as they tried to tally up what they had carried in their pockets. Then they went into a huddle and conferred. Finally, Étienne turned back to us and said, "We think it was about thirty-two dollars and all our pipes and tobacco."

Tom whistled and said, "I think you men were robbed. There's no way you could drink all that up in one night, voyageurs or not!"

They all began grumbling angrily, looking ready to storm Jake's cabin. Tom held up his hand and quieted them.

"Let me look into it; I don't want to have to lock you all up again!" Tom declared.

They all grumbled but nodded their heads in agreement.

"We will wait here," Étienne said.

I handed them a pail of porridge from the cookhouse, and because we had lost all our utensils in the river, they hungrily scooped two fingers of food into their mouths before passing the pail to the next man. So round and round it went until Jean scraped his fingers around the bottom for the last bits. I took no joy in watching this display.

Two hours later, we were sitting on the bank watching the river go by when Tom returned. He smelled of liquor, and I saw the still-wet stains on his boots and pant cuffs.

"You were beaten and robbed after you got too drunk to defend yourselves," Tom began and was interrupted by angry curses. He held up his hand and continued. I was fascinated with his power to quiet four tough men with his steady gaze and a small but firm gesture. The man, young as he was, had a commanding presence.

"I've received complaints of this happening before but have never been able to prove them until now," he said. "I arrested Jake and Jim, confiscated your thirty-two dollars, and destroyed their moonshine liquor."

"Can you do that?" I asked. "I mean, legally?"

"They resisted arrest, and in the struggle that ensued, all the moonshine containers either tipped over or broke. Nasty stuff. It's no wonder you were incapacitated." He handed over the money, pipes, and tobacco to Étienne and watched them divide their possessions among themselves. "In the end, Jake confessed to stealing your money and possessions. And, don't forget, you owe Jacque here the money he paid for your release."

"But if they are victims, should they have been imprisoned and fined in the first place?" I asked.

Tom looked at me appraisingly and said, "You know, I hadn't considered that. Come to my quarters, and I will return your money."

"What about Anton?" I asked as we turned to walk away. "He would have been robbed too."

"Don't worry about Anton. I'll see that he gets what he deserves."

Tom turned back to the four men who were practically doing a jig and said in a firm voice, "Do not give me pause for what I have just done for you."

When four uncomprehending faces stared back at him, he added, "Don't go getting drunk again! You all owe Jacque here a big favor. Had it not been for him, you would not have gotten your money back." He then turned and winked at me. I heard a chorus of cheers involving my name as I fell into step with Tom.

We walked in silence for several minutes until Tom stopped and pointed out Jake's cabin. The door was hanging by one hinge, and broken kegs and empty bottles lay strewn about the yard along with some broken furniture.

"Get away from there, Absalom!" Tom yelled at a man picking through the bottles and tilting them skyward to drain the last drops into his mouth.

Absalom peered at Tom with one rheumy eye and said, "Why? It's just going to go to waste."

Tom sighed and said, "Stay out of that cabin!"

Absalom waved a hand dismissively as he searched for the next bottle.

Tom shook his head, grinned at me, and then continued walking. We entered a small log cabin that served as Tom's quarters. A cot lay against a wall across from a wood-cook stove, and below a small window in the back sat a table and two chairs that apparently also served as his desk. He sat on one chair, gestured for me to sit on the other, and wrote on a couple pieces of paper for several minutes. Then he opened a trunk that sat at the foot of his bed, took out four one-dollar banknotes, and set them on the table.

"Sign this, Jacque," he said and slid the papers in front of me. I scanned them quickly and signed the bottom. He handed me the money, which I was grateful to get back.

"Are you going to release Anton?" I asked.

"Not for a few days," he replied. "When do you go back to Fort Chipewyan?"

"Soon, I hope."

"I'll stop by the Hudson Bay Company's office and explain the situation," Tom said.

"I appreciate all you've done, Tom." I stood and held out my hand.

"It is me that should be thanking you, Jacque," he replied as he shook my hand. "I've wanted to shut Jake and Jim's operation down for a while."

* * *

"I'm a little tired; I think I'll go to bed now," Little Crow said. "No reflection on your storytelling, Jacque, but I've heard it many times."

Little Crow and the others had finished playing cards and were now sitting in the parlor with Jacque and Edward.

"Of course, Little Crow, I will try to continue without your presence," Jacque replied, "but you're going to miss the best part."

"Let me know what he adds to the story this time," Little Crow whispered to White Dove, but not low enough to be out of Jacque's earshot.

"I think you may have me mixed up with a certain Arapaho storyteller!"

The two old friends chuckled as Little Crow left the room.

"I think I will stay; this is my favorite part," Genevieve said.

"Before you continue, Jacque," Edward said, "I have a question for Genevieve."

"Oh?" Genevieve said with a raised eyebrow.

"Yes, why did you give Jacque beef instead of the pork he had ordered?"

"I detest the smell of cooked pig meat."

"What about bacon?" Jacque said. "You like bacon."

"I do."

"And ham!" Annie said. "I saw you eating ham last year."

"Well, ham is good too, but nothing from a pig besides ham and bacon are any good."

"What about salt pork?" Jacque asked. "You use it in your pea soup."

"Yeah, okay," Genevieve said, "but pork chops stink to high heaven!"

"Well, I guess that answers my question," Edward said.

"What question?" Jacque replied.

"Not important. Please continue your story."

17

"Okay. Where was I?" Jacque asked.

"You just got your four dollars back from Tom," Edward said.

"Oh, yeah."

* * *

So, while waiting for orders from the company, I became bored and decided to go into the forest and cut wood for the cookhouse. I selected dead standing trees or windblown ones held off the ground by their branches. The cook and owner, Theophile, lent me an axe and a Swede saw, and told me he would send a draft horse to haul the logs in once they'd been cut. He had offered to pay me, but I told him it wasn't necessary. He replied that all my meals would be free while I was supplying wood. On the second day of cutting, I watched as Genevieve wove her way through stumps, piles of branches, and cut logs. She had small metal pails, one in each hand. Genevieve sat beside me on a spruce log and handed me the pail with water. After quenching my thirst, she passed me the second pail. I lifted the lid and smelled the delicious aroma of moose stew.

"Mmmm, if I had a tail, it would be wagging!"

She smiled and said, "Theophile wants to send a horse for the logs this evening. He's worried others will take the wood while you're away."

I nodded and looked around. There were a lot of logs. They were about twelve feet long and lay where I had felled and limbed them. I realized that I must have stunk to high heaven, all sweaty and gummy with spruce sap.

"Sorry, I must reek."

"I don't mind the smell of a hardworking man," Genevieve said. "Don't ever forget that."

I looked at her, and my face was drawn to hers before I could think. She responded and leaned closer for the kiss. I struggled to stop kissing her, but she grasped my shoulders and gently but firmly pushed me away.

"I have to get back now," she mumbled, picked up the empty pails, and walked briskly away. I watched her, and after walking twenty yards, she turned back to look at me and smiled. Then, with renewed energy, I attacked the trees once more.

I found a dead jack pine that was tall and still standing. It would easily make three twelve-foot logs. The very top looked dry and spindly, so I took the axe, slammed its flat side against the tree, and jumped back. As expected, the top six or seven feet broke off and fell with a crash in the spot where I had just been standing.

"I'm glad you're careful, Jacque."

Maggie's voice made me jump. She was sitting on a stump a dozen or so feet from me.

"Have to be, all alone out here. It's not like I could go for help if something happened." I turned and began chopping tree.

"No, I suppose not," she said. "You going to marry that girl?"

"I don't know."

"For Christ's sake, don't be so daft! Marry her, and I won't bother you again."

"You don't bother me, Maggie; I enjoy your company."

"Well, that's awful nice of you to say."

"You should move, Maggie. This tree is about to come down in your direction."

"In a bit, young feller. Did I ever tell you about the time I was one of Napoleon's consorts? Not the famous Napoleon, of course. Anyway, I would be summoned on a summer's eve and—"

"Watch out!"

The tree slowly tipped toward her and then picked up speed as it fell. It crashed into her while she was in mid-sentence of her tale. I ran and frantically searched for her, but she had vanished. I never saw her again.

129

The incident left me unsettled, and it was a relief to see a man walking toward me leading a large horse.

"You look like you saw a ghost!" the man said when he reached me.

"It's the heat," I said, mopping my forehead and face with my neckerchief.

"I'm Marcel. I've come to haul the logs for Theophile."

"Alright, tell me what to do."

Later, as we walked the horse with the last of the logs to the back of the cook cabin, I thought that someday I would own a farm and have a fine horse like this one. This revelation surprised me. I hadn't thought much about what I would do after voyageuring, but farming would be a good option, especially with Genevieve by my side.

Marcel glanced at me and frowned. I couldn't blame him; I must have looked a sight, sweaty, grimy, and grinning like a fool.

"Now, Jacque, you have a chore ahead of you," he said.

"Eh?"

"You cut the logs. Now you have to buck them up into stove lengths."

I looked at the mound of poles, and my heart sank.

"And then, you have to split them!" he cackled and led his horse away, shaking his head.

"Tabernac!" I cried.

I washed up at the back-porch basin, and when Theophile stepped out to inspect the logs, he rubbed his hands together and smiled.

"My, that is a good haul!" He gushed, pleased at the sight of all that firewood.

"I will begin bucking it all up tomorrow," I said, half hoping he would tell me it wasn't necessary.

"Norbert will help you," he said instead. "Come, have your supper. I have a good moose stew and some fresh bannock."

The next few weeks consisted of Norbert and me sawing the logs into sixteen-inch lengths and then splitting them in half. The boy was strong as a bull. My evenings had been spent making sure my crewmates stayed out of trouble, often having to talk one or two of them into calling it a night and walking them back to camp. One day, just as I was stacking the last of the split logs, Gabriel came running up to me all breathless and cried, "We leave tomorrow!" And then he was off again, searching for the rest of our crew.

Later, after the dinner crowd had left, I sat with Genevieve on a wood bench on the back porch. It was a pleasant evening, not too hot, and I sat up a little straighter as I saw her admiring the long rows of split firewood.

"Those will be enough for the whole winter."

"It will have to be; I won't be back until next summer."

"Oh."

"Genevieve?"

"Yes."

"I have been thinking," I cleared my throat and wiped my damp palms on my pants, "after my contract is up, I would like to rent a farm, and maybe buy one someday."

"Here?" I could see the excitement in her posture.

"No, this is not good farmland. Maybe farther south, along the Red River, or maybe the Assiniboine."

"Oh."

"I would like you to be there with me."

"Okay."

"Okay, you will?"

"No, you haven't asked me yet."

"Oh. Okay, will you come with me?"

"That's not the question you are supposed to ask."

"Eh?"

"Ask her to marry you!" Theophile hollered from inside the cabin.

"Ah, okay," I stammered. My face turned beet red, and I felt like bolting, but I took a deep breath and asked her.

"Genevieve, will you marry me?"

"Yes."

* * *

"I remember that as if it were yesterday!" Genevieve said. "I didn't know you were that nervous."

"Oh, yeah!" Jacque said. "I just about wet myself!"

Everyone laughed; Jacque just grinned.

"Oh my, it's after midnight!" Jacque said. "Can we finish tomorrow before we board the train, Edward?"

"Of course." Edward said, even though he was disappointed to have to stop.

"You can sleep here on the couch, Edward," Gabriel said.

"Uh, thank you for your hospitality, but I better get back to my room and pack for the train."

"Oh, are you on our train, too?" Jacque asked.

"Yes, I have to meet with Harper's Magazine in New York with the stories."

"Well, then we can continue on the train."

"Yes, good night, all!" Edward said.

"Good night," almost everyone said, Genevieve being the exception.

After he left, Genevieve spoke up. "I just don't trust that man; there's something about him. And what's with his eye?"

"I noticed that, but I didn't want to embarrass him." Annie said.

The conversation then turned to how much money Jacque, Little Crow, and maybe Tom would get for their stories.

18

Edward was having breakfast when he saw the policemen enter the restaurant, and he almost choked on his toast. Did they suspect he was the one who stole Eddie's money?

"Mr. Humphries, may we have a word?" Constable Jackson asked.

"Sure, have a seat James, Liam." Edward was surprised at how calm his voice sounded.

The two constables pulled out chairs, sat down, and James waved away the waiter heading their way.

"We arrested two men last night, Patrick and John Donnelly," James said. "We need you to come to the station and look at a lineup."

"A lineup?"

"Yes, we put several people in a lineup in front of you, and you tell us if one of them is your assailant, or assailants, in this case."

"Uh, they will be right in front of me?" The thought of facing these men sent fear coursing through Edward's body.

"We will be right there beside you," Liam said. "No one will hurt you."

"I have a train to catch in an hour and a half; I can't miss it."

"We'll try to get you there in time," James said.

"That's not good enough!" Edward said with more force than he thought he could muster. "At a quarter of ten, I am walking out of your station, no matter what."

"Sure, sure," Liam said and looked around at the opulence of the room. "Are you staying here?"

"I was."

"Looks expensive."

"I suppose."

"Funny thing, we received a complaint of loud noises last night, and when we went to investigate, there were the two suspects," James said. "They were hammering on a safe, steel on steel, making a hell of a racket."

"What's so funny about that?" Edward asked.

"Well, they weren't able to open the safe."

"Still not funny."

"Eddie gave us the combination after we told him we recovered his safe. But when we opened it, the money was gone."

"And?" Edward's palms were sweaty, but he kept his voice level.

"Eddie told us he also gave you the combination."

"Yes, but the Donnellys showed up and took the safe before I had a chance to open it."

"Huh," Liam said. "Nice suit, by the way."

"I've had it for a while."

"Looks new."

"Thanks. We better go if I'm going to make my train."

"We have a wagon outside. It won't take long," James said. "The train station is only a twenty-minute walk from the police station."

Edward was sure he had been caught. He suspected the request to view a lineup was a ruse to get him to the jail, grill him, and then arrest him. But what choice did he have?

The wagon had two benches. Liam sat in front, holding the reins, while James sat beside Edward on the second bench.

"What happened to your carpet bag?" James asked, eyeing Edward's new leather bag.

Damn, why had he spent so much money right away? Why couldn't he have wait until he got to New York?

"Clasp broke."

"Uh-huh."

What did that mean, uh-huh?

The central police station had four levels. The lower level was half below ground, with concrete walls and barred windows that sat just above the street. The next three floors were clad in stone and plaster. Edward looked up at the towering building as the constables led him toward a heavy steel door at the building's side entrance. Edward jumped when the door slammed shut behind him with a clang of metal on metal. He felt the fear tingling in his backside, and his head was buzzing. Edward wiped his sweaty palms on his trousers and looked around for an escape route, but there was none.

"The lineup is ready for you," a constable informed them as they entered the building.

"Thanks," James said and then turned to Edward. "Hey, don't worry, they cannot hurt you here."

Edward nodded and followed the constables into a large room. Against the back wall stood ten men, almost shoulder to shoulder. Edward saw the two Donnellys right away. He leaned toward James and said out the side of his mouth, "The one third from the left end and the one second from the right end."

"You are sure?"

"Positive; no doubt about it."

"Everyone except number three and number nine may leave," James announced.

Of course, the Donnellys turned to leave and were physically held by two burly constables. And, to no one's surprise, they commenced throwing vulgar insults and threats directed at Edward who visibly shrank back and then moved behind Liam.

"Thank you, Edward," James said. "You are free to go after you sign a statement identifying these two men and another statement confirming you did not open the safe or remove any of its contents."

Edward felt his stress level begin to drop after the Donnellys were led out of the room. With renewed bravado, he checked his pocket watch and said, "It will have to be quick."

"It won't take long."

It did take long. After signing both documents, Edward ran out of the building and didn't slow until he got to the train station with only minutes to spare. He had purchased passage in a sleeper car the day before, so all he had to do was present his ticket to the conductor and be directed to his seat. Finally seated, Edward let out a sigh of relief. He had gotten away with it. He hoped to never have to come back here.

He decided to wait until they were well underway before going in search of Little Crow and Jacque. In the meantime, Edward removed his journals and stowed his bag. He pointedly ignored the couple seated across from him and shooed a boy out of his side of the booth. The boy, who appeared to be about five years old, would not move.

"This your son?" he asked the man.

"Yes, but surely he can stay where he is," the man said. "There's not enough room for three to ride comfortably on one side."

"Sorry, you should have thought of that when you purchased your tickets."

"Come here, son," the man ordered.

The boy glared at Edward and slunk across to squeeze in between his parents. Edward ignored them, brushed off imaginary dirt from the seat beside him, laid out his journals in the boy's place, and then looked out the window at the station platform. He was no longer worried about the Donnellys; Doyle and Siobhan were in Saskatoon, and their cousins were currently in a Winnipeg jail. His pockets were full of cash, and he had a meeting with an editor at Harper's Magazine. He smiled and was unaware of the looks he was getting from the couple sitting across from him.

A half hour after the train had left the Winnipeg station, Edward rose, turned to the couple, and said, "Keep him off my seat." He didn't wait for a reply. Little Crow and Jacque would probably be ahead in one of the other economy cars, so he walked through the car corridor into the next coach. There they were, halfway up the car. Little Crow, White Dove, Jacque, and Genevieve sat in one booth and were conversing with a couple across the aisle. The man had a large scar on his left cheek. In the train car's lights, the scar appeared to glow. That must be the policeman, Tom, and his wife, Annie.

"Edward!" Jacque cried when he neared their booths. The man was in good spirits.

Edward greeted the four travelers he knew and waited to be introduced to their companions.

"Edward, this is our good friends, Tom and Annie Flynn."

"Nice to meet you, Edward . . .?"

"Humphries."

"I've heard a lot about you this morning," Tom said. "I understand you are a writer?"

"Yes, I write articles for newspapers and magazines."

"Ah, I see," Tom said, turning to Little Crow and Jacque. "Perhaps the four of us could find a table in the dining car?"

"Yes, that's a good idea," Edward agreed. He was uncomfortable standing in the aisle on full display to all the other travelers in the car. "Lead the way."

The men found an empty table and ordered tea all around, except for Edward, who asked for coffee.

"My friends have discussed your venture with a lawyer, a Mr. Bertram Carmichael," Tom said. He was obviously the group leader as far as legal matters went, not surprising considering his career with the Mounties.

"I see, and what was his advice?" Edward said with what he hoped was not a condescending tenor.

"Well, he prepared an agreement, which he said was standard, for the right to use our stories, assuming you want mine also."

"I will have to hear them first, Tom," Edward said. "Am I right to assume you are the Tom Flynn that Jacque met at Grand Rapids?"

"The one and the same."

"Alright, I'm beginning to see how you and Jacque here met, but when did you meet Little Crow?"

"In due time, Edward, you'll hear how our paths eventually crossed."

"Alright, I look forward to hearing your story."

"Yes, but business first; the agreement is for a fifty-fifty split of all revenue," Tom said. "Half to you, and Little Crow, Jacque, and I will get the other half."

Edward's first impulse was to push back on the ratio, but then he realized that the money was not as important to him as having his byline appear in Harper's Magazine. At least now that he had money in his pocket.

"Alright, that sounds reasonable."

His answer obviously shocked the three men who seemed prepared for a debate.

"Shall we sign the copies?" Tom asked.

"Well, I still have to determine whether your stories will be included," Edward said.

"If they're not, then you can't use mine," Jacque said.

"Or mine," Little Crow added.

The table went quiet until Tom said, "You will see, Edward, that our stories intertwine."

"Okay. Who wants to go next?" Edward asked, laying out his journal and pencils.

"I think Little Crow should continue his story," Jacque said, "while he's still awake."

"Hey, I can still work from dawn to dusk and then go dancing all night!" Little Crow boasted and pantomimed dance moves as he remained seated.

"What kind of dance is that?" Jacque asked. "Looks like you got some of those hemorrhoids!"

"Okay, Little Crow, please continue," Edward said with a grin after the laughter died down.

* * *

About the time Edward was meeting with Little Crow, Jacque, and Tom, Doyle Donnelly stepped off the train in Winnipeg. He went straight to the ticket agent, who visibly shrank back at the sight of the angry man standing on the other side of his cage.

"I'm looking for a small man, round wire glasses, goes by the name Edward Humphries," Doyle demanded.

"I, uh, I can't give that information out, sir," the agent stammered.

"You know, by the time someone comes to your aid, your face will resemble a bloody stump."

"Uh, he boarded the train to Toronto this morning."

"Dammit," Doyle yelled, turning several heads, then in a quieter tone asked, "When's the next train?"

"To Toronto?"

"Yes, dammit! What were we just talking about?"

"Uh, tomorrow morning, sir."

"Give me a ticket."

The ticket agent selected a ticket and set it on the shelf between them with a shaky hand. "That will be—"

"Thanks," Doyle said and grabbed the ticket, "and there had better not be any police waiting for me when I show up for the train tomorrow. Because if there is, I will find you."

"Yes sir, I mean, no sir."

Doyle walked out of the station and let out an angry, futile yell.

The ticket agent shuddered and then removed his billfold, counted out the ticket amount, and put it into the till. It took almost all his funds.

Doyle stood on the sidewalk, hailed a cab, removed a piece paper from his pocket, and showed it to the driver. On the paper was the address of one of his cousins, Patrick Donnelly.

19

Edward watched Little Crow as he stared at the dining car's ceiling, and then, as if coming to a decision, Little Crow began speaking.

* * *

It was the third of May in the year 1877, in Montana territory. I had just returned to Sitting Bull's camp, after a week of fruitless hunting, to find tipis coming down and people loading travois and carts. Yet there was an air of excitement not usually present when we were forced to relocate. Cut Nose was the first person I met upon my return, and I pulled him aside to ask him what was happening.

"We are going to the white grandmother's land, across the spirit line," Cut Nose said. His excitement was palpable.

"Where does this grandmother live?"

"The white grandmother? She lives far away, across the great water."

"And we are going there?" I asked, ignoring the condescending look he gave me.

He chuckled and said, "No, we are going to her land in the north."

"How far?"

"Across the spirit line."

"Okay, Cut Nose, what is the spirit line?"

"Ah, hie!" he cried, exasperated. "The border into Canada!"

"Well, why didn't you just say that instead of trying to sound like a wise man?"

Cut Nose and I didn't get along, not since I had turned down his suggestion that I court his daughter.

"Little Crow," he sighed, "you are lucky you have nothing to pack. Go help the old ones."

"Alright, what do you need help with?"

It took him several seconds to realize I had answered his insult with an insult, and then he turned back toward me with a knife in his hand. But I was prepared for a move like that; Cut Nose was not one to fight fair. So, I jabbed the tip of an arrow to his throat and held him out of knife range. A bulb of blood appeared under the arrowpoint at his neck, and his eyes bulged.

Was it fear?

Or anger?

"Little Crow!" Sitting Bull called from a hundred yards away. His eyes had clouded some over the years, and I wondered if he saw what was happening here. "Come here," he ordered.

I stared Cut Nose in the eyes and flicked the arrow point upward, maybe more forcefully than I should have, and scratched Cut Nose's skin from neck to chin. Blood filled the scratch, and he grabbed his throat with one hand. He turned and hurried into his tipi, calling his wife as he stumbled over the bottom flap.

"When surrounded by enemies, it is not wise to make more at home," Sitting Bull said when I stopped in front of him.

I nodded and then asked, "We are going to Canada?"

"Yes, there is nothing left to hunt here, and the soldiers have us cornered."

"Is Crazy Horse coming too?"

He sighed and said, "No, Crazy Horse is surrendering; he is surrounded in the Black Hills, and his people are starving."

I was stunned. The Crazy Horse I knew would have fought to the death rather than surrender. But I suppose he had to consider his people's needs above his own. Our way of life was over in this land; I hoped it could continue in Canada.

Two days later, we crossed the spirit line. It looked the same as the land we had just left; wide-open grassland. Sitting Bull called for me, and I rode up beside him. He sat at the front of our tribe with chiefs Spotted Eagle and Swift Bird.

"What is that?" Sitting Bull asked and pointed to a dot in the distance.

"A buffalo bull, two years old. There's a fly on his left ear."

He looked at me in disbelief. I grinned, and Spotted Eagle chuckled.

"It is a buffalo," I confirmed.

"Then go get it, Little Crow," Sitting Bull said.

I galloped forward and wished Two Elk was beside me. When I approached it, the bull turned and ran, but my pony was at full gallop. My pony, a good buffalo runner, matched the buffalo's pace and galloped alongside as I shot an arrow into the bull's ribs. It stumbled and fell. My pony slowed and turned back to the dying animal. As I was gutting the bull, I grabbed a buzzing fly and killed it. It was not squashed, so I placed it on the dead animal's right ear.

When everyone arrived, I stood, handed a piece of liver to each of the three chiefs, and drizzled bile from the gall bladder over the meat. Swift Bird was staring at the bull as he chewed. I looked and said, "That fly is still on its ear."

"Huh," he grunted, and he stared at me for several seconds.

I saw Sitting Bull out of the corner of my eye and noticed that he hid a smile behind his piece of liver. The great chief always appreciated a good practical joke. Someday, he would tell Swift Bird of my deception with the fly, and they would have a good laugh over it.

I looked around and saw several riders suddenly appear over a low hill about a mile away.

"Soldiers." I pointed, and the chiefs looked in that direction. "They wear red coats."

They grunted and then trotted out to meet them. I watched the chiefs and the redcoats talk for several minutes, and then they parted. I was disappointed when they rode by me without stopping. What had they talked about? We feasted that night, and the next day, we found our new home. It was in a sheltered area three days' travel from the spirit line, two if by horse. It was encouraging to see an abundance of animal tracks, and there was plenty of water. It was an excellent place to camp.

That first year in Canada was good for the Hunkpapa Lakota, with plenty of animals to hunt, good water; maybe it was a little colder in the winter, but not by much. The redcoats left us alone as long as we obeyed their laws, and we did, for the most part. But the next few years were difficult. The number of buffalo began to diminish from over-hunting by different tribes, Métis, and buffalo hunters. Soon, we were destitute. We traded with a local trader, Jean Louis Légaré, who was honest with us. Over time, Jean Louis became a trusted friend of Sitting Bull.

As the buffalo herds dwindled, we had to swap most of our weapons and ammunition for food. We wore rags and were hungry all the time. Our survival was becoming precarious. It came to a point where Sitting Bull finally agreed to lead his people back over the spirit line and surrender to the American army to save his people from starvation. But Sitting Bull would only go if were assured by his trusted friend, Jean Louis, that the Hunkpapa would not be harmed by the Americans. Légaré assured him they would be treated fairly. I later learned that Jean Louis expected to be paid by both the Canadian and American governments for talking Sitting Bull into returning to the US.

I had my doubts about our safety south of the border since receiving the news that Crazy Horse had been killed in captivity by US soldiers a few years before. And there was also a story about some of Chief Gall and Crow King's warriors being attacked when they attempted to surrender. So no, I did not trust the white soldiers' promises. But Sitting Bull had no choice; it was surrender or starve to death.

Then in May of 1881, Légaré and some of his Métis hunters arrived to accompany Sitting Bull and his followers across the spirit line to Fort Buford in Dakota territory. I stood with a few warriors and their families who had decided to stay. In the group leaving with Sitting Bull stood Zeke and his family. He saw me looking, said something to Walking Woman, and then walked over to me.

"Goodbye, Little Crow," Zeke said.

"I wish you would change your mind and come with me, Zeke."

"I have my family to consider. Otherwise, I would."

"Yes, I understand," I said and held my hand out to him. He brushed it aside and embraced me in a bear hug.

"Good luck, my friend," Zeke said before releasing me and walking back to his wife, who linked arms with her husband as if to hold him beside her. It was the last time I saw him.

I turned my eyes to the Métis hunters. I was fascinated by these men. Most spoke French, which I struggled to understand; they seemed to say everything backward. Maybe if I were a contrary, one who does everything opposite, I could understand French. But then I recognized one Métis man who spoke English and who I had talked with before to practice my English.

"Hello, Little Crow," Jacque Daoust said when I walked over to him. "You are not going with Sitting Bull?"

"No, Jacque. I do not trust the Americans," I said. "Why are you going?"

"You remember how I told you about my farm on the Red River?"

"Yeah."

"Well, we had a few bad years, that's why my wife and I are here, working for Légaré. So, when he asked if I wanted to earn some extra money scouting for him, I had to agree."

"You didn't want to?"

Jacque looked around to make sure he would not be overheard and said, "I have a bad feeling about this enterprise."

"What do you mean?"

"I mean, I don't think Sitting Bull should go."

"Neither do I, and believe me, I did try to convince him not to go, but his mind is made up."

Jacque shook his head and then asked, "What are you going to do?"

"I will go north; there are more animals farther north."

"Yeah, there are some left," Jacque said. "Go to the North Saskatchewan River. You will not starve there."

"Is it far?"

"Yeah, it is, and it's in Cree territory."

"I have no fight with them."

"But they may have with you."

"Why?"

"You are Lakota."

"I am Arapaho," I said, "and maybe the only Arapaho in this land. How can they have a fight with someone they do not know?"

"You got me there, my friend," Jacque said. "Your English is good, but you should learn Cree."

"How do I do that?"

"Find a Cree wife!" Jacque said, and he chuckled as he walked away.

"So long, Jacque."

Jacque turned to face me but continued walking backward. "Goodbye, Little Crow, we will meet again!"

At the time, I wondered if that would come to pass.

* * *

"I remember that, Little Crow," Jacque said.

"Yes," Little Crow replied, "and you were right; the Sioux should have stayed in Canada."

"It was just a feeling I had."

"Did anything interesting happen next, Little Crow?" Edward asked, trying to steer the conversation back to his stories.

"Well, I met Tom. That was definitely interesting."

"Okay, good, please continue."

"Maybe Tom should tell that story. All I did was save his life."

"Yeah, you did do that, my friend," Tom said.

Edward looked at Tom and said, "Okay, Tom, I guess you're up."

Tom rubbed his hands together, leaned forward, and began his tale.

20

I was born Thomas Flynn in 1858 near Trois-Rivières, Quebec. My father, Liam, was adopted by a French farmer who needed a farmhand, and a free ten-year-old Irish orphan fit the bill. My grandparents, Nevin and Fiona Flynn, died crossing the North Atlantic Ocean on one of the coffin ships bringing refugees to Canada from Ireland during the potato famine.

What is that you ask, Edward?

Coffin ships?

Well, coffin ships were those that set sail during the Irish potato famine of the 1840s. Most were unseaworthy, crowded, lacked adequate supplies of drinking water and food, and had poor sanitation. Many Irish died on the journey, including my grandparents.

So, after years of physical abuse and backbreaking labor, my father walked away from that farm on his eighteenth birthday, and he didn't stop until he reached Toronto. Those first years must have been difficult for him, a French-speaking young man in a predominantly English-speaking city. Yet, he prospered, working for many years as a laborer and learning the English language. Then, one day, when I was twelve, he rushed into the house, scooped my mother up, and twirled her around, crying, "I got the job!" The job was that of a city constable.

That all sounds impressive; an orphaned Irish immigrant does good and becomes a city policeman. But the important word in all that is "immigrant." Being an Irish cop in 1870s Toronto had its challenges. Being Irish anything in those days was hard. But he endured, as I have.

I guess with every adversity comes some benefits. I learned how to fight with my fists, and maybe more importantly, how to avoid fights. I knew I would be a policeman by the time I was seventeen, just not in Toronto. Reading about the American Indian wars in the newspapers and about western outlaws in dime novels made me determined to venture west. So, against my parents' wishes, I joined the North-West Mounted Police.

My first posting was at Grand Rapids at the northern end of Lake Winnipeg. That is where I met Jacque, but he has already told you that story. So, I will skip ahead a few years to my next posting at Wood Mountain. My duties included a weekly patrol north to Prince Albert and back. It was on one of these patrols, in 1882, when my partner and I were a day's ride from Prince Albert, that I saw my first murder victim. It was December, and the victim was a trapper who hadn't been seen since early winter. So, my partner, Constable John Edwards, and I approached the cabin of Shorty Jonsson, a Swedish immigrant who's real first name was Knut, and found it empty. As with most places back then, it was not locked.

"Do you notice anything missing, Tom?" John asked as he scanned the interior of the cabin.

John was older than I by ten years and had grown up in the north.

"Uh, no." I tried hard, not wanting to appear the greenhorn, but did not notice anything that could be missing.

"Where's his fur?"

"Yes, you're right."

How could I have missed that? Shorty was a trapper after all.

"Do you think he took his fur to sell?" I asked.

"I don't think so. Légaré would have mentioned it," John said.

As Little Crow mentioned before, Jean Louis Légaré ran a trading post at Wood Mountain. He was the one who had expressed concern about Shorty, as he usually brought his furs there to sell or trade for supplies and he had not shown up so far that winter. Anyway, we inspected two different trails to determine which one he had used last. Unfortunately, both routes were filled with snow, making that determination impossible.

"We're going to have to split up, Tom."

I nodded, but an unease slowly crept over me. "Is that wise in this situation?"

"Splitting up? Yes, he could be laying out there somewhere, injured and in need of our help. And if both of us check the same trail, it will be dark by the time we finish. If we pick the wrong trail, that could be the difference between life and death for him."

"Yeah, I suppose," I said, but it was obvious it had been a while since anyone had last been here. "Which trail do you want?"

"Doesn't matter," John said and then set off on the trail to our left.

I mounted my horse and took the trail to the right. It was early afternoon, the weather clear and cold. Newly fallen snow weighed down the spruce boughs. I had to be careful not to brush against overhanging branches on this narrow trail lest I get snow dumped into my parka.

As I got farther away from Shorty's camp, I saw more and more offshoots of the trail that lead to trap sets. Some snares held small animals, chewed on by birds and predators, while others stood half-covered in snow and empty. Then the caws of ravens drew me down one side trail, where, to my relief, I saw several ravens feeding on a small animal carcass and not on human remains.

I came to a fork in the trail. Both seemed equally used, so I followed the branch on the right for no particular reason. I hoped that it looped around and would return to the fork, but I could see an opening in the trees ahead and suspected this trail led to a lake.

It did. The trail led directly to a lake with a large beaver lodge near the shore and in front of it were two spruce poles sticking out off the ice. I knew there would be a snare attached to those poles under the ice. The recent snow had blown in drifts, leaving some patches of bare ice. I tied my horse to some willows and walked out onto the ice. As I neared the beaver lodge, I could see where the snow had been packed down by two different sizes of moccasins. It was apparent there had been some sort of struggle here. The trail going past the beaver house looked less defined, leading me to believe that this was as far as Shorty and the other person came before turning back. But what had happened here?

I set my rifle down, walked to the spruce poles, and looked down at the snow. Then, curious to see if there was a beaver in the snare, I knelt down and wiped away the snow until I cleared a large circle of bare ice between the poles. It looked like there might be a beaver in the snare.

I removed my parka and bent over, bringing my face close to the ice and then draping my parka over my head to block out the waning sunlight. The murky depths below the ice became clear, and yes, there was a beaver in the snare. It probably had been there for a while; no sense chopping through the ice to remove it. As I peered at the beaver, something moved in the edges of the cleared ice. Curious, I set my parka aside and brushed more snow away.

What was that?

I bent low, draped the parka over my head again, and peered down, letting my eyes adjust. I let out a shriek and scrambled backward on my ass, using my hands and feet to propel me. It was a human face, the wide-open eyes staring at me from under the ice! I looked around to see if anyone had heard me. The shriek that had come out my mouth sure sounded a lot like a frightened child, or maybe an injured rabbit.

It was Shorty under the ice. Of that, I am sure. I will never forget the look of terror in those eyes, not for as long as I live. I retrieved my rifle and fired a shot in the air. The sun was low in the sky, so I mounted my horse and rode back toward Shorty's cabin. Suddenly, I felt a tingling in my scalp, as though I were being watched.

* * *

"Well, Edward, I think I will head back and sit with White Dove until lunchtime," Little Crow interjected.

"Yeah, me too," Jacque agreed.

"You want to sit with White Dove too?" Little Crow said, feigning surprise.

"No, of course not! Uh, I mean—" Jacque stammered. "Ah, you know what I mean!"

"Hah," Tom laughed, then turned to Edward and said, "I will continue my story if you like."

"Yes, of course, please continue."

* * *

I was approaching the fork in the road where John and I had separated when my horse whinnied and I heard another horse respond.

"Is that you, John?" I called.

"Yeah."

He was hidden behind some willows, sitting on his horse with his rifle across his lap.

Was the tingling in my scalp caused by John watching me?

And why was he aiming his rifle at me?

"I found Shorty," I said, trying to sound calm. "He's under the ice in a small lake."

I rode up to where he was sitting his horse. The sun had set, but the moon's light reflected off the snow, so it was not totally dark.

"What do you think happened?" John asked.

"There are two sets of tracks and marks that indicate a scuffle in the snow. I think Shorty was murdered."

"Huh, let's go," John said and then started down the trail I had just come from.

"I think we should wait for daylight so we don't mess up any evidence." This I had learned from reading some of my father's police manuals.

So, John said, "Yeah, you're probably right. Shorty's not going anywhere."

"Not unless the beavers change their diet."

"Ugh."

We rode back to Shorty's cabin, and I lit a fire in the stove while John took care of the horses. A quick search of the room for evidence of the other man's identity revealed nothing of value. Maybe we would have better luck at the lake. I threw my pack on the lone cot and sat on it to take off my boots.

"Why do you get the bed?" John demanded as he walked into the cabin.

"Because I found Shorty and I claimed it first."

"I'm senior to you."

"Not in rank."

"Ah, fek," John grumbled. "Take it then."

"I'll make supper," I said, trying to appease John, but I saw it was not enough. "But first, I'll go check his larder."

Shorty's larder was a small log structure behind the cabin and set on poles twelve feet off the ground with a ladder for access. It was built high to deter scavengers. I stood at the base of the ladder, looked up, and saw that the door was ajar. Someone – and not Shorty, as he would not have left his own larder door unlatched – had been in there. There was a dead branch at the base of a nearby tree, so I went over and picked it up and carried it back to the ladder. I took hold of the branch with both hands and slammed it against one of the larder poles and then listened. Hearing no reaction from inside the larder, I figured whatever had gotten in there was long gone. But, to be on the safe side, I climbed the ladder with the branch in hand.

Halfway up, I used it to swing the door fully open and listened. Silence. So, I climbed a few more rungs up and peaked inside. Suddenly, I heard a low growl, saw a paw swing toward me, and felt a burning sensation when something sharp cut my cheek. I yelped and slapped a hand to my face, and it came away sticky with blood. Then a ball of snarling fur slammed into my chest. I instinctively grabbed the frantic animal with both hands, and then we were falling. I braced for impact and held my breath as my back slammed into the frozen ground. I lost my grip on the animal and it raced away. Luckily, the hood of my parka and the snow on the ground cushioned the blow when my head snapped back. But the wind had been knocked out of me, and I lay gasping, trying to suck air into my lungs.

When I finally got my wind back, I rolled onto my side and slowly stood. Nothing seemed to be broken. My only injury was the cut on my cheek. Surprisingly, the wound was not bleeding as much as anticipated, but there was enough blood to make it look bad. When I walked into the cabin, John did a double take and cried, "What in hell happened to you?"

"Animal mauled me. It was up in the larder," I slurred.

"What kind of animal?"

"I don't know! I think you need to stitch me up, John."

"Uh, sure, okay. Sit down. Let me see what I can find."

"Is there any whiskey?"

"Yeah, I have a bottle; are you thirsty?"

"No, but I want to clean the wound."

"I suppose."

"I'll replace the bottle, John."

"No, no, it's not that . . . well, okay," John said. "Ah, here's his sewing kit."

"Hand me the bottle."

John reluctantly dug in his bag and produced a bottle of cheap whiskey. I poured a liberal amount over my cheek, grimaced at the sting, and felt it run down my neck and chest. Next, I took the needle John had threaded and dipped it into the bottle. After a few seconds, I removed the needle and handed the thread to John. Then I took a swig of whiskey and felt it burn as it slid down my throat. It was the vilest drink I had ever tasted.

"Give me your hands," I said after I was sure the whiskey wasn't going to blind me.

"Why?"

"I want to clean them before you go poking around my wound."

"Oh, okay."

John held out his hands and then moaned when I poured whiskey over them. He started sucking the alcohol off his fingers.

"Don't do that! Give me your hands again, and this time don't lick or suck on them," I ordered and then poured more whiskey over his hands.

"Okay, sew me up," I said and then gripped the chair's seat.

I had no doubt it would be painful. It was. And I suspect John took some small pleasure in my discomfort. I don't know what was worse, the rough thread burning as it was pulled through my skin or the stabs of the needle. Finally, he was done, and I am not ashamed to say my eyes were moist with tears. I poured whiskey over the stitches, found a clean handkerchief in my bag to cover the wound, and then tied an undershirt around my head to hold it in place. Then I lay down on the bed and closed my eyes.

By morning, the pain in my cheek had turned into a persistent itch. I awoke in semidarkness. The glow from the tin woodstove's vent offered three little triangles of flickering light. I gingerly probed the cut through the bandage; it began an inch from my lips and ran diagonally across my cheek, ending near the top of my left ear. A little while later, John got up and made a breakfast of bacon and coffee, but I felt the skin strain against the stiches when I opened my mouth to eat, so I had to settle for just coffee.

"Are you sure you're okay to travel?"

"Yeah, I'm fine." Of course, I wasn't. My back hurt, and my cheek ached and itched at the same time. But we had a job to do, so I pretended to be okay.

"Take his axe and sled; we're going to need them," I told John. Talking was difficult, and it didn't help when John kept saying "Huh?" every time I spoke.

When we arrived at the lake, we tied our horses, and John pulled the sled out to the beaver lodge. Both of us were scanning our surroundings, looking for anything out of the ordinary. Thin drifts of snow had blown over the ice in front of the spruce poles.

"Prepare yourself," I said as I brushed snow off the ice with my boot. But there was nothing there other than murky water. "I don't understand; Shorty was right here!"

John frowned at me, knelt, and began to clear more snow away in a widening circle. Then he stopped suddenly.

"Here he is."

"Huh, he drifted some."

John nodded and handed me the axe. I shook my head and pointed to my cheek. John smirked and then began chopping. He was taking huge swings as if to impress, so I said, "Be careful, you don't want that axe to go through and hit Shorty."

"I know what I'm doing."

I noticed that he couldn't quite hide the shortness of breath the exertion had caused. But finally, he had chopped a hole large enough to pull Shorty out of the water. When we pulled him out, we laid him on the ice and inspected his body.

"He was in a fight," I said. "His lip is split, and there are marks on his neck. I think someone choked him."

"Look at this," John said.

He pointed to one of Shorty's hands and tried to lift it but the body was stiff. "Looks like skin under his nails."

"That's a good observation, John. You know what that means, eh?"

"Uh, why don't you tell me, see if we're thinking the same thing."

I suppressed a grin and said, "We're looking for someone with scratches on his face."

"Yeah, that's what I was thinking," John said. "Wait, how do we know the killer's face was scratched and not his hand or arm?"

"Come here; I'll show you."

I grabbed John's neck when he came close and started choking him. He panicked and started hitting my arm, but I had a heavy coat on, so he couldn't scratch my arms. When he reached for my face, I released his throat and jumped back.

"What the hell was that?" John yelled between coughs.

"I had to prove I'm right," I said, "and now we know the skin under Shorty's nails are from the killer's face and not his arms."

"Dammit, Tom!"

I turned my head, pretending to scan the area to hide my half grin. I found I could grin but only on the uninjured side of my face.

"We should measure these tracks," I said, "so we can match the size to whoever we find with scratches on his face."

"Hmm."

I could tell he would be ticked off about the choking for some time to come.

So, I took the axe, walked over to the spruce poles sticking out of the ice, chopped a piece off one, and then peeled the bark off with my knife. I placed the stick under Shorty's moccasin, held my thumb to mark its length, and then took it over to the frozen tracks I had seen the day before.

"Okay, the bigger footprints belong to the killer."

I placed the stick beside a large track and cut the twig to the same length.

"There, got it," I said. "Now, let's load him up and head back."

John was still grumpy, so I asked him, "What do you think we should do with him, John?"

I watched him straighten up some, and he seemed to ponder this.

"Well, we're pretty close to Prince Albert," he finally said, stroking his chin. "Let's take him to the church there. They can put him in the dead house until spring."

"Good thinking, and we can check with the fur trader there too."

"Yeah, that's what I was thinking," John said. "There's some blood soaking through your kerchief; do you want me to check your stitches?"

"No. It'll stop, so long as I don't have to keep talking."

"Hmph."

I wound up pulling the sled all the way to Prince Albert with the rope looped around my saddle horn. The cord would begin to cut off the circulation to one leg after a while, so I had to move it to the other side every so often. Riding in the lead, John seemed a little preoccupied, which was fine by me: I was grateful for the silence.

The church in Prince Albert was easy to find, its steeple towering above all the other buildings in this bustling little town. John dismounted and entered the church, coming out a few minutes later with the priest, a tall thin man in his forties with a weathered face. If not for his robe and collar, I would have taken him for a farmer. He took one look at me and said, "You need to go see the barber about that cut. It looks inflamed."

"The barber?"

"Yeah, he's also our dentist and our doctor."

I nodded and then pointed at Shorty's body on the sled, asking the priest if he had seen him before.

"Can't say I've ever seen this man here abouts," he said after lifting a corner of the blanket covering Shorty and peering at his face.

"He was a Swedish immigrant, ran a trapline about twenty miles south of here," John said.

"Ah, might be Lutheran then," the priest said. "All right, let's put him in the shed. I'll see that he gets a proper burial come spring."

"Thank you, father," I said. "Could you direct us to the local fur trader?"

"One block over and two blocks down, can't miss it. The barber shop is a few doors farther on," he said, pointing in the general direction, and then asked, "What about the sled?"

"Keep it," John said, and the priest's face lit up.

"Thank you, son, I surely could use it!"

After we had walked our horses away from the priest, I asked John, "Is it wise to be giving away Shorty's property?"

"Well, Shorty had no relatives here; why not donate it to the church?"

"Are you going to put that in your report?"

John stopped and looked me in the eye. "Not everything has to go in the reports, Tom."

After that exchange, I began to lose any respect I had for the man. I knew one thing though, I would keep my reports well detailed, regardless of how it reflected on me or anyone else.

The fur trader plied his trade from a long and narrow unpainted two-story building. The wood planks between the battens were splintered and cupped. And, although the windows on the second floor were covered in grime, they implied that there were living quarters above the business. I shuddered when I thought of the odor in all fur-trading stores. It was a mixture of musky, pungent, and somewhat rancid aromas that seeped into your clothing if you spent even a short amount of time inside. What it must have smelled like in the living quarters, I could only imagine. So why would they not have the windows open? Even in winter, a window opened just a crack would help. Then a light breeze carried the stink of horse manure to my nose, and I looked at the street and saw all the steaming piles of fresh horse droppings. Then I understood.

"I'll go see this barber while you check with the fur buyer," I told John.

He nodded and stepped onto the boardwalk and entered the building. I tied my horse and walked the short distance to the barber shop.

"I'm told you're a doctor?" I asked the man who wore an apron covered in stains of almost every shade of brown imaginable. My first instinct was to turn and leave, but the thought of John touching my cheek again sent shivers up my spine. This man may well be the lesser of two evils.

"Doctor, lawyer, barber, and dentist!" the man declared, spat a stream of brown juice into a spittoon, dragged a sleeve across his mouth, and said, "Have a seat and let me have a look."

This man was short, potbellied, and bearded, and had a ruddy complexion. But what stood out about him was his forearms. They were disproportionally large and well muscled. He untied the wrap and then peeled back the bandage.

"That doesn't look too bad; your friend did a passable job sewing you up," he said. "Let me clean that up and put a proper bandage on it."

Ten minutes later, I stopped in front of the fur trader's when John came out, tearing a piece of dried buffalo meat off a large chunk. There was the smell of liquor about him.

"No one with scratches on his face sold any fur here lately. In fact, it's been over a week since anyone bought fur in," he said as he chewed.

My stomach growled, and I asked him how much the dried meat cost. He looked at me curiously and shrugged. Dammit! If I wanted to get anything to eat, I would have to go inside.

I breathed through my mouth as I entered and took in the long wooden counter that occupied one side of the front room. Behind the counter were shelves full of everything a trapper would need by way of dry goods and firearms. The other side of the room had barrels, sacks, snowshoes, traps, snares, and clothing. In the middle of the room sat a potbellied stove and several chairs surrounding it, all full. The men sitting in front of this stove were older, unwashed men. Their chatter died when I entered. Some men lowered and set their cups out of sight behind their feet. The plank floor creaked as I walked to the counter.

"I'll take a chunk of dried buffalo and a can of apricots."

The apricots were an impulse buy. I wouldn't be sharing those with John, not after he had failed to offer me some of his meat.

"How much do I owe you?" I asked when he placed my order on the counter.

"Two cents for the apricots. The meat is on the house."

"Why, what's wrong with it?" I asked suspiciously as I lifted the jerky to my nose.

"Nothing, it's free to the law."

"How much is it for anyone else?"

"Three cents."

I dropped a nickel on the counter, glanced at the men by the stove, picked up my goods, and walked out.

"How much did you pay for your meat?" I asked John after mounting my horse.

"Nothing."

"You know he's serving liquor in there?"

"No, I didn't notice," he said and kicked his horse into a canter. I caught up and rode beside him. After a few seconds of silence, I asked, "What now?"

"We work our way back to Wood Mountain, stopping at fur buyers along the way. First stop, Duck Lake."

21

"I'm sorry, gentlemen; we have to prepare for the first lunch sitting," the waiter informed them.

"Oh, is it that time already?" Tom said and looked at his watch. "We can finish after lunch if you want, Edward."

"Sure."

Edward stood and walked ahead of Tom, nodding to the others on his way to the sleeper car.

"Hey," Edward cried when he saw the boy sitting in his seat. "What did I say about not sitting in my seat?"

"Sorry, sir, but you were gone a long time, and it seemed a waste to have an empty seat when we are so crowded," the wife said.

"I don't care," Edward said. "If it happens again, I will lodge a complaint."

"Easy now," the husband said.

"I beg your pardon," Edward roared.

The man stood to his full height and towered over Edward. "I said, easy now."

Edward involuntarily shuddered and hoped it didn't show but knew that it had. He brushed imaginary dirt from his seat again and sat down, making a show of reviewing his notes. However, he didn't have to sit there long. The sleeper car was the first seated for lunch, and Edward jumped up as soon as it was called, requesting a Winnipeg newspaper when he was seated.

He was watching the passing landscapes and thinking about Tom's story so far. He had been pleasantly surprised when the man's stories turned out to be engaging. But of course, Edward thought that he could massage the story by using his superior writing skills to craft a compelling story indeed. Pleased with himself, Edward smiled as he scanned the menu. But his good mood changed when he saw the porter approaching his table.

"Here you go," the porter said and then stood aside as the couple with the boy seated themselves across the table from Edward.

"I don't want to sit beside him!" the boy cried loudly.

"Fred, change seats with him," the woman ordered.

Fred, the husband, stood and grabbed the boy by his shirt and lifted him into the seat beside his mother, bending to whisper something in the boy's ear. Whatever Fred had whispered was effective, as the boy sat quietly and looked down at his lap. Then Fred sat beside Edward and spread his elbows on the table, staking claim to more than his share of the table.

"Sir!" Edward called the porter, "may I be seated elsewhere, somewhere more private?"

"Sorry, sir, all seating is assigned according to your berths."

To say the situation was uncomfortable would have been an understatement. Edward had to endure Fred's wayward elbow bumps and the boy's glares. The wife, Fred had called her Jane, gave him an apologetic half-smile twice during the ordeal.

"Excuse me," Edward said to Fred after rushing through the meal.

Fred, who was only halfway through his meal, said, "Just a minute." He then continued to leisurely eat his chicken alfredo.

"Fred," Jane said, "let the man out."

Fred made a show of setting his cutlery down, wiping his mouth with a napkin, and heaving his bulk up. Finally, he stood near the end of the bench, forcing Edward to squeeze by him.

Edward, red-faced and furious, strode back toward the sleeper car, meeting the conductor along the way.

"I want to change berths," he demanded. "The couple and their brat are insufferable!"

"I'm sorry, sir, but we are completely full."

Resigned to his fate, Edward used the time alone in his berth to begin reviewing and drafting Tom's story. He would need to align all three narratives in a chronological and intertwining order that led toward a unified ending. He relished the task and made good progress as time flew by until his tiresome seatmates returned. Sighing, Edward gathered his scattered notes and put them in his bag. He opened the newspaper, blocking his view of the family, and began scanning the pages for any mention of the Donnellys' arrest. He was interrupted by the boy who had slouched down in his seat and begun to kick the empty seat beside Edward.

"Control your bra—child," Edward said without lowering his paper.

Nothing happened until Jane admonished the boy. The boy stopped, and Edward continued to read the newspaper from front to back. No mention of the Donnellys or the break-in at the book store. But then again, the paper was a day old. He reread a few articles, killing time until the lunch hour was finished, and then rose to go see if Tom wanted to continue. He sure hoped so; the thought of sitting here with these people any longer was unbearable. He laid his newspaper out so that it completely covered the bench on his side of the booth.

"Please do not disturb my papers," he said and walked away before they could respond, but he did feel the man's eyes boring into his back until he exited the car.

He found Tom waiting for him and was pleased to hear he was anxious to continue his story. They moved back to the dining car and had to stand and wait until the staff cleared and wiped down the tables before being allowed in. Once seated, Tom picked up where he had left off.

* * *

Back then, the contrast between Prince Albert and Duck Lake was significant. Where the population of Prince Albert was large and predominantly English Métis, Duck Lake was small and populated by French Métis. We stopped in front of the log trading post, a one-story structure with an outbuilding in the back, presumably for fur storage.

"Go ahead, Tom," John said when we tied our horses to the rail in front of the store. "I'll wait out here."

Now it was my turn to look at him suspiciously, but I shrugged and walked inside. The smell and setup were the same as the fur trader's store in Prince Albert but on a smaller scale. The difference here was that the seats around the woodstove were empty.

"Hello, constable, what can I get you?" the man behind the counter asked. He was a stout man with a weathered face that resembled spruce bark and was partially covered by a full beard. He made no effort to hide his stare toward my bandaged face.

"Has anyone sold you fur in the last week?" I asked, ignoring the question on his face.

He turned and spit a stream of tobacco juice into a brass spittoon at his feet before answering. I don't know why that act riled me, but I maintained a professional demeanor despite my initial impression of the man.

"Well, yeah, several men came in."

"The one I'm looking for may have had scratches on his face."

"Yeah, he was here a few days ago," The man said. "Sold me a bunch of furs. Didn't buy anything. Just took the cash and left."

"Métis?"

"Yep."

"Did you see which way he went?"

"Sure did. He took the south road. Rode a brown horse with a white blaze. A real buffalo runner by the looks of him."

"I'll need a list of the furs and the amount you paid him."

"You're not going to confiscate those furs, are you?"

Another stream of tobacco juice hit the spittoon.

"No, but I need the list for my report."

"Okay, you can copy it out of my ledger."

"Is the man's name in your ledger?" I ask, holding my breath.

"It is. Louis Riel."

"You're joshing!"

Another spit, but this time the wad of tobacco came out.

"That's what I said. But the man insisted that was his name, saying that impostor who had stirred everything up had stolen his name. Crazy bastard. I was glad when he left."

We both grinned and shook our heads. Wait till John hears this one, I thought. He'll have a good laugh. You see, Louis Riel's fame had begun in 1869 during the time when the Métis living in the Red River Valley were worried that they would lose their farms after the Canadian government had sent land surveyors to the valley. The problem was, the Métis farmers in the valley didn't have clear title to their property. So, in November of that year, Riel organized a resistance, beginning with the formation a provisional government. But he made the mistake of allowing the execution of one Thomas Scott. Mr. Scott's crime? He had assaulted and threatened Riel. Outraged at this turn of events, Canada then sent 1,200 soldiers to deal with the resistance, which the government had dubbed the Red River Rebellion. Riel realized all was lost and fled to the Dakota territory in the United States. To say the man's name is well-known in western Canada would be an understatement.

But back to my story. After copying the fur trader's surprisingly detailed listing of furs and prices for each piece, I walked out onto the boardwalk to fill John in, but he was gone. Our horses were there, but John was gone. Cursing, I looked up and down the street but didn't see him anywhere. What was he up to now?

I turned one way, stepped off the porch, and walked toward the hotel. The town's buildings were spread out, fifty to a hundred feet apart. I was nearing the hotel when I heard a slap and a woman's scream. No one was on this side of the two-story building, so I ran toward the back with my hand on my service revolver and peered around the corner. Nothing. So, I went to the other corner and poked my head around, and there was John, about twenty feet away at the foot of a set of stairs leading up to the second floor. He was holding a struggling woman against the wall.

"John! What are you doing?"

"Go away, Tom! This is none of your concern," he yelled back.

"The hell it isn't; let her go, now!"

A man peered around the front corner of the building and quickly pulled his head back. John leaned his face in inches from the woman's ear, said something to her, and then pushed her aside and stomped toward the street. I started to follow him but then stopped by the sobbing woman and asked her if she was okay.

"Leave me alone!" she shrieked and began climbing the stairs.

I watched her until she went through the upstairs door, and then I walked back to the horses. John was mounted and waiting for me.

"What did you find out?"

"Are you going to tell me what happened back there?"

"No. What did you find out?"

I sighed. "The killer was here. He sold some furs and then headed south."

John nodded and turned his horse south.

"It's almost sundown; we should get a couple rooms and start fresh in the morning."

I watched his back stiffen. Then he said, "We still got a good hour of daylight."

Well, I wasn't about to sleep on the frozen prairie an hour away from a warm bed. So, I untied my horse and led him toward the hotel.

"Do what you want, John, but I'm getting a room. I'll catch up with you tomorrow."

I didn't look back. After securing a room, the hotel clerk directed me to a stable, and I took my horse there before heading back to the hotel's dining room. There were only two small tables, each with two chairs, so I took one near a large window facing the street. There was no sign of John anywhere. A Cree girl approached and told me the special today was buffalo stew and bannock.

"What else do you have?"

"Well, we have bannock, and we have buffalo stew," she said with a smirk. I laughed and ordered the special.

"Good choice," she said with a smile. "What happened to your face?"

"Rassled a bear. Oh, he put up a good fight, but I got the better of him. He won't be bothering me again."

She stared at me for several beats, nodded, and walked away, looking back once. It was easy to maintain a straight face when half of it was stiff as a shoe. Anyway, after the meal, of which I had seconds, I leaned back and sighed.

"It was good?" the girl asked.

"Yes, very good!"

"You are married?"

"No."

"Do you come through here often?"

"No, it's a little off my patrol route."

"Where do you live?"

"Well, for now at Wood Mountain."

"Is that where the Sioux are?"

"Yes."

And with that, she walked away and once again looked back before pushing through the batwing doors leading into the kitchen. It was a pleasant evening, not too cold, so I took a leisurely stroll around the village and smoked my pipe before heading back to the hotel and going to bed. There was still no sign of John.

* * *

Edward, who had his head down while transcribing Tom's words, looked up when he had stopped talking. Edward watched as Tom looked around the dining car, and even though there was no one else within earshot, leaned forward and lowered his voice.

"Last night, Annie and I discussed how much detail I should go into regarding our, uh, courtship," Tom explained. "So, I need your assurance that you will not embellish what I am about to tell you."

Edward, ever the newspaper writer, leaned forward and instinctively replied, "Of course, sir, you have my word."

Tom studied Edward for a few seconds and then nodded.

* * *

So, sometime later that night, a tapping on the door gradually drew me out of a deep sleep. I lay in bed thinking it was a dream and then tap-tap-tap.

"Who's there?" I called.

"Me. Annie."

I walked to the door and said, "What do you want?"

"Let me in," she whispered, "before someone sees me."

I opened the door, and she brushed by me and crawled into my bed. Her hand emerged from under the covers and dropped her nightgown to the floor.

"Hurry, I'm cold."

Damn! I hesitated for a second, then removed my long johns and crawled in beside her. Then, as Annie and I were getting to know each other, I thought I heard a muffled scream from somewhere in the hotel. I lifted my head and cocked an ear, but then Annie pulled me back under the covers, and I forgot about everything else.

In the morning, I woke up alone. As I lay there thinking about Annie, I realized I didn't know her last name. After a quick birdbath at the wash stand, I packed my kit and went downstairs for breakfast. An older lady was waiting tables, so I asked her if she knew where Annie was.

"She works evenings," she said and, without taking my order, set a plate of bacon and grease-covered eggs in front of me. But I didn't complain; the coffee was strong and the food was good, once I had scraped as much grease off as possible. I drained my second cup, paid, and was about to leave when the hotel clerk ran in and grabbed my arm.

"Come with me; there's been a murder," he whispered. He led me upstairs to a room at the end of the hall, three doors down from the one I had slept in. He unlocked the door, swung it open, and stood to the side, reluctant to enter. I peered in and saw the same woman John had altercated with the previous afternoon. Her bloodshot eyes stared blankly at the ceiling. From the bruising on her neck, I suspected she had been strangled.

"Who else checked in yesterday?"

"Just you. This is, was, Marguerite's room, Marguerite Baptiste. She, uh, offered a service to lonely men."

"Do you know who she was with last night?"

"No."

I scanned the room, unsure what I was looking for, and then I checked her fingernails. There appeared to be one coarse black hair stuck between a split in one of her nails. A beard hair? I took my handkerchief out, removed the hair, wrapped it, and put it in my pocket. I would have to remember not to blow my nose with it. There was also some dried mud on the floor.

Mud? I thought. It's the middle of winter.

I knelt, lifted a clump to my nose, and sniffed.

Horse manure.

"Okay, I'll make my report."

"That's it?"

"That's all I can do without any witnesses."

"But what do I do with her?"

"Call the undertaker."

I heard him mumbling about who was going to pay for that as I walked out the door.

My second murder case in the same week.

I saddled my horse and handed the stable owner a quarter. He shook his head and said, "It'll be fifty cents."

"Fifty cents? For a stall and feed?"

"Yup, for two horses."

"But I only have the one horse."

"Your partner said you'd cover his stable fees. And he slept in the loft, but I won't charge you for that . . . this time."

"John?"

"I guess so. The Mountie you rode in with."

Suddenly, I had no doubt that my partner was responsible for that dead woman in the hotel. Should I arrest him? I had no evidence other than seeing him argue with the woman yesterday. Should I keep looking for Shorty's killer or ride hard to Wood Mountain and report my suspicions about John to my commander?

"You going to stand there and gawk at the wall all day?"

I looked at the stable owner and then shook my head and led my horse outside. The morning was clear and cold; crisp was how I thought of these mornings. I made up my mind to follow Shorty's killer while his trail was still somewhat fresh. There was no sign of John anywhere, but when I left the village, I saw his tracks.

22

"Coffee, gentlemen?" a waiter asked.

"Yes, I'll have a cup," Edward answered.

"Can I get a cup of Earl Grey?"

"Of course, sir."

After they had been served their drinks and an assortment of cookies, Tom continued his narrative.

* * *

The trails, those of Shorty's killer and John, led to a Métis encampment where I found a disturbance involving dozens of armed men. I rode up to the crowd and pushed my way in with my horse. Disgruntled men cursed and voiced their anger at me, but I continued forward to the man in the middle of the circle. It was John, and he looked like he had been beaten.

"What is going on here?" I demanded. "Who did this?"

The crowd grew quiet at the authority in my voice. John looked up, but I couldn't tell if he could see me as both of his eyes were swelled shut.

A Métis man stepped forward and declared, "This man shot Louis without warning!" Murmurs of agreement rippled through the crowd.

"John!" I demanded. "What happened here?"

"Killer." He was on his knees, groggy, and swaying slightly as he mumbled through his split and swelled lips. "Shorty."

I dismounted and knelt in front of John. I removed the hair I had taken from Marguerite's nail and held it next to his beard; it appeared to be a match.

"John Edwards, I am placing you under arrest for the murder of Marguerite Baptiste!" I declared for all to hear and then turned to the apparent leader of these men.

"Where are his weapons?"

He looked around, shrugged, and then said, "Are you not charging him, for what he did to Louis?"

"Louis Riel?" I asked.

Despite the situation, a chuckle rippled through the crowd, and then the leader said, "That was his joke. He did look a bit like Riel, but his name was Nault, Louis Nault."

"I will have to get Louis's side of the story before making any charges," I said. "Is he able to talk?"

"No."

"Why not?"

"He's dead."

"Ah, shit."

"Yeah."

"Hey, did you say Marguerite Baptiste from the hotel at Duck Lake was killed?" a man called from the rear of the crowd with concern in his voice.

"How do you know her?" a woman behind him demanded.

"I, uh . . ."

"You cheating bast—" she began, then chased after the man, who I suspected was her fleeing husband, as the crowd erupted with laughter.

"Tie him up, James," the leader said to a man near John after the laughter died down.

"Tell me what happened, . . . ?" I asked, not knowing the leader's name.

"Guillaume," he answered. "Your man, his name is John?"

"Yes, Constable John Edwards."

"Yeah, well, John here came into our camp uninvited and demanded to know who the last person to enter our village was. I told him, 'You are.' He got angry and grabbed my shirt and growled, 'Who else?' That's when Louis jumped on his horse and galloped away. So, your man jumped on his horse and chased after poor Louis, God rest his soul, who pulled his rifle out of its holster and held it out to his side as he rode. Then John pulled out his pistol and started shooting at poor Louis. Louis got hit and fell off his horse. So, John rode up to Louis, who tried to raise his rifle in self-defence, and John shot him dead."

"No!" I gasped.

"Oui! So, a bunch of us, we grab our rifles and chased after this man, John, but he just sat there looking down at Louis, so we dragged him off his horse, and he fell to the ground. That is how John hurt both eyes, his mouth, and his ribs," Guillaume said with a straight face.

"That was quite a fall."

"Oui, oui, quite the fall." Nodding solemnly.

I shook my head and then asked to see Louis's body. I was not surprised when I saw the scabbed-over scratches on Louis's face. After I placed the measuring stick against Louis's foot and saw that it matched the length of the killer's foot perfectly, I had no doubt he was the man who had killed Shorty.

"He robbed a trapper; did you know that?"

"No, he said he played poker with a trapper and won a bundle of furs, which he sold."

"I'm not sure if that's what happened, but I do know that Louis and the trapper, Shorty, struggled and Shorty wound up dead."

"Ah, so that is why you were chasing Louis."

"Yes. You do not look surprised."

"Well, Louis, God love him, had a reckless nature and a temper to match."

"Did he have any money on him?"

"Uh, yeah, he did. His mother has it," Guillaume said, "but, you know, she's in a bad way; her only son dead this day. She won't have anyone to provide for her now."

I nodded and said, "Well, it was only a dollar, right?"

He looked at me, and a smile slowly formed. "That sounds about right. What's your name, constable?"

"Tom Flynn," I answered and then added, "Can you give me a hand loading my prisoner on his horse?"

"Horse?"

"Yes, his horse."

"Well, uh, that horse, he ran off when we, uh, when John fell off it."

I looked around for John's horse, but Guillaume took my arm and steered me away.

"We don't have any spare horses, but you know what?"

"What?" I sighed.

"Well, Louis, being dead and all, he won't be needing his cart anymore. I'm sure his mother will sell it to you, and dirt cheap too!" Guillaume declared and then pointed at a big two-wheeled cart with long arms sitting half-buried in uncut grass and snowdrifts.

"How cheap?"

"For you, twenty dollars."

"Twenty dollars!"

"Yes, it is handcrafted from only the finest of hardwoods and is capable of hauling five buffalo carcasses."

"Five, you say?"

"At least five, maybe more."

"Alright, but I'll have to write a scrip for it. She can take it to any of our posts for payment."

"Ah, no, that will not do."

"Well, that's all I can do; I only have two dollars on me."

"Ach! I'll tell you what, Tom Flynn, because you have been respectful with us, I will let it go for two dollars."

"Shouldn't you ask Louis's mother first?"

"Eh?"

"Louis's mother, isn't she the owner of the cart now?"

"Uh, yeah, well, I can speak for her."

So, I handed him the two dollars and had him sign a bill of sale so I could get reimbursed. Then Guillaume called two young men over and ordered them to shovel out the wagon and bring it to us. They look toward the cart, then at each other, then back at Guillaume, and one said, "That old piece of junk?"

"Just go do it now!" Guillaume shouted, and they wandered off to look for shovels.

Guillaume looked at me and shook his head sadly. "Young men these days! They are so lazy and impudent. Come, have a cup of tea with me while we wait for your cart."

The hot tea he served was delicious. I detected a hint of blueberries and maybe ginger.

"What kind of tea is this, Guillaume?"

"Ah, that, my friend, is a family secret," he said and then refilled my cup. "May as well have some more. Those boys will be a while."

I gratefully accepted the tea. It seemed to energize me.

"What happened to your face, Tom?"

"An animal."

"What kind of animal?"

"I don't know. It was dark and it happened too fast for me to see what it was."

"Huh, what did the tracks look like?"

"Uh, I don't know. Never looked."

"Seems like a natural thing to do, look at the tracks. Have you never hunted or trapped before?"

"Hunted some," I said, embarrassed that I hadn't even thought to look for the tracks the morning after my encounter with whatever had clawed me. Thankfully, Guillaume let the matter drop, and then he stood, signaling it was time to go.

When we walked out of his cabin, we stopped and watched the two men drag the cart toward us. I could not help but notice how wobbly the wheels were, not to mention how loud the screech emanating from the axle was.

"Your outhouse, where is it?" I asked, suddenly feeling the need to urinate.

"In the back."

When I walked around the back of Guillaume's cabin, I looked in all directions but did not see any sign of John's horse. Maybe it had run away. I wouldn't be surprised, given the crowd of angry men that had pulled John from its saddle. I returned to the front of Guillaume's house and saw my horse had been crudely harnessed between the poles extending from the cart. John sat bound in the back. Up close, I saw the wagon was huge. I walked over and inspected the cart. There was a portion on each wheel that looked somewhat brittle, the parts that had sat in the dirt, I suspected.

Five buffalo! It would be lucky to hold up under John's weight.

"I doubt this will last all the way to Wood Mountain."

"Do not worry, Tom Flynn, it's a strong Métis cart," Guillaume said, pounding his chest once.

"I'm cold," John grumbled.

I threw my bedroll over him, mounted my horse, and urged him forward. The horse struggled, and I saw Guillaume nod to the two young men who pushed the cart from behind. We moved forward and what emitted from the axle was the worst sound I had ever heard! As the wheels of the wagon turned, an ear-piercing squealing erupted.

Had they never greased them?

I looked back, but Guillaume and the two men had disappeared from sight. After a few hours, the squealing wheels and John's constant complaining about the noise had given me a pounding headache. I stopped for a break and rubbed my temples. When I looked up, a mounted Indian sat in front of me, making me jump.

"Why are you scaring away all the game?" he demanded in English.

"Can't help it. I am transporting a prisoner to Wood Mountain."

"Is he crippled?"

"What? No."

"Then why doesn't he walk?"

"You know what, friend, that is the best suggestion I have heard in some time," I said. "Who are you?"

"I am Little Crow, son of Tall Pony and Morning Star."

"I am Tom Flynn, son of Liam and Agnes Flynn," I replied.

"Where did you get this wagon?"

"From the encampment a few hours back."

"Ah, from Guillaume?"

"Yeah, how did you know?"

"He is not an honest man. The rest of the village, they are honorable people. I consider them friends, but this man, he gives the village a bad reputation."

"I see."

"Burn that wagon, Tom Flynn, son of Liam and Agnes Flynn," Little Crow said and then turned his pony and rode away.

John had craned his neck to watch this interaction. Once Little Crow was gone, he turned back to face the rear, grunted, and lay back down.

"Get up, John," I said. "You're walking from now on."

"What? I can't walk all the way to Wood Mountain. I'm injured."

"Bullshit."

So, we abandoned the cart. We topped a hill, and I turned in the saddle and saw the cart was in flames. There was no sign of Little Crow, but I suspected he had something to do with the fire, and I grinned.

"Well done, Little Crow, son of Tall Pony and Morning Star," I said and heard John snort.

That night, we slept under the stars in a spruce-ringed clearing. It must have been at least fifteen below, but with a bed of spruce boughs under our bedrolls and a well-banked fire, it was pretty cozy, as long as I kept my head covered. I heard movement sometime in the night and peeked out from under my blanket. It was just John adding more wood to the fire. I retreated back into my cocoon and drifted off again.

My eyes flew open. I didn't know how long it had been since I had seen John stoking the fire—without his bindings! I jumped up and looked to where he had bedded down. There were only spruce boughs left. Fearing the worst, I looked toward my horse. It was also gone. My rifle too, but I still had my pistol. There was no point trying to chase him in the dark on foot while he was undoubtedly galloping away. So, I threw a few sticks on the fire and watched the shower of sparks fly. After making sure no embers landed on my blanket, I dove under, and my body racked with shivers while my teeth chattered. No sense getting up until daylight. And, against all odds, I fell asleep.

It was not much warmer with the sun out. I quickly realized that John had taken everything; I couldn't even make coffee. I was left with nothing but my clothes and blankets. Luckily, I had used my parka as an extra layer of bedding the night before, and my boots were still at the foot of my bed.

I walked out to the trail and saw that John had gone straight west. I looked south, in the direction of Wood Mountain, a hundred and sixty miles away. Usually a week-long ride on horseback. Since I would never make it there on foot, I turned north and started walking back toward the Métis encampment.

I didn't make it to the encampment. An Indian rider sat on top of a low hill a mile away, watching me. I wondered if it was Little Crow. I kept walking and, after a while, I looked back and saw the Indian was now behind me, still too far to tell if it was him. He galloped away to the west and then turned north into a coulee. I kept putting one foot in front of the other, dizzy from hunger. My feet felt like two blocks of ice.

Was that wood smoke I smelled?

I topped a hill and down below sat an Indian in front of a fire. I smelled meat cooking, and my stomach growled as I stumbled down the incline.

"Are you hungry, Tom Flynn?" Little Crow asked without looking up at me.

I tried to speak, and it came out in a mumble; my cheeks were stiff with cold.

"Sit, get warm, and have some squirrel." Two squirrel carcasses were roasting over the fire. "They're almost ready. Do you want some tea?"

I nodded, and he handed me a steaming enamel cup. It felt good, warming my hands as I sipped the hot liquid. I wasn't much of a tea drinker back then, but that was the best drink I'd ever had in my life!

"Take your boots off and warm your feet by the fire," Little Crow told me.

I set the tea down and tried to pry one boot off using the other, but that didn't work. So, Little Crow knelt in front of me and pried them off my feet.

"Pooh, your feet stink," he said. "You need moccasins. These boots are no good in the cold."

I drank the tea and worked my cheeks until I was able to talk.

"Where'd you learn to speak English?"

"Wood Mountain. I was there with Sitting Bull. A Métis man taught me."

"Yeah? That is where I'm stationed now. Were you at the Little Bighorn Battle?"

"At Greasy Grass, yes, the fight with Long Hair."

"You are Hunkpapa Lakota then?"

"No, I am an Arapaho warrior."

"Arapaho?"

"There were five of us there."

He picked up one of the squirrels by the stick and passed it to me. I began gingerly tearing off little pieces of the steaming meat and then devoured it once it had cooled. Little Crow watched me with a smile and poured more tea into my cup.

"What happened to your face?"

"Animal clawed me."

"Why?"

"He was hungry."

"There are far better things for an animal to eat than you, Tom Flynn. Maybe next time an animal tries to eat you, take off your boots!"

Little Crow chuckled, and I let him have his joke since he had just saved my life.

"You will come back to my lodge. I will sell you a horse and maybe find you a pair of moccasins."

I nodded and struggled to keep my eyes open. The sun had set, and the fatigue from walking and shivering all day had caught up with me. My chin touched my chest, and I rested my eyes, just for a few minutes. When next I opened my eyes, there were clouds above me and frost from my breath rose and drifted away to nothing. I was moving, bumping along as I heard a horse's footfalls. It was a travois I was lying on; I had seen them before.

Do you know what a travois is, Edward?

No? Well, a travois is a simple sled consisting of two poles pulled behind a horse. The ends drag on the ground, and they have either wood cross pieces or fabric stretched between the poles to carry a load. In this instance, several spruce branches were tied between the poles, and I was the load.

Anyway, I craned my neck and saw the backs of a horse and Little Crow. It was warm under the buffalo robe that covered me, and I soon drifted off again.

I must have only been dozing because I opened my eyes when the horse stopped. We were in front of a crude cabin built into the side of a low brush-covered knoll. I got up, and a wave of dizziness washed over me. There was nothing wrong with me; why was I dizzy? Little Crow led me inside and sat me down on a stump, obviously his chair.

He knelt in front of me and removed the bandage from my face and inspected the wound. He then bent down and dug around in a sack until he found a small glass jar. He unscrewed the top and dipped his fingers inside, coming out with a dollop of something that looked like rendered fat. Little Crow leaned toward me and spread the greasy salve over my face. It had a faint earthy odor and was instantly soothing.

"You do not need this bandage anymore," he said and then tossed it into his wood stove.

"I have to track John before his trail is lost."

"It will be dark soon; you should leave in the morning," Little Crow said.

That evening, after a delicious meal of fried moose meat, onions, and potatoes, we sat and talked late into the night. He told me about Greasy Grass, Sitting Bull, American Horse, Zeke, and life before the soldiers had come. I felt a sense of inadequacy when I realized I had very few adventures, good or bad, to recount.

"Put these on," Little Crow said as he handed me a pair of moccasins the next morning, "and then you can go choose your pony. As there is only one pony to choose from, it will not take long."

I looked at him to see if he was joking, but his face was impassive. The moccasins were thick tanned buffalo hide and were a bit snug but surprisingly warm and comfortable. Little Crow had two ponies, the one he rode yesterday and another smaller one.

"I will have to write you a scrip for the pony," I said, watching for his reaction.

"What is this scrip?"

"A piece of paper that promises to pay the bearer a certain amount of money. You can take it to any of our posts."

"Who is this bearer?"

"That would be you."

From the look on his face, I realized he did not know the term.

"A bearer is the person holding the paper."

"Then why didn't you just say that?"

"I don't know," I said. "How much for the pony?"

"Ten dollars."

"Okay." I looked around and realized my scrips were gone with everything else John had taken off with. "Uh, I don't have a scrip with me."

"So, you are not a bearer either then?" he said with a smirk.

"No," I sighed, "I guess not."

"You will pay me someday, Tom Flynn. Do you need a saddle?"

"Yes."

We walked outside and into a small open-walled lean-to built onto the side of his stout cabin. He pointed to a saddle sitting on a railing. I looked it over and saw "US" stamped on one corner. I wondered if it had belonged to one of the fallen soldiers from the Little Bighorn Battle, but I didn't ask.

"I will travel with you for a while. If I find game along the way, then I will return home with it," Little Crow stated.

"I will be glad for the company."

We traveled light and fast across the prairie, and I found myself hoping we wouldn't encounter any game; I was enjoying Little Crow's company. We shared more stories, and I was jealous that he seemed to have had more adventures in his short life than I could ever hope to have. My admiration grew for this young warrior because that is what he was, a warrior. The weather continued to be bitterly cold. On the second day of pursuit, we found my police-issued horse lying on its side, frozen.

"He abused this horse," Little Crow said.

That didn't surprise me, and I felt anger for the treatment of my horse. I dismounted and tried to remove the saddle. One side of the saddle was frozen between the horse and the ground. Impossible to break free, but I did manage to work the saddle bags free. The next day, late in the afternoon, Little Crow held up a hand. I stopped and looked in the direction he was facing. I did not see anything.

"There he is."

I squinted but still did not see anything.

"I will leave you here, my friend," Little Crow said, and before I could protest, he tossed me the jar of salve, wheeled his pony around, and trotted away.

I rode forward and eventually saw a form lying on the ground.

Was he aiming a rifle at me?

No, he was facing the other way.

I rode toward him, my revolver cocked and in my hand. When I neared him, it became apparent John was dead, frozen solid. No sign of injuries, other than those he had already sustained, so he hadn't been killed. He must have just fallen, too exhausted to get back up, and then froze to death. As if on cue, an icy blast of wind blew across this exposed hill. I looked around and saw a stand of spruce trees. I rode there, built a fire in a spot sheltered from the wind, and then cut some spruce poles for a travois. I made it similar to Little Crow's, but mine was definitely cruder than his. When I was finished, I tied it to my pony and went to get John. It would be a long ride to Wood Mountain; the little pony would need frequent rest stops. But, to Little Crow, I would be forever grateful, not only for rescuing me from the bitter cold and giving me a horse, saddle, and moccasins but for also teaching me how to build a warm and comfortable shelter on the prairies. I truly believe the latter had saved my life.

* * *

Tom stopped there and said he wanted to spend some time with his friends.

"Where did you get the rope?" Edward asked.

"Eh?"

"The rope to make the travois and tie it to your pony."

"I used the reins from my dead horse to tie the travois poles together, and I had a coil of rope in my saddlebags. I used the rope to secure the travois to the pony."

"Ah, I see. Could you ask Jacque if he would come here?" Edward asked.

"Okay. What he will tell you is true, Edward. Do not question his honesty."

"Uh, okay."

His interest piqued, Edward ordered more coffee and waited for Jacque.

23

"Hi, Jacque."

"Edward." Jacque nodded. "Tom said you wanted to see me?"

"Yes. Can we continue with your story?"

"Well, okay," Jacque said, "I suppose there will be plenty of time to spend with my friends once we get to New York."

"Yes."

"Okay, let see now, I think I will continue my story in 1884. September, I think it was, at my farm near St. Francois Xavier, west of Winnipeg."

* * *

One evening, at suppertime, there came a knocking on my door as I was saying grace. I muttered an amen, glanced regrettably at the fried pickerel and baby potatoes on my plate, stood, and strode to the door.

This had better be damned important to interrupt my dinner.

I glanced at our two-year-old daughter, Angélique, asleep in her crib, and I was relieved that the knocking had not woken her. The harsh words I had rehearsed in my head died in my throat when I swung the door open. There stood a man with a bushy mustache on his stern face and dressed in a military uniform.

"Jacque Daoust?"

"Yeah."

"I am recruiting voyageurs for an expeditionary force to Sudan. Are you interested?"

"Sudan?"

"Yes, in Africa."

"Africa?"

"What is he saying, Jacque?" Genevieve asked from the table.

"I don't know. What are you trying to say, captain?"

"Colonel!" he barked, then he took a deep breath and said, "I am Colonel Denison of the Canadian Militia."

"Okay; what do you want?"

"Are you interested in joining an expeditionary force to Sudan?"

"Expedi—?"

"Expeditionary." Colonel Denison sighed and drew out the words. "A military force."

"I've never been in the military."

"It pays forty dollars per month for six months, and a uniform is supplied."

"You had better come in and explain, cap – I mean colonel," I said, opening the door wide and standing to one side.

"Would you care for some fish, colonel?" Genevieve slowly stood, heavy with our second child, and prepared a plate without waiting for his answer.

"Sit, sit," I said and pointed to an empty chair.

The colonel removed his hat and took a seat. He looked uncomfortable until the plate was placed before him, and his nostrils flared at the aroma.

"Thank you, ma'am, that smells delicious."

Genevieve blushed and eased herself into her chair. We watched the colonel, who was ravenously forking in the fish. Well, the man had some sense, so Genevieve and I ate our meals, and I waited until everyone had finished before asking him to explain his mission.

"The British are pulling out of Sudan, in Africa –"

"Africa!" Genevieve gasped.

"Yes, Africa," Colonel Denison continued. "There is a revolution among the natives, and General Gordon's forces are under siege. We need voyageurs to carry munitions and troops up the Nile River to rescue them. There is no time to waste." He said this as he wiped a finger on his empty plate and then put it in his mouth.

"Natives, like the Cree?" I asked.

"No, well, I suppose somewhat like them. African natives."

"Would you like some more fish, colonel?"

"Why yes, I would, thank you ma'am."

"Why come halfway around the world for men? Why not use local boatmen?" I asked.

"Lord Wolseley himself believes that only voyageurs can get the job done."

"Well, if I agree to go, and I'm not saying I will, I would need at least two months' pay in advance."

"Ah, that's highly irregular."

"My wife will need money if I am going to be gone for six months."

"Alright, I am sure we can work something out."

"I'm not saying I'm going. Six months is a long time; I will miss the buffalo hunt, the harvest, and a good part of trapping season." I glanced at Genevieve and added, "And the birth of my child."

"I understand, but I'm afraid you will have to decide tonight, Jacque. The train leaves in the morning."

"Can I have a word with my wife in private, colonel?"

"Certainly."

So, I poured the colonel another cup of tea, and Genevieve and I went into the bedroom. I was surprised when the first words out of Genevieve's mouth were, "You have to go. It is too much money to pass up." And, I must say, I was grateful she said that. Maybe she saw the excitement on my face, I don't know, but I truly was excited at the thought of a grand adventure halfway across the world. And Genevieve's brother, Norbert, would be here to look after her. So, with the decision made, we went back into the dining room.

"Okay, colonel, I will go."

"Excellent," Colonel Denison stood and shook my hand. "The train leaves first thing in the morning, and I will arrange for two months' pay to be sent to you, ma'am."

"Thank you, sir," I said. "I will see you at the train."

"No, I have some more business to attend to before I can leave. But I will see you in Montreal."

"Montreal?" This was getting interesting.

"Yes, from Montreal, we will board the Ocean King and sail for Egypt."

"Egypt?"

"Yes." The colonel drank down his tea and set the cup down on the table. "Now, if you will excuse me, I must be on my way. Thank you for your hospitality, ma'am. The food was sumptuous."

My wife blushed once again. I wondered if she knew what the word sumptuous meant; I sure didn't. After the colonel left, I sat heavily while Genevieve poured me some tea.

"Forty dollars a month! For six months," she said. "We could build a bigger house."

I nodded as I looked around our little cabin. My father, Francois, and I had built it several years before. Each spruce log was cut, limbed, debarked, notched, and fitted by the two of us. I would never forget that summer with my dad. We laughed together, yelled at each other, helped each other up when we fell, and worked shoulder to shoulder, and now he was gone.

"Maybe," I said.

"What do you mean, maybe? We can't raise a family in this little cabin."

Suddenly, the door banged open and Norbert stomped in. The young man was a bull.

"I am starving," he declared and headed straight for the table. He lifted the lid off the pot that had once held the fish. Finding it empty, he checked another container and found one lonely little potato in it. The bannock plate held only crumbs.

"What the hell," he cried.

"Uh, we had unexpected company," Genevieve said.

"There's some pemmican in the larder," I added.

He gave us a disgusted look and cried, "Tabernac!"

"I am leaving for Montreal in the morning."

"Montreal! Why are you going to Montreal?"

"It's my first stop on my way to Africa."

"Africa!" Norbert gasped.

"Yes, so I will need you to sleep in the barn tonight."

"The barn? The mosquitoes will eat me alive out there," Norbert whined. "Why do I have to sleep out there?"

He saw Genevieve blush, and then he said, "Fine!"

I saw him glance at her extended belly with a look of consternation on his face.

"You will be on your own looking after the farm for six months," I told him.

He sighed heavily and grabbed some pemmican from the pemmican barrel.

"I'll make you some bannock, Norbert," Genevieve said.

He grunted and skulked out of the cabin. There was no bannock made that night.

"How come I can't go with you?" Norbert asked me the next morning from his seat in the bed of the wagon.

"You're too young, and you were never a voyageur," I replied. "Besides, I need you here with Genevieve."

Genevieve and I sat up front on the bench with Angélique. We owned the horse and the wagon but not the farm or, for that matter, the cabin. We leased the land from Theophile, who had shut his cook cabin down in Grand Rapids after the decline of the voyageur brigades and had purchased land along the Assiniboine River. The house my father and I built on Theophile's land was considered an improvement, along with the clearing of the bush. Theophile had told us that we would get compensated for that if we ever moved. The money from this expedition would give us enough to buy the land from Theophile. Norbert and I could expand the cabin over time when we weren't working the fields.

I had taken a few dollars from our savings can and left the rest for Genevieve. The excitement had been building all morning; the prospect of journeying to Montreal and then across the ocean to Africa had me on pins and needles. Even though I would be away from Genevieve for six months, I looked forward to a new adventure in an exotic location. The trepidation of entering a war zone had not sunk in yet; that would happen in Africa.

I saw many voyageurs waiting on the platform when we arrived at the train station. A chorus of cheers and whoops erupted when Genevieve and I alit from the wagon and embraced.

"Jacque!" someone called.

I scanned the crowd and saw my old friends Gabriel and Jean waving their arms. After my final goodbyes, I raced to meet them and scooped up Gabriel in a bear hug. Not to be left out, Jean embraced both of us as we whooped and danced in a circle.

"Where are the others?" I asked when we had settled down.

"We are all that are going," Jean said, knowing I meant the others from our original canoe crew. Of course, there had been a few other voyageurs after that first trip, but the men who had survived those rapids had a stronger bond.

"Really? I thought for sure Étienne and Pierre would come."

"No one knows where Étienne went after that last trip in from Fort Chip, and Pierre's all stove-up. He went logging and tore his back up pretty bad, trying to prove he could keep up with the younger men. I glanced back and saw Genevieve and Norbert's backs as the wagon headed home.

"Anton is here," Jean said.

He was the last man I wanted to meet again. I would have to watch my back. The next day, Gabriel, Jean, and I, along with 383 other voyageurs and loggers of Métis, French, and Indian descent, boarded the SS Ocean King bound for Alexandria, Egypt. I tried to avoid Anton as much as I could. However, I often caught him glaring at me from across the mess room during meals and knew it was only a matter of time before I ran into him. I had put on a lot of muscle since my encounter with him at Grand Rapids, but he was known for his fighting skills, whereas I had minimal experience. Who knew what dirty fighting tricks he would have up his sleeve?

One day, I was leaning on a rail, looking out at the vastness of the ocean. The ship cut through waves that must have been at least twelve feet high, yet they only tilted the ship moderately.

"Be a shame if someone fell in," Anton said and slapped my back hard.

My grip tightened on the rail as my upper body was pushed forward by the impact. I kept looking out to sea while I composed myself, and then I turned and looked Anton in the eye and said, "It would be. You should be very careful." We stared at each other for several seconds before he broke off and forced a laugh. His face had paled, and he seemed at a loss for words, so he turned and walked stiffly away. It was my last encounter with the man.

After twenty-three days at sea, we arrived in Alexandria. To say we were dumbfounded would be an understatement. Every building appeared to be whitewashed brick or stone, and the people wore flowing robes, mostly white.

Some of the men wore little red hats, some with a tassel hanging from the top, while others had cloth wound around their hair. And, despite the heat, many women wore scarfs covering their heads and most of their faces. Maybe it was to protect them from sunburn. And the trees looked funny; all the branches and leaves were at the top.

The excitement among my friends was palpable. They were all talking at once, pointing here and there and giddily crying, "Look at that!" When we disembarked, any hopes of sightseeing were dashed when we were formed into columns and marched toward the Nile River. We eyed the keeled boats moored there. They looked somewhat like the York boats from back home, but keeled boats are much harder to navigate through rapids. And, we were told, the Nile had rapids.

Well, we'd see about that!

Soldiers were loading artillery pieces, ammunition, food, and tents into the boats when we arrived. These supplies, along with hundreds of soldiers, would be our cargo. We joined what was called the River Column. Before disembarking the Ocean King, we had changed into our uniforms, and I longed for my comfortable clothes. Gabriel, Jean, and I stayed close together. We were thus assigned to the same boat with nine other voyageurs, only a few I recognized. We sat on benches facing the rear and pulled oars. There were sixteen soldiers and various crates in our boat. I looked over the side to gauge how much freeboard the craft had, and I was surprised to see quite a lot. These were good boats. Without much ado, we pushed off from the shore and began our long journey against the current of this large river. Three hundred and eighty men belted out voyageur songs. It must have been heard all across Alexandria! We stayed close to the bank, where the current was not as strong. It was not long before we saw our first strange sight.

"Jacque!" Gabriel whispered in awe. "What are those things?"

I looked at Gabriel's saucer eyes and then in the direction he was pointing and gasped.

What the hell was that?

Soon, the entire brigade was chattering excitedly, pointing and gaping at these strange animals. They had a coat the same color as an elk, long skinny caribou-like legs, long necks with a head similar to a pony but with floppy lips, and large humps on their backs.

"Look!" someone shouted. "They're riding them!"

I looked ahead, and sure enough, there were six dark-skinned men in flowing white robes riding atop these animals near the river's bank. As we passed them, they saw the excitement they were causing, so they decided to put on a show for us. Whipping their animals into a run, they raced alongside us; more than a few hearty voyageurs eyed these foreign beasts with trepidation. They looked ungainly, but boy could they move.

I heard the word "camels" filter through the brigade. It would not be the last time we encountered these beasts, and I wondered what other wonders we would see in this land. And, as it turned out, I did not have to wait long.

"Is that a beaver?" I asked no one in particular.

"Watch yourselves, men," a captain yelled. "Keep your hands inside the boat."

We pulled on our oars, watching this creature as it neared the shore, and then it climbed up onto the bank. Gasps and yells erupted from voyageurs as more crocodiles could now be seen on the bank.

"Those are crocodiles," the captain called. "They will grab you, pull you under the water, spin you until you drown, and then they will eat you."

Three hundred and eighty voyageurs shuddered as one. The soldiers, on the other hand, appeared to be used to these animals.

"What other horrors await us?" one man angrily demanded.

"Well, there are hippos and a variety of deadly snakes," a soldier said.

"What the hell is a hippo?"

"A water animal as big as a buffalo."

"And the snakes?"

"Yeah, I'd advise against going for a swim."

After the excitement died down some, we resumed singing our songs, but some of the robustness had left our voices.

"Mon Dieu!"

I turned and looked over my shoulder and gaped at what we were heading into. Rapids like no rapids I had ever seen before. They were massive and continued beyond our sight. The soldiers called these "cataracts." I guess the word "rapids" did not do them justice. What made entering these cataracts all the more terrifying was that we had our backs to them. I looked over at Gabriel and saw the anxiety in his eyes as the front of the boat rose and the first mist of water splashed against our backs.

24

It took us ten days to get through this cataract. At times, we had to tow the boats from the banks, but mostly we muscled our way up the rapids, paddling thirteen hours a day. We were told it took local boatmen thirty days to navigate through these rapids. Our elation on getting through was dampened when we were informed there were five more cataracts. Well, that was why we got the high pay, I supposed.

* * *

"Was it hot there, Jacque?"

"Oh, my, it was hot! Not the heat we have here; theirs is a dry heat. Cooks your brains from the inside out."

Edward thought about that statement and could not understand it, but he let it pass.

"Then what happened?"

"By October 26th, I think it was, we made it to Wadi Halfa."

"Wadi Halfa?"

"A large village bordered by farmland along the river. Being a farmer myself, I had been wondering how could anything grow in such a hot, dry land. But then I saw how they irrigated the land, and I was not the only one fascinated by the ingenuity of these farmers."

"How so?" Edward asked.

"Well, they had set up a water wheel in the river, but instead of mounting paddles on the wheel, they had mounted woven baskets angled toward the riverbank. As the wheel turned, the baskets would scoop up water from the river and then, on the downward rotation, deposit the water into channels leading to the fields."

"And the river turned the wheel?"

"No, well, maybe a little bit, but here is where the ingenuity I mentioned earlier comes in. A shaft like a wagon's axle ran from the water wheel to a second vertical wheel on the bank that had cogs all around its outer edge. Then a third wheel, sitting horizontally above the second wheel, also had cogs around its rim, and the cogs of the second and third wheel fit together. So, when the horizontal wheel turned, it also turned the upright wheel, which then turned the water wheel by its axle."

"Okay, so how did the horizontal wheel turn?" Edward asked.

"By an ox!"

"An ox?"

"Yes, an ox with a yoke was attached to the third wheel's shaft, and it walked around in circles, all day I suppose. Not a pleasant existence for the beast."

"No, I expect it wouldn't be. This was in 1884?"

"Yes."

"Okay, shall we continue?"

"Yes, of course."

* * *

We were part of the British army's mission to rescue Major-General Gordon and his forces. They were under siege by al-Mahdi's Sudanese forces at Khartoum, six hundred miles away. Upon arrival in Wadi Halfa, General Wolseley was informed that Gordon's forces could only hold out for another forty days. So, Wolseley addressed the voyageurs, imploring us to proceed with all haste in this rescue attempt. His speech was so impassioned, all us voyageurs belted out a deafening cheer.

We left Wadi Halfa singing at the top of our lungs; some soldiers tried to sing along, which was good but mostly funny. Then, on the first day out of Wadi Halfa, we saw our first hippopotamus.

"Hey, Jacque," Gabriel called from behind me. "Would you rather have an ox or one of those beasts pulling your plow?"

I watched one hippo lumbering toward the water and said, "An ox, of course. Look at how slow those things are."

"They look strong, though," Gabriel said.

"Which one do you think would win in a fight?" Jean interjected.

"I would say an ox because they are faster and have horns," I said. "These hippos wouldn't have a chan—"

I stopped short when the hippo opened its mouth wide and roared. The huge gaping mouth bore massive curved teeth, and the roar reminded me of an angry mamma moose.

"I change my mind," I said. "I pick the hippo."

My crewmates and the soldiers within earshot found this exchange hilarious. The hippo charged into the river with deceiving speed and swam toward us. Needless to say, our rowing rhythm increased substantially. Several soldiers aimed their rifles at the beast but held their fire. The hippo, having defended his territory, turned and swam back to his harem.

We frantically paddled, dragged, and towed our boats through cataracts for forty days and forty nights. However, we were still far from Khartoum after the allotted time. Christmas came and went, and we were still battling through massive cataracts. We lost seven voyageurs in those rapids. Each time, crewmates of the lost man would place a cross on the bank near the scene of his demise.

One day, we were surprised to see hundreds of camels under the control of a handful of locals standing near the shore. We were ordered to put to shore, and most of the soldiers, led by General Wolseley, disembarked and mounted these animals. It was a sight to see. Camels knelt down while the soldiers climbed aboard, and then they galloped away, toward, we were told, the siege at Khartoum.

With the majority of the troops and munitions disembarked from our boats, Colonel Denison stood on a crate and addressed us. He said our six-month contracts were nearing expiration. Most of us voyageurs had not been counting the days, so our reactions were a mix of relief and regret. I for one felt we had not completed our mission. And that is what it was, a mission to rescue trapped soldiers, and we had not accomplished that yet. So, to my relief, he gave us the choice of returning home or remaining for several more months to facilitate the return of troops and munitions from Khartoum. Knowing that some voyageurs were anxious to get home, the colonel informed us that he was authorized to offer an additional twenty dollars per month for those who stayed.

Gabriel, Jean, and I huddled together to discuss our options.

"What are you going to do, Jacque?" Even though I was younger than my two comrades, they seemed to respect my opinion on some matters. Maybe it was because I had remained sober, bailed them out of jail, and then gotten their money back from the bootlegger-robber in Grand Rapids. Whatever the reason, I had been elevated to the leader of our little group.

"I will stay," I replied without hesitation. "I need the money for my family."

"I will stay too," Gabriel said.

We both looked at the silent Jean. He had his head down, was staring at the sand, and then slowly looked up at us. "I want to go home."

Both Gabriel and I were aware that Jean struggled in the African heat. We both placed a hand his shoulders, and I said to him, "Of course, Jean, but you do know it's the middle of winter back home?"

His face brightened, and he said, "I have dreamed of snow."

"Could you take a letter to Winnipeg and post it for me?" I asked, and Gabriel said, "Yeah, for me too."

"No, I will not post your letters," Jean said, and then quickly added, "but I will hand-deliver them to your homes."

After Gabriel and I signed new contracts, we finished the letters we had been working on in the evenings. We added that we would be gone longer than intended, and then we gave them to Jean. It was hard to see Jean go; we had become brothers, the three of us. Only eighty-nine of the original three hundred and eighty voyageurs opted to stay.

On February 5th, 1885, a messenger informed the colonel that the Khartoum defenders had been overwhelmed by al-Mahdi's forces just two days before Wolseley's camel brigade had arrived. They had found no survivors. Details of the collapse of Khartoum filtered down through the river brigade. The most shocking fact was that the bodies of General Gordon and many of his officers had been partially dismembered. The outrage among the soldiers was palpable, and we, too, shared their anger.

"We cannot blame ourselves, Gabriel," I said to my friend.

"It was our job to get the soldiers to Khartoum, and we failed," Gabriel said. He was sitting on the ground, despondent.

"It was an impossible mission from the start, Gabriel. You know that. We gave it everything we had."

"But they were counting on us, and now they are dead."

"The rescue mission was doomed before we even arrived in this country; they wasted too much time."

"But what they did to their bodies . . ."

Like many of us, Gabriel had tears in his eyes.

On February 9th, we were approaching the hills of Kirbekan when a soldier from the camel brigade charged alongside us on the river bank, yelling for us to stop. General Earle called a halt and sent our boat ashore to receive whatever message the rider had. The rider told us there was a large enemy force ahead, and we were to wait for the rest of the camel brigade to arrive.

We paddled over to the general's boat and passed along the message. The general nodded and ordered all boats to shore.

"Do you think we will see battle, Jacque?" Gabriel asked, his body twitching with nervous energy.

"We are non-combatants, remember?"

"But what if they need our help?"

"Then we will help," I responded. Neither of us had been in a gunfight in our lives, and I liked to think neither of us would fail to answer the call to arms. In fact, we would welcome the opportunity to make up for our failure to get the reinforcements to Khartoum on time. The camel brigade arrived the next day and immediately began preparations for the attack on the Sudanese occupying the hills. We were awed by the precision with which the British forces maneuvered into battle readiness.

When the soldiers moved out, word had spread that the voyageurs wanted to participate in the fight. The general ordered us to stay put, assigning a few of his men to ensure we obeyed his order.

"Come on," I said to Gabriel a half hour later. I stepped forward, and after a brief hesitation, Gabriel followed.

"Halt!" a soldier yelled.

"If we cannot participate, we are going to watch!" I replied.

I could see the consternation on the soldier's face. His orders were to prevent us from participating; nothing had been said about observing. His predicament was resolved for him by a surge of voyageurs who followed Gabriel and me up the side of a hill where we would have a good view of the coming battle. We stood or sat in full view of both sides yet well out of rifle range.

We could see a line of British redcoats marching double time in a gully that would place them behind the enemy. At the same time, other units moved into position for a frontal assault. Then we watched in horror as the enemy spotted the soldiers in the gully and poured fire into the redcoats. We saw the commander go down as his troops sheltered in rocks and returned fire. The British frontal assault then began from two units. The gunfire was so intense we could feel the concussions through our chests.

Nevertheless, with their superior weaponry, the far outnumbered redcoats soon routed the enemy. We struggled to see through the vast dust clouds and then cheered the victory, but the soldiers with us were less than enthusiastic. Then I saw why: many red-coated soldiers were lying motionless on the field of battle. The voyageurs soon realized this, and we offered our condolences to the soldiers.

The British buried sixty redcoats that day and left two thousand Sudanese soldiers dead on the field. Gabriel and I had seen dead bodies before, drowned voyageurs, but seeing bodies dead by the violence of others affected us differently. We admired the bravery of the fallen men we had known, even in passing, and grieved their loss. However, my feelings were conflicting because, at least in my mind, the Sudanese were only protecting their land from foreigners. It was something I would think about for many years to come, that and the image of hundreds of dead bodies lying in the sun. To this day, I don't know the cause of the conflict. Anyway, shortly after the battle, we received word that the column was returning to Egypt. Thus, our time in Africa would soon be over.

The journey back to Cairo was much quicker as we were traveling with the current. When we arrived, we were told that we, the voyageurs, were in for a treat. A carriage ride through the city was planned, which would be followed by a lunch in the shadows of the great pyramids. When we arrived, all we could do was gape at the massive structures.

"How were these built?" I heard someone ask.

"With slave labor," our guide responded.

"Why?"

"Why did they use slaves?"

"No, why were they built?"

"They are tombs for the emperors, preparing them for the next life."

"Huh, how did that work out?"

"No one knows."

"Why did they use slaves?" another voyageur asked.

Before the guide could explain, someone exclaimed, "What the heck is that?"

There, in the distance, was a strange statue.

"That is a sphynx," the guide said. "It is a mythical creature with the body of a lion and the head of a human."

"Mon Dieu, did such a creature exist?"

"No, like I said, it is a mythical creature."

When we finally departed from the pyramids, we were given gifts of pipes and tobacco. I didn't smoke back then, but I liked the pipe. I gave my tobacco to

Gabriel, who tested it out right then and there. His coughing and watering eyes were a source of amusement for our Egyptian guides.

The next day we took a train to the Suez Canal, where we boarded a ship that would take us home. Once onboard, we lined up to collect our mail. I received two letters from Genevieve. Aside from how she missed me and all, the first letter informed me that Theophile had agreed to sell us the land at a better price than I had hoped for. She said it may be because of the size of her belly, or maybe it was little Angélique sitting on Theophile's lap staring up at him with her large eyes. It was good news indeed! The second letter told me I had a son, and his name was Honoré. Voyageurs and soldiers alike cheered loudly when I shouted the news. The captain himself presented me with a cup of rum. I took a sip and tried to hide my grimace before sneaking it to Gabriel, who swallowed it in one gulp, smacked his lips, and sighed. I laughed when I saw his glassy eyes and goofy grin.

On the voyage home, an outbreak of smallpox struck the voyageurs. Sixteen voyageurs had died on this expedition from drowning and illness. Anton was one of the last to die. He did not have many friends, and despite our troubled relationship, I felt a heavy sadness when I thought of him dying alone in the infirmary.

We received little fanfare when we finally arrived in Montreal. We learned that the voyageurs who did not reenlist had been given a rousing welcome upon their return. But in our case, we were crowded onto a train with dozens of Canadian militiamen who eyed us suspiciously. We found out why when we heard about the rebellion going on in the west. Métis, a people most voyageurs belong to, had engaged the North-West Mounted Police in armed resistance. According to the soldiers, they were on their way to help suppress the savages. They were obviously trying to provoke us, but we did not rise to the bait. We just wanted to get home to our families.

When I disembarked from the train in Winnipeg, I spotted Genevieve standing at the end of the platform holding a swaddled baby in one hand and Angélique's hand in the other. It broke my heart momentarily when Angélique hid behind her mother's leg, but I coaxed her out, and then she seemed to remember me and jumped into my arms. I lifted her up, and Genevieve lifted the blanket to show me my son's face.

"Merde!" I gasped, then quickly laughed when I saw Genevieve's shocked expression.

"Tabernac, you shit!" She cried and punched my arm, but she was grinning at my joke.

"He is perfect," I said, rubbing my arm as we walked to the wagon. "Where is Norbert?"

Genevieve lowered her head and said, "He has joined the Métis."

"What do you mean, 'he has joined the Métis'?"

"He is fighting with Dumont and Riel."

"Shit!" I cursed and then glanced guiltily at Angélique, who continued to cling to me.

"I tried to talk him out of it, but he wouldn't listen. Jacque?"

"Yeah?"

"Can you go get him and bring him home?"

I looked at her and saw the worry on her face. The last thing I wanted to do was leave home so soon after returning, but he was family.

"Alright."

I spent an entire day at home and then prepared to leave once again. Angélique's crying broke my heart, and I almost changed my mind and stayed home. But in the end, Genevieve pried Angélique's arms from my leg, and I climbed aboard our wagon.

25

After all these years, the memory of leaving Angélique that day still seemed to evoke tears in Jacque. He paused his story and looked away, wiping his eyes.

Edward cleared his throat and checked his pocket watch. "It's an hour or so before the dinner seating. Do you need a break, or do you want to continue for a little while longer?"

"I am nearing the end of my story; let's finish it."

* * *

In Winnipeg, I learned the Métis rebels were massing at the village of Batoche, and that is where I decided to go look for Norbert. The fastest route was by rail from Winnipeg to Qu'Appelle and then on horseback north to Batoche. I loaded my horse onto a boxcar full of several other horses that I later learned belonged to Canadian militiamen. I would have to avoid these men as much as possible during the train ride. Animosity toward the Métis and Indians was high among the militia and, truth be told, among most of the white citizenry. I sat in the back, slouched low in my seat, and hid behind a newspaper whenever someone walked by. But I could not hide forever, and I got some hard looks when I unloaded my horse at Qu'Appelle. Before anyone could approach me, I mounted and rode away at a gallop. Looking over my shoulder, I saw a few militiamen pointing my way and hurrying to unload their mounts.

The following seven days were spent avoiding the militia and the North-West Mounted Police. However, the people that did confront me turned out to be the Métis themselves. I had been looking over my shoulder, checking to see if I had any followers, and not seeing any, I turned forward and quickly reined my horse into a skidding stop. Riding quickly toward me were twelve heavily armed Métis.

"Where are you going in such a hurry, friend?" one of them – the leader, judging by his demeanor – asked.

"Batoche."

"Why are you going there?"

"I am looking for my brother-in-law."

"And what will you do when you find him?"

"Take him home; we have no fight with the government."

"Are you with the government?" he asked, and twelve rifles swung toward me.

"No, I am a farmer looking after my family."

"What is your name?"

"Jacque Daoust. I have a farm at St. Francois Xavier."

"Then you know Pelletier?"

"Isidore? Yes, he is my neighbor."

"So, you are Métis; you will come and fight with us." It was not a suggestion.

"I am a Métis, but I will not fight."

"Then we will have to consider you an enemy of the Métis. Are you an enemy of our cause, Jacque?" he asked and cocked his rifle.

"What is your cause?" I asked.

I knew it was because of the Canadian government surveying the Red River Valley. I, too, was worried they would take Theophile's land and evict us, but I wanted to see if these men knew what they were fighting for. They did. The leader stated the same worries about losing their farms as I held.

"Now, you will join us? We will give you a weapon when we arrive in Batoche."

"I don't see how I have any other choice."

"Bon! I am Joseph," the leader said. "Hey, why were you looking behind you?"

"Militiamen. They have been chasing me since Qu'Appelle."

"So, you have led them here?"

"No, they were already coming here; it is no secret the Métis are at Batoche."

"How many?"

"Militia? Hundreds, I would guess."

They looked at each other with concern, then turned their horses, and we rode away at a gallop. Two of them stayed close behind me. So, that was my conscription into the rebellion. When we got to Batoche, I was ordered to help dig a rifle pit on the banks of the South Saskatchewan River. There was still some frost in the ground, and I was given a pickaxe. I did not see Norbert, but the Métis had numerous rifle pits beside the river and near heavily wooded areas along the trails into town. After a day of digging, I was sent with a crew of men to chop trees for fortifying the rifle pits.

It was there that I spotted Norbert; the trees were still leafless, and it was not hard to differentiate the huge man from the others. They were sure making good use of his muscle. I saw him effortlessly carrying a green log out of the woods on his shoulder while two stout men struggled to carry a similar log. He was several hundred yards away and didn't hear my shouts. But now that I knew he was here, I could wait for the right time to approach him. Norbert would resist my request to leave and go home. I was sure of that.

Early the following day, I was in a rifle pit, muscling a log into place with another man, when we heard a ship's horn. A rifle and ammunition bag were thrust at me, and I joined the men at the front of the pit. The pits were basically a wedge dug into the earth. They sloped from ground level down at about a thirty-degree angle until it was four feet deep. Then three rows of logs were placed above the deep end. Gaps were left between the first and second row, which we could shoot through, and I found a spot in the middle. Through the gap, we saw a steamship puffing toward us, its horn blaring so loud it hurt my ears. I could see sacks of grain and hay bales stacked on the deck, so that was where I aimed when the firing started. The sound was deafening; most guns were lever-action rifles, although mine was a single-shot carbine. The ship ran the gauntlet between rifle pits on both banks. Several of the men beside me climbed out of the pit and followed the boat, firing from the river bank. I soon realized this may be a good opportunity for me to go in search of Norbert.

So, I followed my pit mates, occasionally firing into the water below the ship, and waited for my chance to slip away. And then, all of a sudden, there was a shriek and groan of tortured metal followed by two whumps as the ship's smokestacks crashed to the boat's deck. It was then I saw the ferry cable that had been strung high for just that purpose. At the sight of the damaged ship, the Métis cheered and the Indians whooped their war cries.

What's that, Edward?

Yes, there were many Indians taking part in the fight.

Anyway, guns continued firing at the ship as it floated downstream. It seemed to have lost its steering as it slewed first one way and then the other. When the boat was out of rifle range, I realized I had been so mesmerized by the sight of the floundering ship that had I missed my chance to sneak away. I was ordered back to the rifle pit. I was the only one sent back there while the others were moved into positions along the trails leading into Batoche. I was considering my options when I heard the first shots from the east. A rattling fire erupted as if a gun was shooting nonstop and was followed by thumps of cannon fire. It made me shudder. Should I stay there and continue watching the river for more ships or join the battle in hopes of finding Norbert?

After an hour or so, I could not stay still any longer. The gunfire from the east had been steady and intense.

"To hell with this," I declared to no one.

My mind made up, I climbed the incline out of the rifle pit and ran low along the riverbank toward the fight.

"Hey!"

I jumped and then felt relief when I saw a small group of Métis and Cree Indians. A Métis man was waving me over. There was a sense of urgency in his motions, so I ran at a crouch to him.

"Where are you going?" he asked.

"To the battle," I answered.

"Come with us," he said, and then he ran along the river and the others followed.

"Where are we going?" I asked a Cree man in the rear when I caught up to them.

He responded by holding a finger to his lips, silencing me. We followed the river until we came to a ridge on our right. When we climbed the hill, I saw what looked like a cannon, but the barrel looked funny. Then I saw flames and smoke coming out of several rifle barrels that rotated around the center barrel, followed by the staccato of shots I had heard earlier. How was that possible?

"What is that?" I asked.

"Rababou."

"Eh?" I was not familiar with this word.

"Noisemaker," he said. "We are going to capture it."

I wondered how. As soon as the man firing the noisemaker saw us, he would no doubt turn that fearsome weapon on us. I now know the rababou, or noisemaker – what I thought looked like a cannon barrel with rifle barrels all around it – was actually called a Gatling gun.

So, we ran toward the Gatling gun crew with the intent of capturing the gun, hopefully before they saw us coming, when all of a sudden, other Métis fighters began shooting across our path toward the Gatling gun crew. We had run into a cross fire. We immediately dropped to the ground and then crawled back to safety. That was a close call, almost getting hit by friendly fire. When we made it back to the river, we followed it until we came up behind the cemetery.

* * *

"Excuse me, Jacque," Edward said, "was the battle in the village or on the prairie?"

"Both. We had some rifle pits out on the prairie, but the church and cemetery are at the south end of the village."

"Ah, I see, thank you. Please continue."

***

So, then we climbed the bank and approached the graveyard when suddenly I heard a thunderclap. I looked skyward for storm clouds, but the sky was clear. Then the earth erupted before us, and we dropped to the ground and covered our heads as frozen clumps of dirt rained down on us. The thunderclaps came one after the other, and we were afraid to move. Then we saw one of the cannons come closer, but as luck would have it, its barrel exploded, and that was all the opportunity we needed to make our escape back to the river.

We were badly outgunned. Sitting under cover behind the river bank, I refocused on my intent here. It was not to fight; it was to bring Norbert home before he got himself killed. But where was he?

It was late afternoon when I saw a line of smoke across a ravine. The unmistakable smell of burning grass hung in the air. Soon, we heard gunfire and the rat-a-tat of the Gatling gun. When next there was a lull in the fighting, I snuck away from the group I was with and resumed my search for Norbert. Then I thought I heard distant drums, so I stopped and cocked an ear westward. There was drumming! I was elated to know more Indians were preparing to join the fight.

Why was I elated?

Had I subconsciously picked a side and embraced the rebellion?

I had no quarrel with the Canadian government, and I certainly had no fight with the Métis. I was just a farmer trying to make a living. Maybe I felt elation thinking that if we drove the North-West Police and militia back, then Norbert would be safe and I could take him home. Yet I still felt joy in the fact that reinforcements were coming and that victory was possible. So maybe I did pick a side in this fight after all.

Anyway, I worked my way past the church and looked over the bank. I could see the North-West forces were constructing a zareba in a field to the east. A zareba looks like a large coral reef and was made by plowing a large circle, mounding the perimeter with the excavated soil and sod, and then fortifying it further by encircling it with hay bales and wagons. The police were setting up camp there, on the bald prairie. I suspected it would be suicidal for the Métis or Indians to attempt a frontal assault against it.

"Have you seen a large man?" I asked a nearby Métis fighter. "His name is Norbert."

"I know Norbert, but I haven't seen him since this morning."

"Where was he when you saw him?"

"In one of the north rifle pits. Why are you looking for Norbert?" he asked.

"He is my brother-in-law; I want to make sure he is alright so I can rest easy tonight."

Although this was true, my real intent would not have been well received. But then, I thought, taking him home during a fight would permanently damage our personal relationship and our reputations within the Métis community. On the other hand, staying may result in our deaths, either on the battlefield or as prisoners facing possible execution. I already knew getting Norbert to leave may not be possible anyway. Should I stay with him? If we both died, Genevieve would be left alone with two children to look after.

"Sorry, I don't know where he is, but you had better get some rest. No telling when the fighting will start up again."

I nodded and then looked for a dry place to lay down.

The Indians harassed the zareba all night with steady rounds of gunfire at ten-minute intervals. Yet, surprisingly, I slept through the night until the cannons woke me at first light.

All morning, the cannons boomed, the Gatling gun chattered, and the rifles cracked. Then, I saw a contingent of Sioux arrive and take up position near the cemetery. So now there were Cree, Assiniboine, and Sioux Indians on the side of the Métis.

We might win this fight after all.

Early that evening, the order to harass the soldiers was given. Even though my life had been threatened for two days by these soldiers, I was still determined not to harm them. So, I spent the evening pretending to be constantly on the move to cover the fact that I wasn't engaging the soldiers. Exhausted by the subterfuge, I sat down on an old tree stump to rest when a group of Sioux in full war paint passed by my spot. I supposed all the dirt and grime on my face was my war paint. Although, I suspected these warriors would disagree. I watched them as they walked past me and one of them seemed vaguely familiar. Did I know him? I didn't see how that could be possible. The only Indians I knew were Sitting Bull's followers, but most of them went back to Montana. Although, I had heard that a few did go north.

Could it be —? Nah.

After a supper of dried meat, I decided to work my way to the northern positions where Norbert was last seen. I followed the top of the ravine and ran low on this exposed path, but no bullets came. I was almost to the north line when I was tackled to the ground.

"Are you daft, man?"

"Maybe a little," I grunted.

"Huh. Well, you could have been shot up there."

"I could get shot anywhere, Norbert."

Norbert had a distinctive body odor, not particularly offensive, but the big man sweated profusely, even when resting. And his heavy body was now on top of me. There was no mistaking that much weight.

"What?" he rolled off me and looked at me closely, confusion on his face.

"It's me, Jacque."

"Jacque, what are you doing here? I thought you were in Africa."

"I was, and then I came to get you."

"Get me? I'm not leaving. Wait, did Genevieve send you?"

I thought about it and decided not to tell him, lest it create bad feelings between them.

"No, I need you back at the farm now that you have a niece and a nephew there."

"A nephew!" Norbert whooped. "It's a boy?"

"Nephews usually are."

"Well, that is great news, but I can't leave while we are in the middle of a fight."

"Once this fight is over, win or lose, will you come home with me?" I could see there was no way I could convince him to leave right away, so I offered the alternative.

"Uh, I guess."

Not very convincing, but it was better than nothing, and from what I'd learned over these last few days, this battle was probably the resistance's last stand, and it was not going well so far.

The following day started out calm. Several Métis had approached me asking if I had any extra ammunition. I had told them I was running short too. Norbert had taken it upon himself to be my protector, which was a strange reversal of roles after I had helped guide him into adulthood.

At midmorning, the order came down the line to retreat toward the church. Shortly after we arrived, we heard Gatling and cannon fire coming from the area we had just left. But by noon, it once again became quiet. Then all hell broke out. It was a mass attack; infantry, cavalry, and artillery opened fire on us. Soon, all of us, Métis and Indians alike, were running perilously low on ammunition and had to fall back toward the village. I was running beside Norbert when something punched into my rear, making me stumble and fall on my face. Norbert stopped, scooped me up, and threw me effortlessly over his shoulder. I watched the ground go by as I bounced upside down on his shoulder, all the time expecting another bullet to slam into me. He ran into a firing pit along the river's bank, near the one I had been in when we had fired on the ship. That seemed like weeks ago instead of days. He set me down gently on my stomach near one of the sidewalls. We heard someone approach, and Norbert turned his rifle to the top of the pit's slope. A Mountie appeared, rifle at the ready, and Norbert shot him. The policeman grunted and fell to his knees before pitching forward and rolling down the slope into our pit. He landed at the feet of an Indian we had not noticed until now, and there was another Indian lying behind the first. I held up my hand in a gesture of friendship. The Indian nodded and knelt beside his friend and whispered something to him. Norbert kept his rifle pointed at the Mountie who was moaning and clutching his shoulder. Norbert whispered out of the corner of his mouth, "My gun is empty." All of a sudden, the kneeling Indian began to sing.

* * *

"Sorry, gentlemen," a porter said as he approached their table, "but we must prepare the tables for the supper seating."

"Yes, of course," Jacque said and rose from his chair.

Edward gathered his journals and pencils and followed Jacque out of the car.

26

On their way back to their seats, Tom had informed Edward that his party wanted to spend the evening together, so further interviews would have to wait until the following day. Edward was okay with that; he had a lot of notes to review and draft into readable copy. What bothered Edward most was having to spend time with that deplorable family. His anger rose when he arrived at his booth and found the little boy stretched out asleep on his seats, his newspapers scattered on the floor.

"What the hell?" he shouted at the parents.

"I'm sorry, he was exhausted," the woman, Jane, said. Fred looked like he was about to rise and punch Edward on the nose before Jane placed a restraining hand on his wrist. She then stood and lifted the boy who woke and immediately began wailing. Passengers from nearby booths glared at Edward, who ignored them, gathered up the newspapers, sat down, and arranged his journals beside him.

"Is there a problem here?" the conductor asked.

"These people keep using my seat against my wishes," Edward responded, waving a dismissive hand toward the family.

"If you're not using them, what's the problem?"

"I paid for these seats!"

The conductor turned to the couple and said with an apologetic shrug, "I am sorry, but he is right; please respect his space."

"Asshole," Fred muttered in Edward's direction after the conductor had left.

Ignoring the comment, Edward closed his eyes and waited for the call for supper. As he sorted through the three men's stories in his head, the clickety-clack of the steel wheels on iron rails gradually lulled him to sleep. His own loud snoring woke him with a jerk.

"I hope you're not going to snore like that all night," Fred said with disgust when Edward looked his way.

"Oh, probably," Edward said. "I have been told I snore loudly from the time I fall asleep until I wake up in the morning. So, you are in for a treat."

"Asshole," Fred mumbled again. This time the boy giggled and cried, "Asshole!"

"Basil!" Jane cried and grabbed his arm.

Edward smirked.

"That does it," bellowed Fred, who jumped up and grabbed Edward by the lapels and dragged him to his feet. He bent low so he could be nose-to-nose with Edward and began cursing him.

"You should learn to brush your teeth; your breath smells like carrion," Edward said when there was a break in Fred's cursing.

Fred's eyes bulged, and he brought his right fist back for a punch when the conductor grabbed his wrist.

"There will be none of that, sir," he said to Fred.

"This – this person –" Fred sputtered. "Get him away from my family."

The conductor seemed to consider this, then his eyes lit up.

"Sir, there is an empty table in the first-class lounge," he said to Edward. "You could attend the first-class supper seating, if you wish? But you will still have to use your sleeping berth here, I'm afraid. Would that be acceptable to you?"

"It would be," Edward replied with a smile.

He had walked through the first-class lounge and had debated upgrading his fare to the exorbitant first-class price, but back then, the sleeper car had seemed adequate.

"Hey, how come he gets upgraded to first-class?" Fred complained. "He's the one causing all the problems here."

"Well, sir, there is limited room in first-class, enough for one person, not a family," the conductor said, "and you get the extra seats here."

This seemed to appease Fred, who looked at his wife and returned her nod. "Fine by me."

Now, this was better! Thought Edward. Thank you, Basil, you little shite.

Edward sat in a luxuriously upholstered armchair and was immediately waited on by a waiter clad in a crisp white uniform.

"Can I get you anything, sir?"

"Could I get a snifter of brandy?"

"Of course, sir."

Edward followed the brandy with forty-year-old scotch as he worked on the stories, trying to organize them chronologically. He realized that, as much as he trusted these men, he should check historical facts. That would be time-consuming. Ah, to hell with it. He'd just tell Harper's that he had. If they didn't believe him, they could check the facts themselves. After they'd paid him, of course.

Long after supper, the setting of the sun, and several more glasses of scotch, the waiter informed Edward that the lounge was closing for the evening. He then handed Edward a leather folder resembling a billfold.

"What is this?" Edward slurred.

"Your bill, sir, for the drinks."

"They weren't complimentary?"

"No, sir."

Edward lifted the flap and gawked at the amount. It was almost as much as his original fare.

"I didn't drink that much!"

"Yes, sir, you did," the waiter said, "and I did not include the one you knocked over."

Edward grumbled but reluctantly paid the waiter and then attempted to stand. Fortunately, the waiter caught him when he threatened to fall over the table.

"Do you need assistance to your berth, sir?"

"Hell, no," Edward slurred, "I'm not drunk."

He focused all his attention on appearing sober as he staggered toward the sleeper car.

"I have been informed that your bed has been turned down, sir," the waiter said and then rushed to find the conductor and inform him a man would need assistance getting into his sleeping berth.

Edward stopped in front of the latrine door and tried to slide the door lock. It wouldn't budge, so he tried again, rattling the mechanism.

"It's occupied," came a call from within.

Edward, swaying, closed one eyed and peered at the round cylinder above the door latch, which displayed the word "occupied." Suddenly, Edward's urge to urinate increased in intensity. He rattled the lock once more.

"Hold your horses!"

"I don't have any horses," Edward shouted, snickered, then cursed when he felt his bladder threaten to release.

"Hurry up!"

The door flew open, an angry-looking man emerged, and Edward immediately pushed him aside as he forced his way into the latrine. He fumbled with his trouser fly as he hopped from one foot to the other, barely noticing the wetness on the front of his pants. Urine streamed across the wall before finally hitting the commode as he fumbled with his aim. As a steady stream splashed into the toilet and on the seat, Edward accompanied the sound with an off-key rendition of a song he had once heard in a smoky barroom in Saskatoon. His bladder finally empty, Edward stumbled out of the latrine and into the arms of the conductor who grimaced at the condition of both Edward and the interior of the commode.

"You will have to stop singing, sir," the conductor told him. "There are other passengers who are trying to sleep."

"Of course," Edward slurred, putting a finger to his lips. "You are a good man; did you know that?"

"Yes, sir, I am aware."

When they got to Edward's booth, the conductor struggled to help him up into his overhead sleeping bunk all the while trying to avoid coming into contact with the wet spot on the front of Edward's trousers.

"Dammit, can't you move him somewhere else?" Fred grumbled from the lower bunk he, his wife, and his son were crammed onto. "Toss him in baggage; he won't know the difference."

The conductor chuckled softly, but Edward was already asleep and snoring like a Swede saw cutting through a tin roof.

"Good Christ; the man just keeps finding new ways to irritate me!" Fred cried, and despite the situation, ripples of laughter floated throughout the car.

* * *

"Where's our little friend?" Tom asked the next day when his group prepared to go to the dining car for lunch.

"I don't know; maybe he's busy writing our stories," Jacque replied.

"I don't trust the man; there's something sleazy about him," Genevieve said.

"Yeah, I get that feeling too," Annie agreed.

"Did you all sign that agreement that lawyer, Carmichael, wrote?" Genevieve asked the men.

"No, not yet," Jacque replied.

"Well, you had better! We paid the lawyer out of our vacation money. Don't tell Edward anything else until you get a signed copy."

"Yeah, okay." Jacque rarely argued with Genevieve when she used a certain tone.

"Sleazy man, makes my skin crawl," she said and punctuated it with a shudder.

"I thought he was okay," White Dove said quietly.

"No, I agree with Genevieve," Annie said. "There is definitely something shifty about him."

Edward didn't leave his seat until the following day when they disembarked at Toronto's Union Station. As always, White Dove gaped at the grandeur of these types of buildings. She stood inside and turned in a slow circle, gazing up at the high interior ceiling while the others waited for her with smiles on their faces.

"Edward, there you are!" Jacque said, spotting the writer walking toward them.

"Yes, I have been under the weather."

"Was it something you ate or possibly drank?" Tom said with a raised eyebrow.

"Maybe," Edward replied. "When can we meet for more of your stories?"

"I'm sorry, Edward, it will have to be on the New York train," Jacque said, glancing at Genevieve. "We have plans for our time in Toronto."

"Yes, and we will need a signed copy of the agreement before any more stories are told," Genevieve added.

"Of course," Edward said. "I can sign now if you wish."

"It can wait; I'm not going to dig through the luggage here," Genevieve said.

"Okay, well, I guess I will see you all in two days," Edward said. "Enjoy your stay."

They watched him walk away.

"Did you smell him?" Annie whispered just loud enough for the others to hear.

"Yes, it's the same smell drunks have after an extended drinking bout," Tom said.

"Great, not only is he sleazy but he's also a drunk," Genevieve muttered.

27

The following day, Doyle arrived in Toronto. But, to his annoyance, the ticket agent here wasn't going to be intimidated, as there seemed to be a police presence in the station more often than not. And, as luck would have it, two policemen came strolling by as Doyle stood at the ticket counter. They looked at Doyle longer than what he thought was necessary, so he walked away, glancing over his shoulder before going around a corner. The policemen were talking to the ticket agent.

So, Doyle had a decision to make: try to find Edward in the city or wait here to see if he boarded another train. If Doyle left the station, he might miss Edward leaving town. On the other hand, if he stayed, Edward may never show up. Another option occurred to him: question the hansom cabdrivers. It would cost him, but it seemed the best opportunity open to him.

The third one remembered the bespectacled traveler. The foolish driver demanded five dollars to disclose where he had taken Edward. Doyle, short on patience at this point, dragged the driver from his cab and began beating him.

"Tell me where you dropped the man or you will die here!"

"Queen's Hotel," the trembling man lisped through broken lips.

"There, now was the so—" Doyle began but was tackled by a burly Irish policeman before he could finish his sentence.

The force of the hit threw Doyle several feet past the astonished cabdriver, who clambered onto his cab and snapped the reins, intent on putting as much distance between himself and Doyle as fast as he could. Meanwhile, Doyle and the cop rolled on the concrete, punching away at each other. They were both tough Irishmen and seasoned fighters, neither giving any quarter. That was until Doyle rolled on top and cocked his fist for a devastating punch. But before he could deliver it, a boot kicked his head, knocking him out cold before he hit the concrete.

"About fekking time, Owen!" Constable Paddy O'Shaughnessy cried.

"Ah, Paddy, you know you were enjoying the fight," Owen Gwynne, also a city of Toronto police constable, replied.

"Aye, that I was," Paddy said. "Come on, let's get this arsehole into the wagon before he wakes up."

Doyle woke several hours later in a jail cell full of other toughs. He stood and patted his pockets, finding them empty.

"Which one of you slimy rodents took my money?" he roared at the suddenly wary group.

"No one, you fekking idjit," one brave soul said. "The guards emptied your pockets before putting you in here."

"Hmph," Doyle grunted and then sat down, holding his head.

Two hours later, he began shaking the bars and yelling to be released. Finally, the door to the cell area opened, and the Irish cop he had fought in the street came strutting in, grinning at Doyle.

"Oy," the constable said, "are you enjoying the accommodations?"

"Let me out of here, gobshite!"

"Aye, I will do that, but only when you are to appear before the judge, not before, boyo."

"The judge? For what?" Doyle demanded.

"For breaking the cabdriver's cheekbone, idjit."

"When?"

"Are you daft, man? Earlier this morning, before I laid a beating on you."

"No, ya dumb copper, when do I go before the judge?" Doyle said.

"Tomorrow, maybe the day after."

"What? I can't stay here that long!"

"Well, me bucko, it may be longer by another day, depending on his honor's mood."

"Fek you!"

"And you as well."

Doyle spent a sleepless night sitting in a corner, not daring to close his eyes in the presence of the rough crowd in the holding cell. So, when the Irish cop and his partner, the one who had kicked Doyle in the head, came to take him to court, he was too exhausted to make a fuss. Doyle watched the Irish cop, who he learned was named Paddy O'Shaughnessy when he was sworn in, read the charges against Doyle to the judge. After hearing the details of the assault, the judge asked Paddy how much money Doyle had had on him when they had arrested him. Paddy told him, and the judge said to Doyle, "What a coincidence, that is how much your fine is."

"What!" roared Doyle before quickly saying in a lower voice, "Sorry, sir. Thank you."

"You are welcome," the judge said. "By the way, are you familiar with the city of Toronto's bylaws?"

"No, sir."

"Well, one of them deals with vagrancy."

"Huh?"

"It means if you are stopped and searched by the police, such as Paddy or Owen here, and you have no money on your person, you will be arrested for vagrancy."

"So, I am supposed to run once I'm released?"

"Yes, and you shouldn't stop running until you get back to wherever you crawled out from," the judge said and then slammed his gavel down. "Next!"

Paddy led Doyle to the exit and said, "I will give you a half hour head start, boyo!"

This time, Doyle kept his mouth shut; freedom was just a few steps away, after all.

Doyle stepped onto the sidewalk, turned, and headed straight for the Queen's Hotel.

"I'm looking for Edward Humphries; he is a guest here," Doyle said as nicely as he could to the front desk manager.

"I'm sorry, sir, Mr. Humphries checked out this morning."

"Ah, darn," Doyle lamented, trying, with a herculean effort, to appear polite. "Would you know where he went? I, uh, need to find him; there is a family emergency."

The man snapped his fingers, and the doorman scurried over.

"Do you remember Mr. Humphries?" the manager asked.

"Short man, scratched up face?"

"Yes, that's him. Did you hail a cab for him?"

"No," the doorman said, "I offered, but he said he was going to walk to the station."

"The train station?" Doyle asked.

"Yes, he was quite excited to see New York City."

"New York?"

"That's what he said," the doorman confirmed. "You'd never catch me going to New York, let me tell you."

Doyle turned and walked toward the door without another word.

"Well, that was rude," the doorman said.

"Why wouldn't you want to go to New York?" the manager asked.

Doyle stepped through the door and couldn't hear the rest of the inane conversation between the two pompous arses. So, now he was presented with another problem: how would he get to New York City with no money?

28

While Doyle was leaving the Queen's Hotel, Edward was sitting on a bench on the platform at Union Station waiting to board the train to New York City. The train was sitting quiet alongside the platform, but he was not able to board yet. For the fifth time since arriving at the station, Edward patted his suit pocket, verifying his boarding pass was still safely tucked inside. He suppressed a smile, thankful that, after disembarking two days earlier, he had had the forethought to purchase a private sleeper car for this leg of the journey.

Edward gently ran his fingers over the blood-encrusted scrapes on his face and groaned as he replayed the events of the previous night in his mind. He remembered spending the evening drinking in a series of barrooms, each descending deeper into disrepute as the night progressed, until he had found himself in a distinctly seedy taproom. Edward groaned again as he remembered playing the big shot and slapping dollar bills onto bars, buying drinks for anyone who would listen to his boasts of writing for a national magazine. Faces of drunks, bartenders, and the doormen who had tossed him into the street when he had become unruly, flashed through his mind. One of the last memories of the night was being led into an alley by a woman of ill repute who had offered him her services.

As Edward replayed the incident, he suddenly remembered the gravel surface of the alley coming at him at great speed and then the impact of the side of his face hitting the ground. He recalled his ears had rung upon impact. Someone must have pushed him from behind, and then the lady and a man Edward remembered as being the bar's bouncer had begun rifling through his pockets as he had lain face down on the ground. When they had rolled him onto his back, Edward had made a feeble attempt to fight off the pair, and the last memory of the night was the man's fist coming toward his face.

Edward shuddered at the memory of the stray dog who had woken him by licking the dried blood from his face. He had pushed the malnourished animal away, sat up, and grabbed his head as the breaking dawn's early light had seared his eyes. Intense pain had stabbed through his head with each beat of his heart. Not surprisingly, his pockets had all been turned out, everything gone. They had even taken the shoes he had purchased in Winnipeg. As Edward recalled stumbling into the street, he remembered being grateful for two things: one, he had wisely left the majority of his funds in the hotel's safe, and two, the city had not yet begun to stir. But the adventure had left him physically scarred.

Glancing to his right, Edward saw Little Crow and the others approaching and wondered how they were going to react when they saw his face and, how was he going to try and explain it away. The group stopped short when they saw Edward sitting on the bench, angry red scrapes on his cheek glowing like beacons below a swelled purple eye.

"What happened to you, Edward?" Tom asked.

"An unfortunate encounter with ruffians."

"Did you report it to the authorities?"

"No, I saw no reason. They didn't get much, and I was not going to stay in this city any longer than I had to."

"Hmph." Tom was obviously not satisfied with Edward's response.

Genevieve and Annie's suspicious looks were also not lost on Edward. But he didn't care about them, just so long as he got their husbands' stories.

"I have a private berth where we can finish the stories," Edward said, hoping to change the subject.

"Uh, before we do that, there are a few things we need to discuss first," Tom said.

"Oh?" Edward asked.

"Yes, we need to have the agreement signed before continuing, and we want to be there when you present the stories to Harper's Magazine, or any other firm, for that matter. Also, we will accompany you to the bank to cash the check and receive our share of the funds," Tom said. "Is that agreeable to you?"

"Yes." Edward was disappointed but knew he had no choice in the matter. He had toyed with the idea of skipping out on them with all the funds but then realized they may complain to the magazine. "Do you have the agreement handy?"

"I have it in my bag," Annie said.

"Little Crow, Jacque, and I will meet you in your booth for the signing once we are all settled and the train is underway," Tom said.

"Perfect. Little Crow, could you continue with your story after the signing?" Edward asked.

"Yeah, sure."

An hour later, Edward, Little Crow, Tom, and Jacque gathered in Edward's private booth and signed two copies of the agreement. Tom and Jacque left with their copy of the contract, and Little Crow settled in to continue his story.

* * *

It was an early morning in July of 1883, and I was near Beaver Creek when I saw a dozen Indians on horseback. A hunting party by the look of them. That morning, I had had good luck harvesting a lone buffalo cow that was now dressed and wrapped on a travois behind my pony. It was more food than I needed; my hunger that day was for human interaction. So, coming to a decision and making sure my rifle was fully loaded, I walked my pony in their direction.

I had come across these Indians before, but I had avoided them, not knowing their intentions against intruders in their territory. I was a third of the way to them when they spotted me. I raised my right hand in greeting, and I was relieved to see a few of them return the gesture. When I reached them, I was surprised to hear them speaking Dakota Sioux.

"I have meat to share," I said in Lakota, which equally surprised them. Although Dakota and Lakota are dialects of the Siouan language, they differ somewhat, mainly in pronunciation.

"Who are you?"

"I am Little Crow, son of Tall Pony and Morning Star."

"You are Lakota?"

"Arapaho."

"I am White Hawk," one of them said. "Are you the Arapaho Little Crow who fought at Greasy Grass?"

"Yes, with Crazy Horse."

Whoops erupted, and they dismounted and approached me with outstretched hands. I received many slaps on my back from the grinning hunters.

"Did you kill many soldiers?"

"No, but I counted coup on twenty soldiers."

"You will come and be our guest; Chief White Cap will want to meet you."

"Okay." I remembered what happened the last time I was invited to an Indian encampment. Although, this time, I didn't expect a huge encampment like the one at Greasy Grass. They looked at the bundle of meat and one cried, "We will have a feast!" I noticed how thin these men were; some had protruding ribs.

Because of the food I provided, I was heartily welcomed into the camp, which was even smaller than I had expected, maybe fifty lodges. As promised, I was led to Chief White Cap's tipi and told to wait outside. White Hawk stood outside the door flap after announcing himself and was then told to enter. A few minutes later, Chief White Cap himself came out and approached me.

"Are you truly Little Crow, the Arapaho?"

"Yes. I bring you a gift of buffalo meat."

"It pleases me," White Cap said. "I have heard Sitting Bull left Wood Mountain last year. Where have you been all this time?"

"An hour's ride south of here, along the river."

"How come we haven't seen you?"

"I have the eyes of an eagle; I spotted your warriors before they could see me. Because I did not know if I would be welcome, I avoided your hunters."

"Huh. And you fought Long Hair at Greasy Grass?"

"Yes."

White Cap nodded, turned, and addressed the crowd that had gathered around us. "Tonight, we will feast in honor of our guest, Little Crow, the Arapaho warrior!"

It pleased me to have provided meat to the tribe; I had seen the look of hunger on the older warriors and the children and suspected they had probably been surviving mostly on what fish the river gave up.

"You will tell us stories of your brave deeds tonight," the chief shouted for all to hear.

I did not look forward to that.

So, we danced until the meal was served, and then it was a chorus of smacking lips, groans, and sighs as we ate. Several dogs lurked around us, waiting for a scrap of meat to fall, and when one did, a dog would snatch it up with lightning speed and lope away, growling at the dogs who chased him. Finally, when we could eat no more, we rested.

A man was shaking my shoulder, dragging me from the depths of sleep. When I sat up, he said, "White Cap is waiting for your stories."

"Okay."

"He expects you to play out your stories."

"What do you mean?"

"Well, if you are telling about fighting someone, you have to show your movements, like a dance."

"Ah, hie," I cried, not looking forward to making a fool of myself.

For the next several hours, I told them of my struggles over the last few years. I first told them about the Battle at Greasy Grass where Crazy Horse had given me the eagle feather. Then I described the attack at Slim Buttes and the siege in the cave with American Horse. Next was the march to Deadwood, the escape from the jail with Zeke, and the fights with the Crow. Finally, I told them of my time with Sitting Bull at Wood Mountain. I was shy to perform the movements at first, but I really got into it after hearing the cheers and laughter from my hosts. I had noticed a girl watching me and being teased by her friends. I smiled and looked directly at her, which caused her friends to shriek and poke at her. I really put on a show then, and the crowd cheered louder. Finally, exhausted, I fell to the ground and said, "That is all."

White Cap asked, "How many snows have you seen, Little Crow?"

"Twenty-three."

"Twenty-three!" He cried. "You have had a lifetime of adventure, and you are only twenty-three?"

"Yes. And now, Chief White Cap," I said, "let's hear a few of your adventures."

A few people gasped, and then you could have heard a pin drop. White Cap's eyes grew, and then he laughed.

"That is only fair, my young friend," he cried, and whoops erupted from the gathered crowd.

White Cap spoke about his exploits in the Minnesota War alongside Chief Standing Buffalo and Chief Little Crow against the American army. He smiled at the mention of the chief who had the same name as me. By the time he had finished, dawn was beginning to break, and everyone slowly went to their lodges to sleep. I got up and took my pony to the river and then tied him to a sapling with plenty of grass within reach. Then, I took my blanket and lay down near him.

My eyes popped open, and my hand went to my knife. Someone was sneaking toward me. I closed my eyes to slits and watched the shape approach. It was a girl! And she was carrying a blanket. I pretended to sleep as she covered me with the blanket and then crept back to the camp. I smiled when I realized it was the shy girl.

It was afternoon when the camp awoke after the festivities of the previous night.

"Do you have a tipi, Little Crow?" White Cap asked.

We were walking among the tipis, White Cap, White Hawk, and I.

"No, I built a shelter of wood and sod."

"You are welcome to live here with us."

I nodded and said, "I will go there today and return tomorrow."

I had had enough of solitude.

"I will go with you, Little Crow," White Hawk said.

"That is good."

"I must leave you here," White Cap said. "I haven't danced like I did last night in many moons."

He did look weary, so we said our goodbyes, and he walked back toward his lodge.

"I will get some food for our journey," White Hawk said.

"No need, my friend; I have lots of food."

"You are a better hunter than us, Little Crow."

"No, I have food because I only had to hunt for one person."

He nodded, pleased with my response. Then, from a tipi fifty feet away, the shy girl emerged and stretched, straining her tunic.

"Who is that girl?"

White Hawk squinted in the direction I was pointing.

"Her?" he said. "That is White Dove; she is Rain in Face's woman."

"They are married?"

"No, but he has made his intentions known."

"Does she agree?"

"It doesn't matter; he is Rain in Face."

"Is he a chief?"

"No, but you do not say no to him."

"Why not?"

"He is a dangerous man."

"Where is he?"

"On a vision quest," White Hawk said. "I hope he dies out there; everyone is afraid of him."

Our path led us near where White Dove stood. I had the blanket she had covered me with that morning draped over my shoulders, and I do not know why, but I walked straight toward her. She lowered her head, shyly looking at her moccasins, and then I lifted one side of the blanket and held it out. Several gasps could be heard, and then she raised her eyes and looked with fear into mine. I smiled and kept the blanket raised until she took a deep breath and moved under it. Then I lowered the blanket over our heads and listened to the murmurs rippling through a suddenly large crowd of observers.

Under that blanket, White Dove warned me about Rain in Face, and I told her I would deal with him. She said she would marry me if I survived the expected encounter with Rain in Face.

"Are you crazy?" White Hawk asked when we walked away.

"Maybe," I said. "I need ponies to give to her father."

"I think I know where you might be able to trade for a couple of ponies."

"A couple is not enough, not for a woman with White Dove's beauty."

"Ah, okay," White Hawk said. "How many then?"

"Twenty."

"Twenty! For White Dove?" White Hawk cried, then quickly said, "Sorry, White Dove is indeed beautiful, but I have never heard of giving the father of the bride twenty horse before. Maybe five, at the most."

"No, it must be twenty."

"Okay then, tell me, how will you do that?"

"I don't suppose there's an enemy camp nearby?"

"No, there isn't. Why?"

"The way I see it, I will have to borrow twenty ponies from an unfriendly tribe."

"Why would an unfriendly tribe lend—oh."

White Hawk thought for a few seconds, then brightened and said, "There are Blackfeet to the west of here. I can take you there."

"They have ponies?"

"Yes, lots of ponies."

"I will get White Cap's permission first," I said. "Go get your pony and rifle, White Hawk."

He whooped, turned, and ran to the field where the ponies were grazing, and I walked to White Cap's lodge. I explained what I wanted to do and why. White Cap was reluctant to stir up hostilities with the Blackfoot Confederacy, but he eventually agreed, as long as we kept our identities hidden. He was also worried about what would happen when Rain in Face returned, so he told me to wait until I met Rain in Face before I left.

"I may not have to worry about Blackfoot revenge if you are not alive to make the raid," he said solemnly.

"I will be fighting for my future family; he will only be fighting for his pride," I responded.

"But Little Crow, Rain in Face will also be fighting for his future family and for his pride."

"Huh." I hadn't thought of that.

"Since Rain in Face has been on his quest, these last few days have been peaceful in our camp. But, as great a warrior he is, it would not be a bad thing if you won."

I nodded and stood to leave.

"His right knee," he said as I walked out the door. I stopped outside, but I couldn't go back in without being invited. Maybe that's why he had said it when he did.

His right knee.

I met White Hawk leading our ponies.

"We will have to wait, White Hawk, until I meet Rain in Face."

His face paled, then he turned around without responding, hung his head, and walked away. All that day and the following morning, I kept an eye on the horizon where White Hawk had said Rain in Face would come from.

* * *

A knock at the door interrupted Little Crow's recitation.

"Coffee or tea, sir?" a voice asked through the door.

"Would you like tea, Little Crow?" Edward asked.

"Yes!" Little Crow rubbed his hands together in anticipation.

Edward opened the door and ignored how the porter's head slightly jerked in reaction to seeing his face.

"Coffee for me," Edward said. "Two lumps and cream."

"Ooh, I'll have some of those cookies," Little Crow said, "and tea, black."

"I don't think tea ever gets black, Little Crow," Edward chuckled. "Just dark brown like swamp water."

"Eh?"

"Never mind."

They sat quietly and enjoyed their drinks. Edward watched as Little Crow poured some tea from his cup into the saucer, blew across its surface, and then tipped it to his lips. He smacked his lips after slurping all the tea from the saucer, sighed, and then dipped his cookies into the cup before eating them.

What an odd ritual.

29

Doyle sat and watched people walk by while he kept a wary eye out for policemen, particularly the one called Paddy.

Now there was a worthy foe!

He would have liked nothing better than to have another go at the man. But that would have to wait; for now, he had to come up with the money for a train ticket to New York. He wondered what had happened to his Winnipeg cousins. They hadn't met him at the station, and they obviously hadn't caught Edward for him.

Ah, well, he'd deal with those two knuckleheads on his way back to Saskatoon.

Doyle began walking and, not surprisingly, gravitated to the rougher side of town. Walking by one seedy-looking saloon, he spotted a help-wanted poster. "Bouncer required immediately," it read. He went inside and stood in the doorway until his eyes adjusted to the gloom. Then, seeing a man standing behind the bar, Doyle walked up to him and said, "I'm here about the bouncer job."

The bartender looked Doyle up and down, nodded, and said, "It pays fifty dollars a month."

"I only want to work tonight," Doyle said. "I need train fare."

"I don't normally hire someone for a day."

"Fine," Doyle said and turned to leave.

"Wait!" Ned, the bartender, called. "I'll give you two-fifty for the day."

"Five."

"Ah, alright, but you start now. We close at 2:00 a.m."

"Lunch and supper included."

"What?" Ned said, then sighed. "Fine."

Doyle looked around. There were only two old men nursing glasses of beer at separate tables. Shrugging, he took a seat near the door and waited. He needed more than five dollars for the train ticket, but his plan was to make up some excuse to bounce some men who looked to be flush with cash out of the bar and then rob them in the alley.

The day passed slowly, so slowly that Doyle at one point yawned mightily and began to question his decision to take the job. That all changed at ten in the evening when six burly rugby players, fresh off a hard-fought victory, with bruises and swellings on their faces to prove it, entered the bar.

Doyle sized them up and quickly determined they were not candidates for his bounce-and-rob plan. Any altercation with one would probably end up involving all of them. By midnight, the rugby team was getting rambunctious. Then three tough-looking men – shipyard workers, Doyle guessed – entered the bar, sat at a table, and ordered drinks. Doyle sighed when he saw one of the rugby players accidentally bump one of the shipyard workers on his way back from the toilet. Nothing would have come of it had the rugby player apologized, but he didn't.

"Hey, arsehole," the worker yelled. "Watch where you're walking."

The barroom went silent as the player turned.

"What did you call me?"

"Arsehole. Are you deaf, too?"

As one, the other five rugby players stood and advanced on the workers who, to their credit, did not back down.

Ah, shite.

Doyle pushed off the wall and went to intervene.

"Outside," he yelled.

"Fine by us," one of the players, maybe the team captain, said, and they filed out the back door.

"You boys are outnumbered," Doyle said in a low voice to the workers. "No one will think less of you if you leave out the front door."

"Fek that!" one said, and the other two, who seemed to have considered Doyle's suggestion, slowly followed their friend out the back door. Doyle saw the first worker slip a leather blackjack, called a sap by those who carry one, from his pocket.

Maybe they had a chance after all.

"You want me out there, boss?" he called to the bartender.

"Fek no, I don't care what happens outside my doors."

"Well, I'm taking my break, and I'm going out to watch."

"Suit yourself. Don't take long."

Doyle walked to the back door, stood on the sill, and leaned against the door jamb. He watched with a smirk as the two groups circled each other, throwing insults back and forth, but none seemed willing to make the first move.

"Bunch of fekking chickens," Doyle grunted.

The rugby players turned toward Doyle and began swearing at him. The worker with the blackjack took advantage of the diversion and rushed forward, slapping the weapon across one player's head, dropping him instantly. The others wasted no time, and they charged each other. Doyle grinned, now thoroughly enjoying the fight. The rugby team soon had the upper hand because of their numbers, but Doyle waited until the pummeling started to get out of hand before he stepped in.

"That's enough!" he yelled to no avail.

Fekkers!

Doyle stepped forward and dragged first one, then another rugby player off a worker. He was moving toward a third when the first two tackled him. He was soon overwhelmed as all the players jumped on him. They were kicking Doyle as he curled into a ball and then took the brunt of the kicks on his back and shins. Then the kicking stopped at the unmistakable sound of a bullet being jacked into a Winchester rifle.

"Be off with you lot before I start shooting," the bartender yelled.

The rugby players helped their unconscious teammate up, and then they limped down the alley, yelling and laughing, proud of their second victory that night. Doyle sat up, and the bartender tossed a five-dollar bill at him and told him to fek off.

Doyle picked up the money and looked at the three shipyard workers on the ground. They were beaten almost senseless, so he went to the man with the blackjack and pried it out of his hand. It would pair well with Doyle's prized set of brass knuckles. He rifled the man's pockets, took a wad of bills, and then moved to the next man.

"What the hell do you think you're doing?" the man cried, and Doyle whacked him over the head with the sap. He then rifled through this man's pockets as well as the third man's, coming away with a total of thirty-two dollars and sixty cents.

Not a bad haul; they must have just gotten paid.

Time to find a cheap hotel, somewhere to get cleaned up and catch some sleep.

I'm coming for you, Edward Humphries.

He patted the blackjack in his pocket and grinned.

* * *

When they finished their tea and set aside their cups, Edward asked Little Crow, "Shall we continue?"

"Yes."

* * *

It was midday when I saw dust rising above the distant horizon. Rain in Face was coming. I stood near my pony and watched him ride by. He looked at me for a long time as he passed, turning in his saddle before looking forward and continuing on. He was a formidable-looking man, tall and muscular with a knife scar on one cheek and a bent nose from an old break.

How long would it take for him to find out about my proposal to White Dove and then come for me?

It was not long. I heard Rain in Face bellow and White Dove shriek.

Had he hurt her?

My anxiety was replaced with anger when I pictured Rain in Face hurting White Dove. I let my anger simmer into a rage as I waited for him. I moved to the other side of the trail so that the sun would be at my back when he arrived. And then he came, walking in long deliberate strides, and a crowd followed him to watch the fight. I noticed a slight hitch on his right side and a knife belted on his breechcloth. I touched the thick buffalo-hide neckband that White Dove had given me along with a pair of wristbands. At that moment, I realized why she had made them for me.

As he closed the gap between us, Rain in Face increased his pace until he was running, and then he pulled his knife from its sheath. I held my ground and then dropped to my left just before he reached me. He skidded to a stop, and I kicked out hard at his right knee. He grunted as his knee bent inward, and then he went face-first into the dirt. I stood with my knife in hand and waited for him to get up. The crowd cheered, which was puzzling since I was a stranger and he was one of their own. Rain in Face then rose slowly, and the fury on his face was so intense his eyes hemorrhaged. The crowd gasped as one when both of Rain in Face's eyeballs flooded red.

Could he see?

He limped toward me with his knife extended. I circled to his right, forcing him to put as much stress on his knee as I could. Usually, I would detest using a foe's weakness against him in such a way, but I felt I had no choice because of his superior strength and reputation as a skilled fighter.

My suspicion that he might not be able to see through his bloodshot eyes was quickly dispelled when he leaped forward and slashed his knife across my midsection with alarming speed. I instinctively stabbed at him, feeling the blade hit ribs. He staggered, and I jumped forward, drove my knife under his ribs and upward toward his heart, and twisted. He gasped and slashed his knife across my throat before falling backward. I jumped back and bent over, grabbing my throat to stem the bleeding, but there was only beaded blood on my neck. The thick, hide neckband came away in my hand, having been sliced through to the skin. I stood hunched over and held my stomach where there was a lot of blood with my other hand while I watched Rain in Face lying on the ground, twitching. I slowly walked over to him. He was looking up at me with bulging eyes, blood-engorged eyes.

Then he died. Despite my anger toward him for hitting White Dove, I took no pleasure in taking the man's life.

Then the crowd surged forward and surrounded me, some congratulating me while others whooped their war cries, and I saw White Dove. I pushed through the crowd toward her. She removed her scarf and pressed it to the gash in my midsection. I held up the cut neckband and said, "You saved my life, White Dove."

She shrugged and said, "Of course."

She led me to her family's tipi, and we were followed by a small crowd. An older man was standing beside the door. He nodded and said, "You won."

"Yes." Knowing this man was White Dove's father, I said, "I am Little Crow, son of Tall Pony and Morning Star."

"I am Lame Elk. This is my wife, Running Deer."

I grinned, and Lame Elk asked sternly, "What is so funny, Little Crow?"

"I am wondering how a lame elk could catch a running deer."

They gaped at me, and then Running Deer whooped laughter, and then Lame Elk smiled and he too laughed.

"It was not the elk who chased the deer; it was the other way around," Running Deer said to much laughter from the small crowd behind us.

"Come, we will see to your wounds," Lame Elk said after he had recovered.

Later, we sat together, Lame Elk and I, outside his lodge.

"I want to marry your daughter."

"I know."

"I will bring ponies for her."

"I have no use for ponies."

"Then what gift shall I give you for your daughter?"

"You have already given me enough."

"Huh?"

"You have killed Rain in Face, he who beat my daughter. One day, he would have killed her. I am grateful to you, Little Crow."

I nodded and said, "Then I will bring you a buffalo."

"Kill it first."

We laughed, and then he filled his pipe and we smoked. Then, out of the corner of my eye, I saw White Dove's face grinning through the door flap. It was a good day. That was in 1883. White Dove and I were married after my stomach healed, and I was able to bring a buffalo to Lame Elk. For two years we lived in peace, and in that time, White Dove bore me a son who I named Zeke, in honor of my friend. We have three children now, two boys and a girl. She and I had agreed that I would name the boys and she would name the girls. The firstborn, as I've said, was little Zeke. Our daughter was born next, and White Dove named her after her mother, Running Deer. The youngest I named after my friend, Two Elk. His was a difficult birth; White Dove never had any more children after that. But all was good in our lives.

Now, back to my story. Like I said before, we enjoyed two years of peace, and then came the spring of 1885.

30

We were living south of what is now called Saskatoon, and one day, White Hawk and I were out hunting for moose. I shaded my eyes as the crusted snow sparkled in the low midday sun, and I saw three men approaching. I recognized Charles, our friend from the neighboring Métis camp. The other two, also Métis, I did not know. White Hawk and I watched them through the frost rising from our ponies' noses. Their ponies' hooves crunched through the snow, alerting any game within miles of their presence.

"Hello Little Crow, White Hawk," Charles hailed.

"Charles, it is good to see you, my friend," I called back.

I stared at the other two, and Charles introduced them. They nodded imperceptibly but did not smile.

"This is Pierre, and he is Michel. They are from Batoche. They have come to speak with Chief White Cap."

I nodded and whispered to White Hawk, "Ride ahead and let the chief know these men are coming." White Hawk galloped away, and I could see these two Métis were not pleased with this development. However, their reaction was of no concern to me, so I turned my pony and trotted toward our camp. Charles rode up beside me, and we talked about the lack of game in the area. The other two, not content to be in the rear, rode a little ahead on either side of us.

Charles and I stopped and dismounted well back of White Cap's lodge, but the two Métis continued until they were within ten feet of his tipi. Angry murmurs rippled through the crowd of Sioux at this blatant show of disrespect. Finally, Young White Cap emerged from the tipi and stood before the two Métis men. An uncomfortable silence followed until one of the Métis said something in Michif, the Métis language. Young White Cap stood firm, brow wrinkled, not understanding the words. Then Charles walked forward and said to Young White Cap, "They would like to speak to your father."

"I will see if he's available." The anger on his face was apparent as he turned and entered the tipi. And then we waited. The Métis were shifting impatiently on their ponies.

246

"You should move back a respectful distance and dismount," I said in Michif. My friend Jacque Daoust had taught me the language years ago. I had regularly practiced the language with Charles and other Métis from the nearby camp. Pierre and Michel looked at me, surprise on their faces, and reluctantly nodded and turned their ponies. I followed them, and they dismounted and were about to walk toward the tipi before I stopped them.

"You should wait here," I said quietly.

They stiffened and looked at each other. Finally, with a shrug, they stood and waited. A few seconds later, Chief White Cap emerged from his lodge and beckoned them forward. I smiled as I saw the anger on the Métis's faces. White Cap had just taught them a lesson in manners.

Charles and I followed to act as interpreters. Although these Métis could probably speak Cree and Assiniboine, they would not know the Sioux language.

"We are here on behalf of Gabriel Dumont to ask you and your warriors to join us in the defense of Batoche."

Charles looked at me, so I translated between the Métis and my chief.

"What is happening at Batoche?" White Cap asked.

"It is where we will meet the white soldiers."

"Meet? You mean fight the white soldiers?"

"Yes."

"Why?"

"They've refused to recognize that our farms are ours. That can only mean one thing: they plan to steal our land from us, plain and simple."

"And what does that have to do we us?" White Cap asked.

"Many of your people have family living in Batoche, including you, Chief White Cap. We must stand together to protect them."

"You know my daughter?"

"I know her husband. He's one of our best fighters."

"This is my decision. We will help defend Batoche, but only if you do not molest any white settlements along the way."

Pierre and Michel bent their heads together in what appeared to be a heated discussion. Finally, Michel looked at White Cap and said, "You have our word."

"Then my warriors, those who choose to fight, will come to Batoche."

Murmurs suddenly rippled through the gathered Sioux, some excited, most anxious.

White Cap turned to Charles and asked, "Your people are going too?"

"Yes," he replied without enthusiasm.

White Cap nodded, mirroring Charles's lack of enthusiasm.

A week later, fifty of us armed warriors, plus our families, had set up camp a few miles from Batoche. We were approached by two Métis men whom we had not met before, and they told us the battle had started and we were to join the fighting. However, White Cap told them that we must first prepare for the fight.

"You need to come now," one of the Métis demanded, and I translated for my chief.

"We will prepare for war first," White Cap replied.

I told the Métis firmly that we would come only after we have performed our war dance. They cursed and then rode away at a gallop. I heard a thump, like a tree falling, and then another. I had heard that sound before; it was the sound of distant cannon fire. I went back to our tipi and sat in front of White Dove so she could apply the paints she had prepared to my face and chest. Our three children were safe at home. Lame Elk had become increasingly fatigued over the year prior to the journey to Batoche, so it was decided that he and Running Deer would stay home and look after our children.

"You are a fearsome-looking warrior, Little Crow," White Dove said when she had finished applying my war paint. "The white soldiers will tremble when they see you coming."

I smiled and said, "Let's go; the dancing will start soon."

"Wait." She entered our tipi and came out holding my headband with its two eagle feathers. Sitting Bull had given the second feather to me after hearing of the battle at Slim Buttes.

"There." She put it on my head, stood back, and nodded. One feather stood straight up, and the other was at an angle.

We walked to the large fire everyone had gathered around. Across from the fire, I saw Chief White Cap in full headdress with Young White Cap on his right and his adopted son, Blackbird, on the left. The chief saw me and beckoned me over.

"I will be back," I whispered in White Dove's ear, breathing in the heady aroma of wood smoke in her hair. I worked my way around the crowd and stood before White Cap.

"Stand with us, Little Crow."

I was stunned and unsure what to do, and I was grateful when Young White Cap chopped his hand to his side, indicating for me to move beside him. He smiled and eyed my eagle feathers before nodding a greeting. I leaned forward and looked across White Cap and saw Blackbird grin when he saw me looking. White Cap's request initially made me worried about how his sons would react, but they seemed okay with their father's wishes. I looked across the crowd and saw White Dove smiling proudly. I did not realize it as I stood with the chief's family that the tribe would hold me to a higher standard from that day forward.

Then drummers began drumming and singing, and four warriors in full war paint stepped forward. Carrying their lances and tomahawks, they started their war dance. Soon, everyone was singing. More warriors entered the dance. Whenever someone moved out to rest, others immediately replaced them. I longed to join them, and I think White Cap sensed this. So, he gestured for his sons and me to join the dance.

Before dawn the next day, we rode into Batoche. The dancing had continued well into the night, but I had left early to spend time with my wife and to get a few hours of sleep. I was grateful for the rest as I studied the warriors around me; most dozed on their ponies while others, anxious for the coming battle, stared straight ahead with bloodshot eyes. I looked back and saw our wives, several children, and older men following on foot. They would watch the battle from a safe distance.

The Métis leader, Dumont, met us and asked us to take up positions behind the village's cemetery. The man was running here and there, giving orders and moving his fighters. It was a wonder he did not get hit by the soldiers' bullets, especially from that strange gun that shot from many barrels. On the way to the cemetery, I stared hard at a weary-looking Métis man sitting on a stump. His face was covered in sweat-streaked dirt. There was something familiar about him, but I couldn't place him. If I did know him, he must have been one of our neighbors or maybe one of the hired men at Légaré's trading post in Wood Mountain.

Could it be –? Nah.

We did not engage the enemy that day, at least not in the way Sioux or Arapaho warriors fight. We did as the Métis chiefs ordered us to. We hid behind berms or in pits and fired our guns at the soldiers from cover.

"This is not how a warrior fights, Little Crow," Young White Cap said.

"No, it is not," I said, "but your father has told us to follow the Métis commander's orders."

"I know."

I watched my friend and saw the frustration etched on his face.

But that night, after it got dark, we were told to harass the soldiers' camp. Young White Cap was clearly excited at the prospect. I stayed close to him as we crept toward the corral.

* * *

"A zareba," Edward interjected.

"Is that what they call it?"

"Yes, Jacque told me."

"Huh, I don't recall him ever saying that word," Little Crow said.

* * *

So, we crept toward this "zareba" that the soldiers had built with earth and wagons. Some of our warriors were content to shoot arrows high in the air to land inside their camp, but not Young White Cap. With knife in hand, he lay on the ground and began to crawl toward the zareba. Handing my rifle to Blackhawk, I said, "Wait here."

"No, he is my brother. I will go with him."

"It will not be good if Chief White Cap loses two sons this night."

"That is not for you to say, Little Crow."

And before I could respond, he dropped and crawled after Young White Cap. They disappeared into the darkness halfway to the zareba, and I wondered if I would see either of them again. A few minutes later, I heard the first scream.

Shots erupted from the zareba, lots of shots, like hail on stretched hide. Then quiet. I waited with other Sioux warriors, watching for the brothers to return. And then another scream and more shooting. Then, a little while later, out of the dark came Young White Cap and Blackbird, both running in a crouch. I saw their teeth flash and knew they were both grinning. They slid down beside me, both breathing hard, I suspect more from their exhilaration than from exertion.

"What happened?" I asked them.

"We got to the wall. Blackbird went one way and I the other."

"I came upon a soldier and he saw me, so I jumped up on the wall and he screamed," Blackbird said. "I didn't even touch him and he screamed! I stopped, wondering what had happened to him, then everyone started shooting at me."

"Soldiers were running toward Blackbird, so I reached over the wall and grabbed one, but he screamed and dragged me over and inside the wall." Young White Cap said, "Soldiers turned and started shooting at me, but I felt bullets hitting the soldier I was struggling with, he being between me and them. When they stopped shooting, I pushed the dead soldier away and leaped over the wall."

"I heard Young White Cap laughing, so I followed the sound and met him on the way back." Blackbird said.

I looked from one to the other and then shook my head.

The next day, the soldiers mounted a heavy offensive. Cannon fire pounded our positions, and the noisemaker, or rababou as I heard the Métis call it, strafed our lines while soldiers charged. This was where Blackbird got separated from Young White Cap and me.

We were running along the riverbank when the noisemaker began firing on us. I dropped immediately and saw Young White Cap standing and doing a jerky dance, and then I realized he was being shot. I grabbed his foot and pulled hard. He fell, and I dragged him below the river bank. He had many wounds. I couldn't leave him there, so I lifted my friend, threw him over my shoulder, and ran. The other warriors had kept running north, followed by the noisemaker's bullets, so I ran south.

My legs were about to give out when I saw the rifle pit. I ran down the slope and laid Young White Cap down gently. My friend was dying; I counted nine bullet holes, two of which would kill him. He clutched my hand and struggled to speak. I bent low and put my ear near his mouth.

"I fought bravely, didn't I, Little Crow?" he whispered.

"Yes, my friend, you fought bravely." I removed one of my eagle feathers and placed it in his free hand. "You have earned this, Young White Cap."

He smiled and then grimaced and exhaled his life breath. I moved his hands to rest on his chest and placed the feather between them when a large Métis man ran into the pit. He carried another Métis man over his shoulder like I had carried my friend. He hadn't seen me yet, so I picked up my rifle and quietly reloaded.

The large Métis suddenly turned and fired his rifle toward the top of the pit's ramp. Then I heard someone grunt and roll down the incline, and I saw it was a redcoat. He bumped up against Young White Cap's feet and lay there staring at the sky. I began singing my death song for my friend and maybe for me too.

"Quiet!" the large Métis demanded, but I continued singing.

He pointed his rifle at me, and I aimed mine at him. We stared at each other, and then I continued singing.

"Little Crow?" the Mountie whispered, startling me.

* * *

There was a knock on the door followed by a voice that announced the first lunch seating was about to commence.

"That is a good place to stop, Little Crow," Edward said.

"Yes. I should get back to my seat."

31

After lunch, Tom agreed to come to Edward's cabin to continue his story. But, to Edward's annoyance, Annie had decided to join them.

* * *

Annie and I were married in Duck Lake, and she came to live with me in Wood Mountain. She would travel with me once a year back to Duck Lake, where she would spend a month with her family. Over the years, I cultivated several friendships within the community and thoroughly enjoyed my visits there. Annie and I would take walks around the neighborhood after supper, stopping to chat whenever we encountered someone sitting on their porches enjoying the evening air. Everyone knew, of course, that at the time I was a constable with the North-West Mounted Police, even though I would dress in my civilian clothes while in the community. I considered myself off duty during those visits.

On one such visit, during a pleasant July evening in 1884, we were on one of our after-dinner walks when we came across a couple working on their house. The woman was holding a rickety ladder while her husband was climbing up to fix their roof. Well, he had started to climb but had come to a stop halfway up the ladder, and I could see his knees were shaking.

"You need some help there, Barney?" I asked, stopping at his gate.

"Eh?" he said. "Who is that?" Barney's knuckles were white, his hands in a death grip on the ladder. He stared upward and seemed unable to look our way.

"It's Tom Flynn."

"Oh, Tom! Yeah, I could use some help. Our roof sprang a leak."

"I can help you with that. Why don't you come down and tell me what you need to be done?"

"Okay," he said and slowly slid one foot down to the next lowest rung, making sure it was firmly planted before sliding his other foot down. The process was slow, and his wife, Denise, was about to say something when I touched her arm and shook my head. She smirked but kept her comments to herself.

When Barney was firmly on the ground, he let out a big breath and backed away from the ladder. Sweat had beaded on his forehead and upper lip even though it was a brisk evening, an evening with increasing winds that carried the scent of impending rain.

"I tossed some wood shakes up there already. They just have to be nailed in place," Barney said.

"That ladder looks pretty flimsy if you don't mind me saying."

"No, you're right; it has seen better days."

"You're heavier than me, Barney. Maybe I should climb up there while you use your muscles to brace the ladder."

"Yeah, that's a good idea."

He handed me a hammer and some nails. We made eye contact, and I could see the relief and gratitude in his look. I was nailing the last shake in place when I felt the first fat drops of rain land on my head. I climbed down and handed Isidore his hammer. "Finished just in time," I said. "We better be getting back before it begins to pour."

Barney clamped his left hand on my shoulder as he shook my hand.

"Thank you, Tom."

"Anytime, my friend," I said, and then Annie and I ran down the street to her parents' house. We almost made it, but we were soaked through by the time we stood on the covered porch and looked out at the falling rain.

The next day, Annie and I were invited to supper at the home of Barney and Denise. The conversation revolved around hunting, fishing, farming, and of course, the latest rumors involving other Métis. But I sensed something was on their minds.

"What is it, Barney?"

"Eh?"

"Is something troubling you?"

"Uh . . ." Barney hesitated, glancing at his wife.

"Our daughter, Sylvie, she married a Cree man last year," Denise said and then took a deep breath and twisted her apron in her hand. "We haven't heard from her since."

"Have you gone to see her?"

"We tried a few times," Barney said, "but they always seemed to be away, hunting or fishing, whenever we went to the Cree camp."

"Where is the camp?"

"Three days' ride east of Prince Albert, along the North Saskatchewan River."

My regular patrol took me north from Wood Mountain to Prince Albert, then southwest to Duck Lake, and then back to Wood Mountain. I would have to go there on my next patrol in about three weeks or backtrack and go to the Cree camp now. Looking at Barney and Denise's anguished faces, made my decision for me. I would send a letter back to Wood Mountain from Prince Albert letting my commander know where I was going and why. I had no worries about going off my regular route. My job was protecting people in the territory after all, no matter who they were.

"Okay, I will go there and check on your daughter."

Denise jumped up and rushed around the table to embrace me. I could feel her trembling as she sobbed on my shoulder and muttered "thank you" several times before releasing me. Isidore was standing behind her, and when I stood, he grasped my hand and pumped it, a broad grin creasing his wet cheeks. I looked over and saw Annie smiling at me. Was she happy or proud? Probably both. I was determined not to fail.

"Be careful, Tom," Annie said as I mounted my horse the following day.

I wore my uniform that morning.

"I will be back for you next month, Annie."

"I will be ready."

Barney and Denise were standing by their front gate as I rode by.

"I made you some bannock, Tom," Denise said and handed me a cloth-covered bundle, "and some marrow butter too."

"Oh, thank you, Denise."

What a treat! It had been a while since I had had bannock topped with rendered bone marrow. I would have to stop for an early lunch.

"Barney, I will need to travel south to Wood Mountain afterward. I will try to send word, but you may not hear from me for about a month."

Barney nodded, trying to hide his disappointment, but he knew I had other responsibilities.

"Safe travels, my friend," he said as I rode away.

It surprised me that many people had come out of their houses and waved to me as I passed by. Several women handed me sacks of food. It seemed Isidore had told his neighbors of my mission.

Three days of steady travel brought me a mile from the Cree encampment. It was dusk, so I decided to bed down for the night. I built a large fire the next morning, made coffee, ate some of Denise's bannock, and waited. I didn't have to wait long. I had just drained the last of my coffee and had begun putting my kit away when they showed up.

Five well-armed and mounted warriors circled my camp and sat quietly watching me. I took my time as I put away my coffee pot and tied my blanket behind my saddle. Only then did I step forward and address the warriors.

"I am Constable Tom Flynn of the North-West Mounted Police," I said in Cree. Thanks to my wife, I had become nearly fluent. "I have come to speak with your chief."

I mounted and waited for them to lead the way. When it became apparent that they were unsure how to proceed, I kicked my horse forward and walked through them. Their ponies moved out of the way of their own accord, yielding to my larger horse. They turned and galloped so that one was in front of me and four were beside me, two on either side. They attempted to intimidate me with their menacing glares, but I ignored them.

We arrived near a tipi, and I dismounted and stood by my horse and held its reins. The chief emerged from the tipi and strode toward me. This man possessed the bearing of an army commander, and I realized I had straightened my posture and was standing at attention as this man came to a stop in front of me.

"I am Chief Long Claws."

"Constable Tom Flynn, North-West Mounted Police."

"What brings you to our village, Tom Flynn?"

"I have come at the request of Mr. Barney —" I suddenly realized that I could not remember Barney's last name. "He asked me to stop and visit his daughter if I ever passed by here." Of course, the last part was a lie, but forgetting Barney's family name had rattled me.

"I see. What is the name of Mr. Barney's daughter?"

"Sylvie, a Métis girl."

"Ah yes, of course, Sylvie," he said, shaking his head sadly. "An unfortunate situation."

"What do you mean?"

"Come with me," he said, and we walked to his tipi. "Loud Duck will see to your horse."

A boy whose eyes jiggled off-center ran awkwardly toward me, yelling, "Gimme the horse, gimme the horse!" Not knowing what else to do, I handed him the reins, which made him giggle, and then he turned and tried to run away, but my horse dug his hooves in and refused to budge. Loud Duck kept running anyway, and when the reins jerked taut, his feet flew out from under him. He was airborne for a second and then fell flat on his back, still holding tight to the reins as my horse snorted and backed away, dragging Loud Duck along, who lived up to his name by quacking loudly.

I grabbed the reins and calmed my horse, and the chief said, "Maybe it's better if Calling Elk sees to your horse. Loud Duck, you go home now."

Loud Duck, tears streaming down his face, trudged away, rubbing his backside and mumbling something under his breath. I was just entering the chief's tipi when I heard a loud quack from behind me.

"Loud Duck tries, but sometimes he gets too excited," the chief said, switching to English.

"I see."

What else could I say?

"Are you hungry, Constable?"

"No, I just had breakfast. Call me Tom."

"Okay, Tom, I am going to have some tea. Would you like some?"

"Yes, thank you."

A woman about his age, who I assumed was his wife, scurried outside to make the tea. I waited for him to tell me about the situation with Sylvie, but he just sat there studying me. I looked around his tipi, noting the weapons and their placement, a habit I would carry for life.

Only when we were served our tea did he begin to speak.

"When Big Bear first brought Sylvie home –"

"Big Bear, you mean Chief Mistahimaskwa?" I asked.

"No, no. Same name, but two very different people."

He laughed and then continued his story.

"Our people welcomed Sylvie, and things were good for a while. Until the troubles started."

Here, the chief paused as if weighing how much he should disclose.

"Sylvie was a very jealous woman, always accusing other women, even married women, of trying to entice Big Bear into their lodges. There was no truth to her accusations, though Sylvie could not be convinced. After a while, the abuse began."

"Big Bear hit her?"

"No, even though Big Bear is one of our fiercest warriors, he was the one being abused."

"I . . . um."

"Yes. Sylvie would hit him with whatever came to hand when she was in one of her rages. Everyone would hear the screaming and gather near their tipi in case they were needed to rescue Sylvie. But then Big Bear would hurry out, covered in blood, and Sylvie would appear and hurl insults after him."

I was still speechless as I looked at the chief.

"I felt shame for Big Bear; he lost a lot of standing in the tribe," he said, shaking his head. "I met with the elders to discuss the situation, and we decided that Sylvie had to leave our camp. But before we could inform Big Bear and Sylvie of our decision, Big Bear's sister took matters into her own hands."

"And?"

"Big Bear's family are all big. His parents, brothers, and sisters are all big strapping men and women. Well, Speckled Fawn, Big Bear's younger sister, who could carry a buffalo quarter over her shoulder for miles, stepped in. She entered Big Bear's tipi and dragged the screaming Sylvie by the hair from her lodge and proceeded to beat her. It took three strong men to pull Speckled Fawn off Sylvie."

"Was Sylvie injured?"

"She survived the beating, but a week later, Big Bear came to my lodge and told me she was missing. He had been out hunting and had been gone most of the day. It was evening by the time he had returned and found Sylvie gone."

"What did you do?"

"We formed search parties and went looking for her, but we found no trace of her. That was two months ago."

"Do you think she is in the river?" I asked.

"It is possible."

"Can I speak to Big Bear?"

"He is no longer here. After the suspicious looks he was getting, he also disappeared."

"You have no idea where he could be?"

"No, but I'll find out, sooner or later," he said. "He may be with another tribe, perhaps Chief Short Claws'."

"Short Claws?"

"My brother. He is also a chief. His camp is west of here. Check back in a few months; we may know where he is by then."

* * *

"We should go back to our seats; it will be suppertime soon," Annie said.

"Yes, of course," Tom said, and then he looked at Edward and added, "We can continue after supper."

32

"So, you left Chief Long Claws' camp, and you went to Chief Short Claws' camp?" Edward asked later that evening.

"No, I stayed a little bit longer," Tom replied.

"Is it of interest to the story?"

"I don't know, but I would like to tell you about it anyway."

"Alright."

* * *

I thanked Chief Long Claw for his hospitality, but he wasn't ready to end my visit just yet.

"Come with me, Tom Flynn. I want to show you something."

I wanted to be on the trail while the sun was high, but it would have been considered an insult to refuse his request, just as it would be an insult to refuse a gift. So, I followed him out his tipi.

"When the buffalo herds began to disappear, I-we-realized that we needed to change our way of life," he said. "The days of following the great herds were over. We needed to find a place where there was a renewable source of food, and then we found this place."

"Why here?"

"There was plenty of moose, deer, fish, and good water. What more could we want?" he said. "Now we are coming to our garden. But keep in mind, Tom, we still have a lot of work to do."

We could see several adults and children weeding a vast communal garden.

"We have potatoes, turnips, carrots, corn, and onions."

I could hear the pride in his voice as he spoke.

"And on that side are saskatoon berries."

"Huh, I never heard of cultivating saskatoons before."

"Yes, and we have apple trees throughout the camp."

I turned and looked back the way we had come and saw the trees. How could I have missed them?

"Everyone shares everything. We have hunters, fishers, and foragers. Come, I want you to see our storage."

We walked toward a low hill where several men were working.

"This is our root cellar. The boys are digging it deeper for more storage."

"Is there food in there now?"

"Yes, do you want to look inside?"

"I do."

The temperature dropped several degrees as we entered the cellar, and I smelled earth, cured meat, and smoked fish. I was surprised to see fish and meat hanging above piles of vegetables that sat on a lattice of poles.

"You have everything in here," I commented.

"Yes, it keeps all our meat and fish, fruit and vegetables from spoiling."

"This is impressive. Are there more tribes doing this?"

"Not at this level, as far as I know, but my brother is looking at doing this. Although, I don't know how far he has gotten with it."

"Well, I guess I'll find out," I said. "I'm going there next."

"If you see Big Bear, tell him he is always welcome here."

Big Bear was indeed at Chief Short Claws' encampment. I was met by a group of warriors on horseback, seven in all. They did not speak English, and I wanted to keep the fact that I knew Cree quiet for the moment, so I rode straight ahead into camp, under escort, without saying a word.

The chief met me, and I asked him in Cree if Big Bear and Sylvie were in the camp. He said Big Bear was and then asked why I was looking for him. But before I could answer, a large man rode out of the camp at a gallop. Guessing it was Big Bear, I remounted and chased after him. I could hear whooping behind me and knew the warriors that had led me into the camp were chasing after me. The hairs stood up on my neck.

Would they shoot a Mountie?

Our horses thundered over the prairie, and I was conscious of the danger that mole holes presented. One step into one of those holes would break a leg and end a horse's life. Big Bear had a faster pony, but his bulk was wearing down the animal's stamina, and I slowly gained on him. I didn't dare look back; all my attention was on the ground in front of me, searching for obstacles or depressions.

Soon, Big Bear's pony slowed and then walked despite Big Bear's encouragement. Finally, he stopped the heaving animal and dismounted. I rode up beside him and dismounted just as the others arrived in a cloud of dust and formed a circle around us. They held their weapons at the ready but lowered them when Big Bear waved them off.

"Why were you chasing me?" he asked me in broken English.

"Because you ran and I wanted to talk to you." I surprised him by responding in Cree.

"About what?"

"I was sent by Sylvie's father to check on her," I said. "Will I be able to tell him his daughter is safe?"

"Ah, no," he said, lowering his head. "Sylvie ran off. I tracked her to the river; her tracks told me she had fallen in."

"No tracks came out?"

"No, I rode up and down both banks for several miles; she is gone."

"Okay, thank you for telling me," I said, "and Big Bear?"

"Yeah?"

"Chief Long Claws says you are always welcome back home."

Big Bear nodded and turned his face away. I left him then. I believed Big Bear's account and would write in my report that her death had been accidental. I did not look forward to breaking the news to Barney and Denise.

* * *

Edward heard the cart rolling down the aisle and asked Tom if he would like a coffee.

"Tea," he replied.

Edward nodded and opened the door to place their order.

"I think I will jump ahead to the rebellion in 1885," Tom said after they got their drinks and cookies.

"You were involved in all the battles?" Edward asked.

"No, just at Fish Creek and Batoche, where I was wounded."

"Okay."

* * *

In April of 1885, I was sent to Winnipeg to join General Middleton's forces. Among the nine hundred men in his command were many untrained volunteers from down east. I had hoped to avoid conflict with the Métis and Indians, many of whom were friends and some may well have been my in-laws. But it was my duty and I had no choice. So, after loading my horse, I boarded the train bound for Qu'Appelle and reported to the general. I noticed a man on the train, a Métis man who hid behind a newspaper when I walked by. I wondered about that man, traveling on a train full of soldiers heading toward the conflict between soldiers and

Métis. This man was either an innocent civilian or a spy. I decided that I had better keep an eye on him.

When we arrived at Qu'Appelle, an officer spotted the Métis man removing a horse from the horsecar and then galloping away. Suspecting he was a spy; the officer ordered a couple militiamen to unload two horses and go after the man. Then he told me to go with them when it became apparent the militiamen were not adept at riding horses.

We chased the Métis man for many miles, but it became clear we would never catch him. I probably could have caught up to him, but the two militiamen slowed me down. One took a nasty fall, and I suspect he had a few cracked ribs. So, we gave up the chase and rode to rendezvous with Middleton's forces. We knew they would eventually have to cross Fish Creek at Clarke's Crossing, so that's where we headed.

We were a few miles from the crossing when we heard shooting coming from that direction. But we were not alone. The militiaman on my right grunted a split second before the rifle's report. He had been shot in the chest and fell off his horse, dead before he hit the ground. I bent low and looked for the shooter, and then I saw them, a band of Indians charging toward us. The remaining militiaman and I turned and ran our horses, looking for cover.

Ahead, there was a dry gully. I pointed at it and yelled, "Drop into that gully and let your horse go!" He shook his head, so I yelled "That's an order!" and pointed my finger at him. He didn't acknowledge my command, but he followed my lead when we came to the gully. We reined our horses, jumped out of the saddles, and dropped into the depression. We had our rifles, pistols, and cartridge pouches, and nothing else.

Taking aim, we opened fire on the Indians, Cree by the looks of them, and they turned away, riding out of accurate rifle range. I knew they would tie their ponies and crawl toward us; it was a precarious position for us to be in. Glancing at my partner, I was sure he was not aware how dire the situation was, and I saw no benefit in enlightening him.

"Save your ammunition for sure shots," I said to him.

He nodded, and I looked into his eyes. The man was terrified. In the distance, we could hear cannon and small arms fire.

"Sounds like we are taking it to them!" I said in an attempt to calm him. He didn't say anything, just kept staring straight ahead. He wiped his face with his sleeve, and it was then that I noticed tears running down his cheeks.

"It's going to be all right; we just have to remain calm and make our shots count."

I saw movement and was shocked at how close the Indians had gotten in such a short time. So, I tracked one warrior, shot the feather from his headband, and then yelled in Cree, "The next shot will be between your eyes!"

Suddenly, the militiaman jumped up and ran in the other direction. A bullet slammed into his back and he fell forward.

"You sons of bitches!" I yelled and wasted a few shots.

The next half hour was a lot of back-and-forth shooting. I didn't hit anyone, but I did have a few close calls of my own. After the half hour, I was out of rifle ammunition and only had one bullet left in my pistol. One Indian quickly jumped up and down, and I fell for it, shooting my last round. It got quiet, and I was sure they suspected I was out of ammunition, but they weren't taking any chances. I could see them circling me and knew this was the end. So, I stood in a crouch empty-handed and yelled at them to come and get me. There was silence, other than the distant thumps of cannon fire and the pop-pops of rifles, as I waited for a bullet to find me. Then a warrior stood and walked toward me. It was Big Bear, husband of the late Sylvie.

"Tom Flynn," he said and then pointed toward my horse grazing a hundred yards away. "You fought bravely. Go now."

I nodded, picked up my rifle, and walked away. I could hear angry voices behind me, but no bullets were fired. Unfortunately, I had to leave those two militiamen behind. I caught my horse and rode hard for the crossing, but the fighting was over by the time I got there. Our forces were in full retreat when I caught up to them. The Métis had won that skirmish, and I could see the shock on the soldiers' faces. They now knew they were in for a fight against tough men who were also excellent marksmen. I learned later that some of the soldiers had been unsettled by the presence of Sioux warriors in full war paint. It is impossible to describe the terror evoked by the sight of painted warriors bearing down on you. Some of the soldiers had a haunted look about them.

* * *

"It's getting late, Edward," Tom said. "We'll have to finish tomorrow."

"But we arrive in Buffalo early tomorrow morning."

"Oh, yeah. Well, after that then," Tom said and tried unsuccessfully to stifle a yawn.

"Good night, Tom."

"Good night."

33

Edward spent the rest of the evening charting the three biographies, Little Crow's, Jacque's, and Tom's. First, he put dates along the chart's left column – in years and months, and in some places, days – and then the three names along the top row. Next, he began entering what they were doing at those times until he had filled all the dates. Edward then drew lines between squares where two or all three were at the same place simultaneously.

When he was done, a clear picture of how he would proceed with his writing emerged. With that determination, he began writing and did not stop until the words on the pages started to flicker and his hand cramped. He looked out the window and was surprised to see the sun peaking over the horizon. He lay down and slept until there was a knock on the door and a voice announced, "Buffalo." Edward sat up and looked out the window, expecting to see the beasts, but what he saw was the outskirts of the city.

Buffalo, of course.

Sleep was no longer an option, not with all the clamor of travelers excitedly chattering away as they passed his berth, so he continued writing. But then he glanced outside and saw his six acquaintances walking into the station. The women were talking excitedly, and the men gave each other bemused looks. But, all in all, they looked like they were enjoying their time together.

What must that be like, having a wife and good friends like that?

Edward had had his romances, but they had never seemed to work out. There had always seemed to be a prettier woman or a more easily attainable woman, predictably ending with Edward alone once again. But he had no regrets. He preferred the freedom to pursue any woman that took his fancy, single or married, and on occasion a lady of the night. Sure, he got scratched up and robbed now and then, but that was all part of the excitement, the element of danger, whether it was an opportunistic working lady or an angry husband. Still, he could not shake the feeling of envy as he watched these people.

Later, when the train had left the Buffalo station bound for New York and the noise of embarking passengers had settled down, Edward lay down once again to catch some sleep before lunch. All too soon, he was awoken by a rapping on the door followed by a voice announcing lunch. Edward had not eaten since supper the previous evening, and his stomach rumbled loudly as he left his cabin for the dining car.

After lunch, Edward organized his writings. These pages were loose, not like the pages of his journals, which he only used for notes and rough drafts. He found it easier to use loose paper for his final drafts so he could discard pages he wasn't happy with rather than having to tear them out of a journal. A knock on the door interrupted his organizing, so he roughly demanded, "What is it?"

"Uh, it's Tom. If this isn't a good time, I could come back later."

"Oh, sorry, Tom," Edward effusively apologized as he opened the door. "I thought it was a porter; they have been interrupting my work all day."

"Should I come back later, then?"

"No, no. Do you wish to continue your story?"

"Uh, yeah, sure," Tom said, noticing the scattered papers lying about.

"Sorry for the mess; I was organizing the three stories. Have a seat, and we will begin." Edward moved some papers and sat down with his journal. "Okay, please proceed."

* * *

I reported to the general, and he told me the retrieval of the two militiamen's bodies would have to wait until the current threat of attack from the Métis and Indians had passed. He seemed to be preoccupied or maybe flustered. Whatever it was, it was not very encouraging, considering he was our commander.

We marched to the South Saskatchewan River, where we waited for the Hudson Bay Company's steamship. This was how the general decided to advance on Batoche. We all knew he was worried about another defeat by the hands of the Métis on land, so we sat and waited for the ships to arrive. The morale of the men diminished daily.

Finally, the ship arrived, but we still did not advance. The general wanted it armored, so the metal plates he had ordered with the boat had to be hung over the sides. Bales of oats and other supplies were also stacked on the ship's deck. Only then were we allowed to advance. And you would think that after all that preparation, we would float into battle unscathed. Not so.

We steamed into a hornet's nest. A hail of bullets came from Métis and Indians in firing pits along both banks of the river. We tried to return fire, but raising our heads above the bales would be suicidal, so we hunkered down and waited. The plan was to float by Batoche, gather some information about enemy positions and the size of their force, and then disembark and advance on the town. But that did not happen. Instead, a ferry cable the Métis had set high up clotheslined our smokestacks and knocked them onto the deck. It was a brilliant move on their part, and it effectively crippled our ship.

Our ship lost power, and we floated downstream. We managed to get the boat to shore when we were far enough away from the Métis positions and then disembarked. We joined with Middleton's main force and advanced toward the town's church with cannons and a Gatling gun. For some reason, the Gatling gun was set up and had opened fire on the rectory until a white flag appeared, and then the deadly gun went silent. The rectory door opened, and several women, children, a priest, and some nuns emerged with their hands in the air. That was unfortunate, but it got worse. Cannons were wheeled to a ridge, and they opened fire on the town itself, destroying several houses. I don't know if the families were home. I like to think that they were not. I tell you this, Edward, with a heavy heart. I was doing my duty, of course, but still, I questioned why I was there.

Anyway, as other units deployed, our group was kept near the church. Then, suddenly, a group of Métis rushed our artillery, clearly bent on capturing the pieces and turning them on our troops. But they were forced back by a fusillade of bullets from the Gatling gun. We then moved back, and that was when the Métis moved to outflank us and we came under heavy fire. The battle raged into the afternoon, and then a lull in the fighting ensued. Finally, the general ordered us to retreat to the outskirts of town where we were told to build a zareba.

* * *

"Do you know what zareba is, Edward?"

"Yes, Jacque explained it."

"Ah, that's good."

***

So, we hunkered down, but the Indians pestered us at night. We got very little sleep. For the next few days, we gained ground and lost ground. One night, two Indians breached our defenses. We lost one man, but we fired so may shots, I am sure we hit those two Indians.

***

"You didn't," Edward said.

"Eh?"

"Ask Little Crow about it."

Tom stared at Edward, then said, "Alright."

***

Anyway, the Métis and the Indians were well entrenched and had put up a fierce defense. But we suspected they were running low on ammunition. Métis men could be seen crawling over the battlefield, seemingly to collect spent rifle slugs. So, on the fourth day of battle, we stormed the town in an all-out attack. It worked; the defenders fought hard, but they were no match for our superior numbers, and as suspected, they were indeed low on ammunition.

I saw a couple of Métis men: one was large and the other average sized. I am ashamed to say I fired at them and hit the smaller man in the backside as they were retreating. The large man lifted his partner off the ground and threw him over his shoulder. I continued chasing them, and then they just disappeared. When I neared the spot where I had last seen them, I slowed and had my rifle at the ready in case of an ambush. I peered down a clear path to the riverbank, and a bullet hit me in the shoulder. I fell down an incline that turned out to be a rifle pit and came to rest beside a couple of Indians. One was severely injured, and the other had started to sing.

It was Little Crow! The one singing, not the injured one.

***

"Wait, Tom," Edward said. "Let's stop there."

"Okay, but I'm not tired; I can finish the story."

"Actually Tom, from this point on, I would like all three of you to tell me the rest. Together."

Tom considered this and then nodded.

"That's a good idea, Edward. I'll run it by Jacque and Little Crow."

"We should finish tonight; the train arrives in New York early tomorrow morning."

"Yes, after supper then."

34

Despite the inflated price, Edward had purchased a bottle of champagne to be opened after completing the three narratives. He was determined to finish taking down the remainder of their stories after supper. Tom had asked if everyone could come, the three men and their wives. It would be tight, but Edward thought it would be okay.

When they arrived at the appointed hour, Edward was prepared for them. His bag and all his papers were stored out of the way, and the champagne was on ice. They all came in and seated themselves. The three men and Genevieve sat across from Edward while Annie and White Dove sat on either side of him. As it turned out, there was plenty of room.

"You have this room all to yourself?" White Dove asked.

"Yes."

"How much did this cost?"

"Uh, a pretty penny," Edward said, uncomfortable with the line of questioning.

"Really?" she said. "It must have been real pretty."

"So, what do you think about our husbands' stories so far?" Genevieve asked.

"Fascinating," Edward said. "They certainly have lived remarkable lives."

"We are still having adventures," White Dove said.

"Yes, next year, we will go to the Grand Canyon and camp there," Tom said.

"I want to ride a mule," Little Crow said.

"A mule?" Jacque asked. "Why?"

"I heard they are stubborn."

"Huh?"

"Well, I figure after living with White Dove all these years, those mules will seem tame in comparison."

They all burst out laughing, except White Dove who cried, "Hie!" But she did it with a grin, and Edward was once again struck by how close these couples appeared to be.

"Shall we begin?" he asked.

The banter was all well and good, but he had a story to finish.

"Yes, of course," Tom said. "Who do you want to start?"

Edward checked his notes and then said, "Let's start with Little Crow, and you and Jacque can interject whenever you like."

"Inter—?" Little Crow said.

"It means they can speak up whenever they want to say something," Edward said.

"Yeah, they're good at that," Little Crow said with a grin.

* * *

As I said before, Tom here was shot and rolled down the hill right up to Young White Cap's feet. I did not know it was Tom until he rudely interrupted my singing, something he is fond of doing, by the way. Anyway, I was singing a death song for my friend, Young White Cap, who had just died, when Tom said my name. I looked closely at the Mountie and saw that it was none other than my old friend Tom Flynn. I was shocked.

* * *

"Wait," Edward said. "Jacque, you were not angry at Tom for shooting you?"

"What?" Jacque cried and looked at Tom. "You shot me?"

"You know it was me."

"The hell I do! Now I'm going to have to shoot you to even things up. Fair is fair."

"You are not going to shoot my husband, Jacque Daoust," Annie cried.

Jacque began chuckling, then said, "Yeah, I know it was Tom. I'm just thankful he's such a bad shot, or I wouldn't be sitting here."

"Arse," Annie said.

"I told him years ago," Tom said to Annie.

They all chuckled at Jacque's joke, and then Edward tried to get them back on task.

"I can imagine your shock, Little Crow; it was quite a coincidence to meet Tom there," Edward said.

"No, I was shocked that he'd survived that long."

There was more laughter and some grumbling from Tom.

"But what I don't understand is, how are you friends now when you fought on opposite sides at Batoche?" Edward asked.

"We have discussed that, over the years," Tom said. "You see, Edward, the rebellion was not welcomed by any of us. Jacque was only there to bring his brother-in-law home, and Little Crow and myself were only doing our duty."

"But still, you shot at each other and then became such close friends afterward."

"Edward, we were close friends before the battle," Little Crow said, "and now we are brothers."

"And we are sisters," Annie added.

Edward watched the group smile at each other and felt affection for each member of the group.

"Little Crow, could you continue?" he asked hoarsely.

***

Yes. So, I continued my singing until I was sure Young White Cap had passed over to the other life, and then I looked at Tom and said, "Hello, Tom Flynn, son of Liam and Agnes Flynn."

He replied, "Hello, Little Crow, son of Tall Pony and Morning Star."

And then we heard, "For fek's sakes, keep it down. Can't you see I'm hit?"

We looked and saw the large Métis man holding a man in his lap.

"It's me, Jacque Daoust," the injured man said.

"Jacque Daoust, son of who?" I asked. Of course, we both knew who Jacque was.

"Son of Francois and Antoinette!"

"So, what brings you to a place like this, Jacque, son of Francois and Antoinette?" Tom asked.

"This big idjit!" Jacque grunted. "I came to take him home."

"What's your name, son?" Tom asked Norbert.

"Norbert, son of, uh . . ."

"He's my brother-in-law," Jacque said.

"Wait a minute, are you that little boy who used to wait on tables at Theophile's cookhouse in Grand Rapids?" Tom asked.

"Yeah, that was me. Hey, I remember you!"

"Why'd you shoot me?" Tom asked.

"It wasn't, uh . . ." Norbert stuttered.

"It's alright, son; I respect the fact that you're fighting for something you believe in. There's honor in that. Still hurts like the devil, though."

Shooting then erupted near their rifle pit, and I swung my rifle toward the entrance. Tom looked at Norbert, the only other person with a firearm.

"It's empty," Norbert said.

That is when Tom said that we had better get out of there.

"To where?" Jacque asked. "And who is the captor, and who is the prisoner?"

"Little Crow, with your face painted, no one is going to recognize you," Tom said to me. "I think you should leave now and go home. The fight is over; you cannot win."

But I resisted. It was a hard decision. I had never run from a fight before, and I didn't want to then, either, especially with Young White Cap lying dead beside me. I felt the need to avenge his death. But then I remembered how Crazy Horse and Sitting Bull had surrendered. They had reason to keep fighting, to avenge deaths, but they eventually saw the futility in it, and at that moment, so did I.

* * *

"What convinced you of the futility?" Edward asked.

"The noisemaker." Little Crow sighed. "If the soldiers had a gun that could fire like ten guns, then we were doomed."

"So, you left?"

"Yes."

* * *

So, I left Young White Cap where he lay. Tom assured me he would get a decent burial. Then I followed the riverbank, hiding in bushes whenever soldiers passed. When I got to our camp a mile away, I told White Dove and the others that we had lost a great battle and Young White Cap had died bravely. There was loud wailing, and I encouraged everyone to leave before the white soldiers came for revenge. Every Indian knew of the white soldiers' need for revenge. They had heard the stories of women and children being cut down by the whites' long knives, so we packed up and went home, unmolested.

* * *

"It took Little Crow several years to get over that," White Dove said quietly.

"I would have dreams where Young White Cap was calling to me for help, and I would turn my back on him and walk away. His calls would turn to screams, and I would look back and see him engulfed in flames," Little Crow said, and Jacque placed his arm around Little Crow's shoulders and leaned his head against his friend's. Edward was taken aback by the display of affection between the two men. He had never seen anything like it before, not even at funerals.

What would it be like to have friends like that? he thought and then realized he would probably never know.

Little Crow nodded and cleared his throat. "I have other bad dreams. The ones about the cave at Slim Buttes are the worst, but I have accepted these as a way to remember the people and how bravely they fought in those battles."

"Hear, hear," Tom said, unashamed that tears had filled his eyes.

"Shall we take a break?" Edward asked. "I can order coffee or tea."

"Tea would be nice," Annie said.

"I can continue while we wait," Jacque said, "if you want."

"Yes, okay."

* * *

So, after Little Crow left, Norbert pulled my pants down and inspected my wound.

"There's a field hospital set up at the church," Tom said.

Norbert nodded, folded his handkerchief, and pressed it against my wound. Next, he turned to Tom and helped him remove his coat. Then, Norbert tore both of Tom's shirt sleeves off, wrapped his shoulder with one sleeve, and used the other for a sling.

"The bullet almost made it right through," Norbert said. "I can see it under your skin. See?"

Tom looked down at his shoulder and said, "Oh, yeah, there it is."

Then Tom said, "Let's go; you two will be my prisoners."

Tom held up his hand, quieting Norbert's protests, and said, "Look, if you run, they will capture you or shoot you. But if you help Jacque and me to the hospital, they will show mercy. I will speak on your behalf."

I nodded to Norbert, and then Tom asked him to drape his redcoat over his shoulders so there would be no doubt that he was a Mountie, even from a distance. Then Norbert scooped me up against my will and threw me over his shoulder. He then placed an arm under Tom's good arm to support him.

"Let's go," Tom said. "I need to pick my rifle up when we get to the top."

* * *

A knock interrupted Jacque.

"Ah, tea is here!" Little Crow said, rubbing his hands together.

Edward opened the door, and the porter poured and handed cups of tea to everyone.

"There are cookies and fruit too," the porter announced.

"Yes, we'll take a plate of cookies," Edward said. "White Dove, would you care for a long berry?"

"Yes, please."

Edward winked at the porter, selected a banana, and handed it to White Dove.

After the tea break, where the men drank from their saucers and nibbled on cookies while the women seemed to chatter at once, Edward asked if they were ready to continue.

"Maybe Tom should take it from here," Jacque said.

"Alright."

* * *

I told the soldiers we met that Jacque and Norbert were my prisoners and that we were headed for the hospital. No one seemed to care. When we got to the church, the doc cut the slug out of my shoulder from the front and then sewed up both holes.

After I was patched up, and after a few other soldiers who had minor injuries were looked after, Jacque was finally lifted onto the bloody table. You should have heard him yell when the doc began digging for the bullet!

"I still say he was rougher than he needed to be!" Jacque grumbled.

Tom grinned and then continued.

* * *

Norbert, of course, was taken to a makeshift stockade, which was a fenced garden guarded by half a dozen soldiers. That's where they took Jacque after he was stitched up.

I sought out the general, and when he did not appear too busy, I approached him and petitioned on behalf of Jacque and Norbert. I told him Jacque had served with the British army at Khartoum, which greatly impressed the general, and that Jacque was only there to bring Norbert home. That, of course, was all true. The deception came when I told him Norbert had been threatened by Métis men to join them or be considered a traitor. So, Norbert was forced to join them, but he always aimed high and never shot at any of our forces.

He asked where they lived, and I said a farm near St. Francois Xavier. He seemed to ponder this, and then he signed a letter granting them amnesty and told me to send them home without any firearms. So, we found Jacque's horse and off they went, Jacque lying forward on his horse's back while Norbert walked alongside.

* * *

"That was one long, painful ride, let me tell you," Jacque said.

"Well, Edward, that ends our story."

"Alright then," Edward exclaimed. "Let's open that champagne!"

He opened the bottle with a loud pop and the liquid spilled over the top. White Dove let out a little scream at the sound, and Genevieve quickly moved the champagne bucket under the bottle.

"Grab a glass, everyone." Edward began filling them and then toasted, "Here's to reading your stories in the most famous magazine in the world."

"Hear, hear," Tom said, and they all drank, Annie and White Dove making faces and Jacque guzzling his down in one tilt.

"But how did you wind up meeting every year for a holiday?" Edward asked after refilling Jacque's glass.

"It is not a holiday; we are visiting," Little Crow said.

"Right, but how did it come about?"

"Well, I was in Saskatoon one year doing some training and decided to stop in at Little Crow's reservation when I was finished," Tom said. "There had been a drought in Saskatchewan that year, and hay for cattle and horses was scarce. The little feed available was grossly overpriced."

"Our tribe had developed a large cattle herd for our own food, and we sold some too," Little Crow said, "but that year, we almost lost everything."

"I took the train back to Manitoba and went to see Jacque," Tom said. "I knew he had hay, and I was going to see if he had any to spare."

"I did, but not enough to save Little Crow's herd. So, in addition to what I gave him, Tom also purchased as much hay as he could and filled a railcar with bales and took it to Little Crow's reserve."

"It saved our herd."

"We still haven't been paid for the hay, by the way," Jacque said.

"Hey, did I ask you to buy us hay?" Little Crow said.

They all laughed heartily, Jacque and Tom wiping their eyes.

"But did Little Crow's tribe ever reimburse you?" Edward asked Tom and Jacque.

"Not necessary; we were helping a friend," the glassy-eyed Jacque said, his brow creased as if the idea of expecting pay was an insult.

"Well, that is the last of the champagne," Edward said. "If you'll excuse me now, I'll finish writing the final draft for the magazine."

They all stood to leave, and Tom asked, "So we will meet at Harper's offices day after tomorrow at one o'clock?"

"Yes, wait for me outside the building, and we will go in together," Edward replied. "I will ensure we receive separate checks so you can be on your way once the agreement has been signed."

"Good," Tom said, extending his hand. "It has been a pleasure, Mr. Humphries."

"The pleasure has been all mine, sir."

* * *

"How come you didn't tell him Little Crow's band paid you and Jacque back for the hay?" Annie asked Tom.

"They paid Jacque back," Tom said.

"They paid you, too," Annie said.

"They tried," Tom said, "but I owed Little Crow for a horse and saddle, and for saving my life."

"And besides, it sounds better the way I tell it," Jacque said. "Now, let's go to the dining car and have another drink!"

"Do you think that's wise?" Tom said. "We have to get up early to see our train going under the Hudson River."

"I still don't think that's a good idea." Little Crow shuddered. "I wonder if they can drop us off before the tunnel and we can paddle across?"

"Paddle what?" Tom said. "Do you think there'll be canoes just lying there for the taking?"

"I will make a canoe!"

"And I will help you." Jacque slurred.

"We've talked about this already; it's perfectly safe," Tom said, exasperated.

"Fine, I'm still going for another drink. Little Crow, do you want to join me?"

"Darn right I do."

35

The day after Edward arrived at New York's massive Pennsylvania Station, Doyle stepped onto the same platform. Looking around at the sheer number of people bustling about the station, Doyle realized questioning anyone would be a waste of time.

How was he going to find him? So far, Doyle had discovered Edward had been staying in upscale hotels on this trip. Where had he gotten the money?

He began his search by walking up Seventh Avenue, looking in the windows of all the hotels he passed, and hoping to see Edward sitting in the restaurant or lobby. He knew it was a long shot, but what else could he do?

He was walking by an optometrist's shop with a large wooden pair of glasses, less the glass, mounted above the entrance. Doyle walked by and stopped in his tracks after glancing through the door's window. Sitting in a chair and looking back at him was none other than his nemesis, Edward Humphries.

Doyle stared at the man, ready to charge in if Edward tried to run out the back, but he just sat there staring back at Doyle. It was unnerving. Then it hit Doyle. Edward wasn't wearing his glasses, but he was now reaching for them. Doyle leaped out of sight beside the door, bumping into a man.

"Excuse me," the man said and then entered the optometrist's shop.

* * *

Edward had sought out an optometrist after walking through the streets of New York and realizing many of the sights he wanted to see were blurry. But he did see the large prop of eyeglasses cantilevered out from a building. Edward knew this symbolized an optometrist's shop, so he entered and inquired about new glasses. The optometrist seated him in a chair facing a wall that held an eye chart and began determining Edward's prescription. While the optometrist selected lenses from a box, Edward turned his head and looked out the glass door. He was surprised to see a man looking back at him. Edward squinted but could not make out the man's features. Fear coursed through him as he stared at the man.

Was that Doyle?

Panicking, Edward reached for Eddie's glasses and slipped them on just as the door opened and a stranger entered. Relief washed through Edward.

"Be right with you, sir," the optometrist said to the stranger and then sat down near Edward. "Try these lenses, sir, and read the first line."

Edward went through the optometrist's procedure until he found lenses that Edward could see perfectly through.

"These are the ones, doc."

"Okay. Would you like to select the frames now?" the optometrist said, waving his arm to a counter that held an array of frames.

"Could I have them placed in frames like these?" Edward asked, holding up Eddie's glasses. He liked how comfortable they were, and he could keep the old ones as spares.

"Of course. The glasses will be ready for you to pick up tomorrow morning."

* * *

After Doyle was sure Edward hadn't recognized him, he walked to the corner and crossed the street. He hid behind a delivery wagon and watched the optometrist's shop. First, Doyle would follow Edward and find out where the man was staying. Then he would find a spot to lie in wait. Doyle had seen the scratches on Edward's face and wondered how he had gotten them.

He'd find out soon enough. Doyle savored the anticipation of the coming encounter with the little shite. Sitting so smug in that chair, getting new glasses. He'd shove those glasses up –

Before Doyle could finish his thought, Edward suddenly emerged from the optometrist's just as the delivery wagon began to move. But, as luck would have it, Edward turned and walked in the opposite direction. Doyle left the cover of the wagon and followed along, keeping his distance. Finally, after several blocks, Edward turned into a large building. Doyle looked up and read the name: the Knickerbocker Hotel.

Of course, where else would the pompous arse stay?

Doyle eased into an alley where he had a clear view of the hotel's front door and settled down to wait. He stifled a yell when a rat scurried by his feet. He gagged when the stink of garbage wafted by from further down the alley.

Edward, the son of a bitch, would pay for this.

* * *

At precisely six o'clock that evening, Edward entered the Knickerbocker's dining room for his supper. He almost blanched at the prices but hid it well and ordered a steak, rare and bloody. Edward waited for his meal and considered going for a walk later in the evening but dismissed the idea. He had to complete the final draft for the next day's meeting with the publishers at Harper's Magazine. Once again, he felt the tingle of anticipation. After some deletions and additions, the stories really took shape. But he had to be careful not to laud Little Crow's battles with white men. Some wounds were still fresh among the Americans.

The steak arrived swimming in blood, making Edward salivate. After his meal, Edward wandered to the hotel's front door and once again considered a walk.

"Out for a walk, sir?" the doorman asked.

"No, I don't think so," Edward said. "I have some work to do. Just getting some air."

"Very well, sir."

Edward stood on the steps and inhaled the evening air deeply. A chill ran up his back, and he sensed that someone was watching him. He looked up and down the street but did not see anyone looking his way. Edward shivered once again and then went back inside.

* * *

Doyle watched Edward from his nest in the alley and willed the man to walk away from the building, but maddeningly, he went back inside. Dammit! Ah, well, if Edward didn't come out in the next couple of hours, Doyle could find a place to sleep for a few hours without having to worry about the little shite disappearing on him. He just had to be sure he was back early so he could wait for Edward to emerge from the hotel. And then Edward would pay, one way or another, for all the grief he had caused Doyle and his mam.

His hatred for this man threatened to overwhelm Doyle's judgment, so he breathed deeply and tried to calm down despite the smell of rotting garbage. He slipped the blackjack from his pocket. The act of slapping the sap into the palm of his hand seemed to have a calming effect.

The following morning, Doyle arrived at the alley across from the Knickerbocker Hotel at 9:30 a.m. He had rented a room in a rundown hotel, the first hotel that would agree to rent a room to the brutish man who smelled of garbage. But unfortunately, the hotel was many blocks away from the Knickerbocker, in a seedier part of the city. And, due to doors banging and people yelling, it had taken Doyle several hours to fall asleep. Finally, he had woken at 9:00 a.m. and had run all the way back to the alley. He had not washed or eaten since the night before.

Was Edward still in there?

Doyle cursed himself for giving his prey a window of opportunity to once again escape his clutches. But a half hour later, Edward came strolling down the sidewalk, whistling and staring up at all the tall buildings. Doyle could see Edward's glasses glinting in the sunlight and realized the man was returning from the optometrist with his new glasses. Good. Well, maybe not all good. With Edward's vision renewed, Doyle would have to ensure he stayed well out of sight while following him.

Edward entered the Knickerbocker, and Doyle's stomach growled loudly. He was so hungry, he felt like vomiting. Poking his head out the alley, he saw a grocer's fruit display set up on the sidewalk in front of his store on the next block over. Taking a chance that Edward wouldn't slip out of the hotel or happen to look out his room's window and spot him, Doyle jogged to the grocer, asked for a bag of apples, paid the man, and jogged back to the alley. As he ate his apples, Doyle was sure Edward hadn't left the hotel.

At 12:30, he saw Edward emerge from the hotel, look both ways, and then walk briskly down the sidewalk. Doyle trotted out of the alley, crossed the street, and narrowly missed being run down by a horse pulling a large wagon. He ducked behind the wagon as the driver loudly cursed him. He saw Edward glance back and then continue on. Doyle increased his pace and closed the distance between them.

The wind had picked up since the morning, and Doyle had to quickly duck into an alley when a sudden gust blew Edward's hat backward off his head. Edward turned in Doyle's direction and chased his rolling bowler, finally catching it right in front of the alleyway. Doyle, not three feet from Edward, held his breath as he watched Edward pick up his hat, dust it off, press it down on his head firmly, turn away from him, and continue walking down the sidewalk. Doyle let out a breath and then cursed himself when he realized he had just missed a golden opportunity to grab and drag Edward into the alley. Fuming, Doyle left the alley and walked swiftly behind Edward. He was within ten feet of his prey when Edward hailed and waved at someone across the street. Doyle stopped and looked to see who he was waving at and saw three women and three men waving back at Edward.

Shite!

All of a sudden, a trolley car stopped to let people off and on, blocking the view between the group and Edward. Seeing that Edward was standing near a back lane between tall buildings, Doyle decided this would be his last chance to grab him. He palmed his blackjack, ran up behind Edward, and slapped it across the back of his head. Edward crumpled, his glasses flying off his head and landing several feet in from of him as Doyle grabbed Edward around the waist and dragged him into the alleyway. If any pedestrians saw them, they chose not to intervene.

Doyle threw the groggy Edward against a brick wall and grabbed the leather bag he still held with a surprisingly firm grip. Doyle punched Edward in the stomach and felt his grip on the bag's handle loosen. Then Doyle yanked the bag away, rooted around inside, and his hand finally emerged with the remainder of Edward's money.

"What do we have here, you pathetic little shite?" Doyle said.

Doyle thumbed through the cash and quickly determined that it was more than Edward owed his mother for rent. He pocketed the money and then grinned at Edward, who was still slouched against the wall, bloodied and too terrified to move.

"Now, little man, it's time to play."

Doyle grabbed Edward's shirt with his left hand, cocked his right fist, and laughed when he saw a wet spot forming on Edward's trousers. His laughter stopped abruptly when he heard a shout. He turned his head to his left and saw one of the men from the group Edward had waved at earlier running toward the alley. Doyle cursed and drove his fist with all the force he could muster toward Edward's face, but Edward jerked his head to the side at the last second, and Doyle's fist ricocheted off of Edward's cheek, and then slammed into the brick wall. Doyle bellowed as extreme pain shot up his arm, and he knew that he had broken several bones in his hand. He cast a murderous glare at the terrified

Edward, who suddenly fell to the ground in a dead faint. Doyle turned to face the man racing toward him, but something about this man caused Doyle to turn and run. He justified his decision to run on the fact that his right hand was broken and useless, even as he tried to ignore the foreign sensation of fear that radiated throughout his body.

Doyle ran to the end of the alleyway and into the next street, narrowly missed being hit by a streetcar, and continued running across the street and into the next back lane. At the end of that alley, Doyle stopped, bent over, and put his good hand on his left knee as he gasped for breath. He glanced back into the alley and was relieved to see that it appeared empty. After he caught his breath, Doyle stepped out onto the sidewalk and looked up and down the street and then heard the rapid footfalls behind him.

36

Little Crow looked across the street after the trolley had passed. Edward had disappeared. His gaze shifted to the alley as he let his eyes focus on the dark passage.

"Where'd he go?" Jacque asked.

"Edward's in trouble," Little Crow cried and then ran across the street.

Tom and Jacque looked at each other and then followed Little Crow.

"Stay here!" Tom hollered to Genevieve over his shoulder.

Little Crow stepped onto the sidewalk, saw a much larger man about to punch Edward, and yelled, "Hey, leave him alone!"

He watched with dread as the man drove his fist toward Edward's face, but then he saw the man hit the brick wall as Edward moved his head out of the way.

Good for you, Edward!

The man had cried out and was holding his injured right hand with his left when he turned to face Little Crow. Suddenly, the man turned and ran the other way. Little Crow slid to a stop in front of Edward and knelt down in front of him. Relief washed over Little Crow when he saw Edward's chest rise and fall. The right side of Edward's face had begun to swell, but other than that, he appeared to be okay. Little Crow looked up and saw Tom and Jacque enter the alleyway, so he stood and ran after Edward's assailant. He heard Tom call after him but he ignored the cry as he focused on catching the man who had hurt his friend.

Little Crow ran to the end of the alley and stopped on the sidewalk. He looked to his right and to his left. There was no sign of the man.

"He went that way." A boy of about ten pointed across the street toward the opposite alley. "What did he do?"

"Something bad," Little Crow called as he ran through a break in the traffic.

The buildings on either side of the back lane were several stories high and blocked out the sunlight. Little Crow could only see twenty feet or so into the alley, so he proceeded with caution. He gave every ash can and every container a wide berth lest Edward's assailant was lying in wait for him. Then he saw the man's frame silhouetted in the sunlight at the end of the alley. Little Crow ran hard toward the sidewalk, and just as the man turned to look back, Little Crow drove his shoulder into the man's midsection. Little Crow's momentum carried both of them off the sidewalk and into the street. Screams erupted, horns sounded, and young boys cheered as Little Crow rolled on top, his face a mask of rage directed at the man who had beaten his friend.

But before Little Crow could swing his fist, something slapped against the side of his head, and he saw stars flash as he crumpled to the ground.

* * *

Doyle stood and looked down at the man who had tackled him. His broken hand throbbed after the shock of inadvertently trying to stop his fall with it. The intense pain had almost made him black out but not quite. He still had the presence of mind to slip his blackjack out of his pocket with his left hand and slap it across the man's head.

"Hey!"

Doyle turned and saw two men emerge from the alley, two pretty tough-looking men.

Shite!

Doyle turned to run, saw a large fist come toward him, felt the impact of a powerful punch, then nothing.

* * *

Little Crow's eyes focused slowly. Someone was kneeling over him. He felt a surge of panic when he remembered the fight.

"It's me, Tom," Tom said. "Are you okay, Little Crow?"

"Mmph."

"Can somebody call an ambulance?" Tom yelled to the bystanders, one of whom rushed toward a phone box.

Tom looked up and saw a large woman wearing a butcher's apron and massaging her right hand.

"That was quite a punch," Tom said.

"Wasn't right, that man using a blackjack."

Then Jacque arrived, bent over, pressed his hands on his knees, and gasped for breath.

"Are you okay, Jacque?" Tom asked. "Should we call an ambulance for you too?"

Jacque, still breathing raggedly, looked at Tom, jerked his thumb toward Little Crow, and asked, "Is the Indian alright?"

"Fek you," Little Crow grumbled, "and no, half-breed, I am not. It feels like a mule kicked me upside the head."

* * *

An ambulance arrived and the attendants loaded a groggy Doyle into the back. A New York policeman climbed in to accompany Doyle to Bellevue Hospital. Tom had assured the two policemen who had arrived on the scene that Edward would be filing charges against Doyle. The other policeman took statements and then offered Little Crow a ride to the hospital to get looked at for cautionary purposes. Little Crow refused, then staggered and would have fallen had it not been for Tom's quick actions to catch him before he fell. Tom helped load Little Crow into the squad car, and then turned to look for the woman who had knocked Doyle out. She was gone. Tom suspected he would find her in the meat shop a few doors down, but first he needed to go check on Edward.

"Let's head back, Jacque."

"Oui."

"This is a bad day, my friend."

"Oui."

They walked back through the alleys and were not surprised to find Edward gone and Genevieve, Annie, and White Dove waiting on the sidewalk across from the Harper's Magazine office building.

"Edward was taken to Bellevue Hospital," Annie said.

Tom noticed Edward's bag in Genevieve's hands.

"Is his manuscript in there?"

"I don't know."

Tom glanced at Jacque, who looked back and then nodded.

"Here, let me have a look," Jacque said to his wife.

"Do you think you should?" Genevieve asked. "It is Edward's personal property, after all."

"I think he should," Tom interjected. "If Edward's writings are in there, then we should keep the appointment with the publishers, explain what happened to Edward, and pitch his story."

Genevieve pondered that, nodded, and handed the bag to Jacque.

"It's here."

"Then let's go," Tom said.

Three hours later, Genevieve, Annie, Tom, and Jacque sat on hard wooden hospital chairs while White Dove paced the waiting room.

"What's taking them so long?" she asked for the fourth time since they had arrived.

A doctor walked into the waiting room and asked, "Are you all friends of Edward Humphries?"

"Yes, how is he?" Tom asked as he stood.

"Edward suffered a facial fracture," the doctor said and then pointed to his cheek. "His cheekbone. He will be released tomorrow morning."

"What about Little Crow?" White Dove asked.

"Who?"

"Little Crow, her husband," Genevieve said. "He was brought in the same time Edward was."

"Have you asked at the nursing station?"

"Yes, they said he was still in the examination room."

The doctor looked at White Dove, saw the worried look on her face, and said, "I'll go check on him."

"Thank you, doctor," White Dove said.

Tom watched as Genevieve guided White Dove to a chair beside Annie and then sat on the other side. Both women comforted White Dove, who kept twisting her handkerchief in her hands.

Finally, the doctor came back and told them that Little Crow had wandered off, but he had been found and brought back to his room.

"We want to keep him overnight for observation, but he should be able to go home in the morning," the doctor said. "We put him in the same room as Mr. Humphries."

"Thank you, doctor," White Dove said.

"I'll call an orderly to take you to their room."

Tom glanced over at Jacque, smiled, and nodded.

Their friend was going to be okay.

***

"They won't let me leave." Little Crow said to White Dove when the group entered the room.

He was sitting up in his bed, and a few feet away lay Edward, who's face was swelled and purple. One of his eyes was closed, but he was awake.

"Edward!" Tom said. "How are you feeling?"

"Like a mule kicked me."

"Hey, that's my saying!" Little Crow cried.

Jacque grinned and said, "Edward?"

"Yeah?"

"I hope you don't mind, but Tom and I took your manuscript to Harper's."

"Uh, I would have liked to have been there. You should have waited."

"Edward, they want to publish your book."

"Really?"

"Yes, they want to meet, when you are well enough, to negotiate royalties."

"Thank you, Jacque, Tom."

"What are you going to do with all your money, Edward?" Annie asked. "Travel the world?"

"Travel? Yes, but only as far as Winnipeg." Edward stared at the ceiling and said softly, "I have some unfinished business there."

Edward's Books and Stationery
Winnipeg, Manitoba
1911

"Look at Little Crow," Genevieve said. "He's in his glory."

Genevieve, Jacque, Tom, Annie, and White Dove stood in front of the bookstore's long front counter watching Little Crow telling a rapt audience how he counted coup at the Little Big Horn Battle. It was supposed to be a reading from Edward's book, but Little Crow preferred to relate his adventures while standing and acting out some of the movements, much to the delight of his audience.

"He is a gifted storyteller. Would you agree, Edward?" Eddie said.

"I would, Eddie."

Genevieve grinned at the two, who she suspected purposely wore matching suits for the occasion. They were almost indistinguishable, like identical twins.

"So, you two are equal partners in this store?" she asked them.

"Yes, Edward and I had a long talk when he came back from New York, and we worked everything out," Eddie said.

"All my royalties from the book goes right back into the store," Edward said.

Genevieve suspected there was more to their story, but decided it wasn't any of her business. She was just glad that Edward was happy.

I always liked him, she mused.

Loud applause drew her out of her reverie as Little Crow's performance came to its conclusion and he theatrically bowed. Genevieve smiled as she looked around at her friends and joined in the applause.

The End